Offbeat / Quirky

OQ

Offbeat / Quirky

an anthology

Edited by Eckhard Gerdes

Journal of Experimental Fiction 73

Offbeat/Quirky Books

an imprint of
JEF Books/Depth Charge Publishing
Aurora, Illinois

Logo by Norman Conquest

The cover art, which is in the public domain, is from hypnotism posters that were the product of The Donaldson Lithographing Co. based in Newport, Kentucky, and date to around 1900. More information about these and other similar images can be found at *The Public Domain Review.*

ISBN 1-884097-73-1
ISBN-13 978-1-884097-73-7

ISSN 1084-847X

Offbeat /Quirky Books
an imprint of JEF Books/Depth Charge Publishing
The Foremost in Innovative Publishing
offbeatquirky.com
experimentalfiction.com

JEF Books are distributed
to the book trade by SPD: Small Press Distribution
and to the academic journal market by EBSCO

Introduction by the Editor

A few years have passed since the last anthology issue of the *Journal of Experimental Fiction* was published, and of course, much has happened in the interim.

The origins of JEF go all the way back to 1986, when I published my own little chapbook of experimental fiction called *Projections* in conjunction with *NO* magazine, a delightful little press in Chicago. From that experience, I came up with the idea of starting my own press, and using the name Depth Charge Publishing, published two paperbacks, my novel *Ring in a River* in 1994, and a novel by Arthur Winfield Knight called *The Darkness Starts up Where You Stand* in 1995. But the name *Journal of Experimental Fiction* wasn't used until the anthology *Belighted Fiction* was published in 2001.

Including the proto-JEF titles, the book you are now holding is the 57th book we have published. Many of the writers we have published in our anthologies have gone on to great acclaim in their careers, and we couldn't be prouder to have noticed their talent so early. Daniel Borzutzky, for example, was just awarded the National Book Award for Poetry, and he appeared in the *Belighted Fiction* anthology and in other issues of *JEF*, as did the wonder-inducing story writer Amina Memory Cain. And they are by no means alone.

From editing these anthologies, I have met some of the most interesting writers of our era, many of whom have gone on to publish books with *JEF*. Meeting so many great writers, whether in person or via correspondence, has been one of the great joys of my life. And even though *JEF* is by no means a great money-making operation, the rewards I get from doing this work are immense indeed!

I am very happy to introduce the following authors to *JEF*'s readership. Let me introduce them, in quite Midwestern fashion, in the order of their first names. Many of them, are, of course, already familiar to most of you and are well established in the realm of innovative writing. But you will also find some very fresh and interesting voices here that you may not have heard before. I hope you enjoy the width and breadth of the visions that are collected here.

This anthology is also a step in a new direction for us. I have wondered for a while now if the monicker *Journal of Experimental Fiction*, albeit accurate, wasn't perhaps a trifle academic. Not that I have any problems with academics. I teach college English classes myself, and have taught creative writing at universities before. But I don't want to give readers the sense that we are part of an insular community that only feeds off of academe.

Indeed, much of academe ignores our efforts entirely. And many, many of our writers are just "regular folks," not academics at all. So I have decided to start an imprint of JEF Books called Offbeat/Quirky Books to signify that what matters above all to me and to JEF's readership is not the achievement of academic credentials in order to acquire some sort of scholarly validity. What matters, purely and simply, is the quality of the work. The writers you will find here have unique voices and will challenge what you think writers can do with fiction. And the innovations herein are not all cerebral calculations based on theory, but many are those that come from instinct and heart.

That some hearts are offbeat is fascinating, and perhaps a little dangerous, but why should we all beat in unison? That some instincts result in quirkiness is more than eccentricity for eccentricity's sake. It is the claiming of the individual in a sea of conformity.

I have said this before, but it bears repeating: I tell my students and anyone else who is forced to or cares to listen that I believe firmly that the measure of great work is if the creator can look at the work when it is complete and say to herself or himself, "Only I, of all people on the face of this planet, could have written this work." If the creator can say that honestly, then she or he has added something to the sumtotal of human knowledge, and for that we should always be deeply grateful.

Eckhard Gerdes

List of Contributors

9 Alec S. Scott
18 Aria Riding
31 Arnold Skemer
35 Austin Brookner
51 Ben Pullar
56 Ben Slotky
59 Carla M. Wilson
63 Carolyn Chun and Deborah Chun
68 Carolyn Chun and Layal Hakim
77 Carolyn Chun and Peter Hobson
79 David Ableev
81 David Wirthlin
84 Denis Emorine
86 Don Skiles
88 Eckhard Gerdes and Peter Cherches
90 Ernestus Jiminy Chald
96 Evan Gulford-Blake
98 F. Ghisalberti
102 HB Berlow
111 Jamie Popowich
127 Jane L. Carman
136 Jeremy Thompson
142 Jerry Vilhotti
143 Jim Meirose
153 Joel Allegretti
157 John J. Trause
159 Jonathan Plombon
170 Joseph Bouthiette Jr.
176 Kay Merkel Boruff
198 Larry Smith
211 Mark Axelrod
235 Martin Heavisides
238 Michael Koenig
248 Michael Oppermann
253 Nick Romeo
256 Norman Conquest
258 Peter Cherches
261 Peter J. King
272 Peter Wortsman
275 P. K. Garrison
306 R. Bremner
309 Ryan Forsythe
325 Shane Jesse Christmass
327 Steve Pastis
334 Thaddeus Rutkowski
338 Ute Carson

Offbeat / Quirky

Alec S. Scott

Victory for Jesus

By Raisin Kane

Staff columnist and Staph infection for Where Does My Garden Grow? *

WHITE POPE – A realgood funtime was had by all or *nearly* all last night, at White Pope Parish High's new art-of-the-State Spirit Dome, where the Jiminy Christs of Jesus, Louisiana, played the Blue-tips of Canton, Ohio, for the coveted title of "National Champions of Infringement." The Jiminy Christs won, of course, but the visiting Blue-tip teammates, their mismatched matchheads burning hot and bright with blue-limned self-knowledge, put up an admirably vicious if ultimately fruitless fight.

The final score was 546 to 12, or 423 to 21, depending on when and where you were sitting or standing; the final death-toll (on the field) was 8 ½, an unlikely yet prophetic figure, which -- when divided into the expiration date on the back of any given box of Merit's *Crunchy-soft Cereal* -- equals the total number of deaths of The Ones Who Rule But Cannot Rule that will be necessary for the End-Times to restart. (As many of my older readers may recall, the End-Times stalled like a lemon about 150 years ago, when The Ones Who Breed Inadvertently inadvertently bred, and dammed the dimmed light that leads and lays, and we've been waiting lost and lusting for its aching return *ohmygod* ever since.) ["Coin us 'Interruptus'" is our motto, and for good reason, too; not even the Creator its *bad* Self hears our sepia-honed pleas of "Please please me." –Ed]

And speaking of breeding (is such a thing still aloud?), the 12 to 13 Nuvian Prom Queens who comprise the Jiminy Christ Cheerleading Squad – their candied apple-asses shining sweetly under plaid and pleated playedwith skirts – begged more sideline score-change than a baboon for their beloved home team, 37 times succeeding (and so having to perform acts of copulation and repopulation with the judges -- male, female, and Other -- that even *this* over-seasoned reporter has rarely witnessed -- and never, by God, actually experienced I wish); 58 times failing. [Videotapes of these failures and their

* The official organ of the Holy-Unholy Church of the Creatureman

subsequent punishments will be sold at next month's fundraising banquet for the Women of White Pope, being held at the Juliet Baptist Secretion Center near the edge of town, just three miles west of Totem McCoy's Burning Field of Desire. – Ed again]

At the center of the White Pope Dome bootfall field throughout the night, excitedly keeping watch over the citizens, the players, and the game's wildly oscillating score as he swam frenzied figure eights in the fetid murk of his crystal-clear bulletproof tank, was His Master's Serpent and Private Heresist (whom celebrity stalker and domestic terrorist Victor Noonan once called "the Creatureman's very own Left-hand Man"), Flannery "the Black Flame" Williamson. In a mid-game radio interview with TV reporter Chris Meager, conducted by megaphone from a helicopter circling 200-feet above the reptilian changer of See-changes (thanks entirely to the Dome's innovative retractable protoplasmic roof), the Black Flame said that he was enjoying his vacation from the state's capitol immensely, loved all of Jesus equally (though he admitted to loving some parts of Jesus more equally than others), and then reiterated his disquieting invitation, uttered psychically several times earlier to those assembled, to "come on down" to his tainted tank and feel his Lovely Lost Loneliness firsthand.

As always when the Black Flame is near, members of the audience were advised by the continuously speaking, endlessly echoing PA system that to view His Master's Serpent in the "flesh," one must first load two DD batteries into a flashlight receptacle meant for three, then shine the Blue Beam of Loneliness into his or her own soul – not the Serpent's, or the Serpent's vapor-tail – to catch even a peripheral glimpse of His Needless Harm and Repentant Willful Failure; failure to look away from His Master's Serpent's Gaze, should it fall upon you during your encounter, could/would result in death, rape, or even existential evisceration by Mr. Williamson (never all occurring at the same time, so at least you'd have a fighting chance), "so keep the little ones drugged and blindfolded when meeting the Main Man's main man, and don't say we didn't warn you!*"

Perennial favorite and Jesus socialite/power broker Becky Bourgeois was also present at last night's game, and in apparently good spirits as well, reading aloud from

---

* This year's cheerful yet sinister play-by-plays and PSAs were delivered by celebrated Asian educator and child Psychologist, Verne Faust.

volume 8 of *The Right Thing to Say* (during which she added 7 unofficial slogans of her own, my personal favorite being, "She says she tried to reach me on the *Tele*-cat, but I must have been asleep at the time") before generously donating her desiccated head to the night's blood spattered events, despite her much-publicized criticisms of her home team's head coach, Louie Samifer, late last week.

In a nutshell, during a press conference intended to promote the grand opening of The Devil's Shame, Ms. Bourgeois' antique and baked goods boutique, she not only called into question the 8-foot tall, 7-foot wide half-man's covert tactical strategies for the recently empowered Fascist Absurdist Regime – of which she and Mr. Samifer are both senior members – but also frowned upon his repeated use, despite several admonitions and fines from the Guilt Branch of the JSL, of the word *poltergeist* while on the field, citing its evocation of less enlightened times as an impediment to the morale of the Jiminy Christ bootfall players – many of whom are themselves second-generation Hillbilly, remember – and therefore to their performances in recent troubled though nonetheless triumphant games. This, in turn, led the coach to fire back long dead accusations that Ms. Bourgeois (who had killed the accusations herself) had ingested the protective wrapping of three of his four offspring's souls at once, just because, she felt, "my teeth were in danger of never falling in love."

But there were no such statements from either party last night.

All that was witnessed by those who gathered in the spectral glow of the Spirit Dome's séance-powered lights, was the willingness of a tired and bitter old coach-thing to be silenced by blood-tainted hush money, and a touching if tritely theatrical testament to one old Coozie Suzie's dignity, devotion, and lust as she shouted nonstop encouragements and come-ons to the Jiminy Christ bootfall team members when their sprits or hard-ons were low, and growled vile and unpronounceable epithets – all the while biting and snapping like a thing possessed – at the freakishly tall, thin, buck-naked players of the opposition team (it's true, their honey-dipped genitalia just hung and swung, bees a-buzzing, for all-too-many to see); and all who looked upon the singular spectacle of her proud, eagle-wedged face being repeatedly, repugnantly toe-nailed from one end of the field to the other by the bare sweat-soaked feet of muscular young boys, felt some arousal mixed with disgust that, to be quite honest, glowed proudly inside their plastic heart sheaths nonetheless.

Immediately after the game, when body and head had been reintroduced and improperly reprimanded (they just tossed the bruised and battered cranium in question into Old Ma Moneybags' lap, those filthy Guilty Branchers!), Ms. Bourgeois said happily of her experience, "I loved cheering my righteous Brother Brutalizers through every step of their victory in tonight's championship game. A more beautiful and stinking 24 feet I have *never* seen and licked!" And here the 86-year-old hussy was observed to smack her swollen lips and drool uncontrollably, so potent was the mere mention of her notorious and unaccountable fetish for the odorous feet of her 17-year-old homeboys. "I felt like I was the Belle of the ball," she added with a sly half-smile. "I loved being kicked in the punt like a piece of sweetbeat meat." And then the plaid and pleated playedwith skirt that some call curtains and others call home, closed around her collapsing laughing head, and thunderous applause was heard throughout the hall of Midwives and Minors, Whose Sins, However, are Outsized by All . . .

Ms. Bourgeois' longtime lover and personal assistant (as well as onetime political rival and potential assassin), the ever-regal, ever-beautiful Ms. Greta Guilt Tree Napes of Norway was also available during the game's Halftime Repression for stern talking-tos and impersonal dust jacket signings, at a small yet elegantly decorated sacrificial picnic table near the rear of Smiley's Snack Shack (officially known as the White Pope Dome Food Exchange). Her three most recent books, *To Name Him is to Know Him*; *Once for Now, Twice for All-eternity*; and the critically acclaimed historical thriller, *The Kings of Kunnyville Manor*, were all on prominent display behind her, while her three earlier works, *Menstruation Nation*; *The Sex lives of Septuagenarians, or: The Shape of Things that Come*; and the much maligned yet highly popular mind-manual for young and old foot fetishists alike, *The Metaphysex of Sox*, were still sadly nowhere to be seen -- the first two having been banned over a decade ago by the then ascending Fascist Absurdist Revolution, while the third was later demonized by Ms. Napes of Norway herself.

[This demonization, which some feel Ms. Napes of Norway was coerced into, was conducted in the Reaction Room just off the east hall of the White Pope Parish Courthouse, the dark and empty corridor of failure's shame repeatedly penetrating the anus-eyed angel of Ms. Napes' rumor-headed burden, 'till it came a-bleedin', by God, like a righteous ragling waterfall of pink, pigtailed pain. – Ed 'n out]

Poor lovely lesbian. Said she to me once, in a brief and slurring moment of Blue Heaven-induced candor, "When given the opportunity, a man will steal your lighter and squash your purse, then fuck you in the ass and call it a quickie – while a woman, in my experience, generally won't. Plus, women are the cat's meow when it comes to eating pussy . . ."

In the more palatable if less appetizing category of Recent Edible Treasures, Billy Badass's carnal confection, the Frozen Stiffy; country singer Jack Farber's homemade fermentation, Narcoleptic Wine (which will put you to slow, sad, country/western sleep); and the Odontoid Tumors of Grover's Palate (somewhat spongier than last years', but still rather excellent), were all available throughout the night at thirteen different booths in the White Pope High School parking lot, each of which had been painted red, white and blue by its ostensible owners, the Nomore Teacher's League in Favor of St. Starla's Choice, and then arranged with its twelve counterparts to form a composite image, viewable only from high above, of a giant five-pointed star, in an apparent parody of the Women of White Pope's five-pointed Star of Virtue. (The Teacher's League left out the winking eye at the center of the star, thus, I suppose, the joke.)

Having recently been bought and broken, like so much else in town, by The Reality Pros, Inc. (who last year discovered the Skull of God half-buried in the marshy outskirts of White Pope, and have sold it since, piece by piece, shard by shard, to the Vanquished Nuns of St. Clementine's Heart), the Nomore Teacher's League members, haughty hotties all – their big buoyant breasts already lactating for the upcoming Post-millennial Breast Fests – told me that my presence was no longer welcome in their quarters -- hind, fore, or otherwise -- but that new quarters and bills, freshly minted and printed after recent ratification of the Bill of Wrongful Rights, would gladly be accepted, even from the lowly likes of me, at anytime.

As my mother is the founder of their betters and predecessors, the Teacher's League of Nomore in Support of St. Starla's Choice, I possess incoherent feelings of retribution and flame toward this particular order and its associates' disowning of one who had all but worshipped their delightfully shallow form of femininity. But in the interest of objective journalism and in honor of last night's civic spirit (s), let me enthusiastically report that the order's lower level representatives, the White Slave Faces -- who ran the concessions, fake beards, clown shoes and all, with unskilled wits near wits' end -- were ever the models of decorum and gentle gentile condescension which our parish charter explicitly directs, and our citizens have rather impudently come to expect.

But that's all neither here nor there.

It was near the end of the Post-game Snack Break that four full cries from the Air Raid Sirens of Yore called everyone back to their jagged and misshapen plastic seats (a honey-slathered loaf of bread now waiting like a graduation gift under each one), and high priestess and head prostitute of the Church of the Creatureman, Ms. Kathleen "Kitten with a Whip" Whipcord -- who was recently appointed to be the Creatureman's tri-city troop liaison -- arrived in a sleek stretch Limbo at the edge of the once-manicured but now mangled bootfall field.

Wearing nothing but a pair of blood-red stiletto heels and a gleaming gold navel ring -- through which a giant black bow had been teasingly tied -- Ms. Whipcord rose like the proud Fascist Absurdist she is from the passenger side of the idling incorporeal conveyance (whose name, I think, was once Mathew, or might have been Molly, or possibly Molloy?), strutted on slowly swaying hips across the crowded sideline to a Living Microphone being held out for her by the excited and trembling sausage fingers of Bastard Coil of Newbury (his clerical collar as yellow as the pissed in snow), and said to the spectators, rather charmingly and disarmingly, I thought: "Sorry I'm late, but I've been at the Club all night . . .*"

Some in the audience booed, others shouted that Ms. Whipcord was "being too ambiguous," but most cheered the lovely lady and her compelling candor; and slurping down what remained of my Frozen Stiffy (whose genderless, disembodied voice cried out with what *I* believe to be the best climax of its short-loved life), I tossed my least favorite part, the panty pink wafer-cone, into the wastebasket next to the entrance of Men's Room One -- where I had simultaneously been eating my edibles and

---

* The exclusive and elusive, not to mention notorious, Bapho-Metro Dance and Trance Club, located in the lower Midregion of Baphometropolis -- or so the legend goes . . .

committing random acts of verbal violence -- before quickly making my way back through the throng of jubilant militants and milling moderates to the oppressive smoke-filled press booth, where I would shortly observe, along with my journalistic brethren and a handful of Humanistic Shaman, the Golden Jackboot Ceremony, or "Final Triumph" as it is known to be known, from a clear and unfettered vantage point.

After taking the microphone from Bastard Coil and grunting into it with feral ferocity for several confusing minutes, Ms. Whipcord then blew three sharp times into a solid silver P.E. whistle she had produced from What-knows-where, as if calling a Canine Squad from the neighboring town of Thanatos (Creator forbid), or a pod of Zombie-dicked Dolphins from the New Florida Keyes (even worse!).

As the nipples of her notably ample breasts engorged and pointed imperiously, two Jiminy Christ linemen kicked and shoved the shackled and chained captain of the opposing team, Jack Flair of the aforementioned Blue-tips, out from behind the bleachers and onto the field, while two Blue-tip linemen (their bulbous, lopsided heads glowing like dying embers out of solid, solemn respect) pushed the ceremony's namesake -- the 12-foot 12-inch tall gold-plated jackboot -- from the other side on a broad wooden platform with small squeaking wheels.

Reaching the presently empty center of the bootfall field simultaneously (Flannery "the Black Flame" Williamson had been hoisted by helicopters, tank and all, back to Baphometropolis at the game's zenith on the usual dubious grounds of "security concerns"), the linemen of both teams shook hands in a curt yet courteous manner, and Ms. Whipcord introduced the captain of last year's losing team, Hector Hegel of the Studs of Independence, Iowa, who stepped out of the back of the Limbo to a smattering of applause, and then limped slowly through the sideline crowd of empty-eyed onlookers to stand beside her like a nervous, skeletal pet.

With a bit of awkwardness -- his head and body having been rejoined by a court-appointed Metaphysician only yesterday morning, so give the poor guy a break -- Mr. Hegel intoned the time-honored mantra, "Head to Toe, Joe, Head to Toe," three times into the throbbing microphone that Ms. Whipcord held up before his gaunt and frail face, and then the hulking Coach Samifer, obviously drunk and belligerent, reappeared at the far end of the field to wild applause, the Golden Hatchet gripped tightly in his right hand.

(Rumor has it that he's kept Our Sacred Cleaver of the Hard-hearted Hard-on, the sacrilegious old goat, in a cobwebbed corner of his dingy garage for the past 11 months!)

Mr. Flair, meanwhile, kicked off his phantom boots and polka-dotted socks, made his way over to the tall, narrow stepladder that now stood beside the Golden Jackboot, and climbed it with quiet dignity -- the spectators chanting "Das *Boot*! Das *Boot*! Das *Boot*!" as a form of hilariously cruel accompaniment -- to the very top.

Bowing his blazing red and white phosphorous head over the cushioned edge of the Jackboot's shining heel shaft, Mr. Flair mouthed a silent prayer to the God of Where He Lives, and Mr. Samifer, who was in no mood for such staid formalities, finally arrived behind him huffing and puffing like a thing without lungs (which he most certainly once was). And then, without warning, Coach Samifer lunged halfway up the stepladder, grabbed Coach Flair by the back of his ceremonial gun belt, and swiftly swung the Golden Hatchet at the X-marked sweet spot at the base of his adversary's neck. With this simple savage act he promptly extinguished his poor opponent's head, and sent it smoking to the bottom of the giant boot heel, where it rolled around in elliptical circles (or so we like to imagine) for several seconds, before settling, as always, in the cold confined space of the giant boot's tempered-steel toe.

At this the devoid devoted roared monstrous approval, and Ms. Whipcord, from my relatively close point of view, could be seen to reach down between her thighs, her long slender hand hidden behind her big black bow, whereupon she feverishly began fingering herself . . .

As the White Pope High School marching band began to play the Idiot Elite's unofficial anthem, "Smalling Flesh and the Goat-cheese Lyre," with little skill but much enthusiasm, Coach Samifer stumbled down the stepladder, shouted incoherent obscenities at the surrounding spectators and dispersing linemen -- giving them all, just briefly, two of his three middle fingers – and lurched with bloodless Hatchet back off the field.

Coach Flair's body, which had stood up straight and almost fallen from its petite perch after being so hastily separated from its Reason for Being (or so the head likes to think), was immediately arrested and taken away to the Dietrich Detention Center in Jesus, where it will reside in servile solitude, as did the body of Coach Hegel before it, until exactly one year from now -- when, That Which Is Unknown Willing, the entire pointless yet crucial process will begin anew . . .

Well, that about sums up the night.

The Jiminy Christs of Jesus won their sixth consecutive victory as "National Champions of Infringement," a happy goodtime funreal was had by all or *most* of all, and everything ended as it always does and always should -- in the Belly of Sin and Redemption, which every one of us, even when we swim with the Scumsluts of Badlands and Bad Favors, carry in our hearts and souls forever.

Amen, a men, a man . . .

Assignment: Read the above Archived Article carefully, as you will be tested, each and every one of you when the time comes, on its value as an illustration of all that was wrong with the right-world of The Ones Who Rule By Insemination.

-- Mr. Male

History Teacher

Mt. Herewith High School on a Friday afternoon

Aria Riding

The Argon Men

She had her cramps for three days (and then three more days and then three more days…), beginning soon after we arrived in Oualidia from Safi. She had begun planning to have her cramps well ahead of time, when we were still in Safi, at the moment she learned that thermal radiation was leaking into Safi's famous sardine factory and into all the ground and water of Safi—and into all the people. She decided on the magnitude of her future cramps when she learned about the great number of Safi children being born with deformed genitals and strange glandular conditions. She decided resolutely that she would have a miscarriage (although she was not pregnant) when we learned about the phosphorous in the air that consumed the oxygen inside our bodies when we breathed it in and gave our skin a slight, tremulous glow. She decided to die in solidarity with everyone's suffering, whether or not it helped, when we learned about the toxic gases still contaminating everything, settling into the crops and livestock and then emanating from them in gentle auric waves.

Nevertheless, we ate a great deal and drank a great deal while we were in Safi. We kept our faces scrunched up because all the food and drink had a black, acrid aftertaste, although to be fair, when one scrunches up one's face, every flavor becomes tinged with the sour and the bitter.

She held herself together, she stayed strong until we departed.

…………

She bit her lip and watched the countryside and all the gum covering the back of every headrest and now and again the people vomiting into the stairwell of the bus and how they lay into that crevice at improbable and intimate angles, embracing their low ribs. Then we had to take a taxi for a few hours. Cramped between everyone, she knew she would suffocate, "Your hip is hurting me," she said, again and again, "Can you not get away?"

There was sweat on her upper lip and she had to close her eyes because the world was so cruel to her, and she could not escape. In her mind's eye she saw a skull on a toilet paper tube, filled with flowers, stood upright on the dispenser, a phosphoric aura of pollen falling towards the tiles, the hole. It traveled with her, dancing over the hillside shrubs festooned with plastic bags and leaking chemical containers, over the goats and the dirt farms.

Her cramps finally began when she went to toilet a few minutes after the taxi left us at a gas station overlooking thousands of empty tourist bungalows cut into the cliffs and gleaming and shimmering with heat and she felt smugly certain that this would be the end of her. The beginning of the end. She felt cold sweat burning her brow. She kindled the flame and grew pale. "I have even, very little blood," she told me. "I have not enough."

Having not planned my martyrdom ahead of time, I did not get cramps like hers. But her weakened condition inspired me. I meditated on her pain; I tried to get sympathetic cramps; I visualized her cramps floating from her body into mine and thought about intentionality. When none of that worked, I ate food I knew I could not digest properly and did receive some pain, but not the right kind. Fortunately, through a stroke of carelessness, I had forgotten to protect myself from the sun: my skin started to burn. Badly. It became much worse with rubbing. This trial was all mine.

She was walking ahead, weaving back and forth unsteadily in the road, looking for a hotel. I trotted to catch up with her; I was a little nauseated from anticipation—I was so eager to show her my skin burn. She didn't want to see it. She didn't want to hear about it. No matter what I put myself through, she would never allow me to experience suffering like she did. Any time I suffered, she considered it a theft.

"My shoulder is quite bad," she said, and left me with her bags and went on ahead.

....

The first few days we stayed in a room on a hill high above the ocean. The building was gone but the room remained, surrounded on three sides by row after row of large apartment complexes, all empty except for the proprietors.

It was quite hot and unusually humid, this was important—she cared about weather more than anything else, and I learned that, if one is a sensitive person, a weather report is the only divination that will accurately foretell one's quality of existence, whether or not one's life will be worth living for the foreseeable future. She liked the heat, but sobbed from the humidity. Her body at this time was in terrible conflict. She wanted me to keep the shutters closed and to know the weather from the condition of her body and spirit. She said, "I do not understand people who joke about talking about the weather. It is everything. In fact, it is, sure, the only thing that really interests me." She said, "I have a kind of constipation of my spirit. It's really a catastrophe, this weather, not?"

With total concentration, we poured over the weather diagrams, charts, the little pictures of clouds, of sun, of rain in the papers, we studied them again and again although we could not read the language, and from the diagrams we could not be certain whether here, in this place, this was sun, and this was rain. We looked at the symbols in the paper and looked at the sky. We could not be certain. Each day, deciding when to go outside was as complicated as planning a bank robbery.

Whenever we mustered all our heroism—and managed to open the door to the outside world, we would scamper perilously through the muggy heat to the café, she shielding herself from the sun, I not doing so. We ate the same food and drank the same water and used the cafe toilet, impatiently waiting for each other, very stressed to be out of the room. Although our existences and diets were now identical, our symptoms and impairments refused to become the same, and this incongruity hurt me, but, at least our conditions continued to worsen: her cramps wracked her back and forth, her belly got sicker and sicker; my glands reddened and burned, I began to have difficulty breathing and seeing and my skin began to rub apart like wet paper and gave off a peculiar odor that made her scrunch up her face involuntarily, as if she was eating. At this development (my skin smell), she became jealous and swore that she also couldn't breathe or see, "Even I am quite blind, quite breathless, and really, between us, I am the one who is not ok." She grew quiet for a while, and then blurted out that she did not think the smell was from me, even she was not convinced that I had any odor, for to her, at the moment, everything smelled very, very bad. She said, "My sinus is a catastrophe. I cannot stay in this room."

Then we dragged our luggage down the side of the cliff, and teetered along the empty streets for a few hours. Finally, we rented a dark, wet basement in a stone house, with only a sand dune separating us from the ocean. It looked like the coldest possible place. She paid for the apartment; the fat landlady was kind to her and would not look at me; I tried not to feel too forlorn, "It's because my condition is worse than hers," I comforted myself. When we put our bags down, moisture seeped up into them.

Having been outside for so long had hardened us. We went for a stroll without difficulty. A few old men sitting outside empty apartment complexes called out to us that it was necessary to receive their massage. Their anger was not much obscured. There was no one else about. The weather was already turning. We went to a seafood restaurant. Everything they served came covered in melted cheese. She trembled and drew into herself, straining to furrow her brow until it beaded with pained perspiration, "I'm weak," she said. She was too weak to say more.

In the darkness, in the wet stone house basement, she lashed out at one mosquito all night. She had her earplugs in and couldn't hear the mosquito's relentless approach and struck out without waking from time to time hitting my arms and the sides of me and my face sometimes striking my hands and spraining my fingers as I scratched away at my falling-apart skin without sleeping, but she said she was the one who wasn't sleeping, which enraged me after a few hundred sleepless hours.

Since finally we were at the beach, the rain began and never relented.

The rain burned our skin; nevertheless, we spent much more time exposing ourselves to this dry rain than we had to the wet sun. Either we were in the burning rain or we were inside the basement in the damp, cold dark. I looked at my face in the mirror and scratched it back up into place and cleaned something she had dirtied and picked at myself and washed and cleaned; I couldn't stop cleaning; I cleaned to stop myself from scratching, which I did anyway, until the surface of everything, had there been any light inside the wet stone house basement would have gleamed like a pearl inside of which I loped like dull rust-colored meat, pushing around rags with my toes.

She lay about here and there in the moist beds or on the soggy, mildewing couches and dripping verandas or on the cold wet tiles or went to the sea and lay on the wet sand so she could feel damp and sick in the rain that burned her skin at the water's edge, not touched by the tide but drizzled by its flying droplets of foam. She lay next to a dead dolphin, and cried to herself for three days, feeling they were one, and saying, "It should have been anyone else, why not me?" The dolphin's belly expanded and she felt connected and held fast to her own taut, protruding belly and fell asleep in her wet clothes and did not wake except when the men woke her to warn her that she had to let them cook for her in return for a little money. The men became angry when she told them she was too sick to eat and they said that if she did not eat their families would starve. Then, although they were still angry and becoming ever angrier, they patiently held her down and squeezed argon oil all over her. They did this, they explained, because argon oil is like no other oil and this must be done. And the angry men patiently massaged her deep into the sand rubbing her body up and down and exfoliating her with junk bracelets that were scratched by the sand so that, the men explained, she had ruined them and had to buy them, and this made sense to her. And the men said, "We are the Argon Men." And The Argon Men explained to her that every European woman needed to pay to be healed and purified by the touch of an Argon Man and his oil of argon, because every European woman had grown sick and impure through her whoredom, the whoredom of being seen and coveted and touched, and, the Argon Men cautioned, although the oil of argon and the massage of the Argon Men would help a European woman recover a great deal of her purity, the only way she could truly be cured was by making love to an Argon Man under the stars while his family waited for him at home never once questioning him and being grateful since he was working selflessly for their welfare and the greater good of all peoples and in any case the Argon Men's families would never have understood how civilized and liberal and European the Argon Men had become through exposure to sick Europeans and plus also, God. Here, the angrily patient Argon Men explained to her, gesturing in all directions, being a whore was bad business: here you had to pay the men who accosted you and raped you for the privilege of their consent, but it was all for the best, for it began the journey to purification, to salvation which could only truly be traveled by marrying one of the Argon Men so he could get a visa and come live with you and all your endless wealth in Europe and leave his family behind in a stone house never going out, just sitting, sitting and sitting—their obscured bodies shrinking and their eyes getting bigger and bigger in the near dark. She hadn't really been listening. But she had heard the word, "Purity." It resonated with her. "Although quite angry, the Argon Men patiently explained all this to me," she told me, as we lay side by side being massaged into the sand.

"Anyway they said something like this.... Of course, here I'm quite exotic.... In any case, I want to be pure," she said. And she recounted everything to me in her restless dreams, crying out loudly at me as she hit me, unable to hear herself because of her earplugs, as I lay beside her and the dead dolphin and a single female mosquito, all of us coated in argon oil and massaged ever deeper into the sand.

"A boy, maybe thirteen, maybe fourteen came up to me behind the dune," I said. "He said he had a condom and he took it out of his pocket and showed it to me. So I did not think I had a choice."

She didn't say anything. She was asleep.

....

After being pressed down into the sand by the Argon men for several weeks, after her resistances had been oiled and sanded smooth as bloody pearls, she agreed to let the Argon Men cook for her and some portion of their anger receded. Momentarily. And, not too reluctantly, their fingers released their pressure on her smoothed-out body, and not too begrudgingly, they allowed her to sit up and after eliciting many promises that she would never leave under any circumstances, they ran off to pretend they were going to find very special fish for her, from someone they knew who they swore did not sell rotten fish, unlike, they said, the fisherman who were standing at their little cooking stands ten meters from the sea, they who pretended to take fish from the sea and who stood near the sea, but whose fish were old and from far away, far inland, from a destitute place of torment and deformity.

And now that the Argon Men were gone, she dragged herself like a mermaid up the beach towards our wet stone basement apartment, trying to decide which one of the Argon Men she had to marry, leaving a slick of argon oil behind her. For a moment she felt a little energy: thinking about gossiping over meat and cheese plates with shrunken old ladies in the kitchens of little Swiss villages where she was quite the celebrity, about the looming specter of rape that she barely outwitted at every turn in these savage countries, unlike the unfortunate Swiss couple who would be captured and beaten a month later in India, where the young man was tied and forced to watch the five men rape his older female companion as just cause for being unwelcome; where, thereafter, a part of the Indian government agreed that the white people were to blame, and the world got excited. She stopped for a cigarette and remembered that her belly was wracked with pain and made a face before dragging herself down the steps to the wet stone basement, proudly thinking, "I don't care at all about my celebrity."

She lay there, hour after hour in the near-dark dampness, too tired to try to wipe off the sand and the argon oil and certain she would be deadly ill if water from a faucet touched her hair. Without needing to look in a mirror she was satisfied, confident that her countenance remained quite blanched and fragile, delineating her ordeals and the ordeals of the world as she watched the first of the Argon Men tumble down the rain-slicked stone steps and splatter through the puddle of the tiny courtyard, where they paused to tear open their sacks, scattering through the air the grains and vegetables and animals they had brought for her. Food hung all around them, suspended, uncertain. The Argon Men leapt into the wet stone basement and poured her seven hundred glasses of sweet mint tea from seven hundred different tea pots and cried out, "Traditional sweet mint tea: sugar with tea, not tea with sugar!" They explained she had purchased all the tea sets in good faith at the moment they had been set before her, and it was a good thing too, for if she had not done so, misfortune would have befallen all of us. This made sense to her. She stretched her fingers on her stomach and said, "Of course, but just now I'm really too weak to go about searching for my money case."

Gesturing wildly, sometimes at her with angry patience, but overall with furious impatience at each other, the Argon Men retreated to the courtyard and cried out that she must not look away from the ceremonial preparation of the meal which would help her determine her future, her future husband, and they began to cook, batting about and stirring the grains, the vegetables and the animals that had for all this time remained–hovering in the burning rain.

When all was done, the Argon Men captured every morsel in tajines as if catching fireflies in a jar. Smiling without veiling their hatred for her, they poured back into the wet stone basement like the contents of an endless tea kettle, cascading in on her with their scents and their oils and with so many meals for her, so much food that she thought their families could eat, and eat and eat. And she could not eat. Even the smell of food made her retch and spit out her cigarettes and her empty, taut little belly was vibrating and contracting all the time. Her condition was more and more real. All of the overcooked vegetables from the tajines piled up on all of the surfaces of the wet stone basement, all these bright colors smooshing down into browns and blacks and gray molds and couscous piled up on the floor tiles like little sand dunes that I, having also dragged myself in from the shore–even pulling the dead dolphin and the mosquito behind me (I too was a mermaid in an oil spill, I wasn't copying her)—would try to sweep outside, but the sea wind pushed all the couscous back in on us with the wet dust and wet sand until there was a dune that filled our wet stone basement apartment and cracked the ceiling and the ceiling after that, and the ceiling after that, and pushed the fat landlady up through the ceiling of her house, and for this the fat landlady blamed us (though she would not look at me) and screamed at her, "Now you will have to pay for renting the more expensive floors, and for what, to stay with an American, what do you think this one can really love you?" And this made sense to both of us. And the couscous piled in and piled in until you couldn't see the house anymore—a tajine of couscous and sand had taken its place with the beds and pillows sticking out of it like mildewing animal bones and purple carrots.

She retched and trembled. She convulsed. Not wanting to offend anyone, we explained these gestures were part of a traditional western dance of erotic enticement. She threw up. She pleaded again and again with the Argon Men, begged them to stop, moaned that they were cooking too much food, far too much food, but this only insulted them and angered them into heaping higher piles of food on top of the greater amounts of food they were already bringing us as hospitable punishment for failing to consume, to consume, and they flung the hot tajines at our heads while ignoring us and fighting amongst themselves about who would get to marry her and purify her and leave their family who they loved more than anything.

The whole while, as the Argon Men argued, I was pounding and kneading argon oil into her sick belly, not taking no for an answer—which was the right choice, for she never stopped begging me to stop pounding and kneading argon oil into her poor belly, never stopped moaning that my attentions were only making her already depleted condition more dire. Like any hero concerned for their own future I was determined to heal her no matter how many times she vomited into the growing plata terra of steaming dishes piling on top of each other on the floor. I pounded and pushed away on her, doing everything but love her, "Don't worry," I crooned, "I have learned the esoteric secrets of the culture." In fact, there was a book on the tea table, *The Esoteric Secrets of the Argon Men,* but I hadn't bothered to crack it. Sometimes it's enough that something is there.

Although the Argon Men never looked at me, I knew we understood each other. I made a tremendous display for them, massaging her into the wet stone, because I had to let them know she was my meal ticket, mine, not theirs. I had already given up my wives and husbands and children and families to try to get a marriage and a visa from her. She was mine, although I could never love her, not as they could love her, because like all Americans I was incapable of love, and I wanted them to respect that. She was mine, she was my new native territory; as I massaged her I was becoming her. Picking and choosing the things I liked about her. I felt such sympathy for the Argon Men, for myself. That all our destinies were tied to her. It started to work me up and I massaged her harder and splattered the burning rain that fell through the holes in the ceiling with Argon Oil. She was an ungrateful person who didn't allow anyone else to be as sick as her, who didn't even appreciate the angry hospitality and enforced massages and threatening influx of food she was intimidated and worn down into paying for, who even wanted to steal death from a dolphin. She pleaded with me to "Please stop this," to stop pounding on her, to stop kneading on her, to stop staring meaningfully at the Argon Men as they ignored me and argued amongst themselves; she entreated me to eat some of the food, to eat some of the food, and the truth is I had gotten bored and had stopped massaging her, but I was too busy to eat because I was washing the mosquito and the dead dolphin—and at the same time, to save resources, I was washing our clothes again and again, trying to get the food and the rain out of them that had already starched and filled them so they stood about like partial men and women, judging everyone in the scene, and nodding approvingly at me, as if to affirm: though incapable of love, I was industrious, a good person.

The Argon Men cooked more food in the tiny courtyard, screaming at each other, flooding us with spices, with growing heat, drowning us in their voices. Angrily the tajines clattered through the air and their hot clouds spread from them as they opened. So many colors.

She barfed up acid from her empty, distended belly as she cried and moaned that she would pay the Argon Men in any case, but could they at least give her a moment's peace, could they let her rest, could she breathe, could they cook at home? The Argon Men became furious and began to bring us cartloads of food, dragged by the poor, straining donkeys that materialized from the energy of her unjust desires. The Argon Men screamed at her, "Do you want our families to starve in front of you? Why do you come to this country? I hope you profit very well from all of your comforts!" She choked on her stomach bile and pleaded with me to talk to them for her, to speak to them, not to speak for her, for surely I would get it wrong, and I had no right, but somehow to reason with them, to show her a little mercy if I ever loved her.... But really, I was too busy cleaning everything in the wet stone basement and I had to do this while scratching at my body, my terrible skin, my poor skin which seemed to be coming away in fistfuls; every time I touched something my touch dirtied it; I had to clean it again; it's not that I was unsympathetic; I felt warm to her, but her lack of consideration wounded me; I couldn't see how she could remain unaware of my responsibilities, first and foremost, for the upkeep of all our things. And me, in my own state. And so we continued: she, the dead dolphin, the mosquito, the Argon Men, the donkeys, and I, aggressively ignoring each other but forever and ever connected, growing close.

In the end she became dramatic and threw up the lining of her stomach into her mouth as Dihrams spouted from her fingers and she whimpered, "Please take this money and at the same time feed your starving families with all this food." And the Argon Men were so enraged that she suggested that they consume this food—this food that they had made only for us with their relentless, merciless hospitality—that they shouted at her, "Are you crazy?" And in snarled whispers the Argon Men confided in us that they themselves could not eat what they prepared for us because Coastal Argon Men have always grown quite ill, deathly ill from eating of their own food and thus for the last hundred years they have only been able to get any sustenance by watching others eat, which partly but not completely justified their distemper. They shouted again, "Are you crazy? For this insult, we will invite you into our homes and you will eat there in front of our families and drink our traditional sweet mint tea, sugar with tea, not tea with sugar!"

This is how they threatened her, and they piled their carts high as the city walls with all the food in North Africa and their donkeys strained and strained to pull all the food in North Africa to her in the wet stone basement; the donkeys strained until their hearts gave out and they died, but the Argon Men kicked so wildly at the sides of the dead donkeys with their heels rattatatattatting in and out and beat them at the rear with such ferocity that the dead donkeys continued their stiff, short-stepped little trots, and the Argon Men, in such a hurry to prepare their sand dunes of food, used the burning rain to set their carts on fire and thus the carts became stoves, so by the time the dead donkeys trotted through the doorway of the wet stone basement, they were fully cooked and the vegetables fell on top of them so that they were hidden, like the meat is always hiding, underneath and buried in all the tajines that she was too sick, too sick by half to eat and that I was also completely too busy to eat with all my cleaning responsibilities, even though I was very, very hungry.

Poor me. Oh poor, poor me. Not only was my skin depleted of all four humours and falling away like water before the glimmer of summer, not only were my sleep patterns quite distressed, not only did I have to take care of everything and continue to give healing argon oil massages to her and the dead dolphin and the female mosquito and the dead donkeys and with increasing frequency to the angry cooking Argon Men who denied it was happening by pretending not to notice it was happening, not only all this, and on top of it all my cleaning, my cleaning of everything and everyone, on top of it all, I was completely hungry. But I had no time! She was no help at all: she was so sick, as she always was so she wouldn't have to do anything, she was busy with this struggle just to exist, and the dead dolphin, like her, did nothing, and the angry Argon Men and the dead donkeys were busy, always coming in and out in and out of the wet stone basement and screaming and bleating and arguing and kicking and whinnying, and the landlady was busy shrieking above us, and the mosquito was busy trying to suck us all; everyone was too busy to help me; I had to do everything, I had to fix everything. In truth, I felt self-conscious in the face of all their busyness, self-conscious and nervous like I had to do something all the time to prove I wasn't a good-for-nothing, so I scratched down parts of my body away from my body and washed and washed and washed. I washed the clothing for days and days without stopping. I washed our socks until they disappeared. I washed the mosquito until it was smaller than a flea. I washed the dead dolphin until it was as translucent as a jellyfish. I washed our undergarments so feverishly they caught fire and did not go out and burned us as we always had to wear them to remain decent in front of the Argon Men. I washed and wrung out our clothes and towels until I couldn't use my wrists anymore and had to hang everything to dry with my feet. I was very good at this and it took me less than a minute, much less time than it would have with my hands, but, as it was always raining the clothes became damp and moldy again immediately and anyway, by the time I had hung the clothing with my feet while standing on my head and scratching at my falling apart skin with my cramped, locked-up wrists and hands, the wind had blown rotten vegetables and sand and couscous all over the mildewed clothing and blankets which were already half-full of holes that I could not mend with any amount of washing and scratching and even when I did mend them, it didn't do any good, because every piece of fabric around the house was being constantly chewed on by flocks of Argon Moths who could not fly away because their wings had been pelted through by the burning rain and falling pieces of cooked donkeys and other foods and burning pieces of carts. At this point, I was a little reduced, and could no longer see (as from my sickness I could not see) or feel (as I had washed away my nerve endings) or smell (I was a little ill, I could not smell) the difference between any piece of wet, moldy cloth and my own falling apart skin ...

I cannot eat, she said, I cannot eat. But the Argon Men had already contacted their friends at the restaurants and the fishermen who they had insulted before in front of her, but who they were secretly buying the fish from now that she was not looking, these fishermen who cooked their catch for you right there on the beach under big umbrellas that protected the flames from the wind, but as soon as they handed you a fish from the grill the wind would push a dune of sand right over you and your plate. And the fishermen all had starving families and so the Argon Men let her know she had to go and eat all their fish, and the waiters and the cooks and the owners of the restaurants all had starving families, so she had to go and eat all the beards of the muscles which they served covered in melted cheese. All the restaurants in the town were seafood restaurants that covered their plates in melted cheese, it was a part of the mystique of this place, and there was so much food to eat and all the families were starving and when she begged to leave, the cooks and the waiters and the restaurant owners and the realtors and the fishermen all followed her back to the wet stone basement and started melting cheese all over all the clothing I was trying to clean and all over the translucent membrane that was all that was left of the dead dolphin, and all over the atom that was all that was left of the mosquito and all over the dead donkeys and everything else in the wet stone basement and the fishermen stuck their fishing poles into the frayed burning holes in everything and when a fish jumped into the house they would immediately hook it and gut it and grill it as it hung twisting in the air, so its guts fell onto our shirts and towels and hot fishy oil spattered over all of our cheese-covered clothing that I had just finally hung out to dry in the burning downpour.

She had already been thin before she stopped eating and now she fell away until she was nothing more than a stick, an arm of a sundial in the rain, not even a body, but the sliver of a shadow cast by a choked-off voice, whispering, "I cannot eat this."

And the Argon Men came around, with all the food in the world and screamed at her to eat, for the sake of all their starving families that they never wanted to go home to see again.

And I realized, in all this burning rain, that there had been no drinking water in weeks, that not one of us had held a single drop on the tip of our tongue, and soaked to the bone, I was very, very thirsty. As I washed into dissolution a little whisper of some shred of cloth, or perhaps it was her, or a piece of my skin, whatever it was it was the last thing I could find, my thoughts of my poor state were disturbed by a tiny shadow of a whisper–trembled from somewhere unseen, "I am thirsty, I am the one who is more thirsty."

Probably she would never notice.... Probably she would die before she noticed.

Nevertheless, I decided to wait to tell her I was pregnant.

Arnold Skemer

Argentinian Asseverations

1

Argentinian administration advocates Antarctic annexation. Army assembled arouses autochthonous animals avian and aquatic. Asphyxiate anomie and all antipathies across Argentina. Administration anticipates admirable Argentine ascendancy adumbrating advancement and authoritarian awakening. Argentinian acquisition of Antarctica advances autarky and ancient ambitions. Advancing ascendancy asserts awestruck ambitious Argentina. All admire army's arrogance advocating Argentinian assertion and associates antipodean ambitions. Attenuate anxieties. Advance admirable Argentina. Acquire adjoining areas as Argentina administers all adjuncts adjacent. Assail anomie and anti-social attitudes. All Argentinians adhere. All anti-state activities are asinine and are abolished. Angola, Andorra, Afghanistan, Albania, Algeria, Anguilla, Antigua, Armenia, Aruba, Australia, Austria, Azerbaijan affirm affinity and Argentine aspirations. Assertive Argentina authorizes australopithecine auxiliary against armies arrayed against Argentinian ambitions. All allies align against Argentinian adversaries. "Antarctica Always Argentinian abode!" Argentinian adherents assemble, assail anti-Argentine arrogance. All Argentina assembles as administrative adjuncts augur awakening across all areas as Argentine anthem arouses ardor. Aboriginal Argentinians acclaim Antarctic acquisitions, affirm adherence among all areas. Argentinian autocracy and army ascendancy affirm acquirement. Atrabilious asseverations assault ancient attitudinal assertions and absurd antediluvian attitudes anemic across all administrative areas. Assiduous ascent accumulates at atrium and anvil assisting Argentine advanced authority. "ARGENTINA AWAKE! ARGENTINA ADVANCE!" Aver animation astir across Argentina. Attenuate all accusatory attitudes. Army acknowledges Antarctic accumulations, asks all acrimony and all anachronistic attitudes abandoned. "ALL ADVANCE ARGENTINA!" Applause attends all assertions.

"ARISE ABUSED ARGENTINA," affirms army," and accelerate Argentine ascendency at Antarctic abodes. Acknowledge Argentine acquisition and all additional areas." Adamant advocates attain adeptness at administering Antarctic Anschluss. Align Antarctica along Argentine ambitions. Amity among antipodal associations attains ascendancy. Amicability advances and antipathy anathema among all. Animosity arrested. Antithetical animus abjured. Apothegm appears: "ALL ANTARCTICA ARGENTINE!!!" Argentinian ardor affirms annexation. Audible appraisal animates Antarctic animals. Auspicious axis affirmed as azure atmosphere acclaims advent an all azimuth alliance among Argentina and Antarctica. Argentina ascendant. Argentina Advances Always.

2

Buenos Aires begins broadcasts affirming Antarctic acquisition and asserts all autochthonous Antarctics accept biaxial association between Argentina and Antarctica. Argentina beseeches all aquatic animals affirm Anschluss. Bizarre ballet before acquisition belies affection between bilateral allies. Binding affinity affirmed before administrative association. And Anschluss beckons. Army bunkers bring bandoliers before battalions. Bizarre barracks burgeon bearing bazookas. Argentine belligerence beckons beaming beatitudes before beauteous beholdings betokening Argentine bastion. Besiege Antarctic bivouacs bearing anti-Argentine blackguards, blatant bastards all. Blockade! Bombard! Assassinate bothersome brutish adversaries, bubonic bitches. Bullets Argentine bulwark. Bugles arouse. Argentine army bashes belligerent's befuddling Antarctic association. Argentine brigadiers barrage bedeviled bastards befouling Antarctic areas. Baboons! Bandits! barbarians all. Battle becomes Argentinians! Battlefields abound. Beasts beaten. Agony befalls bastards. Bellicose Argentinians bellow, besmirch aliens attempting arresting Anschluss attempt, bizarre blotches, brazen blustering bastards, brothel brothers, bunny brained bastards, buccaneering brutes. A blunder, a big blunder before Argentine army. Argentines administer Antarctic areas bypassing broaching bastards. Beautiful bacchanalian atmosphere affirms balmy beatitudes as bandmasters build accolades, banners assail beneficent actions. Argentinian belligerence baptizing barbaric actions approaching battles. Bedlam bedazzles Buenos Aires before battle's beginning. Belittle Argentine bellicosity and accept anathema among auxillaries. A benignant brutality affirmed among all. Bestow bombast among antebellum Argentine adherents. Billingsgate amongst Buenos Aires bigwigs affirms blameless blandishment. Blatant blather bedecks blaspheming Argentinians. Bloodcurdling bloviations beguile Buenos Aires before army assemblies and attacks Argentine adversaries assembling. Bloodshed becomes all. Battle blur beckons. Blunt bluster betokens boisterous boldfaced bullies bolstering Argentine aggression. Brassy braggadocio brightly betokens brutish bucks. Bugles and butchery bring alarming action and armies assemble.

3

Caryatid cunts before atrium at broadcasting agency at Buenos Aires assert Argentine ascendancy at Antipodes. Cadres activated, advance caissons. Calmly Argentinian army advances against adversarial canaille. Capable Argentinians bring carnage and ceaseless brutality. A certainty arises as army advances. Chilean claims atrophy as Chilean army capitulates before Argentine advance. All alien armies consider. Climax coming? Coercion continues against anti-Argentinian cabal. Cogent contingencies attain coherence. Colorful contingents collude but Argentinian army breaks all alliances against Anschluss. Adversarial carcinoma crumbles before conquering Argentinians. Bellicose Argentinian army asserts coming concord but combat continues. Amoral confederacy against Argentina cratering? Can Argentina compel capitulation? Anti-Argentine carcinoma continues but cessation contemplated. Cancerous amphictyony atrophies against courageous and callous Argentine army. Argentinian army concentrates causing advantageous concatenations and concise axial breaks. Concrete causations confer advantages and Argentinians conceive anticipative cunning countenances. Custom commandoes and cumulous clouds congregate across Antarctic atmosphere. Can cryptic crux adumbrate celebrating certificating asserting Argentine aspirations? All anticipate but can any be certain? Army continues advance against Antarctic climes. Breakthrough can come anyplace. Adversarial armies await annihilation. Audacious Argentinian army acquires advantages against cunning contingents. Consummate Argentine artistry boldly acquires adhesion among Antarctic areas.

Chilean army calculations consume carcasses after carcasses. Can Chile contemplate capitulation? Captivity can come as Chilean army craters before Argentinian assaults. Chilean command contemplates capricious attempts at confronting Argentina. Chileans after all conceived claim concerning Antarctic abode. Chilean claims correct. Chile also affirms Antarctic association, ancient affinities. Chaotic combat, capture, carnage characterize armed actions. Can Argentinian chauvinism confront Chilean claims? Chileans are chauvinists also but are abject cockroaches combat wise. Chile cannot compete with Argentinian audacity, admirable courage, combative confrontational arrogance. Argentina commands and Argentine commonwealth completes conquest. Chile cannot compete. Chile accepts Argentine ascendance and Argentine-Antarctic confederation. All Argentina appreciates Chilean capitulation and congratulates Argentinian army. Consanguineous blood of Argentinians and Antarctics affirmed by Argentinian biologists. An Anschluss affirmed biologically! Consequently Argentine actions affirmed by ancestral affinity. All acclaim consanguinity alliance of the Antipodes, constitutional clarity constructed by applying ancient association. Conserve all Argentinian blood connections as also contiguity appends Argentine affirmations. A binding contract attaches Argentina and Antarctica, controlled, coruscated, coupled and cozily combined. Credulous citizens cackle, cry, cheer caterwauling creations all-Argentinian alliance, Argentina Antarctic cynosure, affirmed, announced and advocated among all. ADVANCE ARGENTINA!

Austin Brookner

Casual Encounters

Misanthropic man seeks....

"I hate improv groups. I think Whole Foods is a disgusting ripoff. I think the people who work at ice cream stores and serve you by throwing ice cream into the air for it to land in a cup are weirdos. I think almost every band I see sucks. I hate those white funk groups that play for white people. There are some things that I really like and am passionate about, but if they happen to be things that you are also into, you will probably repulse me. My occupation is a doggie life coach. In my spare time I am a TV killer (I shoot up television sets). I am not good boyfriend material. I've been told by previous girlfriends that I'm a jerk. Though in my defense I never intended to be. Unless I was planning on breaking up with them. Yet I still would like to find a companion to spend an evening with."

I posted this ad on the Craigslist casual encounters page under the category 'man seeking woman'. It'll be funny to see what kind of maniacs, if any, it attracts. The funny part about it was everything I said was really true. Except for bit about being a doggie life coach. And a TV killer. Although I bet I'd be good at them both. Neither seems too demanding. And considering all the weird crap people pamper their pets with these days, my life coach line didn't seem out of the realm of possibility.

That's one thing I did miss about Texas, though. The dogs. They had real dogs there. My neighbors across the street had four yard dogs with the freedom to run all over the neighborhood as they pleased. The alpha male and his main bitch would sometimes go on midnight excursions to bathe in the river, stop by my place and say hi and get a treat, then continue on their escapade. It was great to see dogs behaving like real dogs. In a pack. Outdoors. What I saw from the dogs in New York would amount to animal cruelty if the dogs didn't already have such dead lifeless expressions in their faces that I couldn't even consider them animals.

I had not yet unpacked my luggage from my flight that morning. I was plopped on the living room couch with a pizza and hadn't moved in hours. When I first arrived at JFK, I had forgotten how big and labyrinthine the airport was. At one point there were two adjacent doors that each said 'EXIT'. One led to a level below and one did not. There was a TSA employee sitting in a chair between the two doors. I asked her which door led to the area where you can get a taxi? Her response was, "What are you asking me for?" as though how dare I make such an imposition on her. Welcome home, I thought.

It struck me how much quieter New York City seemed than how I remembered it. I took it as a symbolic indication that my party days had come and gone. New York was a good town if you were young and full of energy, old and wealthy, or a money-crazed Wall Street broker-type. It's such a big and demanding and expensive city that you need to have boundless energy to keep up, or you need to have a lot of money. I had neither. But my friend Nick, an asthmatic pothead, had come through for me with a place to stay.

Nick was a first generation Polish-American. His parents had emigrated from Poland to Phoenix, Arizona. The details of when they came to this country and what they did for a living had never been discussed between us in our more-than-a-decade long friendship. I liked how with him our friendship was so easy and natural that we never felt the need to discuss those types of things, which strangers rely on for conversation.

Only on a few occasions did him being Polish ever manifest itself in a way that I saw: when he spoke Polish on the phone to his parents, when we went to a German beer garden and a table starting singing German national songs and Nick got visibly red and cursed to himself in Polish and stormed out, and when the New Warsaw Bakery was open late one night making loaves for the next days' run and he finagled buying a loaf off the assembly line for three bucks by negotiating in Polish with the bread makers.

But in all visible ways he was American. He loved Bob Dylan and Willie Nelson and Grant Green and The Rolling Stones. I think growing up in Arizona had a real western influence on him, because he loved that whole cowboy guitar playing and cowboy depiction of America. He wore big cowboy boots, blue jeans, and button down plaid shirts.

He lived on N. Moore St in a neighborhood of lower Manhattan called Tribeca, in a loft that was a huge palace by New York standards. It was one of my favorite streets in the city and one of my favorite apartments to be in. I had crashed there many times over the years when it was late and I had been too drunk to make the trek back to Brooklyn.

To the west was the Hudson River, and the light had a way of hitting the cobblestone streets in the morning and early evening that looked magic to me. The big windows from behind the TV that faced me were grayed with cigarette smoke. His record collection was in shelves to the right of the TV and spilled over onto the adjacent desk.

The place smelled like cigarettes and old New York. It was a little bit cold and archaic, but also homey and beyond perfect for my needs. He rented the apartment from his Uncle who owned the place since the 1970s. His uncle was a guitarist and was in a psychedelic rock band in the 70s and early 80s that had a decent underground following in Europe. They released a few albums on a German label that his uncle still gets royalty checks for.

Nick moved in here when his uncle decided to move back to the other home he has in Woodstock. That was how Nick could afford the place. Nick worked as an investigator for a legal firm, and his public defender salary could never have afforded the place at market price. The details of his job were never totally known to me. I knew he was sent all over the city to investigate little crimes, like lesbian lovers quarrels turned violent.

I had known Nick since I was eighteen years old when we met in college. The first thing he said to me was "Hi, I'm Nick. I'm the best bass player in the world. And the best guitar player." He was a cocky little guy, but we all were at that age, and to his credit, he is pretty damn good on both instruments.

Nick, myself, and my brother had gone together to see one of the greatest, most memorable and life altering performances for me when we saw Iggy Pop and The Stooges. It was when they had just reunited. They headlined a day long festival in Randall's Island put on by Little Stevie from the E-Street Band. Iggy was godlike. And the band was perfect – unbeatable.

They opened the door and gave me a taste of a world that I had never known, and instantly wanted to be in. It was a world separate and apart from the dull, boring, dissatisfying, unconquerable world I had always lived in. A world where, through one's own making, could become exciting, could be everything you wanted it to be, and where you were god.

I kept that experience with me, and the porthole shown through Iggy's eyes, during my life, and I would try to stay true to it, although I failed to more often than I succeeded. But whenever I came to a challenge or a decision that appeared to me to be somewhat important or defining, I kept that thing that Iggy showed us that night in my mind and I made my choice accordingly. I guess you could say Iggy was my moral compass, for better and for worse. Sometimes it felt like I had escaped one prison only to enter into another.

I curled up comfortably in the living room sofa of Nick's apartment with the pizza I had ordered. I was extra cozy. After trying the pizza in Texas, I couldn't bring myself to ever eat it again. I just couldn't stomach paying four bucks for a lousy slice of shit, knowing that I had eaten better pizza for one dollar way out in East New York, Brooklyn at some fried chicken joint. If I'm gonna kill myself on bad food, I want to enjoy it.

Nick had left the spare key under the doormat for me when I arrived because he'd be at work when I got in. He'd probably be getting back from work soon. I felt like killing some time. I thought I'd go for a walk, one of the last remaining luxuries that New York City has to offer. I hadn't gone for a walk in a while without feeling self-conscious for it by the people in cars around me.

I walked over to the West Side Highway, crossed the traffic of cars and bicyclists and strollers. I walked without a destination and without knowing how far I'd go. I felt the breeze from the river. Texas felt like an erased memory. A book that had been closed shut and thrown away forever. And with that, all the voices and noises and people and thoughts that were once me were gone. I felt the weight of it all wash from me and was massively relieved. It was like dying and still being allowed to live. Reincarnated. Alive among the living dead. I felt I could go anywhere, do anything. Get any girl I wanted. This feeling was interrupted.

"Hey man, you got a light?"

"Yeah."

I passed him my lighter.

"Thanks man. I appreciate you."

"No problem," I said.

He was a Hispanic looking man. In his forties I'd guess, and a worker's build.

"Shit man, I gotta get all the way uptown today," he said. "You know a car you keep running and running trying to get it started. Then all of a sudden it starts up. That's what my life is like."

"Can't get going, huh?"

"No man. Like everything is happening crazy right now. Couldn't get nothing going before, and now it's like," he expressed his eyes in a way that finished his thought for him. "I got two plumbing jobs today, both I gotta figure out what to do once I get there. My daughter's giving birth tomorrow. She induced. She's overdue. So I gotta make sure I got the right hospital."

"There's a Bob Dylan lyric that reminds me of," I said. "Something like 'Yesterday everything was moving too fast, today it's moving too slow'."

"Yeah. He's exactly right. That's how it is. Welcome to the world."

"Yeah," I nodded in agreement. "The world of people."

We drew smoke in silent conspiracy.

"Is she having a girl or a boy?"

"A boy."

The man looked way too young to be a grandfather. He himself looked like a young father.

"I like coming out here by the river," he said.

"Yeah, me too. It was better before they redid it with all this kiddie park shit."

"Fuck yeah. But it's better than those parks on the other side."

"You mean with the bums and shit."

"Well, you know I believe in crowds."

"In what?"

"Crowds. Like how they say you become your crowd."

"You are the company you keep," I said.

"Something like that. I really believe that. The people you hang around, they become, or you become like them. You'll become a part of that crowd, whether you mean to or not. Like a lot of my old friends, I don't see them no more. I'll see them on the street and be like 'Hello. Good to see you. I'm good. Okay. See ya later.' Just quick, polite, keep on moving. I had to just cut a lot of people out like that."

"I can understand that."

"Yeah, thanks a lot man. I appreciate you."

"No problem."

I crossed the west side highway back to North Moore Street. I turned my head to the right, in the direction of south, and caught the new Freedom Tower. It was hard to imagine anything being uglier than those two grey monstrosities that were blasted away and gone, but somehow they did it. I mean, my goodness. That Freedom Tower is one grotesque slab of mundane cheap Chinese crap. I hope somebody blows that one up too.

The fucking audacity they have to name it the Freedom Tower. That was the old rallying cry: "they hate us for our freedom." What freedom were they talking about exactly? Can't drive without a license. Can't get a license without paying for a driving test. Can't drive to another state, town, or borough without paying a toll. Can't vote without being registered. And the president doesn't even have to be the person who gets the most votes. The Electoral College can elect someone else if they want to. Every day there's another law being made to take away what little freedom we have left. And they never get rid of old laws. America: land of the free. What a joke.

As I walked I saw a wild looking girl with curly red hair running in my direction. She was awfully cute, but she looked totally insane. She stopped when she got to me.

"Excuse me, sir, do you have a cigarette?"

"No, I don't. Sorry."

She began to run off again.

"Hey, wait a minute," I said.

"What?" she said coarsely.

"Where you going?"

"I'm looking for a cigarette, man!"

"Well, when you find one how 'bout I take you out for dinner."

"I have a boyfriend."

"And he sounds like a swell guy, too, a real papaya. But what'd ya say?"

"Listen, man, I gotta run."

I saw her accost several more people until she found one with a smoke she could grub.

I got back to the apartment on North Moore St. and saw my ol' buddy Nick as I walked in.

"Nicky!"

"Corey! Hey, good to see you."

"My man. Good to see you, my brother from another mother."

We embraced momentarily with our arms slapping one another's back.

"So you made it in alright with they key and everything?"

"Yep. Easy as pie. Got a beard going on, I see."

"Yeah, a little bit. I set up the cot in the office room there for you, don't know if you saw it."

"Yea, I did. I remember that old mama."

"I'm sure you do. So what's the plan? Just hanging in town for a bit? You going back to Texas ever?"

"We'll see. I doubt it. My landlord's cool with me leaving my shit there for now. I don't want to be a bother to you though. I'll get outta your hair here if you need me to. Just needed a change of pace, you know?"

"Hey, man. You know you can stay as long as you want. Happy to have ya."

"Thanks Nick."

"Wanna smoke a bowl?"

"Do girls fart?"

"I'm not sure I know the answer to that."

"Sometimes they do. Nevermind. Pack it up."

Nick went to the desk with the vinyl records on top. In one of the drawers were his weed and his bowl named "Susie" which I remembered from college.

"You still have that thing?"

Nick looked at me for a moment not knowing what I was talking about. "Oh, Susie Q. Yeah man."

"That's amazing you still have that."

"Hey, Corey – do you remember my cousin Sheila?"

"No, why?"

"You don't remember Sheila? I know you guys have met her before. She's from Poland with the thick accent."

"I don't know. Maybe."

"Well she just moved to New York. I told her you were coming. I think she's interested in meeting you."

"That's nice."

"She was actually asking me if we could all meet up tonight."

"Well that's fast. Should I watch out?"

Nick did not say anything. He had a terrible poker face. I was just joking with him, but I could see immediately there was something he was hiding.

"Here let's smoke a bowl," Nick packed Susie and passed it to me.

"What's going on Nick?"

"What are you talking about?"

"Your cousin. Why does she want to meet me?"

"She just does, that's all. She likes you I guess."

"C'mon Nicky. I mean I'm flattered and all, but I know I'm not that special. Just tell me. What's going on? Or you can't have any of my pizza."

"*Pizza. Did someone say pizza?*"

"Cut it out."

"*You said the magic word.*"

"I'm not doing this with you Nick."

"Okay, all right. I don't know, man. I honestly don't know for sure. But I think --- no, I really don't know. I shouldn't say anything."

"C'mon! Hey, tell me or I my answer is no. I may have an internet date lined up for tonight anyway."

"Alright, alright. Geez. *You know I like it when you're pushy.*"

"Nick!"

"Ok. I'm not sure, but I think she may be looking for a green card so she can stay in the country and work."

"Really. Wow. So she wants to get married?"

"I don't know for sure, but I think so, maybe. She's been talking about how her work visa is set to expire and she's not sure if she'll be able to stay in the country. I know she doesn't want to get back to Poland and live with her mother. When I told her you were coming to visit and might be staying for a while until you got your own place, well, she got very interested in meeting you."

"That doesn't necessarily mean anything."

"She's a lesbian."

"Oh, right. Which one is Sheila again?"

"Tall, thin, dirty blonde hair, a little bit proper."

Nick could see I wasn't getting it.

"Really pretty. You've met her."

"Oh....yeah...her. *She likes to go ta bed wit women*?"

"Yeah, you didn't know that?"

"I guess I did," I said.

"I know it's weird, man. She's a strange bird. We don't have to do it. Or doesn't have to be tonight. If you're tired or something."

"Nah, its cool. Let's go out together. Got nothing else to do. Never been proposed to before. I'm kind of curious to see what it'd be like."

"Me too, my friend," Nick said. "Me too."

We all met up that evening at Puffy's Tavern. I was glad to see that Travis, the bartender, was still there. We sat in the corner table by the window. Sheila was not the person I was thinking of. It must have been Nick's sister whom I had her confused with. Sheila was by all accounts, gorgeous. She had the figure of a model, and it came up in our conversation that, yes, she had done some modeling when she was younger. She dressed very conservatively with a sweater and a skirt. Her hair was in a ponytail. She had a figure that was perfectly proportioned so that any clothes, it seemed, would fit her effortlessly and just right. She had some computer job at a tech startup.

"Hey Travis, another round for us here. I got this one guys," Nicky said.

"Thanks Nick," I said. "So Sheila, how long have you been in the states for?"

"Six months, about."

"Uh huh. And do you have to go back to Poland at some point?"

Nick shot me a glance.

"Ya. I got my veesa extended another three mohnths. Then I don't *know*."

Hmm. She's not showing her cards yet. Maybe Nick was wrong. Too bad for me she's not into men. I'd marry this girl for real. Well, it would be for real even if it were a sham.

"Here you go guys," Travis said. "Shots are on me."

"Thanks Travis," Nick said.

Travis brought with him four fireball shots, one for him and three for us, and we clicked our glasses, tapped them on the table, and gulped them down with four throws of the neck.

"Corey –

"Yea," oh man, I thought.

"Nick tells me you have no place to stay."

"For now, yes, I'm staying with Nick until I get my own place."

Here it comes.

"I have an apartment with extra room and bed. You can stay with me but I need a favor."

"Uh huh."

"To stay in the cahntry I need a green card. If you and I get married and stay together for a year, you can live with me and I won't ask you to pay rent, maybe if you get a job you can help share some of the other expenses, but that's all. It wouldn't be romantic. You can see other woman. I see other woman too sometimes. Maybe you can take some time and think about it. But I need to know soon. I got my final extension on my work visa. Cannot get anymore. Can you think about it please?"

"Yea, sure Sheila. You know I'm happy to help if I can. And that's a very generous offer with the rent and all. Please, allow me to think about it."

"Ok. Thank you."

We all took a sip from our drinks and allowed for the silence. It was a hard segue to make from there, but someone had to do it.

"Ya'll wanna go back and get stoned?" I asked.

"Yeah," said the two Polacks in unison.

We landed up getting high and watching TV for the next couples hours and finished the remaining cold pizza slices. Sheila left a little later, taking a cab home. Nick and I called it a night shortly afterwards. I went first to brush my teeth and take a piss. I heard Nick's phone ringing as I was in the bathroom.

"Is she calling back already? My goodness. She's *pushy.*"

Nick's voice fell silent as he listened to what was being said on the opposite end. It was the wrong kind of silence. I could tell Nick wasn't moving, as there were no sounds coming from the wood floor. Whatever it was he was hearing, it was something bad.

I washed my hands and brushed my teeth. I knew as soon as I left the bathroom I would be hit with something unpleasant, though I did not know what it would be. I took my time cleaning my teeth, wishing I didn't have to come out of there to hear whatever the news would be.

I opened the door and walked into the kitchen. Nick was no longer on the phone, just standing with his back leaning on the countertop and his eyes looking at the ground.

"What was it?" I asked out of obligation.

"Nora's dead."

I said nothing. It wasn't like I didn't see this coming. We all knew what she was like in college, and the roads she went down. But it was still a shock.

"How did it happen?" I asked.

"I don't know," Nick said. "Matt didn't know."

"That was Matty on the phone?"

"Yeah."

We both knew how it happened. By not being told how she died, it told us how she died.

"Wow, some first day back, huh?" I said.

"Yeah," Nick kind of laughed. "You should visit more often."

We both kind of laughed.

"Hey, had you seen Nora at all recently?"

"She came and visited me in Texas last Christmas," I said. "That was the last time. How bout you?"

"No. I hadn't spoken to her in years."

"Yeah. I know you two kind of stopped communicating."

"She'd leave messages on my Facebook wall. Sometimes I'd respond with a few words, just like 'Good, how are you?'. Most of the time I just ignored her. Then, nothing."

"She didn't seem well when she visited me in Texas. I should have known."

"Hey, none of us could have done anything about it. You know that. She was gonna do what she was gonna do. You can't think like that."

"Yeah I know. Of course you're right."

After a few silent moments we sat back down on the couch. Nick took a hit from Susie. He passed it to me.

"No, thanks. I'm okay. I'm gonna go to bed, actually. I'm pretty tired."

"Yeah?"

"Yeah."

"Ok g'night Corey."

"Good night Nick."

I decided to wear my good clothes. First, my blue, open-fly under-britches, made of Egyptian lisle cotton. Then, I put on my ribbed under-shirt made of 100% certified Sea Island cotton, my black mid-calf chiffon socks, also made from 100% certified Sea Island cotton, my custom made white mother of pearl buttoned shirt, made from Swiss Alumo fabric, and made by the best and only real tailors left in Manhattan, my black wool trousers, my 100% cashmere sweater from Scotland, my orthopedic leather loafers, my blue Italian made silk jacket that was my absolute favorite color in the whole world, my leather coat with an inside fur lining and a fur collar, a hat, a glove, a scarf, and I was dressed.

I put the cargo in a black plastic bag, already annoyed at myself for committing to lug this thing along. It'll be worth it, I said to myself, hoping that the act of it saying it aloud would make it so.

I walked north to the Mexican joint on the corner of 6th Avenue and Watts Street and placed a five spot on the bar for a cafe con leche to go. The coffee was four dollars and some change. I left the rest for tip. I then turned the corner on Watts and stopped by the cigar bar. The porter let me in, as the bar was not yet open for business. I bought a pack of red Dunhills – the stronger kind. Can't even buy tobacco products from the Dunhill store in New York. I thanked the Dominican porter and walked east with the black plastic bag still in my hand, lighting a cigarette along the way.

I thought back to my first cigarette. Must have been at age 12 or 13 or 14. I was walking back from the park with a friend of mine from the neighborhood. As we were walking we saw a pack of cigarettes on the ground with a little less than half a pack inside. The package was green, so they were probably Kools or Newports. We went back to his house because his parents weren't home. We went into the back yard and had our first cigarettes together.

That first drag. Man. It was like a coalmine explosion in my chest. There might be something to that psychology mumbo jumbo where one tries to re-experience their first high with each subsequent drug experience. Not ever being able to do so, you keep taking the drug in hopes of finding it. Maybe you know that it's impossible. But subconsciously you're not ready to accept that you've already had you're first. You've had your shot and it's over. All you can get now is actually being a smoker. And then maybe cancer. So you move on to new and different drugs that you haven't tried before. But after you've had your first fuck, your first high, your first trip, your first time getting shitfaced drunk, and your first smoke, nothing feels that special anymore, it just becomes slight variations on the larger theme of being fucked up.

We finished all the smokes that were left in the pack. We each coughed liked hell and felt sick, dizzy, lightheaded, nauseous, and paranoid that his parents would come home and smell the smoke and somehow know what we had done and we'd get in trouble. Which of course didn't happen. We took the cigarette butts and buried them someplace in the dirt. I remembered feeling like I had done something wrong. And feeling that way felt good.

I was going to the nexus of the universe (to quote Seinfeld), 1st Avenue and East 1st street; towards the last place I remembered her living at in New York. I had the idea that I would make some kind of gesture. At a certain point along the way, I realized how pathetic it was. I was trying to do something symbolic; it was just so stupid. I second guessed myself and thought about not doing it at all. Then, as I got closer, I figured what the hell. I had come this far already. Might as well go through with it. I turned left on East 1st street towards where my memory told me her building was.

I wasn't sure if it would still be there. Things change over so quickly around here. But yeah – there it was. I recognized the outer part of the building. Address number 68. I didn't remember what the exact building number was, but 68 sounded about right. I was near certain that it was her building.

I reached into the black plastic bag with the cargo in it that I was carrying, and took out my worn black jeans with the big rip in the crotch and placed them on the ground in front of the building's entrance. Not feeling that I had placed them in a prominent enough position, I picked the jeans back up and laid them down with as much length as they could take up, so that the jeans expanded across the entire foot of the door. Looking down at it, it looked as meaningless as it was. Some ugly pair of ripped jeans on an equally ugly tan and black dotted concrete sidewalk. It was depressing.

Was this all that I could offer her memory? Was this supposed to celebrate her life, and all that she meant to me? Some shitty looking pair of jeans strewn out like trash on a stoop? Well, she did always like those jeans. But why was it that every time I tried to appreciate her, I failed? And she appreciated me to such an extent that it was embarrassing, even though deep down I felt it was deserved.

I didn't stay in front of there for long. As I left, I felt not as overtaken with her loss as when I first set out. Part of me was sad that the grief appeared to have left. Whenever a strong emotion blew through me I was sad when it left, whether it was a good one or a bad one didn't make a difference, because most of time there was nothing there at all.

It's a rip-off, I thought. You spend the vast majority of your life not feeling the strongest emotions you have. It's mostly filled with nothing. Feeling bored or indifferent, or slightly annoyed, which is just the same, really; it's not a real emotion. I couldn't even cry yet over her death – but I knew as suddenly as the tears would eventually come, they would leave.

The weight in my hand was lighter as I no longer carried the bag with jeans, and so were my spirits. I couldn't account for it. Maybe it was just getting rid of old clothes that made me feel lighter in spirit. I could go for that. It certainly made more sense than thinking that my gesture had given me some peace of mind.

I remembered the first time we had met. Why hadn't I remembered that story for the eulogy or the memorial service afterwards? Whatever I chose to write and say on those occasions must have been awful. Why didn't I talk about how we met? How could I have forgotten?

It was the very beginning of college. Maybe even the first week before classes had begun. I remembered walking into a room I hadn't been in before, with people inside whom I didn't know. Billy Idol's "White Wedding" was playing and I started dancing. And from across the room, like in a movie, this person came into focus and went right up to me and gave me a giant hug and screamed "Yes!" like she had known me all my life. And that was it. There was Nora.

I had a new friend in life. A friend I would always have. My first friend who was a girl. I had never had that before. I thought it was so cool. It was so cool to have a real friendship with a cool chick. Nothing romantic. And in that way, I didn't have to fear losing it as you would with a girlfriend. I found with Nora a complimentary friendship that I hadn't ever known before. There wasn't that same kind of rivalry that would exist in male friendships.

Nora had a habit of always signing off a letter, email, or birthday card to me with the phrase "Your partner in crime". She was my best, and to this day, my only girl, friend. How do you duplicate meeting by dance bonding to "White Wedding" and instantly hugging? We hugged before we knew each other's names. You can't re-create that. It's a once in a lifetime.

I took out my cell phone from my jacket pocket. I had recently downgraded to the most basic cell phone I could find apart from the Mickey Mouse phone. It was a Samsung Jitterbug that a friend of mine had recommended. The phone was primarily for senior citizens. It had no text messaging, no email or internet, the only buttons it had besides the keypad were "Yes", "No", and the "On/Off" button, and it had a function that connected you to a live nurse. And it was really goddamn loud. It cost me $22.30 a month, including tax, and even that had started to feel like too much to me. I dialed Nick's number, one of the few I knew by heart (the phone had no way to program phone numbers into it, either).

"Hello?"

"Hey Nick. Hard at work?"

"Hardly. Taking my sweet time walking outdoors. On my way to see a guy who robbed a jewelry store. Whats up?"

"Tell your cousin I'm in."

"You sure?"

"Yeah. Why not? I'll marry her. Why shouldn't she be able to stay here if she wants to?"

"Man, she'll be thrilled. But you sure you don't want to take some time to think about it. If it's about staying here, it's no problem, really."

"No, it's not that. I want to do it. Maybe she'll bring a girl home once in a while and they'll be drunk enough to let me in on the action."

"I don't think *that'll* happen, but if you want to get married, I'll call and let her know. Have you ever even lived with a woman before?"

"No," I said. "Have you?"

"No."

"It's different though, right? Since she's a dyke."

"She's still a woman," Nick said.

I took one last moment to ponder. It occurred to me, since dating sites such as tindr (and others whose names are so clever that I cannot remember them) only work with a phone and not a computer, that by refusing to have a phone with text messaging or internet access, green card marrying Sheila, even though she's a bulldagger, is quite possibly that best shot I may ever have to get laid again for the rest of my life.

"Fuck it," I said. "Yeah, I'm in. Call her and let her know. How bad could it be?"

Ben Pullar

Jubilee Discussion

I was in the dark house, the box brownie camera of my Grandma's house, and I was watching the rain, watching the window beaming with rain and light and water, looking through it at the mango tree in the garden. My Grandma was opposite me in the dark side-room of the house, drinking tea, trying to get me to talk. About my future dreams. I was sixteen and I had a few bad dreams. She wanted to hear them.

But I was tired of her questions. All I wanted to do was think about my own things. Spend time with my cousins. Listen to my Grandma's fantastic odd stories. I didn't want to worry about my future. But she kept badgering me. So I gave her an answer to the question of what I hoped to do in the future, with my life, my profession.

'I want to live in a shack in the bush,' I told her.

And she gasped. Sipped her tea. Said, 'You're just like Doug.'

Meaning my uncle, her oldest son. Doug, who lived in a shack in the bush.

'You can't do that,' she said. 'You're just exactly like Doug.'

I didn't think I was. I had only given her a throwaway answer. It seemed to upset her, so I was quite pleased. But then a dreadful thing happened. I actually started to wonder about my future.

What would I do? I couldn't think of anything. Businessman? Scientist? Poet? Nothing really appealed. Taxi driver? Carpenter? I didn't want to be involved in any of those things.

I was looking through the rainy window smeared and fresh and black, through the glass to the mango tree, and my mind started to follow my eyes out. It started to wander around through the rain outside. It started to pay a lot of attention to something particularly interesting that I had not seen before, and that was a mango. The last mango of the season. Somehow having evaded all the fruit bats and my Grandma, there it was. Somehow I had seen it.

I thought, maybe I could learn how to get these high altitude mangoes. These elusive late season fruits. I tried to think of possible ways.

Chainsaw. Seemed crude. I considered a mango pole. Three gaffer-taped broomsticks, one pot plant hanger hook. I imagined threading one up through the tree. Leaves and twigs would fall into the eyes. But I thought I could do it. I thought I could even have fun with a few of these end of season mangoes now and then.

If I got one, I thought I would run through the garden screaming, would run down the street yelling, blasting. I would run north, out to the coast, would wade out into the sea, dip the mango into the surf, turn the waters into a mango soup, a sea of mango juice. I would inspire in the process an entire generation of fish to hallucinate themselves into space, turning the night sky into a deep aquarium. Boiling with life. Death.

In a world like that I would look up to the stars every night in the rain, reaching up now and then to pluck an interstellar fish from a constellation, and I would sell them back to pet shops, make a billion dollars, and I would retire, welt and shrink in the garden of whatever expensive river side house I might buy from the proceeds. And I would reflect in unusual ways. My brain would be altered by years of eating fantastic hallucinogenic mango fish, making me see words differently. Mangomyert. Mangogare. Marrrrrrr. Mangourd. Treme. Toll. Tighs.

And then I thought, no. No. It wasn't for me, that sort of life. Too odd. Too insignificant.

I turned away from the window, ignored my Grandma, who was still shaking her head, and saw my cousins on the couch in the adjacent lounge, watching a rotten old science fiction film with bad special effects. Rain thrummed over the house and darkened the ceilings but the lamps were on, shining orange and green, and my cousins were all rugged up, watching their film, and I thought, 'Those special effects are just old mesh and silk and cardboard, I could do that.'

I could do it easily. I could win contests, win grants and awards and become famous. But then I thought about fame. I thought it would be a bit of a grim prospect in the end.

It would be like rainy 1986 Europe at a Riviera boulevard almost every day. Junkets. Resorts. Film festivals. Many colored umbrellas, hoods, wristwatches, fennel. Critics attacking, obsequious, crawling.

I imagined a normal day, shopping. Photographers would take snaps of me walking through the shopping centre. No peace. I imagined a Sunday afternoon, wealthy, successful, famous, out buying fruit at an elite store. Everyone dripping with water, but they would be noticing me and gawping. It seemed awful. Out of the grime and tumult the local mayor would approach me and ask what I thought I was doing.
'Getting ideas for more films,' I would tell him. It would be a disaster, I knew it.
They would start pinning me down for facts. How are you going to do this amazing thing? They would keep asking me this, and I would fail. I know that I would. I would have to shrink back suddenly. It would not last.

What else was there? I sat in that dark room, looking out the window, and I looked past the tree, the mango, the lens of the window, over the roofs.

A chimney sweep? There were still chimneys in this tin city. Or something different? Something really unheard of? A roof runner, leaping the corrugated iron leaves of tin, house to house, over gardens, turning the rooftops into an offbeat over-running freeway.

I would be a legend of the night, a sub-tropical spring-heeled jack. Tapping the rooftops of every second house, following the cold iron ranges around the city, across the river. I could see a whole other different sort of city from the blurred passing rooftops, and I could write about it. I could write books about that sort of city. Open up new rooms for others following along behind me to explore. I could do that.

But it was ludicrous. Hopeless. All I saw were failed goals. Designs. Graves. On the wet grass below my Grandma's house. I saw myself standing there in the rain, digging the graves of all my dead dreams. When I was done and the dirt had piled up and the holes were filling up with dead seas of mud water I saw myself sitting down in the wet grass under dark clouds and just giving up. Sighing a lot. Sighing as a heavy wind washed in and a crack came and a heavy object landed on my head. Before me, an elusive mango vibrating among the blades of grass.

Running around the garden laughing. Looking up, past the house in the rain, towards the road, and the future.

And then I buried it. I buried all of it in those flooded mental graves. All of my options. Hidden.

In the side-room my Grandma poured me a cup of tea and said, 'You should at least lay down a red carpet if you're going to live in the scrub,' and I looked out through the window and I saw the mango. It seemed to glow up there in the mango treetop canopy. I saw it and I was mesmerized. And as I sat there sipping at the green tea, I looked over at my Grandma.

I saw her old thin arms and her bright blue eyes, more alive than the house and my cousins and the rain. She held her cup in the palm of her left hand, laid the palm of her right hand over the top of it, like it was an urn full of her recently deceased late husband's ashes. My grandfather. It wasn't an urn of his ashes, it was her personal cup of tea, but she was looking at me with her eyes, and I could read them.

'A great disappointment,' she was thinking. She was thinking of where she had come from, her brothers who had died in the second world war, her parents who had come from different countries, who never had to worry about what they were going to do. Who never would have voluntarily lived in the scrub, eating leeches, bees. She looked at me and I knew she thought I was a fool. An idiot. A twit out of the rain. A drip out of the steady drizzle.

A slow learner. Getting slower. I saw it and I thought of her neck and legs and shoes, carrying her through the century, through wars and disasters and failures and disappointments to this table, this side room, this grandson hopelessly lost in his own pitiful world, and I felt bad, and I didn't want to cause her any more problems, so I started smiling in a funny way.

My cousins were still watching their science fiction movie. The bad special effects. Mesh lights on cardboard, silver foil warp-drives wobbling on strings.

Then I turned and looked out the window again and watched a fruit bat claw at the last mango of the season, the last in this part of the world, finally tearing it away from the tree branch.

'I think I will definitely use a red carpet,' I said.
'At some point, yes, but it's not in your future.'
'Not much is now,' I said.
'You'll find that more and more,' she said. 'More and more it'll happen. Part of the design.'

I looked out the window at the bat in the tree. Attacking the mango. Getting it. Flying away with it. Driving it off into the ruins of the rain.

'Anyway,' I said to my Grandma, 'thanks.' She sipped her tea. I got up. I went and sat down on the couch with my cousins and watched the rest of the movie. The afternoon went on. The rain kept coming for a while.

Ben Slotky

All the Ants in Arkansas

It's important to know the facts, it's important to begin a thing. This didn't start here, it couldn't, this is what I'm thinking now, but it's important to lay or lie the facts down anyway. I say lay or lie, I *will* say that when I eventually say this, because I don't know which it is, which we're supposed to do, right here on the ground. This is important to get out, right at the beginning, that I'm on the ground, laying or lying. You should remember this. Once I heard a way to remember whether it was lay or lie that only people lie. I'm thinking about this now and was then. That's important. That needs to be right out at the beginning, and that makes two things. You need to remember two things. Remember this about that. It will lead up to something. I am on the ground. One time a girl told me that the way to remember the difference between horizontal and vertical was that whores laid or lied down. That girl's name was Jane. It still is, even from here. She lives in Austin, Texas, which is not in Arkansas, which is where I am now and was then. My mother's name was Jane, too. She is dead. Jane's mother, not my grandmother, but the Jane who told me about horizontal and vertical's mother is dead, too. A motor scooter accident. Head trauma. Jane, not my mother Jane, used to go out with my friend, not my friend who looks Jewish but isn't, but another guy. The first time they had sex was on July 4th, which is my birthday, mine and America's and my uncle Kenny's. Once I had a dream about my uncle Kenny and ordering pistachio ice cream in a parlor with no attendants and you have to watch this, watch this as it adds up, lines up, before it goes away. It stacks on and on and goes, inexorable, even though all of this is true, all of it happened. These are all things that happened and I am saying it to a pile of ants, all of it.

Where I am is here. I am in Stuttgart, Arkansas, in a hotel lobby looking at a pile of ants, a hill of ants. I am laying or lying on the ground looking at a pile of ants, laying or lying, and you need to remember this. Today I was at Riceland Foods. I was trying to sell them things.

Papers, documents.

One time I wrote a story about how my mother said "Records, cassettes" when I told her I was reading a SPIN magazine. This happened, and is something you should remember. What happened was this. My mother asked what I was reading and I said SPIN magazine and she said "records, cassettes." I have a whole story on that, a whole story on that one scene that happened and I have nowhere to put it. I have nowhere to put this story; it doesn't fit, it doesn't belong. I thought I would put it here, in this story.

I tried.

I cut and pasted and copied.

I changed the font, the spacing. I was going to put it in there to show how there was a connection between when I said "Papers, documents" and "Records, cassettes." It doesn't work, is what I am thinking here on the ground. It can be too much. I am thinking that, watching all these ants.

Personalized documents, marketing materials, four words. I was going to sell them a product that would allow them to sell other products, personalized products, and marketing materials. If you make a product personal, people are more likely to buy it. If it has your name on it, if it looks like this is for you. Like this is for you. You should remember this.

I am explaining why I am here. I am in Riceland. I am in Arkansas. I have been in Arkansas once before. When I was 12, I was in love with a girl named Laura. Her family moved to Arkansas. I was going to save up money and take a train there. My brother sang the Huey Lewis & the News song to me, saying it *does* take money to ride this train. In a book I am writing, I have a story about Huey Lewis and a dog I am going to buy. This is what I'm thinking about, looking at these ants. There are so many of them. They are eating a chicken wing.

This is what is happening.

It is hot outside and this is where I am. It is night, not almost night, not not-yet-night. I have a whole story about the feeling of not-yet-night. I have no place to put that either and I was going to say you should remember that too, but you shouldn't because this is almost over, and this is where I am. And it is hot outside and it is not yet night and on the way to the lobby, the lobby where I am laying or lying with an anthill and a chicken wing, there are two men sitting on chairs outside of their room two, three, four down from mine and they are drinking in the dark. They are quiet and it is dark and they are drinking and smiling, toasting me with their beer cans. And I am looking at the ants and the chicken wing and thinking I don't want to go back to my room.

I can tell you why I am here right now and I already have. I just did. This is when and where. This is why. I am here because of the circumstances that brought me here. An addition. Weight, accumulation. What else can you do? And this isn't a question as much as it is a soft thing you say, you mutter, you don't declare. A soft thing you whisper, lips pressed on harsh carpet, ants walking past, simply, cleanly, inevitably. You could trace this out, if you wanted. You could see how this happened, all of it, lay or lie. I could show it to you and am showing it to you.

Back in my room, the remake of the movie *Assault on Precinct 13* is on HBO. A rapper named Ja Rule is in that movie. He looks like an otter. He has been in thirty-nine movies. That's three times the amount of precincts that are in the movie that was on HBO in the room I am staying in. I know this now, as I'm writing this.

This is me explaining, and it looks like a line, a progression, a forceful, an inevitable, this-means-that, right here, right where I am. Sometimes the sheer weight of circumstance, I am thinking. Sometimes that, I am telling myself, you, these ants, records, cassettes. This isn't even close to all the ants in Arkansas and you need to remember this.

Carla M. Wilson

Ecrire Les Oiseaux

Les Oiseaux

I don't mean to say that the birds were not always in my life. But it was only after several years of not noticing them that they came back. I was living downtown in a dirty loft with two artist friends, boozing it up and making art and every time I think of those times I realize the opportunities that were passing me by. The paintings, the writing, the music, the connections to important people. Only I didn't know, even then.

I could have flown then.
I would have flown high.
I could have grown then,
and touched the sky.

Les Petits

Everyone thinks he or she wants children by a certain age. At around 30 one begins to panic, thinking one must start getting on with life, thinking it's about time one started doing something important, or doing what's expected; not knowing that a decade or two later the person you thought you were will transform into a completely different human being with different thoughts and feelings. You'll behave completely differently, and the possibility exists that you weren't meant to be a parent and you weren't meant to be one thing or another. You'll be forced to come to terms with that and one day, you'll be faced with the question of who you really are.

J'aime bien les petits
J'adore les enfants
Je te manque, mes amis
Je te pense souvent

Des Arts

If I could choose what I'd like to be good at, it would probably be painting. The smell and the thickness of paint, the way the brush feels against a canvas, not to mention all the colors, makes me giddy. There is something about using my hands to create that I find necessary in order to feel fulfilled. Even if I had studied sculpture or ceramics, I think my favorite studio-art medium would be painting. I'd paint swirls of blues and greens mixed with white or yellow on a well-used, paint-thickened palette. I love to squirt the color from a tube, dip my brush into the thick paste, feel the weight of the brush tip, soaked and weighty with color, and slather it on a canvas or any blank surface. The sublime satisfaction of the slap, slap of wet against dry, the splash and tinkle of the swirl of the brush into a clouded water glass for rinsing, water splashing everywhere, getting messy. I would have loved to have made drip paintings, like Pollock, taking up an entire studio floor, walking around and around a canvas, splashing paint, dipping my brush, splashing paint, dipping and splashing, dripping and splashing.

Let me make a mess,
Throw the paint around,
Color on my dress,
Splash it on the ground

Des Animaux

They seem sad, the animals in the zoo. Every time I visit, I walk to the far end of the zoo and visit the elephants. Almost all of them are usually standing with their heads and trunks hanging down, tails swish-swashing slowly, back and forth, heavy metal chains tied around their ankles. I see them standing around in more or less the same place where they eat hay and drink water from the large trough. Occasionally they reach up to curl their soft pink trunks around the fragrant eucalyptus branches that have been installed for them to graze on. One looked at me once with its tiny grey, wrinkly eyes, and I wanted to climb over the ledge and hop into its cage. Once inside, I would climb onto its large, scratchy back and together we would make our way towards the I-5 freeway and amble off into the sunset.

Il y à des animaux

Qui volent souvent

Être banale mais

Je ne les écouter pas

Jamais

Les Chansons

Before I go to sleep I often hear music. Specifically, pop songs pop into my head. Then I must immediately jump up out of bed (even after I've settled in nicely), throw the covers off and make a note of what the song is. Usually one song leads to another, and then I'm up for a couple more hours documenting songs. I don't know where the music comes from; it seems to come from nowhere. But I'm glad music comes to me instead of nothing at all. It's too bad there is nothing genius that comes of it. Only a kind of neurotic tic.

Sing, sing a song

Make it simple

To last your whole life long

Don't worry that it's not good enough

For anyone else to hear

Just sing, sing a song!

Des Arbres

It would be nice to be surrounded by trees. You could listen to the wind rustling the leaves and the birds twittering between the branches. I would attempt to identify the birds and I would never carve words into any trunks. It would be a good opportunity to reflect on and acknowledge the birds that have come and gone. Finches are fairly polite whereas crows and mockingbirds can be noisy and inconsiderate. Black Phoebes are sweet-tempered and sociable, while Western bluebirds are rare and often skittish. Hummingbirds are bold and colorful, yet delicate and charming; some say they are messengers of persistence and escape. Rarely do I see flocks of geese, but often spot hawks, kestrels and blue jays.

JEF 73

il y a des oiseaux

qui se font entendre

car ils sont souvent perdus

Carolyn Chun and Deborah Chun

Incomplete Instruction Set II

You are a lady. What is a lady, you ask? A lady is not a hollow space.

You are a lady. In all things, you are a lady first and foremost, my dear. This fact does not occlude your vision, although it occupies a certain amount of your awareness. It uses the energy that you might otherwise dedicate to making an unintentional, embarrassing flourish, or to beginning a stammered sentence. You are less able to twitter than you would be if the knowledge that you are a lady did not partially occupy you at all time. Not that you lack the ability not to be calm. Consider a deep pool, which contains frantic or graceful worlds, I won't presume to insist upon your constitution, but generally presents a smooth surface. The purposes that you serve are your own, or ones that you have chosen, anyway, and this fact does not occlude your vision, although it occupies, as I have said, a certain amount of your awareness. Overall, however, and this part is a mystery, your vision is enhanced. "Tightened" may be the right word for it.

If this discussion seems quite beside the point, then you are a quick study. Look up from the page and fix your eyes on the horizon, or the far wall, as the case may be. Consider the variety of shades that constitute a single color. Imagine splashing some water against it—how the color would darken and curl.

A lady is not a megaphone. Others may speak to you in order to make their words loud and true, but they mistake their purposes for your purposes. This is not an intentional deception on your part. In fact, this mistake is a mark of your success. You are a lady, and a lady is misunderstood. The propensity of your audience to project onto you their own designs, their perception that you are delighted to be imbued with their aims, is a burden every lady carries. The light that falls down to meet you does not pass through you, my dear. But it does not knock you down.

JEF 73

There will be times, my dear, when you will not know what to say. At these times, you will call out, "Line! Line!" Utter what comes. If there is not a script, there is at least an outline. If there is not an outline, there are at least instructions. For example, when you are in Italy, one instruction is, "Speak Italian." The rest are in Italian.

A lady is a master of extremes, my dear. Consider your present location, and now consider the spectrum that it presents. In your immediate vicinity are a variety of temperatures, volumes, scents, textures, objects that one may take into one's view. The emotional vicissitudes color the air in their own dimensions. Let this pass through you, and not the other way around.

What are you able to say? What do you need to say? If the former set does not contain the latter, and it does not, in your case, then heed this gentle promise: The message always finds a way out. You are a lady first, in everything you do, you are a lady, and so you must be in possession of the messages you contain, as well as their methods and the incidental damage and blessing in their wakes. When you raze your garden to the ground, when you burn the roses alive, when you deliver to the sea your untended jewels, when you smile for the wrong reasons, when you curl your body in the earth, when you commit malice, arbitrage, homicide, suicide, homicide-suicide, when the mouths close down on you, when you are victimized, when your voice cannot carry beyond the moment, when your train of thought is charging right at you, whether or not you've tied yourself to the tracks, when nobody can believe you; you must articulate clearly. A lady is always believed, and yet we have all seen that a lady may fail in delivering her meaning. But you will not fail. I am here to see to that.

A lady can never be captured, because, if she is captured, then she disappears, as the saying goes.

I have not yet told you what to do with your beauty—whether to nourish it or abandon it. I have not discussed giving or receiving insults or praise. How to carry your strengths, your vulnerabilities, your teacup, your knife. My dear, the relevant moment is coming; it is already at your heels. The decision will be upon you just before you have made up your mind about it. However, these aspects, which can feel large, do not compose you. You are a lady. The rest is beside the point. A lady is a garden that nobody tends.

You will be required at times to move on. Or, anyway, you will find it necessary at times to move on. Or else, full disclosure, you will just decide to move on. You are a lady, and a lady can always recognize the hour. In order to move on, whether it is from a topic of conversation, or a meal, or a city, or what have you, first resolve completely to leave behind whatever it is that you intend to discard. If you are not able to completely resolve to leave it behind you, then its shadow may loom over your new direction. It's out of my hands, my dear. You are a lady, and you will or you will not be guided by my advice. Some choose to live with their specters. If you open your hands to release their content, and your eyes fill with the reflected moment and you hesitate, then the departure may never arrive. Let's not dwell on that. First resolve completely to leave. Next, judge whether you have an ally. It may be that you have no ally, but there are also none who oppose you. In that case, resolution, the first step of moving on, is the only prerequisite for executing the final step, departure. In case it is not, then you may find that your intentions align with another participant's. You are a lady, and another's interests aligning with yours indicate the other's good character. Turn your back to the same direction that your ally's back faces. You are now in a position to make your intentions known. The shifts in your constitution may have already communicated transition to your audience. If the audience does not acknowledge the shift, then consider moving on from your present company. Anyway, you are a lady, and a lady is able to rise to those occasions when an amplified signal is necessary; when shifting your vision from the audience's eye to the audience's shoulder will not suffice. You will need to fix upon a new horizon. The audience, which has not yet moved on, will feel disrupted when you bend toward the new aim, when you set down your glass, its contents trembling nearly audibly—is there a ringing sound coming from the glass? Your audience will find your turn sudden, although you've already completed it, since they have continued to look in the direction opposite to your present movement. An apology will be well-received just before you glide past, not tripping on your own feet. You are a lady, however, and only you can say how accommodating you will be.

Departure is best achieved upon the pretext of necessity.

You will have to eat. A lady has appetites. She must dine, she must speak, she must sleep, she must listen. She licks her fingers. She curls her toes. She gnashes her teeth. She closes her eyes. She delivers the mail. She forgets someone's name. She applies the fork and knife to the meat with reckless splendor. Et cetera. Which is Latin, as every lady knows.

A lady is not a layering on of aspects. A lady has her firmament, and her depths, dear, and now is the time to articulate the realization that is beginning to reflect in your features, that knowing that has gestated all along just out of sight: A lady is her own home. This is why your mortality cannot bear another's weight. Yet you must sometimes bear it. That double-vision glare never quite comes into focus. Yet you must sometimes bear it.

You are a lady. A lady is not a vapor or a memory, although these analogies have their value. Analogies may be all we can offer one another. When you are seen by another, the other creates a two-dimensional image of you. This is not intentional, but has to do with the constitution of the human eye. Be wary of first impressions, since a first-time observer is unlikely to ever see the whole, so to speak, picture. If this worries you, then good. Trust your lack of faith in my instruction. Disbelief is the height of femininity.

You are a lady, and a lady is marked by her standards for being addressed. To whom you will grant your audience is your prerogative, but a the speaker never forgets the speaker is addressing a lady. First and foremost. A lady. At the front of each speaker's mind: the shapely fact that you are a lady.

These are not the only instructions you will receive, dear one. The instructions are intended to provide context and clarity, but do not expect certainty. To be certain is to certainly not be a lady.

Carolyn Chun and Layal Hakim

Autoinventio

"What if the characters we are impersonating outlive us?" she wanted to know.

"That would be impossible. They only exist in our heads."

"Who's to say in whose heads whom exists, now?"

"They will die with us, naturally."

"In what form are they alive now, bound together with our bodies? What can be said to exist apart from these words?"

"Now the lines between one character and another are blurred. Now the dividing curtain is rent in two."

"Whom shall I ask for when I go to the front door?"

"Now the eyes close on one future and open on another."

"Will you answer? Or will the man you've invented? Which is the copy? Which is the form, and which the mold? Which the shadow, and which the projector? Among your projections are certain... inconsistencies... suggesting a dynamic formulation of the roles you play. This version holds me a bit too tightly, and that one prefers to be alone in the next room. This one sleeps while that one stays up all night. Still another constantly finds himself singing. And yet who can say where the inconsistency lies? The versions of myself, the perceivers, may contain the inconsistencies: perhaps this one presses against you and that one prefers to be alone in the next room. Perhaps this one of me pulls you close against that cold part of me that becomes a melody in your head."

"Perhaps these characters are the same everywhere for everyone."

"Are the characters interacting with each other? Is that possible? Could it be that one character created the other but in the same mind? Which character dominates the other and leads us to make mistakes? Is one being empowered by the other?"

"How do they change with time? They don't think."

"Time? What happens with time? It could be that the characters evolve into the

other characters with time, and so they never die but only swap. And if they can swap, and be swapped, then they can probably be transferred like energy. Transferred from one body to another. So that is how characters can outlive us."

"When I wake up inside my second thoughts, and not the other way around, I go spinning through possible attributes. I am wild. I am tame. I am a villain. I am a dentist. I put on clothes to be one or the other or a third, and so on. However, there are those for whom this decision is already made."

"If all of us are free to make decisions, then those of us who make decisions to limit the choices of others of us prevent all of us from being free to make decisions. Not that they prevent us all, but they prevent some of us, to the effect that we are not all free to choose whom we will be."

"Ah. You're late. I didn't even hear you arrive."

"Neither shall you hear my departure."

"Hello down there!"

"Who is that coming down the stairs at this hour?"

"Oh, hello! I'm very sorry if we woke you."

"No, I woke without your assistance."

"Those stripes suit you. I like your matching sleeping cap."

"Thank you."

"My love, are you unwell? Can I bring you something?"

"Dearest, will you come to bed? I have suffered a bad dream, the same bad dream as before. The same dream as always. Come upstairs. It's late."

"I am sorry to hear that you've been troubled. We shall send up your designated companion."

"Yes, go on upstairs, oh unanimously selected one."

"Oh, My Love, but what more do we have than this hour? This minute? This one single moment in which to have one's eyes open?"

"The east is beginning to brighten, Dearest."

"Go on, you elected official."

"Do not let us keep you."

"My love, what more do we have than these benches and small tables? What more do we have than the dark windows holding back the stars and dew and one or more spiders?"

"Go on to your striped love, and I will entertain our new guest."

"Dearest, your discussions will not reach a conclusion tonight or the next or the next. Feel free to return to these matters at your leisure once you have accompanied me through slumber to dreams and back again."

"What more do we have, my love, than you folding and unfolding your hands? What more do we have than these few words?"

"You're quite stubborn aren't you?"

"What more do we have than these weakened old walls covered with designed wallpaper? Designed, they are, with blue tulips, so that we don't get bored?"

"Come stand by me and look at that wall on your left"

"Right here?"

"Exactly, that's perfect. What do you see when you look at this wall?"

"I can see cracks in a weak wall and old wallpaper with blue tulips on an off-white background."

"Look closer and think deeply. Then tell me what you can see."

"I can see cracks on some parts of the wall, some are short and some are long, and some are coalesced with each other. On other parts of the wall I can see wallpaper, old and partially dirty wallpaper. There are some blue tulips on a old white background."

"Close your eyes."

"Shall I continue to face this wall?"

"Yes."

"I will tell you when you can open your eyes. When you do open your eyes, you will see what I see when I look at this wall."

"What do you see?"

"I can see movement. The wall is alive. I can see a field. There are two children playing in a field. They are playing with a kite. There's green grass around them and trees in the far distance. The leaves on the trees are blowing, just as the grass, blowing in the

wind. The wind is warm. Look at the sky. There are birds flying in a synchronized way. The birds are of many colors. There are black birds, blue birds, yellow birds. The birds are singing as they fly. They fly slowly in the warm, sweet wind. Look back at the field. There's a cottage on your right. A woman walks out wearing an orange dress, soft and light. She's holding a basket in her hand and many other children run from behind her into the field towards the happy children. The basket has cakes. The woman puts the mat on the grass not far from the cottage door. She bends down as her dress sways and put the cakes on the mat. The children all gather around the cakes. They eat the cakes as the clear, warm, sweet wind blows softly. The singing birds are singing. The happy children are joyful. The green grass is healthy. You can open your eyes now."

"I can see it. I can see the alive wall. It's beautiful."

"What more do we have? We have eyes to see what we wish to see. We have hands to feel what we wish to feel. We have hearts to transmit love and receive love from each other. We have power. The power that allows us to implant feelings in each other. Feelings that make you smile or cry."

"I don't want you to cry."

"These walls are not weak. They are strong. They are so strong that they allow you to see and feel whatever you want."

"I am afraid that we will never be at home in this interpreted world."

"Would you like a cake, my blue-feathered bird?"

"Our imaginations are more grounds for distrusting our perceived worlds."

"Would you like a cake, my hollow-boned bird?"

"A second ago I swear this was a paper-covered wall!"

"Have a cake, my fan-tailed bird."

"Mmffmm."

"There you go."

"Mmm. Yes, you have a certain flair for taking matters into your own hands, when it comes to insisting on cake-eating. I admire that. One relies on the movements of others, the muscles working their skeletons, and the blood cells surging through their brains. One relies on them. These form another house with its own adjustable walls.

And without these houses, we would have no way of knowing which direction gravity pulled."

"Context is everything."

"Context is indeed everything. Until we see God."

"I think this cake is getting to you. Have another piece."

"You see, in the beginning there was void, there was nothing."

"Ah, yes. It must have been hard to know how fast to drive without speed signs."

"God said, Let there be context. And there was context."

"That's not how I remember it."

"It's hard for the mind to conceive of the contextlessness of the world that preceded context. Or perhaps it's not hard, simply unbearable."

"I think I'd prefer it. No traffic signals stopping me. No speed limits. No men at work."

"Didn't we intend to go to sleep? Why now have we eaten cake? The hours are unforgiving. If we lose track of them, then they may lose hold of us."

"No pedestrian crossings. No school zones. No windy bits or slippery bridges."

"And what have we now? A bit of crumbs at the corner of our mouths? An imperfect contextualization of you folding and unfolding your hands on the highway before the dawn of time?"

"You're right. Better keep the hands on the wheel, eh?"

"Good night then. I'll see you tomorrow."

"Aren't we sleeping in the same room?"

"What of it?"

"You don't have to tell me that you'll see me tomorrow. I'll be with you. In fact I'll be inside your dream. I'll make your dream. I know what you will dream tonight."

"Here we go again."

"You can control your dream too."

"And where do you think dreams come from, O wise one?"

"They can come from three places. They can be from God. They can be from Satan. And they can be from one's self thinking."

"One's self thinking... do you mean I can think of something and choose to dream about it?"

"No. I mean, the things you think about on a daily basis or even those things that you used to think about or those things that influence your life and routine. These things can form part of your dream"

"And how can dreams come from God or Satan?"

"I don't know. You would just feel it I guess."

"OK, so come on, control my dream and tell me what I will dream tonight."

"You will dream about another wall, not the living wall."

"Another wall?"

"You will dream of the wall. The wall will be all around you. It will be a closed wall covering the whole room. It will be dark in color. Dark grey skies. You will see black crows flying in the sky. There are clouds, horrible clouds. You never thought that clouds could be scary, but these are terrifying. The sky looks heavy. It seems that it might rain. You know that it won't rain water. It won't rain anything you have ever seen. The crows fly clockwise around the wall, and you, you will be slowly turning counterclockwise watching them fly faster and faster. You become dizzier and dizzier. You can't wake up. The crows are increasing in number. There's about one hundred of them, then a thousand, then a million, then they overlap and they're becoming faster and faster. They start eating each other. Why are they eating each other, you ask yourself. The sky starts raining. It's heavy blood. It's blood, but it's heavy. It so viscous that you can taste it. It won't stop and you're even dizzier than before. You can't wake up. You fall to your knees and continue to look up. The crows are all gone, they have all been eaten except one. The winning crow slows down as it continues to fly clockwise. It slows down. It slows down. It come to rest on its feet not far from where you kneel. He looks at you. He sees that you are covered in blood. You're scared. You can't wake up. He's going to eat me, you think. You know. The crow approaches you. You can't see the clouds anymore. You can't see the dark sky or the blood around you. You can't see the wall. All you see are the crows eyes staring at you. You wake up."

"I worry about you when you use such imagery. I worry about the crows and the blood and the murder. I don't mean a flock of crows, which is called a murder, I mean the killing. If these fill the dream you give me, then maybe they fill your dreams. What fills your dreams may spill over into your waking thoughts."

"Red, red, is the color they bled. We sleep in a bed. We live by a thread."

"Your song does comfort me, I suppose. It's better than dreams darkened by crows."

"Blue, blue, to cover us two. Red for my head. Blue for your shoe."

"You are troubled. Stop pinching me and go to sleep."

"Good morning my dear fellow human."

"Can we have some of that cake for breakfast?"

"You want cake for breakfast?"

"Is there a problem with that? My mouth, throat, esophagus, stomach, both intestines, liver, and pancreas don't seem to have any restrictions on what I eat and when. You see, I was born without a user's manual. So I will live without a users manual. I shall die that way too."

"So tell me, what did you dream last night?"

"You know perfectly well the answer to that."

"No. I don't. You didn't let me control your dream last night remember?"

"The world will not break in half if we put aside the present moment. The world will not unravel if our hands hold each other. Our perspective will not crumple up like a piece of paper if I have a drink of water."

"When one is asked a question, it is polite to acknowledge it."

"Avoiding a question *is* acknowledging it."

"Avoid. A. Void. Void. Voided. Canceled. Reduced to nothing. Nothing. Absence of presence."

"Poof. Gone. A cloud of smoke."

"The curtain drops. Nobody knows whether or not to applaud. The audience is empty. But I digress. Your dream?"

"The dream has mostly evaporated. I seem to recall a pair of dark eyes above a pointed beak."

"Do you recall the feast? Do you recall being devoured? What did dying feel like? My death feels like floating in a warm pool."

"I have cut ties with my past. My dream was dreamt, and now the time for sleep has past. For you, I can see that the way forward is the way back. But not so for me."

"No past. No dreams. No memories?"

"Well one cannot forget everything. But one does not need to dwell on one's memories. I stand before a mirror. I give the expressionless face reflected in the dark glass a quick, dispassionate inspection for dirt and blemishes and then I turn, I push the door open. Now, I am in a new room. Or a kind of corridor. Walking beside you."

"Yes, we do walk together. I'm watching our feet. I see them go. Here, this is our turn. Left. Watch out for the puddle. No telling how deep the water goes. The surface is a mirror into which you might sink. Down and down and down."

"The threat of depth. Plus seven years of bad luck for breaking a mirror. If you believe in that sort of thing. Which I don't. It seems unfair. You accidentally break a mirror somehow, maybe you dropped it, and then there's broken glass shattering, there's a mess, and maybe you don't even have shoes on. Even if you can get the vacuum without stepping on a shard, there's the splinter lodged in your brain, a thought about the glass, that some piece will turn up later on, stuck in a soft bit of flesh. The piece of glass perhaps too small to even see, but the blood drips down anyway. That should coincide with seven years of good weather."

"Down and down and down. For seven years the blood drips down. Oh, careful. More puddles."

"How long before I saw that this is fiction? It took until this very moment for me to know that the story that contains me is its own invention. In fact there are no walls, no rooms, no guests, no dreams, no birds, no cakes."

"Down and down and down."

"What if we did things differently? What if we had done things differently?"

"Differently differently differently. That past has a future that no one will see."

"How amazing would it be? If one movement from one person was done

differently. One word changed. One kiss. One look. One movement. It could have made everything that followed very different. For everyone, everywhere, like resonance. People resonance. World resonance."

"Change change change. Are we there yet?"

"There where? In the new world? I might not be walking with you now in this new world. Then we wouldn't have anywhere to go. Nowhere, like empty space. Or one of us might not have existed, or existed in a different form."

"But it's still us though?"

"Maybe in different bodies, or we might have different minds, different thoughts, different dreams."

"Change change change. New people?"

"Different people. Maybe different species. Harmful species. Harmless species. All from a single change, or two. A big change happening with time, within centuries or a second. A new realm could have come to existence. We would not have been able to go there though. Or shall I say in present tense that we are not able to go there?"

"Can they come to us? These new people in this new world."

"You mean new realm? Are you paying any attention?"

"I'm paying lots of it, and well spent too. New realm. Can they come to us?"

"We don't know. We might never know, since we can't see them, or can we? It might be a realm with the same people in this world except they are living in a different way, with different events. A realm with people like us, with a purpose like us, who eat like us, who love like us, who breed like us who dream like us, who see unlike us. The world has a realm that no one can see."

Carolyn Chun and Peter Hobson

Decoherence

Peter Robert Hobson wrote his dissertation, "The Design & Construction of a Holographic Film Measuring Machine for the Heavy-Liquid Bubble Chamber HOBC and a Determination of the Cross Section for Charm Production by 360 GeV Protons," in high-energy physics regarding holography, bubbles, and a computer controlled film scanning machine "CHIMAERA." He included a quotation from from Book II of Milton's Paradise Lost because of the parallels between the names of his machine and its software and Milton's vision. Unfortunately, Carolyn dropped Peter's dissertation, and the words came loose. She reconstructed the introduction as best she could. The result follows.

A heavy-liquid, frozen, many-fired, rapid cycling bumble chamber, HOBC, with a typical bubble diameter of 10 microns, has been used to charm the total measure of 360 GeV/c protons. The method employs all monstrous, all prodigious things. The lab is haunted by a Hologriffin who mediates parking disputes and nibbles on any graduate student who falls asleep at his post. Students are discouraged from attributing any credit to her for her assistance in staying alert when reporting to funding agencies, as the presence of a Hologriffin in the lab might increase insurance premiums in the H2 beam line at CERN.

The experiment NA25, comprising HOBC, the bumble chamber, and an associate, Muffin the Muon Detector, is described. The buzz of the bumble chamber is calibrated. The Hologriffin and Muffin give complete family histories and Muffin provides iridescent, razor-edged feather samples. The operating conditions of HOBC are itemized by the Hologriffin, and the rocks, caves, lakes, bogs, dens, and shades of death are discussed. The theory that Hologriffins were created for evil is considered in detail. She objects to such consideration so this consideration is conducted at a low volume during her naps, out of reach of her tail point, which occasionally flicks out to whip supporters of the "created for evil" theory.

The effects of the recorded image of laser coherence are not a universe of death. The limitations of God's curse and objective structure are aberrations. Aberrations abominable, unutterable, and worse. The effects of spatial filtering on Hologriffins are considered from a considerable distance. The Hologriffin likes Muffin's feathers but has difficulty holding the feathers in her claws, and has started several lab fires while trying to study the feathers by the light of a flame. Lab fire response protocol is practiced or performed on a weekly basis. (Only one casualty has resulted from a feather-fire incident: one graduate student went to the hospital after suffering from smoke inhalation, but has since made a full recovery and shifted to another lab, in another field, on another planet.)

The design and construction of Chimera, a computer-controlled, film-scanning monster, is described. The design principles, "Where all life dies, death lives, and nature breeds, perverse," are outlined. Chimera discusses his mechanical stages and abominable microcomputer. Particular emphasis is placed on the design of his optical system and the choice of video camera tubes (red ones).

It was hoped that Chimera, hand-raised in captivity by the lab personnel, would naturally attach himself to the workers and provide security during those times that the Hologriffin engaged in abominations inutterable, and worse than fables yet have feigned, or fear conceived. The software, running in a PDP 11/44 minicomputer, providing the guidance and data acquisition for Chimera is described in detail. The software driving the stages, running in an 8085 microprocessor, which allowed the Hologriffin to update the Chimera to fire-breathing status, and replace with evil every good purpose, is briefly mentioned.

The analysis of the data is presented. The backgrounds in each topology are considered. The effects of cuts are described. The costs of medical treatments are outlined. The scanning efficiency and decay visibilities are calculated. The charm production cross-section is evaluated. Finally, the predicted date at which scientists may return to the lab without being eaten is evaluated. Like Gorgons and Hydras, Hologriffins and Chimeras die. Hologriffins and Chimeras die.

Daniel Ableev

Solipsoid (Translated by Dennis Mombauer)

"Soleww activated the vendor, and a tiny, delicate Chrysalid dropped out. Soleww made sure the Chrysalid was assimilating different soul parts of animals (Shobolon, Ingus, etc.) correctly and transferred them through precise instructions into himself. Soleww calibrated the Chrysalid to meet the exact soul requirements, the final step being its deposition in compartment no. 8 of Sansabienne. Immediately afterwards the Chrysalid began to function and dissolved as soon as the animal processes had been implemented completely. Soleww sank, deeply exhausted by his animations, in Plastilence under the Aesthetics Of Darkness And Cinematography Of Sansabienne.

#

After his uncoupling, Soleww puttered around at the vendor until he finally received a brand-new Chrysalid. Instantly, the pertinent animal matrix [Hume] was selected, and the re-charged Chrysalid moved into compartment no. 8 of Sansabienne. Soleww was able to pass the forest only with the help of animal morphemes, while the dolphin-dog soul was being transferred into Soleww's contaQ mask. When the bank of The Light-Lukewarm Night, Respectively The Divine Bliss, came within reach, everything ended in Plastilence under the Aesthetics Of Darkness And Cinematography Of Sansabienne.

#

After his uncoupling, Soleww summoned a Chrysalid that met all of the specific animal requirements. The transfer of a potent Kalǝder soul was programmed and the delicate limbs of the Chrysalid were pattern-rigged in such a way that the forest animatronics made a flawless defeat of the Ultra-Radical Enmity Of Sansabienne possible. Compartment no. 8 was being filled and de-catastrophized employing the formula ╓╒jugnelb═ook╕╖. Straight away, Soleww operated his flesh-It with a lagged animal matrix across the intricately labyrinthine forest trails and swaths of different levels of difficulty, while his contaQ mask was glowing isis-red. At the end of his journey the forest was upside down, which meant his arrival at the bank of The Light-Lukewarm Night, Respectively The Divine Bliss

[Plastilence].

#

After his uncoupling, Soleww approached the vendor inside his formless somamorf and lured the Chrysalid out via a soma messenger. While mentalugging out of his flesh-§§ with restless maggot paws the Chrysalid's limbs through Motors_of_Inhumation, the last soul residue of twelve highly specialized cadavers [Dodoniel] was installed. The somamorf developed a certain amount of protrusions during the charging procedure, among them the bulge form characteristic for gaping. Soleww's little eyes-in-gastric-juice observed his psychical and physical excretions, all of them introversive, very carefully. Stomach joints, a multitude of tendon levers, dystopian genitals, cartilage conditions as well as brain-, nano- and face-enclaves made up Soleww's rich inner life, while on the outside the forest of Sansabienne was being mastered for the trillionth time with brutish perfection. As soon as the bank of The Light-Lukewarm Night, Respectively The Divine-Bliss, came within psychosomatic reach, the 8-singularity relocated into nothingness. Ultimately, Soleww accepted, neither for the first nor the last time, the bliss of the Plastilence," said the General Secretary.

#

Once I had learned to read the peculiar metaphors of this wise creature, I was able to agree: those unscrupulous minions who, just like the vile oppressoR himself, made more and more the impression of primitive flesh hags, should have never conducted the attack. But now it was too late, and the amoral body politics had – by demand of the Commission's almost unanimous decree – to be sanctioned through massive deployment of mortuary distorters ASAP …

David Wirthlin

The Youngling

Hovik nurtures his Xetl tree. He licks the tangy bark, his rough tongue on its smooth surface. It absorbs saliva and quickly turns red, then back to brown. The tree drops several leaves for his use.

He binds his feet, Xetl leaves wrapped tight against skin, props them up, higher than his head. Blood to his feet slows. The Xetl leaves respond, transfer fluid through his pores. Leaves visibly drying; feet invisibly nourished. When Hovik walks, his feet are impervious to the flaws of earth. Sticks, rocks, wet mud, roots, flora, fauna, everything. His feet slide over sharpness, repel wetness, disperse dirt. He doesn't float exactly, but his feet don't touch the ground either.

He gnaws wild beast of prey. Lunch: a bone, kidneys, a hemisphere of the brain.

Other trees fall from the sky each day. Each is launched from a distance, no destruction, no harm, but a nuisance nonetheless. At first there is no pattern. These non-Xetls land, some roots up, others roots down. No matter the direction, each penetrates soil in force, several feet deep, a new permanent fixture of the landscape. Over time, trees fill in around the cottage in abundance. Over time they become patterned, form a wall, a barrier from other trees, from wild beasts of prey. His cottage is protected. Despite the malicious intent of trees, they protect him from the others that will be sent, from anything that might try to destroy him. Over time, Hovik fills in the gaps between trees with mud, spit, and yellow tall grass.

Hovik motions like work every day. While he muds gaps between trees, other trees fall, and their impact loosens his mud. He breaks down more wild beasts of prey, builds storage for the drying of flesh. Their meat stacks up, sometimes goes rancid and becomes fuel. He uses intestines to bind trees, a web of wild beast parts as a surface to bind mud. Then more intestines and more mud. His most complete wall looks only like mud, spit and yellow grass, though it's built upon a foundation of trees and intestinal binding. The trees and intestines form an internal lattice of strength.

Near the silverbrush, wild beasts of prey mingle and watch. Snort here, stamping of feet there, attempts at communication. Hovik does not desire to understand them. They marvel at what Hovik has built, marvel at trees, lament the loss of their kind at Hovik's hand. When he started, Hovik focused on the younglings, their meat tender, their spirits pure, but realized mature beasts could feed him longer, send a stronger message of dominance over wild beasts of all kinds. Most of his storage holds mature beasts. Younglings never last long enough. He breaks them down and consumes them on the spot, his feeding ritual and needs ever expanding.

Hovik rests on the branch of his Xetl tree, feet and hands bound in leaves. A wild beast approaches, a braveness not usually seen amongst the beasts. This youngling stands underneath the Xetl tree, sniffs it, licks its tangy bark. The bark does not respond. Unconcerned, Hovik remains on his branch, lets his bound feet and hands absorb Xetl nutrition.

This youngling will not leave. It lies down at the base of the tree. Hovik considers tearing it asunder and consuming it in kind, but he's curious. He watches the beast, even as he drains leaves of value, and he wonders if the beast understands this tree's worth or if the beast wants something from him or if it's simply a wild beast on a wild beast quest which Hovik cannot understand.

The youngling stands, urinates on the base of the tree, which Hovik doesn't mind, except this is where he urinates too. The youngling finishes, retreats to silverbrush, likely unaware of the damage it will cause. The urine soaks into the bark, into the soil, into the roots. The bark turns green, separates from the tree, falls. Hovik feels the loss, panics, drops to the ground, his feet sinking into the earth. Though his feet are wrapped, he feels earth anew, aware of its various imperfections. He removes leaves from his hands, picks up fallen bark, tries to replace it. It doesn't stay. Hovik licks it in place. No longer tangy, it doesn't change color, doesn't adhere. The tree retreats its leaves. Hovik consumes the bark, but it tastes like wild beast of prey.

The Xetl tree is leafless, patchy in its bark, and, unknown to Hovik, has roots rotting underfoot. Hovik hunts down the youngling, encroaches on wild beast territory, cannot discern between them, and slaughters all in his sight with his hands. He's quick to act in his rage; they reciprocate no violence upon him. He does not eat or store any beasts, but leaves them to rot in a field beyond silverbrush. The youngling laments from a safe distance.

After washing in the river and sleeping some, Hovik finds an egg in place of his Xetl tree. He carefully picks up the egg. He wonders if maybe it could hatch a wild beast, if this was the youngling returned to torture him. What if the youngling has merged with the tree? Would whatever hatches be a treasure or a torment? He carefully weighs it in his hand, considers his options, notices it' s not an egg, but a seed or perhaps a seedpod filled with a multitude of seeds. He tries to squish the seedpod with his fingers, but it doesn't budge. He pushes harder and realizes what he's holding is more like a rock than anything else. It's smooth on one side, more smooth on the other, heavy all over. When the rock hatches, it bears a stone, jagged and hot. He hurls it in the river, and this is the point, just now, he is overcome with a deep, unbearable sadness and drops a tear from his eye. He takes this solitary tear, wipes it on his burlap pants. All this does is transfer tear from face to pants, and when there is no larger reaction beyond evaporation, he dives into the river to retrieve that stone.

Denis Emorine

Death at Half-Mast

(La mort en berne)

Novel

Taken from Chapter One

Translated from the French by Michael Todd Steffen

1

How did their story really begin? He couldn't say. Those near him knew Dominique as an animated yet cautious man. He could get uppity. He could overstep himself in heated debates with friends. High on the list of things he loved, he loved to write. Truth be told, beyond writing little else mattered to him. Now in his fifties, to his great satisfaction he lived, as it were, by his plume. Without looking back, Dominique Valarcher left his job as a university librarian at the Sorbonne, where his wife Laetitia taught French literature and Latin. His books were translated across Europe and in the United States. The writer sometimes had the impression he was better known abroad, which didn't bother him. Though France had recently woken him. He was invited to conferences. He had been granted writing residencies. *Nobody is a prophet at home*, the well-known proverb had applied to him, until these recent years. Dominique Valarcher had taken this late success in his own country with a somewhat affected detachment and a certain satisfaction. Editors in America and Romania offered to publish his collections of poems and his plays in bilingual editions. The writer had never even asked for this attention. Recently he had been invited to Benson College at New York University, an all-female college that touted itself for preparing women to lead the world. Valarcher wasn't persuaded that studying French or reading his books would particularly prepare them for the task though he was flattered that prestigious and highly selective institute of learning had paid him this homage. He relished the idea of speaking in English with the young students also but the

American professor, Jim Cole, had warned him: speaking English was forbidden in foreign language and culture classes. The rule was taken seriously. And in this establishment where the best of the best were recruited to teach, they didn't mess around with the rules.

Don Skiles

Beautiful Shirts

At that time, I didn't have a shirt to my name. The ass was out of both pair of pants I had. . .like Huck Finn's father, whose hat was "like a jint of stove pipe. . .such a hat for a man like me to wear, one of the richest men. . ."

Men today – some men – wear knitted Peruvian peasant caps.

Shirt off his back, he would give you. There was a woman, young, a long time ago, living in a rented house with a hand-built stone fireplace. She wore men's shirts, too big for her (she was petite), they came down to the middle of her thighs.

British shirts. They are expensive; bespoke shirts. Half a dozen at a go. Finest Egyptian cotton. No gentleman wears a silk shirt. Same with silk sheets. The same.

Tuck it in, or leave it out?

Barrel cuff? French?

Top button undone?

Button-down collar? Or wide?

Full-cut, traditional, or slim fit?

There was a time. When men wore paisley patterned shirts, and some wore faded denim shirts with embroidered collars and cuffs, embroidered by their girl friends. Those were beautiful. (It was before tattoos.)

And that's what Daisy Buchanan said to Gatsby, isn't it? As he threw armfuls of shirts onto the bed, a kaleidoscope of colors, autumn leaves falling, that green light glowing at the end of the dock.

"They're such beautiful shirts," Daisy said, crying.

A shirt should break expectations

Wearing an old shirt, faded into faded, at a small scarred desk, with a glass of amber whiskey, a cup of dark coffee, and a leaky window looking out on fog, close.

Dolly out, and up.

Roll credits. Lights up.

Fucking beautiful.

Eckhard Gerdes and Peter Cherches

Portrait of a Tobacconist

Friendly Tobacco. That's the name of his shop. Friendly Tobacco. Emil Friendly is a tobacconist. Your friendly neighborhood tobacconist.

A drug pusher, right? That's what you're thinking, a drug pusher. A nicotine candy man, as it were. Emil Friendly does sell candy too, and breath mints, but tobacco is his stock in trade.

Calling the tobacconist, the main character of this feuilleton, Friendly, that's a joke, right?

No, friends, it's no joke. Emil Friendly is an honorable man plying an old and honorable trade, honorable since women were women and cigars were smokes. There was a time when a tobacconist had to know the difference between Latakia and Perique, Virginia and Burley, Yenidje and toasted Cavenish. How many of you, dear readers, can tell the difference between Yenidje and toasted Cavenish? Emil Friendly can. He can also spot a Peterson at twenty paces. The tobacconist's eye, the tobacconist's nose.

Tobacconist, a quaint yet stately word, so much more elegant than "smoke shop proprietor."

Feuilleton? Can you think of a better term?

Emil Friendly, though always chatty and cordial with his patrons, is something of a loner when not at the shop. So, actually, though his customers consider Emil friendly, he's really something of a...well, misanthrope isn't the word, he doesn't dislike humanity, really, he just lacks interest in his fellow man. We need a term something like "agnostic."

Look over there, to the left. Do you see that house? A two-story yellow brick number in the North Shore suburbs of Chicago. There's a nice yard in front, and an even nicer yard in back (you'll have to trust me). The front lawn (yes, I know I said yard) is decorated with rows of perennial flowers accented by new patterns of annuals every year. This year the last frost happened early, so the flowers are particularly stunning. Of course, the ajugas are beginning to overtake the jack-in-the-pulpits, and the squirrels keep decapitating the sunflowers, but those are the tortures suffered by many gardeners. Emil Friendly often considers poisoning the squirrels, but he can never bring himself to do so.

Ajuga, jack-in-the-pulpit, Yenidje, Latakia, Friendly Tobacco.

Emil had once traveled all the way to Turkey to meet the great Meerschaum pipe artist Ismet Bekler, the Muhammad Ali of pipe carving, so dedicated is he to his trade and its traditions. Some may think me a pariah, but I belong to an ancient and noble profession, Emil tells himself. Still, people are going to think the worst of him, so he buries himself in his gardening to forget his worldly woes.

In his affluent, lily-white suburban community, Emil Friendly is the sole Communist. Even Democrats are harder to find than a needle in the haystack of this overwhelmingly Republican enclave. At "community outreach" meetings, he continually irritates his neighbors by suggesting that the inhabitants of this town, village, hamlet, call it what you will, pool their resources in order to benefit the community as a whole.

Now, Emil doesn't think of himself as a Communist, a "commie," even if his neighbors do. He claims to be an "independent." Of course, that really means next to nothing, as "independent" is a catch-all that has included virulent racists like George Wallace, wacky billionaires like Ross Perot, "soft" Republicans like John Anderson, and petulant consumer advocates like Ralph Nader.

Emil Friendly is an independent tobacconist whose passion is gardening.

An honorable tobacconist. Emil would never sell tobacco products to anyone underage. Why, he'd card anyone who looked a day under 30. And on top of that, he wouldn't even sell to anyone who coughed when asking for cigarettes.

"Excuse me <cough>, <cough> <cough>, a pack of Pell Mell please."

"Pall Mall? No, buddy," Emil would say, "I can't sell to you. You've had enough. Now go home and sleep it off."

Emil Friendly may not care much for people, but he cares about them, as he cares about tobacco and his garden, though gardening he very much cares for.

One Sunday afternoon, a roving philosopher turns up as Emil is tending his peonies and nasturtia. "Neighbor," the philosopher says, "there is a concatenation of all events in this best of possible worlds."

"Whatever," Emil replies. "But let me take care of my garden."

Ernestus Jiminy Chald

"The Way of all Flesh"

Ɑkˈtoʊbər ˈTwɛnti-naɪnθ: Maɪ ɪnˈtaɪər laɪf hæz bɪn ə ˈʤʌmbəld mɛs. Moʊst ɑv ðə taɪm, Aɪ ˈkʊdən't tɛl ɪf Aɪ wʌz ˈkʌmɪŋ ɔr ˈgoʊɪŋ . . . ɔr ˈsɪmpli ˈsteɪɪŋ pʊt. It hæz ˈɔlˌweɪz bɪn ðɪs weɪ. Aɪ rɪˈfjuz tu fɔrs ˌmaɪˈsɛlf tu ɛnˈdjʊr ðɪs ˈmædnəs ˈɛni ˈlɔŋgər. Haʊ ˈvɪvədli Aɪ rɪˈmɛmbər ðə taɪm Aɪ spɛnt lɑkt ʌp ɪn ðæt ˈoʊdiəs ˌsænɪˈterɪəm, səˈraʊndəd ɑn ɔl saɪdz baɪ waɪt: waɪt wɔlz, waɪt ˈsilɪŋz, waɪt flɔrz, waɪt ˈhɑˌspɪtəl gaʊnz. ˈKlɔɪŋ æt maɪ skɪn wʌz ˈnɛvər ə kraɪ fɔr hɛlp ɔr ə ˌmænəfɛˈsteɪʃən ɑv maɪ səˈpoʊzd ɪnˈsænəti æz ðeɪ ɪnˈsɪstəd əˈpɑn ɪnˈsɪstɪŋ əˈpɑn—Aɪ ˈsɪmpli ˈwɑntəd tu ˈblʌdi ðə pleɪs ʌp tu breɪk ðə məˈnɑtəni ɑv ðə waɪt. ˈIvɪn naʊ wɛn Aɪ si ðæt ˈɑfəl ˈkʌlər—ɑn ʃits ɑv blæŋk ˈpeɪpər, ˈɑrtəkəlz ɑv ˈkloʊðɪŋ, ðə klaʊdz ɪn ðə skaɪ, ði ɛgz ɑn maɪ pleɪt, ðə ˈsɜrfəs ɑv maɪ oʊn tiθ—Aɪ æm fɪld wɪð ði ɜrʤ tu tɛr θru maɪ flɛʃ ænd peɪnt ðə wɜrld rɛd. Rɛd, ðæt moʊst ˈsæŋgwɪn ɑv ˈkʌlərz; ðə ˈkʌlər ɑv ˈpæʃən; ðə ˈkʌlər ɑv ræθ. Aɪ daɪd ə ˈθaʊzənd taɪmz bɪˈfɔr Aɪ ˈɛvər ˈtruli ˈstɑrtəd ˈlɪvɪŋ. Jɛt naʊ ðæt Aɪ æm ˈfaɪnəli əˈlaɪv, maɪ ˈʤɜrni ɪz ˈnɪrɪŋ ɪts ˌɪrɪˈvɜrsəbəl ɛnd.

Aɪ æm priˈpɛrd fɔr ðə ˈfaɪnəl frənˈtɪr. Aɪ æm ˈrɛdi tu goʊ aʊt ˌhɔrəˈzɑntəl, tu əˈsum rum ˈtɛmprəʧər, tu fid ðə wɜrmz, tu ˈʃʌfəl ɔf ðɪs gɑdfɔrˈseɪkən ˈmɔrtəl kɔɪl. Aɪ ˈriəˌlaɪz naʊ ðæt ɔl ðə jɪrz Aɪ spɛnt ˈbiɪŋ toʊld ðæt Aɪ wʌz mæd, ənˈhɪnʤd, dɪˈreɪnʤd, ˈkreɪziər ðæn ə ʃɪthaʊs ræt, ˈoʊvər ðə ˈreɪnˌboʊ, ɪt wʌz ˈnɛvər mi. It wʌz ˈɔlˌweɪz ðɛm. Ðeɪ wɜr ðə wʌnz hu kʊd ˈnɛvər ˈtruli si. Ðeɪ wɜr ðə wʌnz hu laɪd tu ðɛmˈsɛlvz ænd tu iʧ ˈʌðər. Aɪ kʊd ˈɔlˌweɪz si. Aɪ kʊd ˈɔlˌweɪz hir. Aɪ ˈɔlˌweɪz nu.

Ænd ðʌs ɪt ɪz wɪð kəmˈplit ˈklɛrəti ɑv maɪnd ænd səˈrɛnəti ɑv ˈspɪrət ðæt Aɪ hæv meɪd ðə dɪˈsɪʒən tu pʊt ən ɛnd tu ɪt ɔl. Ɔl maɪ ˈmɪzəri. Ɔl ðɪs wɜrld'z ɪnˈsɛsənt ˈmædnəs! Aɪ æm ɪˈrædəˌkeɪtɪŋ ɪt ɔl. It ɔl ɛndz wɛn Aɪ ɛnd. ˈƐvriˌθɪŋ ˈtɜrmɪˌneɪts wɪð mi. Bʌt noʊ, Dɪr ˈRidər ɪf ju ɪgˈzɪst, ðæt aɪ æm nɑt ˈgoʊɪŋ aʊt əˈloʊn. Neɪ, Aɪ æm ˈteɪkɪŋ ɔl ɑv ðɛm wɪð mi. Ɔl ðə ˈprɪgɪʃ fɔpˈdudəlz ænd ˈbɑrbərəs laʊts hu mɑkt mi ænd dɪˈraɪdɪd mi ænd traɪd tu hoʊld mi daʊn bɪˈkɔz ðeɪ kʊd ˈnɛvər ˌʌndərˈstænd ðə θɪŋz ðæt Aɪ ˌʌndərˈstʊd. Aɪ wʌz səbˈdud bɪˈfɔr. ˈSʌbʤəˌgeɪtɪd ænd ʃæt əˈpɑn, Aɪ sæt laɪk ə gʊd ˈlɪtəl lun ɪn ðæt əˈkɜːsɪd ˈwilˌtʃɛr, maɪ ɑrmz baʊnd ɪn ˈhɛvi waɪt ˈlɛðər rɪˈstreɪnts ænd maɪ hɛd baʊnd ɪn waɪt ˈbændədʒəz, æz ðeɪ wild mi frʌm wʌn waɪt uːbliˈɛt tu ðə nɛkst. Səmˈtaɪmz, ɪn ən ækt ɑv ˈærənt ɪnhjuˈmænəti, ðeɪ wʊd wil mi bɪˈfɔr ðə tɔl ˈtrænsəm ˈwɪndoʊz ɪn ðə rɛk rum soʊ ðæt Aɪ kʊd geɪz ˈaʊtˈsaɪd æt ðə wɜrld bɪˈɑnd, ə wɜrld fɪld wɪð soʊ mʌtʃ mɔr ðæn waɪt; ə wɜrld wɛr ə mən laɪk mi maɪt hæv hæd ə tʃæns; ə wɜrld wɛr Aɪ maɪt hæv pəˈzɛst ðə ˈfridəm tu stænd ɑn maɪ oʊn tu, tu wɔk əˈmʌŋst ðə triz ænd smɛl ðə sɛnt ɑv ˈfrɛʃli ʃɔrn græs ænd skɪp əˈlɔŋ ðə ˌprɑməˈneɪd; ə wɜrld wɛr ˈpipəl ɑr mɔrnd wɛn ðeɪ daɪ ɪnˈstɛd ɑv ˈbiɪŋ ˌʌnˌsɛrəˈmoʊniəsli ˈkɑrtɪd ɔf tu ðə kriməˈtɔriəm tu bi ɪnˈsɪnəˌreɪtɪd laɪk soʊ mʌtʃ ˈgɑrbɪdʒ; ə wɜrld wɛr taɪm maɪt ˈæktʃuəli pæs ænd wʌn deɪ dʌz nɑt ˈsɪmpli blid ˈɪntu ðə nɛkst; ə wɜrld wɛr lʌv maɪt ˈpɑsəbli bi faʊnd ɪf wʌn ɪz ˈlʊkɪŋ fɔr ɪt ænd rɪˈsɛptɪv tu ˈlɛtɪŋ ˈʌðərz ɪn; ə wɜrld wɛr dʒɔɪ ɪz dʒʌst æz ˈprɛvələnt æz ˈmɪzəri, wɛr ˌɑpərˈtunəti nɑks, wɛr bʊks meɪ nɑt bi dʒʌdʒd baɪ ðɛr ˈkʌvərz, wɛr ɪts ˈnɛvər tu leɪt, wɛr ɔl ðæt ˈglɪtərz maɪt ɔr maɪt nɑt bi goʊld jɛt wʌn ˈdʌzənt maɪnd ˈiðər weɪ bɪˈkɔz æt list ˈsʌmθɪŋ ɪz ˈglɪtərɪŋ.

Fɔr ˈbɛtər ɔr wɜrs, Aɪ æm səbˈdud noʊ ˈlɔŋgər. Maɪ glʌvz ɑr ɔf ænd maɪ ˈtælənz ɑr ɪkˈspoʊzd. It's taɪm fɔr ðoʊz hu dɪd mi rɔŋ tu peɪ ðə ˈpaɪpər, ænd ðə ˈpaɪpər ɪz Aɪ. Aɪ æm ðə wʌn hu wɪl kæʃ ɔl ɑv ðɛr tʃɪps, hu wɪl liv ðɛm dɪˈfʌŋkt, hu wɪl sɛnd ðɛm tu mit ðɛr ˈmeɪkər. Aɪ æm ðə ˈrɛkənɪŋ ɪnˈkɑrnət. Aɪ æm Dɛθ. Aɪ æm ðə ˈtɛrəbəl ˈɛndɪŋ tu ˈɛvəri bʊk wʌn ˈwɪʃɪz ðeɪ'd lɛft ənˈrɛd. Aɪ æm ðə dʒʌdʒ, ˈdʒʊri, ˌɛksəˈkjuʃənər, greɪvˈdɪgər, ænd ˈmægət ðæt kənˈsumz ðə ˈkɑrkəsɪz ɑv ðoʊz Aɪ'v ˌɪnˈtɜrd. Aɪ æm ði ˈɔrkɪˌstreɪtər ɑv ɪˈtɜrnəl ˈsaɪləns. Aɪ æm ðə kənˈdʌktər hu wɪl lid maɪ oʊn ˈpraɪvət ˈɔrkəstrə ɪn ə sɑrˈkɑfəgəl ˈsɪmfəni ɑv ræθ. Maɪ bəˈtɑn ɪz reɪzd.

It tʊk mi ˈnɪrli ə mʌnθ tu kəˈlɛkt ðɛm ɔl. Ðə sænɪˈterɪəm stæf wʌz ˈizi tu træk daʊn, fɔr Aɪ nu wɛr tu faɪnd ðɛm, nu ðɛr ruˈtinz, nu wɛn ðeɪ wɜr moʊst ˈvʌlnərəbəl. Aɪ ˈkæpɪtəˌlaɪzd əˈpɑn ðæt ˈnɑlədʒ. Aɪ ˈtɑrgətɪd ɪtʃ ɑv ðɛm ˌɪndɪˈvɪdʒuəli, æbˈdʌktɪŋ ðɛm wʌn baɪ wʌn ˈoʊvər ə ˈsɪriz ɑv kənˈsɛkjətɪv wiks. Aɪ prɛst ðə snʌb-noʊzd ˈbærəl ɑv maɪ Koʊlt ˈKoʊbrə ˈɪntu ðɛr bæks θru ðə ˈpɑkət ɑv maɪ ˈoʊvərˌkoʊt ɪn ðə ˈmænər Aɪ hæv əbˈzɜrvd ɪn ˈkaʊntləs hɑɹd-bɔɪld ˈgʌmˌʃu fɪlmz, ænd ˈɔrdərd ðɛm tu ˈfɑloʊ mi kəmˈplaɪəntli ɪf ðeɪ wɪʃt tu rɪˈmeɪn sɛnʃənt. Maɪ feɪs wʌz ˈkʌvərd baɪ ə tʃɪp, kɑrˈtuni ˈleɪˌtɛks pɪg hɛd mæsk soʊ ðæt ðeɪ ˈwʊdənt ˈrɛkəgˌnaɪz mi—nɑt dʒʌst jɛt. Aɪ baʊnd ðɛr hændz ænd fit wɪð dʌkt teɪp ɪn ðə bæk ɑv maɪ Rɑdkoʊ ænd droʊv ðɛm tu ðə ˈruənz ɑv ə kən'dɛmd ˌɛlə'mɛntri skul ɑn ðə saʊθ saɪd. Ðɛr, ɪn ðə 'bɔɪlər rum, Aɪ ˌriɪn'fɔrst ðɛr rɪ'streɪnts wɪð roʊps ænd ʧeɪnz ænd fɔrs-fɛd ðɛm dɔg fud tu sə'steɪn ðɛr 'mɪzərəbəl lɪvz.

Ðɛr ɑr 'θɜr'tin ɑv ðɛm wɪð mi ɪn ðə 'bɔɪlər rum naʊ. Ðoʊz Aɪ wʌz ə'neɪbəl tu æb'dʌkt hæv 'iðər pæst ə'weɪ ɔr veɪ'keɪtəd ðə 'sɪti bɪ'fɔr Aɪ wʌz 'eɪbəl tu siz ðɛm. Aɪ du nɑt hæv taɪm tu træk ði 'ʌðərz daʊn, ænd Aɪ æm æt pis wɪð ðæt. Ðə wɜrst ə'fɛndərz— ðə wʌnz hu Aɪ wɪʃ tu 'sʌfər ðə moʊst—ɑr ɔl hir wɪð mi naʊ 'pɛdʒəɹeɪtɪŋ ɪn 'pʌdəlz ɑv ðɛr oʊn fɪlθ. Aɪ stɑpt 'fidɪŋ ðɛm dɔg fud læst wik ænd hæv 'oʊnli bɪn 'gɪvɪŋ ðɛm ʤʌst ɪ'nʌf 'wɔtər tu kip ðɛm 'klɪŋɪŋ tu laɪf ən'tɪl tə'mɑˌroʊ naɪt—ə naɪt nɑt 'ɑrbɪˌtrɛrəli 'ʧoʊzən, fɔr ɪt ɪz ðə 'θɜr'tinθ ˌænə'vɜrsəri ɑv ðə deɪt Aɪ wʌz 'kɑrtɪd ə'weɪ tu ðæt ɪn'fɜrnəl 'mædˌhaʊs. Tə'mɑˌroʊ naɪt, 'ɛvriˌθɪŋ ɛndz.

Fɔr ðoʊz hu faɪnd ðɪs 'ʤɜrnəl—ɪf 'ɛnibədi 'ɛvər dʌz—Aɪ wɑnt tu meɪk ɪt klɪr tu ju ðæt Aɪ æm nɑt mæd. Aɪ æm nɑt ən'hɪnʤd. Aɪ wʌz 'drɪvən tu ðɪs baɪ ðɛm. In ðə 'nuzˌpeɪpərz ænd ɑn ðə 'tɛləˌvaɪzd nuz 'proʊˌgræmz, ðiz 'θɜr'tin 'mɑnstərz wɪl ɪn'dju:bɪtəbli bi rə'fɜrd tu æz maɪ 'vɪktəmz, bʌt ðoʊz hu wʊd bɪ'liv ðɪs 'fɔlsəti hæv ɪt kəm'plitli 'bækwərdz. Ði 'oʊnli 'vɪktəm ɪn ðɪs sɪ'nɛrioʊ ɪz Aɪ. Aɪ æm ðə wʌn hu wɪθ'stʊd jɪrz ɑv ə'bjus ænd 'tɔrˌmɛnt frʌm ðiz 'seɪdəsts. It ɪz Aɪ hu wʌz baʊnd, drʌgd, 'tɔrʧərd, dɪ'sfɪgjərd, ænd 'rɪdəˌkjuld. Ænd fɔr wʌt? In ðə neɪm ɑv 'saɪəns? Bɪ'kɔz Aɪ nu ænd ðeɪ dɪd nɑt? Bɪ'kɔz Aɪ kʊd si wɛn ðeɪ wɜr blaɪnd? Ðɛr ɪz noʊ ˌʤʌstəfə'keɪʃən fɔr wʌt ðeɪ hæv dʌn.

Aɪ hæv bɪn ʃæt ə'pɑn maɪ ɪn'taɪər laɪf. Tə'mɑˌroʊ naɪt—'Dɛvəl'z Naɪt— ðə 'faɪnəl 'kɜrtən ʃæl fɔl. Tə'mɑˌroʊ naɪt, Aɪ ʃæl bi boʊθ ə'vɛnʤd ænd ɪ'mænsəˌpeɪtɪd. Ðə 'fɪzɪkəl rɪ'streɪnts ðeɪ ɪm'poʊzd ə'pɑn mi 'θɜr'tin jɪrz ə'goʊ meɪ bi gɔn, bʌt ðə 'mɛntəl rɪ'streɪnts ðeɪ fɔrst ə'pɑn mi wɪl rɪ'meɪn ɪn'tækt æz lɔŋ æz maɪ breɪn kən'tɪnjuz tu 'fʌŋkʃən. Tə'mɑˌroʊ maɪ breɪn ʃæl sis tu 'fʌŋkʃən. Tə'mɑˌroʊ maɪ hɑrt ʃæl bit noʊ mɔr. Tə'mɑˌroʊ naɪt, 'ɛvriˌbɑdi ʃæl 'pɛrɪʃ.

Aɪ rɪ'mɛmbər 'kripɪŋ aʊt 'ɪntu maɪ 'mʌðər'z 'gɑrdən wɛn Aɪ wʌz ə smɔl bɔɪ ænd kə'lɛktɪŋ æz 'mɛni 'ɪnˌsɛkts ænd 'vɜrmɪn æz Aɪ kʊd: wɜrmz, 'kætəˌpɪlərz, 'leɪdiˌbʌgz, 'sɛntɪˌpidz, 'preɪɪŋ mæntɪdz, 'spaɪdərz, 'græsˌhɑpərz, 'bitəlz, ænd maɪs. Aɪ wʊd pleɪs ðɛm ɪn ə lɑrʤ bɑks wɪð ə 'ʃæloʊ 'leɪər ɑv dɜrt ænd livz æt ðə 'bɑtəm ænd 'mɑnətər ðɛr 'ɔfən 'hɑstəl ˌɪntə'rækʃənz wɪð wʌn ə'nʌðər. Wɛn Aɪ gru 'wɪri ɑv əb'zɜrvɪŋ ðiz

ˈmɪniəˌʧʊr məˈnæʤəriz, Aɪ wʊd daʊs ði ɪnˈtɪriər ɑv ðə bɑks wɪð ˈkɛrəˌsin ænd sɛt ɪt əˈfleɪm bɪˈhaɪnd ˈaʊər gəˈrɑʒ, ˈwɑʧɪŋ ðɛm rɪθ ænd skwɜrm æz ðə fleɪmz kənˈsumd ðɛm. Aɪ hæv spɛnt ɪˈnumərəbəl ˈaʊərz ˈfæntəˌsaɪzɪŋ əˈbaʊt wʌt Aɪ wɪʃt tu du tu ðə ˈθɜrˈtin ˈmɑnstərz Aɪ naʊ hoʊld ˈkæptɪv wɪð mi hir ɪn ðɪs ˈbɔɪlər rum. In ə ˈmætər ɑv mɪr ˈaʊərz naʊ, ðoʊz ˈfæntəsiz ʃæl bɪˈkʌm ˌriˈæləˌti.

Ɑkˈtoʊbər ˈΘɜrtiəθ: Wɛn Aɪ riˈmuvd ðɛr ˈblaɪndˌfoʊldz ænd tɔr ɔf maɪ mæsk, rɪˈvilɪŋ tu ðɛm ðə dɪˈsfɪgjərd feɪs Aɪ nu ðeɪ kʊd ˈnɛvər hæv ˈpɑsəbli fərˈgɑtən, ðeɪ lʊkt laɪk ðeɪ hæd sin ə goʊst. Ænd, ɪn fækt, ðeɪ hæd. Ðeɪ wɜr ˈstɛrɪŋ dəˈrɛktli æt ðə goʊst ɑv ə mən ðeɪ hæd dɪˈstrɔɪd ˈmɛni jɪrz əˈgoʊ— ðə goʊst ɑv ə mən ðeɪ tʊk fɔr dɛd. Sʌm ɑv ðɛm ʃæt ðɛr pænts wɛn ðeɪ ˈriəˌlaɪzd hu ðɛr æbˈdʌktər wʌz; sʌm ɑv ðɛm pɪst ðɛmˈsɛlvz; sʌm ɑv ðɛm ˈfeɪntɪd. Ɔl ɑv ðɛm wɛpt. ˈƐvəri ˈsɪŋgəl ˈrɛʧɪd wʌn ɑv ðɛm. Ænd Aɪ dəˈraɪvd ə greɪt sɛns ɑv ˈplɛʒər frʌm ðɛr tɛrz. Ðə ˈteɪbəlz hæd ˈfaɪnəli tɜrnd. It wʌz Aɪ hu læft ɪn ðɛr ˈfeɪsəz ænd meɪd ə ˈmɑkəri ɑv ðɛr ˈsʌfərɪŋ.

Aɪ riˈtrivd ðə brɔdæks frʌm ðə wɔl ænd tʊk ə fju wɔrm-ʌp swɪŋz æt ən oʊld ˈwʊdən dɛsk tu gɪv ðɛm ə teɪst ɑv wʌt wʌz ɪn stɔr. Ðeɪ gæspt ænd weɪld ænd skwild ænd ˈplidəd wɪð mi, ðɛr ˈfeɪsəz bəˈgrʌtnˌ ænd kənˈtɔrtəd ɪn ˈgæstli ɪkˈsprɛʃənz, bʌt ðɛr ˈpɪtəfəl kraɪz fɔr ˈlinjənsi fɛl ɑn dɛf ɪrz. Aɪ gɑt tu wɜrk ɑn ðə ˈnɜrsəz ænd ˈɔrdərliz fɜrst— ðə ˈlɪkspɪtəlz—ˈswɪŋɪŋ ðæt brɔdæks wɪð ɔl maɪ maɪt ənˈtɪl ðɛr ˈbɑdiz wɜr ˈfʊli dɪˈsmɛmbərd ænd strun əˈbaʊt ðə bɪˈskʌmbərd ˈbɔɪlər rum flɔr. Wɛn Aɪ hæd ˈfʊli rəˈdust ðɛm tu mɪsˈmæʧt paɪlz ɑv ˈmæŋgəld flɛʃ ænd boʊn, Aɪ tɜrnd maɪ əˈtɛnʃən tu ðə ˈdɑktərz ðæt hæd bɪn ðə tru ˈrɪŋˌlidərz ɑv maɪ ˈæŋgwɪʃ. Aɪ tʊk maɪ taɪm wɪð ðɛm, ˈteɪkɪŋ ˈspɛʃəl kɛr nɑt tu ɛnd ðɛr ˈsʌfərɪŋ tu sun. Aɪ ɛkˈstræktɪd ðɛr tiθ wɪð ˈnidəl-noʊz ˈplaɪərz; Aɪ riˈmuvd ðɛr ˈaɪˌlɪdz wɪð ə ˈskælpəl ænd pɔrd kəˈroʊsɪv ˈkɛmɪkəlz ɪn ðɛr aɪz; Aɪ kɑrvd ði ˈeɪnəsɪz frʌm ðɛr ˈhaɪndˌkwɔrtərz wɪð ə ˈrʌstəd ˈbʊʧər naɪf laɪk ˈpʌmpkɪn lɪdz; Aɪ smæʃt ðɛr ˈtɛstɪkəlz wɪð ə slɛʤ ˈhæmər ænd droʊv ˈreɪlˌroʊd spaɪks θru ðɛm. Aɪ ˈwɑntəd ðɛm tu ˈwɑloʊ ɪn ðɛr oʊn ˈægəni æz ðeɪ hæd fɔrst mi tu ˈwɑloʊ ɪn maɪn. Ænd ˈwɑloʊ ɪn ɪt ðeɪ moʊst ˈsɜrtənli dɪd.

Waɪl Aɪ wʌz ˈhækɪŋ ðiz ˈmjuːlɪŋ kwɪmz tu ˈpisəz, Aɪ fɛlt laɪk ən ˈɑrtəst əˈgɛn. Iʧ ˈsɛpəˌreɪtəd lɪm, ɪʧ spɜrt ænd pul ɑv blʌd, ˈɛvəri ʧʌŋk ɑv ˈtɛndən ænd flɛʃ, ænd ˈɛvəri ˈʃætərd boʊn bɪˈkeɪm ə pɑrt ɑv maɪ ˈmægnəm ˈoʊpəs. Aɪ wʌz ˈpeɪntɪŋ ðə wɜrld rɛd ænd ɪt wʌz ə ˈbju:tɪəs saɪt tu bɪˈhoʊld . . . pərˈhæps ðə moʊst ˈbjutəfəl saɪt Aɪ hæv ˈɛvər beheld. Ðiz ˈmɑnstərz ðæt wɜr soʊ ˈhɪdiəs ɪn laɪf wɜr tɜrnd ˈɪntu ə ˈbjutəfəl wɜrk ɑv ɔrˈgænɪk ɑrt baɪ ðə bɪt ɑv ðə brɔdæks ænd ðə bleɪdz ɑv ðə naɪvz Aɪ ˈbrændɪʃt wɪð sʌʧ ˌɪnkənˈdɛsəns ænd kənˈvɪkʃən. Wɛn maɪ ˈmæstərˌpis wʌz kəmˈplit ænd ðeɪ wɜr ˈskwɜrmɪŋ noʊ mɔr, Aɪ daʊst ðɛr dɪˈsmɛmbərd rɪˈmeɪnz wɪð ˈgæsəˌlin ænd sɛt ði ɪnˈtaɪər ˈbɔɪlər rum əˈfleɪm. Aɪ ðɛn stʊd əˈkrɔs ðə strit—gɔr-bɪˈdræbəld ænd dɪˈlɪriəs—ænd wɑʧt æz ði ɪnˈtaɪər ˈbɪldɪŋ wʌz kənˈsumd baɪ fleɪmz. Ænd Aɪ læft. Aɪ læft laɪk Aɪ hæd ˈnɛvər læft bɪˈfɔr. Reɪn bɪˈgæn tu fɔl, əˈkʌmpənid baɪ ˈʌˌprɔriəs ˈθʌndər . . . ðə ˈstændɪŋ oʊˈveɪʃən ɑv ðə Gɑdz. Aɪ stʊd ɪn ðə ˈdɛljuʤ ˈlæfɪŋ ænd ˈkeɪpərɪŋ ænd ˈrɛvəlɪŋ ɪn maɪ ˈvɪktəri æz ðə blʌd wʌz wɑʃt əˈweɪ.

Ænd naʊ hir Aɪ æm bæk ɪn maɪ Rɑdkoʊ pɑrkt ɪn ði ˈæliˌweɪ bɪˈhaɪnd ðə haʊs Aɪ gru ʌp ɪn—ði ˈoʊnli pleɪs ɪn ðə wɜrld Aɪ ˈɛvər fɛlt ˈhæpi ænd ˌʌnəˈseɪləbəl. Maɪ taɪm hæz kʌm. Aɪ æm nɑt æmˈbɪvələnt. Aɪ æm nɑt ˈfɪrfəl. Aɪ hæv əˈkɑmplɪʃt wʌt Aɪ wɪʃt tu əˈkɑmplɪʃ ɪn ðɪs wɜrld, ænd Aɪ æm ˈrɛdi tu muv ɑn tu ðə nɛkst.

Aɪ hæv ʤʌst ˈfɪnɪʃt kənˈsumɪŋ maɪ ˈfaɪnəl mil: ə Dəˈtʊrə ˈsæləd meɪd wɪð ˈflaʊərz ænd ˈsidˌpɑdz pərˈlɔɪnd frʌm ðə Bəˈtænɪk ˈGɑrdənz. Ræɲʧ ˈdrɛsɪŋ simz tu goʊ bɛst wɪð ˈDɛvəl'z Wid; Aɪ ˈseɪvərd ðə dɪˈlɛktəbəl ˈbɪtərnəs ɑv ˈɛvəri ˈmɔrsəl. Ðɪs ˈsæləd wɪl bi ðə ˈlɪtərəl dɛθ ɑv mi. Ðɛr wɪl bi noʊ mɔr ˈfɪgjərətɪv ˈɛndɪŋz. Ðɪs ɪz ˈtruli ænd ɪˈrɛvəkəbli ɪt. Ði ɪˈfɛkts ɑr bɪˈgɪnɪŋ tu krip əˈpɑn mi naʊ ænd Aɪ ˈwɛlkəm ðɛm wɪð ˈoʊpən ɑrmz. Wɛn ju faɪnd ðɪs ˈdaɪəri ɑv maɪn, Dɪr ˈRidər, huˈɛvər ju maɪt bi, ɪt wɪl bi klʌʧt ɪn maɪ koʊld, ˈlaɪfləs hændz.

Pərˈhæps wʌt sərˈpraɪzɪz mi moʊst əˈbaʊt maɪ oʊn dɪˈmaɪz ɪz ðə greɪt sɛns ɑv ˈtoʊtəl ˈklɛrəti Aɪ naʊ fil əˈbaʊt ˈɛvriˌθɪŋ. Aɪ kʊd ˈɔlˌweɪz si, bʌt naʊ Aɪ kæn si mɔr ˈklɪrli. Aɪ kʊd ˈɔlˌweɪz hir, bʌt naʊ Aɪ kæn hir wɪð əˈlɑrmɪŋ fəˈdɛləti. Aɪ ˈɔlˌweɪz nu, bʌt naʊ Aɪ noʊ wʌt ˈoʊnli ðə ˈmɔrəbənd kæn noʊ. Aɪ kæn smɛl ɪt ɔl. Aɪ kæn smɛl maɪ ˈmʌðər'z ˈpɜrfjum; ðə sɛnt ɑv maɪ ˈfɑðər'z weatherbeaten ˈlɛðər ˈʤækət dɪˈpɛndɪŋ frʌm ðə koʊt ræk ɪn ˈaʊər ˈlɪvɪŋ rum; ðə smɛl ɑv draɪd livz ˈbiɪŋ reɪkt ˈɪntu tɔl paɪlz ɑn ðə frʌnt lɔn ɪn ˈƆtəm; ðə smɛl ɑv ˈbeɪkən ˈfraɪɪŋ ɑn ðə ˈkɪʧən stoʊv; ðə smɛl ɑv maɪ fɜrst ˈgɜrlˌfrɛnd'z hɛr; ðə smɛl ɑv ðoʊz ˈkɛrəˌsin ˈsæʧəˌreɪtəd ˈbɑksəz ɑv dɛθ ˈbɜrnɪŋ əˈweɪ ˈsloʊli mɪr fit frʌm wɛr maɪ væn ɪz naʊ pɑrkt. Aɪ kæn teɪst ðə saʊnd ɑv ˈɛvəri ˈkʌlər ænd smɛl ðə ˈtɛksʧər ɑv ˈɛvəri saɪt ðɛr ɪz tu hir. Aɪ kæn teɪst ðiz wɜrdz ænd smɛl ðə saʊnd ɑv ðə ɪŋk ˈlikɪŋ frʌm maɪ pɛn. Maɪ flɛʃ groʊz koʊld ænd ˈpæləd. Maɪ hɑrt bits pɑliˈrɪðmɪkli. Maɪ ˈbaʊəlz ɑr dɪsˈʧɑrʤɪŋ. Aɪ æm ˈspeɪsɪŋ aʊt. Aɪ æm ˈlɛtɪŋ goʊ.

Aɪ æm bɪˈgɪnɪŋ tu luz ɪt naʊ. Aɪ æm ˈfeɪdɪŋ əˈweɪ. ˈƐvriˌθɪŋ hæz bɪˈkʌm soʊ ˈægənaɪzɪŋli braɪt. Jɛt fɔr wʌns Aɪ du nɑt maɪnd ðə ˈwaɪtnəs ɔr ðə ˈtwɪnʤɪz. Aɪ ˈwɛlkəm ðɛm boʊθ. It's ˈhæpənɪŋ naʊ. Aɪ æm ˈslɪpɪŋ əˈweɪ. It's taɪm fɔr mi tu ʌnˈhænd maɪ pɛn. Aɪ'v fərˈgɑtən hu Aɪ æm. Aɪ'v fərˈgɑtən wʌt Aɪ'v dʌn. Aɪ'v fərˈgɑtən ɪt ɔl.

Ænd jɛt ˈɛvriˌθɪŋ ɪz ˈkrɪstəl klɪr.

Evan Guilford-Blake

Gate

I open my eyes.

There is a gate before me. The gate is solid, a gleaming wall of gold or brass. It is enormous, extending higher than I can see into the clear-as-still-ocean sky, and to either side to vanishing points that must be miles away. There seems to be a door; it's locked. The keyhole is within easy reach, but I have no key. I have tried to peer through the keyhole but I could see nothing, and there are no hinges, no handle, nothing that will allow entry if the gate were unlocked.

I stand there, alone, awed. Except for the gate, the landscape is bare: As far as I can see there is only the gleam of light off the brightly polished surface. No trees, no grass, just a softly packed light brown surface that, as I raise a sandaled golden foot, spreads like fine dust. But not far: The air is still, so still that, were there clouds, they would seem not to move.

The dust settles. There is no more motion. Neither is there any sound. I have never experienced being so completely removed from outside sensation. I raise my hand and look at it; the sleeve of my white robe slips down my arm and bunches at my elbow. My hand is golden, like my foot. Like the gate. I squeeze it. It is yielding, unlike the gate. I call out: *I am here.* The sound rises and disappears. I call again, louder. The sound rises and disappears. If there is another being, human or otherwise, within the range of my voice, he or she, or He or She, is choosing not to acknowledge my presence.

It is as though I am at the center of the universe and surrounded by the implacability, the ethereality, of time.

*

I am reminded of when I was a child. I would lie in bed and stare out the window, an act of *boketto*, and, though I did not move -- not even to bat an eyelash -- each moment, each fraction of each moment, would seem a different universe, as though time were not a continuum but a series of planes separated but conjoined, one flowing into, layering on, the next, surpassing it yet remaining intact itself. I floated with those planes, on them, fully conscious of the fact that *they* were unchanging: were, and would remain, for all of eternity, and that I was a new and distinct being in each who, after existing on a billion trillion such planes would eventually disappear from the next and never "be" again.

I could not explain this to my parents. My father existed in, and for, the linearity of the real, the tangible. My mother believed we made our way from God, to God, and that through the journey we became, at its end, part of God and immortal as God. My father believed God was an intangible and thus not real. He would stand with me outside the golden walls of the Church and watch the sky while I stood there, awed, and watched what my mother said was Heaven.

It, too, stretched farther than I could see and neither did I have a key to enter it.

*

On this plane, or rather these planes, nothing changes except me. I can not note how I change, yet I am certain that I do. I must. Man is mutable. Change is immutable.

The gate stands before me, as though waiting for me to pass through it, or to scale it, or to go around it. Each nanosecond passes, a different universe reveals itself.

I close my eyes. I wait. What else can I do?

The end

F. Ghisalberti

Bright and Risen Angelo

The only time I ever used the toilet, one sesame seed came out of me, gleaming, spotless. It leapt upon me. Its kiss was vicious, undeniable—Stephen Crane.

I live in a hole. I did not fall into it, I threw myself into the hole sideways, my ribs cutting a field of flowers like a mower; but I was not ridden by death; I trimmed heads; I left roots. Like another angel. More fertile. Spilling seed from my mouth. Not like an angel. Angel-adjacent. Like someone who met an angel in a bathroom stall. And begged for a ride. Under wings. And was thrown out. The angel threw me; my pride says I leapt; I am sharp-sided and cut those flinging hands as I would cut the flowers, a few moments from now; where I started. I curved as if carried around the earth. I opened the hole before me. By noticing it; by noticing where I was falling after I was inside. It is not the right hole. I did not inspect it from the outside. But from inside it feels wrong. There were no other holes. I carved this wrong hole for myself, inside the hole, from the matter of the hole itself, by flinging myself into it.

When the angel's hands were cut by throwing me, I saw: it had other colors of skin inside. They have them all. They just wear the one you expect on the outside. It is their privilege. Look, I'm lying, because I care about issues and want to politicize them. Real truth: he was named Angelo, but the wings were real; not tattoos; he was an angel; but illegal. He was wearing a suit made of a white person's skin. This isn't something he said. I was there. When he had me buy it for him. At Saint Vincent's. They told us it was the snoopy from the Macy's Thanksgiving Day Parade. Someone (pro-life) had shrunk it down using a blow-dryer and it had taken all night—that's what the saints said. We knew though. All sales-pitch. We checked the tag. All person. No dog balloon. Now, all Angelo. Let's not speak of him again; I'm breaking up with him. I'm the one, who is not feeling it. Angels don't have … it.

Your eyeball, your gaze, gives me hachera! You are the fleshy space that fills the night sky and wakes me up. You raise your eyebrow (it's very big): a freezing wind blows the sheets of skin from the skin of me! And I already start to make excuses, half-asleep, to save face. But, there's no reason to justify myself to you—you are already on my side, on all sides of me, as I am inside you, as I surround you. Why don't I just say, like you, I climbed down, spiraling, into a pile of garbage, following the long trail of my unfurled tongue that had been slashed at by so many bursting tin cans it stopped naming what to put back inside them as it wormed its way to the center of the garbage kingdom, looking for you, mewling in pleasure like a slug gnashing its dentures against a rock, looking to lick you (after licking everything else). Where the heat was, where the steam builds pressure. You took all that pressure into your belly and became a furnace.

My tongue entered you and created a release valve. Otherwise, you would have exploded. Before my tongue entered you, it looped around you several thousand times, drawing at your sweat, your ample hairs (let us call them mushrooms, but they are not, they are just hairs), not touching, but closing in always pulling away ... I expanded you but not so you could see (it was dark), not so you could feel (for the actions of a tongue that orbits you like it once orbited Saturn—it was subtle). Any inward pressure and you would have exploded and ruined this mountain which is all made of garbage, even all the trees and animals on it are made out of discarded waste that you will soon find out that I discarded, that I discarded upon me when I lie (down, and to you), when I take credit for being a mountain, a burgeoning eco-system for all these animals trees rocks and shrubs made out of fish sinew wrapped around hypodermic Kleenex which is blown underneath the skin ... grazing, growing up, out, reaching for the sky, rocks pulling at their soft tits, trying to pin them to a star (everything a hole does, everything a hole reaches for).

If you only let me touch you. You would have ruined everything. Even my tongue entered you without touching. Your organs part, make way, your veins expand ... the holes in your bones ... I fling myself through you, and you are my hole with no boundaries, no corners, no edges; sometimes, when you hold your breath, I am held in a borderless vice for thousands of years.

Outside (this is what was happening with my tongue, but I have my own life), I married a Fairy. Did this happen after I climbed up after you into the deep crevice of a mountain of garbage? I did it before, as a reaction to what I would do later, with you. I married a fairy. She was a city fairy. We went to a verdant field. Allergies killed her, immediately.
I opened a door in her body (in her side, it had already been partially exploded open by her sneeze) and went inside to bring her corpse to her family; they worked in speculation. None of them looked up from their screens, tapping keyboards with every corner of their wings; working fast, never not making mistakes; one of them pointed, I knew it was wrong, went another way; this is the room.

Fairies buried in caskets made out of thumb drives; their names scrawled in pollen. It is very orderly; it is just a big series of piles on top of piles, forming trees of plastic with fairies rotting inside them and one fucking squirrel squeezing them in and out of his cheeks, then replacing them.

I will bury you in garbage.

I buy the whole speculation and turn it into a landfill and recycle all the workers into products to throw into the landfill. Small as you are, my pants are so tight, you cannot fit into the pocket. It is a hole! A vast, flat, hole, with lips pressed against each other, impossible to open. I know it is dying of thirst. I keep my pants wet. But nothing gets in. The pocket will not help itself.

I don't know if this is before or after I met you at the top of that mountain of garbage, deep inside that hole? Did I mention that you were at the top of a mountain? No, I didn't foresee it; I told you already, not here, somewhere else; somewhere prying eyes don't need to know about; let's look up at them; let's confront this: there they are, looking down on us from the sewer; pitying us, who cannot afford to be there; dripping their sepsis on us, sustaining us; look, we're grateful; we're grateful for it; but I'm going to lie to you, I'm looking up at you, and when I lie to you, it is my-sided; this isn't a conversation. I know the right to blink has been taken away from you. You can't avoid this. I am the king of the mountain inside the mountain. The mountain is made out of a hole. A hole, that I married, and dug a grave for: by climbing. When I went inside I met someone. I don't care if it was myself. No one's identity is that clean. It's not about being certain, it's about being incomplete. On top of a mountain in the open air, deep inside a mountain of garbage with no space: gleaming, with no light. I didn't notice it until it happened later; simple; I haven't foreseen it yet, but at the center of this mountain of garbage, where bursting, fetid streams filled with birds groan slogans at us, there is a top of a mountain in the wide open air.

The air, the open air, which is made out of fairy wings, closes in on us. Squishes us. Air tight. What may have been fairy wings before they were repurposed as shrink-wrap and squeezed around bad meat; we decided to do that. We are making worlds here. Just one of these packages is a whole world.

Meanwhile, let us assess just what is going on with my tongue. Left to its own advices during a honeymoon, a death, curling in on itself; an ouroboros we have never gotten out of; let's say you are inside it. I'm saying that: you are inside it. I don't care who you are. I just remember an urgency to bind you by licking you. If I say you are my mother or father, the eyes up there in the sewer will mist over with a sense of significance; they cry every time they can mistake a yes or a no into existence. The tears of the binary fatten the fields of garbage we are tending down here, using real tools almost new, that I stole from a truck; it's just something that happened; these tools, those tears; these materials benefit us in our trap there is no escape from. It's a prayer. And I would say it, if I still had my tongue. But I do not, and I don't want it. As for you—assume it's still around you, still inside you, everywhere. Not touching. Some things won't change. But possession has changed. That is, I lost interest; having lost interest, having tasted nothing sweet, I removed my tongue from the gobstopper it was hanging on inside me (I won't say where but somewhere sexual) and set it free.

I can hear it howling; I'm shit at breakups; you deal with it.

HB Berlow

Let's Talk About My Book

Introduction

It's a compulsion. Once you start it, you won't want to stop. My book, that is. I'm talking about my book, the introduction to which you are currently reading. I truly believe you are going to read it through to the end. Whether it fascinates you, confuses you, irritates you, whatever the underlying personal motivation may be, you will go straight through to the end.

There is the obvious notion of getting what you paid for. The fact that you bought this (hardcover at $22.99 USD, £11.99 GBP or $12.99 as an eBook) means you are not going to waste your money. This is assuming you are not reading an older version and have purchased it at a used book store and got an amazing deal. I have encountered people, mostly men, who with a fanfare of bravado have declared something to the effect of "This is screwed up" or "What the fuck is this guy writing about?" or something Neanderthal and disparaging. Women are much less derisive in their comments and have a greater sense of value with regard to things that are considered amenities in their lives. They will pay a fortune for shoes and clothing and jewelry without batting the proverbial eyelash. But a book or a magazine, despite the comparatively minimal cost, is something that is contemplated with a far more acute sense of value.

Nevertheless, I feel extremely confident that you will finish this book.

We are, basically, as a human race, competitive individuals. Our greatest sense of competition is, surprisingly, with ourselves. We have a need to complete a project, get through a social experience, finish the goals we have set for ourselves, regardless of how unrealistic they may have been to begin with. Professing to start working out or changing your diet for the sake of your health is noble. Maintaining the discipline to do so in a chaotic and clustered world is difficult. Often, we alter the goals to keep within acceptable parameters that we know we can achieve. From five days a week to two days a week of working out. Having a healthy breakfast, lightening up on lunch, but still having escargot and cocktails for dinner. Whatever. You made a change. Of some kind. Pathetically minimal though it was. You achieved your goals.

Completing a novel is a piece of cake.

But this is not a complete alteration of your lifestyle. This is not a dramatic change. Unless you have never read a book in your life and your BFF highly recommended this one as something you personally could relate to, you are in possession of this book because you wanted it. You are a reader, by either first nature or second nature. You did what absolutely every reader does when shopping in a bookstore:

- First, you saw the cover. This was a brilliant concept by a graphic designer who was advised exactly what the publisher needed in order to capture the prospective reader's attention. Right down to the font on the cover, the tag line, the blurb, these meticulous details were designed to grab your eye when you saw it among the other new releases on that special table in front of the bookstore. (The fact that you bought it validates the artistry and marketing.)
- On the back cover, you read the synopsis with fascination. If it's a complex multi-layered novel, let's say like *East of Eden* by Steinbeck, it might be described with allusions to a modern re-telling of a Biblical story (something like that) which will be enough to pique your curiosity. Thrillers or mysteries have the built-in whodunit aspect in their synopsis. These are the appetizer to the main course.
- If you're lucky as an author, there will be blurbs. That's good stuff. Other authors saying cool things about your book. It might be vague and generic comments that can be construed as positive reviews. There might be a lesser known or completely unknown writer who is identified as having won an award that you have never heard of but are still fascinated because he won an award and he's saying something mostly positive about your book.
- Then there's the really good stuff: the author's photo and bio. It's more than likely not a selfie but something with a bit of polish and professionalism. (As the author, you hope it doesn't make you look ridiculous or unreal or, worse, not life-like.) If the author has more than one book, there's something to

identify the fact that he's not a novice. The prior work will be identified in glowing terms such as "best seller" or "highly controversial" or something out of the School of Yellow Journalism. If this is the author's first book, there will be some basic info, something perhaps comical to throw you off, and then the final "This is his first novel" as though you didn't gather that to begin with.

- Finally, you crack the spine and get to Page One. And there it is, the famous First Line that all authors are told will be the make-or-break piece of their work that readers use to determine worth, as though your first impression of a person will eventually decide if you will eventually become lifelong friends. But by then, you have been taken in by all the other marketing points and will buy the book, in spite of the first line (unless it happens to be *It was a dark and stormy night...*).

As the reader/buyer, you are surreptitiously discussing this soon-to-be-yours book with other potential reader/buyers in the store, giving the "What-do-you-think" discussion a drive around the park. You want validation. Perhaps it's there. Perhaps another reader/buyer who is the same gender and age as you and dresses in a similar fashion makes a positive comment reinforcing your decision and you walk gleefully to the register. On the other hand, you get a shake of the head with comments relating to the book having qualities too close to last year's bestseller on the same subject and this author just seems to be glomming on to the current trend. Despite needing validation, you have not read last year's bestseller on the same subject so you will buy this one because it is this year's model and you walk gleefully to the register.

My book, the one you are currently reading, has all the aforementioned qualities. I feel the cover dramatically captures both the tone and intensity of the work. I would like to take more credit for it but I have to admit it was the design of the publishing firm. I can say that I had several conversations with the graphic designer regarding the work as she had not read it. Strangely, the publisher does not allow his graphic design team to read the works. He claims it will falsify his intentions that are necessary for marketing the book properly. Any discussions the author has with the designated designer are restricted to genre, mood, and intention. He must possess absolute faith in his designers. In this particular instance, it shows.

I am fortunate to personally know two award winning writers. One is a female ten years younger than me who has been on the New York Times Bestseller list and writes literary fiction like me. The other is an older gentleman who currently teaches at a major university, has won several prestigious awards, but has never really been a financially successful writer. Nevertheless, the wide range of my acquaintances piqued the interest of the publisher who encouraged me to get a blurb from each. Along with two others from the publishers own stable, the comments on the back of the book make me surprised that I was the one who actually wrote it.

Personally, I wanted to use an older photo, one where I wasn't so gray and didn't have quite as many lines on my face. The publisher said since I was getting more into the literary genre my photo should reflect a more mature version of myself, despite the fact that many who know me, including my publisher, would not have the word 'mature' pop into their head as the first description of me. That being said, I understood the direction he was going in and acquiesced. The actual bio was as colorful as, well, me. I have been published. I have gone to college. I have been president of a writer's group. It's all impressive enough stuff. As long as you take out the fact that: the two previous works were from an independent press that is out of business; I never got my degree; and the writer's group never actually had any national acknowledgement. Hey, but it's on the bio and unless the prospective reader is going to take out their Smartphone to research the veracity of the info, I'm looking pretty good.

You're finally where I want you to be, here, right here at this Introduction. Okay, maybe you bypassed the Introduction in favor of going directly to Page One, Chapter One, the First Line. You read it, huh? Yeah, I know you did. It was moving and grabbing, a little melancholy with a touch of hope. Makes you want to continue, right? Or, maybe you did. Beyond the first line, the complete first paragraph, down to the bottom of that very first page until you...

...turned the page. That's where I got you. That's where I knew you were going to buy my book. I'm glad, more for you than for me, because you WILL be impressed.

Sadly, until that point, you weren't getting ME, who I am as a writer, or anything to do with MY writing. You were getting everything the publisher and the marketing team wanted you to get. You see, they sell a product, which is my book. I want you to buy my book, which is their product. I know it sounds the same but it really isn't. It's a matter of perspective. Yet, I understand their motivation. They are assuming a risk in order to make a profit. They will do everything, short of lying, in order to get you to buy their product, my book. Now, I'm sure you will enjoy my book for all the right reasons. That is, as long as you buy it.

Perhaps you have read some of my earlier work. If so, you will undoubtedly recognize a familiarity and a newness at the same time. Certain diction, word choices, tone are familiar. It takes a deeply conscious effort to subvert the naturalness of a style that has been developed over the years. Notice I did not say it takes a brilliant writer. Even brilliant writers often can not hide their true selves that have emerged through countless drafts and rewrites and revisions. It is the same for all people. The true essence of who we are can not be suppressed any more than a leopard can change its spots. Cliché aside, it is true. Rather, a writer intending to, for lack of a better expression, disguise himself must be aware of all components of his writing in order to avoid doing that which he does as second nature.

To be aware of yourself to avoid being yourself.

That is not what I did.

I felt it was necessary to allow those parts of my writing style that have become familiar to those who have read my books to be apparent while, at the same time, adding in unusual and, perhaps, off-putting elements that would make the reader wonder what the outcome would be. I have found a disturbing trend among many contemporary writers who have written umpteen books and sold millions by which they are more or less predictable. The introduction of characters, set up of the plot, nature of the dialogue, the red herrings and eventual outcome are all rather expected. It would be like having a short order cook grill you the same hamburger over and over again. It may be a damn good burger but after a while you wish there might be something different. Throw in some jalapenos. Use Swiss instead of American cheese. Something.

What I have done with this new novel is akin to using a different meat in my hamburger. You start out with a bite, get a taste for the story, and then realize this isn't ground chuck or ground sirloin. It might be horsemeat and it surprises you. If I had told you it was horsemeat prior, you would have resisted the opportunity to try it. You wanted your traditional burger. Aren't you glad you took a chance?

I recognize there will be hardcore fans that are resistant to this unique style. They want their hamburger. But it is important to remember that writers choose to be artists or assembly lines of non-intrusive literary pabulum. Perhaps the latter category appeals to a particular type of reader, which I know for certainty is not you. You have followed me along a journey to this point and are reading. Because, after all, it is a compulsion.

The decision to alter or vary what can be considered my trademark style was a difficult one to make. It was not an arbitrary decision based on boredom or chance or a malicious desire to test the fans of my work (as has been known to happen with other more literate authors). There was simply a "What if?" moment that came upon me, merging an existing idea which would have run the course of previous works with an alternate ideal. If these two were blended, the result would be confusing at first followed by a sense of enlightenment. The notion of producing such a profound "Ah ha!" moment was just too thrilling of a possibility to avoid. That being said, I understand and respect the rejection of such a work as well.

I thought that, initially, I might write this as I always have and then, in essence, rewrite it during the revision process. However, I set my mind in a firm and fixed manner in order to alter my regular process. I basically thought differently while writing but did not attempt to write differently in the hopes of filtering my regular manner through an alternate voice.

But enough of the writing process, MY writing process, because it is all too complex for a non-writer (i.e. a reader) to absorb. Most folks want a car that runs, which looks good, that gets good gas mileage and that has a few unique perks and amenities. Most folks do not want to know how it was manufactured. This is rather sad considering the process of creation is fascinating, not as much for the details and logistics, but for the spiritual and emotional aspects. There is a great deal of the writer within the work, at times placed there like crumbs along a hidden path, but just as often an unintended consequence of the writer imbuing his work with every essence and fiber of his being, the subconscious dictating the elements with a whisper. It is the writer who, during the long and elusive process of editing, may learn more of himself than a reader could ever dream of doing. Therefore, the writer creates works for the purpose of more fully understanding his own psyche. The entire process is somewhat masturbatory in nature.

There is more to writing a book then self-revelation. There is story-telling, which, for me, is the pinnacle of the craft. Telling a story, presenting characters, bringing the reader on a journey, making them laugh or cry or get angry. There is much that is published that is described as "important" to which we feel less intelligent if we do not clearly see and embrace this importance.

This is a fallacy.

There is nothing more important than telling a story. Themes and deeper meanings emerge but should never be the primary impetus.

Which is why you will enjoy this piece especially, considering the whimsical nature of the main character's journey, a picaresque tale of a lovable modern rogue whose indiscretions pale in comparison to his goodness. Although there will be the desire to cast down the impudent rascal, in the end some benefit or joy or goodwill is passed on to someone more deserving, allowing the reader to see the impudence as a mere character flaw.

This takes a certain degree of skill, to allow the protagonist to be laughed at, be laughable, and additionally to instill laughter within the reader. A lesser writer than myself would simply have told simplistic tales and hoped they became sufficiently stitched together to create a greater whole.

My sincerest wish is that you will pass on this work to your family, friends, and acquaintances who will share in the uplifting tone that I have created. We have spoken at length on how this work represents the financial investment on the part of the publisher; that writers need to make a living as well; and that, while there is Art to consider, the Business of writing also comes to the forefront. However, the intention of writing this piece, I have come to realize in retrospect, was the profound desire to spread Hope at a time when things seem bleakest and Humanity appears to be drowning in Greed and Ignorance and Excess. If in making a profit on this venture (and potentially winning praise and accolades) I am also able to instill the Blessings of future possibilities, perhaps the effort was truly worthwhile. Only time will tell. In the time you have taken to read this, your thoughts have progressed from "What if?" to "Why not?" as you make your way toward the register, the check-out line, the clerk at the front desk. This book will soon take an honored position in your home and be embraced by your family. And your life will be the better for it.

And now, without further ado, I offer you…

Chapter One

Jamie Popowich

absentricity

absentricity (ăb′sən-trĭs′ĭ-tē)

v.

a. When the state of being away from a place or person merges with the physical phenomena arising from a cocktail of electrons and protons sparked by the friction of relationship breakups, particles, and fragmentary thought with an opposite charge of particles, ennui, and repetitive heartbreak with the same charge.

b. The emotional and physical science of such phenomena.

c. Connected to the abstract processes of human flight.

1

Reggie swung his legs out onto the windowsill of his apartment and sat comfortably on the outside of the sill, his purple-socked feet dangling in the air. He was six floors up, easily seen, but at a little past four a.m. there wasn't anyone around to watch. He stood up fully on the outside of the window sill then pushed off the edge with the backs of his heels.

He didn't fall.

He headed toward the roof with his arms and legs pumping, breast stroke style, through the air. He two-stepped on the top of a street lamp, leaving his sock prints in the smog residue and dust.

He aimed higher.

Got beyond.

Then got beyond even that.

2

The first meeting was the clearest memory Reggie had of the Ex who'd nicknamed herself? The Raven? Why The Raven?

Their Meeting:

Him walking confidently along the street.

The Raven walking by him.

Him thinking *that's the type of woman I'd fall in love with. Phooey! I'm not having it.*

Then running after her. His voice cracking as he said, "Hey."

"Hold on," The Raven said into her phone. To him she asked, "I drop something?"

"I don't think so."

"Do we know each other?"

"No."

"Oh. Sorry." Back into her phone, "False alarm."

"Wait. I've got something--"

"Hold up." To Reggie, "Sorry, you want me?"

"Yes. I mean no. No, I don't want you. But--"

Into the phone she said, "I'm going to have to call you back." To Reggie, "Do you stop every woman you see to tell them you don't want them?"

"You're the first."

"You figure my confidence needed to get knocked down a peg?"

"I saw your face--"

"And you thought--"

"I've got to chase you down. To tell you--"

"I'm not worth it?"

"Yes! I mean no. Yes but what I mean is I've got something—I need to find out who you are."

"Who're you?"

"That doesn't matter."

"The same goes for me then."

"There's something about you though."

"What about me? Something that makes you say no to me? Is that it?"

"I don't know. I can't figure it out."

First encounters weigh heavy on the memory. Last encounters hold the same weight. Those are easy markers. The middle is the problem, always submerged, lost in the act of being. Not in the shocks of the beginning and the end.

3

Reggie floated above the telephone wires that lined the streets and crossed themselves like webs over the intersections.

He was moving through The Past a landscape that resembled an industrial wasteland made up of sand, brick, and two-by-fours piled together in mountains. Nothing was concrete, nothing stable. Sifting rubble. The street signs jumbled words or just blank. All the buildings that ran up and down streets, were they factories? skyscrapers? homes? they were all broken windows and no doors anywhere. Some tube lights flickered dimly inside though any light only created shadows, shadows cast on darkness, making a steady trek, a thorough search through this land, nearly impossible.

Reggie landed on the top of a set of telephone wires and tightrope walked them for several blocks, never looking down, always looking forward, hoping to see something that'd catch his eye.

Snow swirled around him as he walked along the wires, piling up inch by inch on the wires.

Below him there was snow falling on top of snow that had already buried snow.

He stopped at a wood telephone pole, sitting down on its corner to catch his breath. He put his hand out and watched flakes land in his palm. The snow lacked cold. Without wetness. Snow with its look but not its substance but that still made the late night look earlier, brighter, than it was.

Two lovers passed below him. Their steps easily in synch with each other. They were a memory. Reggie's memory. But as far as the lovers knew the city was theirs alone. The apartment buildings, the stores, these were all props, all emptied of the extras who had played their roles. For one moment there were no politics, no clash, no mass extinction of centuries of life behind them. There was this one snow swirling moment caught outside the frame of time.

Sitting on the edge of that telephone pole, stretching himself to its very end, Reggie watched as they disappeared and the snow buried the tracks they left behind.

4

On meeting Ex-Lovers (brief conversation & observations):

Nice to see you.

Nice to see you too.

How're things going?

Things are great.

I'm great also.

You keep well.

You too.

A person didn't reminisce with an Ex. This wasn't a friend. And don't use "*but I still want to be friends.*" as evidence There was no friendship. That relationship had a break at its core. If anything, if people were lucky the years apart helped pave over any damage caused. To see one another years later, each having survived the battle of being together, that's not the time to start sentences with *remember when we used to*. That betrayed truth. That admitted that *I remembered when we used to*.

Guess what? They probably don't remember. That's why they look like they want to run away. All they're thinking is, *I haven't thought about you for years.*

5

Reggie often ransacked his own pad, opening his closet, pulling dirty clothes out onto the floor, going into the kitchen, rifling through the drawers. Why are kitchen drawers so messy? Why was one drawer always stuffed full of out of date menus, a few loose buttons, staples, unopened mail?

He found what he was looking for in something like the inside pocket of a jean jacket he'd meant to donate away. He unfolded the letter. The ink on the pages faded even further than last time. But the letter hadn't lost its vigour. It still had all its meaning.

He read and reread the words *I miss you* knowing that *I miss you* wouldn't be written again. At least not by whoever wrote the letter. The name faded beyond recognition. The name forgotten to lessen *I miss you's* impact.

6

Reggie dropped from the air onto a building that was at least forty storeys high. Momentarily he thought he saw someone fall onto one of the ledges below.

The landscape from this high up was city blocks of craters waiting to be filled in by buildings, and skeletons of buildings either becoming craters or becoming buildings. The streets under so much reconstructive surgery, some already collapsing under the weight of their many nips and tucks. A space of flux. Of city planning. Franchises. Corporate big ideas. The promise of. The next bright thing. And always the promise of new jobs. Even in The Past the city already co-opted.

Reggie recognized the shapes of some buildings. That building there with its living spaces, twenty-four-hour gym, coffee shop, knitting store, bar, spa. The corporate sponsors and architects trying to jam as many lifestyle choices inside. A homeless guy he'd met out front, handing out flyers about the building barking *this is the newest in mixed-use A-Ford-A-Bill-Ity*.

Reggie stepped off the edge of the building he was on, letting himself fall a few storeys before kicking off the side of the wall, sending small bits of brick crumbling below as he left.

7

Where heartbreak leaves us …

Lined up at a twenty-four-hour grocery store to buy milk and Cap'N Crutch. A meal break.

The shelves and fridges of the grocery store looked like looters had got to them.

Stoners in line kept spilling their change all over the floor as they salivated over their Pop Tart and peanut butter combo.

8

Erotic desire.

Not the same as sexual desire.

Sexual desire has an intensity that lasts days.

Erotic desire is fun, satisfying, and a good way to release tension in the jaw. But Erotic desire flickers off.

Sexual desire? That gnaws at a person like constant hunger.

9

Reggie'd wake up, certain he was in the midst of sexual desire but as the dream lifted he'd find himself alone jerking off crazily amongst his unwashed bed sheets. In his dream he'd been nothing more than a ghost floating between copulating bodies unable to hold on to anything.

Reggie didn't want damned sexual desire. He didn't want to see the naked bodies running through his brain.

He wanted relief.

10

a comic interlude

performed by a comic standing in front of plastic brick wall

"Anybody out there got the energy for dating?

applause

"Yeah, well try sustaining that into your mid-30s."

ba-ding tch

11

A Sidestep --

Some Reggie Breakups:

Snoob – She asked Reggie to stop shaving his body hair.

"Your stubbly front is scratching up my mid-section when we fornicate."

The body hair issue is what split them up. Reggie couldn't stand the sight of his swirling black chest hair – it looked like some low-end crop circle that pranksters couldn't really be bothered making any artful patterns with.

Violet -- She bolted up from the double mattress on his apartment floor, hands dancing, fingers pointing. "You're making me stressed out, pal. That aftershave you're using is vapours strong."

"I'm not using aftershave," he said.

"What the hell is that then? It's coming through your pores." Violet frenetically smelled her fingertips. "It's like a mixture of garlic, ginger, and," sniff sniff, "sugar."

"Oh. That's sweet ginger garlic chicken from Kingdom Comes Noodles."

"Yes! That's it."

"I'm guessing that it's either the sweet ginger or Violet?"

"Ah, no offense, but I kinda suspect that odour is tatooed on you for life."

Madame LeQuest, -- Madame LeQuest was much older than him or he much younger than her, depending how you stand on these things. Theirs had been an intense summer of repose. Debt, humility, heat, the serial knife fightings that were terrorizing the city, borrowed time, these were as meaningless as the near invisible dust particles that bobbled around rooms. Reggie and Madame LeQuest spent the summer staying up late with the air conditioner on, drinking gin and tonics, and watching her collection of 16 MM film and video tapes of people battling each other with their elbows.

Until the damn past got in their way.

They understood history -- staying stuck in it was easy. But during the fall their histories squeezed each other out. Their pasts became more intoxicating then each other's company.

When viewed one against the other, this trail of breakup lowlights was like a chain with one breakup locked to the next and the next one locked to the last. Each chain responding to the other and all being a part of the whole mass of breakups built on the same interlocking mistakes. Reggie's problem was he couldn't follow the chain back to its end to ever figure where he kept going wrong.

12

Reggied treaded air outside one of the windows of The Merrymount Hotel.

The curtains were brazenly left open. A naked couple chased each other around the room, swinging pillows, laughing, their bodies moving and exposed without hesitation.

Later they watched TV and ate cold pizza.

13

a musical interlude
as sung by a couple of bearded street musicians

How'd the lyrics go?
To absentricity?
Yeah.
Snap your fingers jaunty-style and…

"To witness breakdowns
Of the muscles and memories
O Big Bachelors
Got ourselves

Offbeat/Quirky

Big time

Failures of

That

absentricity."

14

Reggie let himself fall toward the ground, swinging his arms every few seconds in the air so that he didn't crash to the sidewalk but landed on his feet without any pressure on his ankles or his aging knees. He'd learned to do this after several severe drops.

He'd landed in the city's main Square. He walked across its wide intersection, the concrete park to his right, and the blinking video monitors around and above him.

Disembodied voices drifted around him

-I know he doesn't want a relationship

-I'm really glad you said that. Hold up! Yo, guy. What up?

-Darling, we found a German man on the Street who we thought we'd bring to you.

-What if she falls in love with him?

-He would be the last person to know.

-I saw your wheelchair from behind but didn't want to presume it was you.

-She coughed loudly. And that's when I looked up from my melon and realized she was showing me her beaver.

-DeWitt speaking?

-Excuse me, may I have this dance?

then evaporated.

15

When a person lives alone the battle to keep self-esteem high is always a silent, precarious fight. *I'm not ugly. I'll meet someone. That shirt looks good on me.* One thing to do is to stay away from mirrors. Mirrors only undermine the vision of the self. If you look in a mirror expect to hear thoughts like *'You're old' 'You're too fat in the face'*. Those echo in the head for days on end. And all those nights home alone and empty handed, when the sexual force seems more like crumbs, those doubts grow.

16

Reggie, lost in a cavernous building.

A digital clock lying on the floor blinking from 2:30 am to 2:53 am and back to 2:30 am.

Cue *laugh track*.

Moving further into the darkness the *laugh track* louder.

A TV flipped on, the image scrambled, the light revealing a couple opposite it stretched out on a couch. One absently rubbed the arches of the other.

Laugh track.

"And you travel through time, Astra?"

"Just my own time line, Speck."

"What do dinosaurs look like?"

"Speck, I said I travel through my own time line."

"I was hoping dinosaurs would show up again."

"They don't."

"Then the future's not as exciting as I thought. I guess no flying cars?"

"None."

"Any chance of an orgasm."

"Not in your future."

Laughter. Applause.

17

A drink at Batching's Bar. A single's bar where anything **must** happen.

Welcome.

A woman dressed in a toga, a wreath pressed round her head, chased after a shirtless man drinking beer from a pitcher.

A couple of lovers passed out forehead to forehead at the end of the bar while flies circled around the mood-lit candle between them.

Reggie stepped over a couple in a desperate make-out session, pushed through the shoulders of two identically dressed dudes holding hands in their white shirts, red ties, black pants, running shoes, grabbed an empty bar stool and waved a soaked napkin at the bartender, a greeting not a request, who made up a gin and tonic and rolled it to a stop in front of him.

Roaming The Past depleted a person. If you didn't make sure to have regular meal breaks you'd easily end up with your face in the pavement.

18

flying techniques advice

in no particular order (and not to be tried at home)

Erase all traces of your everyday life.

Dial your mental frequencies to past experiences then dive backward.

Become part of this secret society (a secret society not built on, or following any, deadly conspiracies). This secret society is built on centuries of whispers in libraries over old stacks of newspapers, in antique shops, at rummage sales, and bars. Always with the persistent rumour that if you go back deep enough that you could stop living in the present and slip into the past forever.

19

let yourself go

lean back and listen

The sex in the apartments around Reggie's drifted off, put on pause. At most some whispers. Couples making plans. Promising shared dreams. Speaking fears.

Outside the footfalls of a few lone pairs of friends and lovers stumbling home.

listen for the noises that always get blown away by the everyday

The white monkeys eating from the trash.

The soft clicks of the street lights turning colours for no one.

The absence of breath in the bed across from you.

20

'My, how time does fly.'

Reggie had seen time flying in action. An Ex picked up her alarm clock, an old style one with bells like ears sticking out the top, and inside the clock face a hula skirted beach doll shaking her hips as the seconds danced by. The Ex launched the clock across the room at Reggie, the hula doll dancing in the air, the clock cracking the wall beside him.

That was a moment, taken out of its course of action.

What led to the flying clock?

She was yelling at him. Telling him, "Let's go. Now's our chance."

Then she stretched her hand out to grab his, her fingers achingly trying to grab him so they could leave. So they could start a new life together. But he wouldn't take her hand. He didn't want to listen to her. He didn't want things to change.

She walked out the door with her suitcase in hand, sending him a final air-kiss. Her gesture of such cool composure that nothing short of following her would have measured up.

21

Only candlelight illuminated the room.

There were no walls, no chipped paint, no pollution stains on the ceiling from the window being open. There were no clothes on the floor. The couple wasn't boxed in by a low ceiling. Everything was on pause. Everything disappeared.

Are you there?

I'm here.

With eyeliner she'd drawn little wings at each corner of her eyes to give the impression of a cat's eyes. With lipstick, two hearts over her nipples.

Reggie fell off the bed.

Their movements from the edge of the bed to the chair and back to the bed had a grace with each leading the other in quick breathy tune. The lovers' whispers so gracefully close to each others' ears. Those excruciatingly beautiful performances played at such low frequencies that no one was invited to listen. And no recording device, no matter how technologically sound, would have ever been able to capture.

22

Above the clouds.

The air clotted with texture-less dust.

Below, the city stretched out as mass, its meanings, its hold lost amongst the sprawl.

Agonizing.

If only he could stay up here forever.

23

One day Reggie called an Ex. He had no plan. He didn't think through repercussions.

"Hi," said Reggie.

"Who's this? No name's showed up. What's so special about your number?"

The Ex said.

"I'm calling from a pay phone."

"Really? You must have found the last one."

"I did. I'm sorry to call you. I wanted to see how you were doing."

"Kovacs? Kovacs is this one of your weirdo jokes?"

"I'm no Kovacs. This isn't a joke. Normally when a person calls, like I'm calling—Like, what I mean to say is—Oh, jeez—I should have started by saying *it's been a while*."

"Are you an obscene caller? If this is obscene can we do this in two hours when I have more time? And no hot potatoes about hooded men or ball gags. That's not my thing."

"I'm not obscene."

"You should be apologizing that you're not obscene."

"Do you have five minutes?"

"For a mystery caller who isn't obscene? Absolutely. Is there a chance my name came up in someone's will?"

"No."

"Wow. This call is really disappointing. Why're you playing hard to get here."

"It's Reggie."

"Reggie?"

"Yeah. Reggie."

"I don't know a Reggie. Did I have a nickname for you? I usually do. Maybe that's how I knew you?"

"No. I was always just Reggie."

"I don't know Just Reggie."

"Yes you do."

"Do I?"

"Me."

"You?"

"Reggie."

"Right. I know your name but what's that? What's in a name, right?"

"I didn't expect this conversation to go—you sound like you always—I'm enjoying this. This is exactly like how it used to be. Give me one more second."

"Of what?"

"Of this. Of us."

"I have no idea what you're talking about."

Then Reggie knew what he needed to do. "Where are you right now?"

"I beg your what?"

"I'm coming to see you."

"I'm busy."

"You're always busy. Please. You're still in the city. I'll hop in a cab."

"You sound crazy."

"I'm not. It's Reggie."

"Yeah, I got that. But sorry, you've definitely got the wrong person. I don't know you."

"I don't have the wrong person. Are you at home? It's—I know—I sound like a staker—I meant a stalker—. No, I'm not. I'm excited. Trust me. I'm not fooling myself. I'm not expecting the past. Just to—Just in person. To see you. To put things right. I—I used to call you—The Raven. I used to call you The Raven."

"Oh. *That* Reggie." Pause. "I'm sorry to do this but--"

She hung up on him.

He left the telephone swinging in the air from its cord.

24

a sports interlude

(aka place no bets)

"In this core-nah, weightless in flight…

May I present--

REGGIE!

"And coming into da rang! Bringing everybody down!

IS--

The final. Crushin. Blow. Of the defeatahhhhhhh'd."

25

To say that accumulated, continuous, breakups were Reggie's final note, a stake through his heart for good measure, well—Cynics! Pessimists! Go away! We live in the age of Factless Pessimism. If a person can't give up on the past, if they fully embody it like Reggie did, eventually they forget who they are and channel backward into the hope of youth. Not the folly! But the hope!

And one day, Reggie dropped out of the sky with a headful of hope.

Crashing into a woman as he landed.

As convenient as that may sound that's often how these things pan out.

They decided to go grab something to eat. Got to make sure there was no short term crash damage. Nothing guaranteed. No promises made. No ties binded. They ran down the block, flush with the excitement that had befallen them. Hailing a cab. Blindly heading further into the city.

Two people wondering, briefly, if this was going to lead to anything.

Sometimes that's as good a start as any.

Jane L. Carman

WORD!

A goose is a goose is a goose.

A goose is a goose it is true, but the goose is more.

The goose is a goose in that she honks in that she is feathered on the body, webbed on the feet, in that she is motion and emotion.

The goose is a goose in that she swims in that she waddles, although swimming and waddling are not exclusive to geese or old women or hefty men who live near beaches like Siesta Key and Anna Marie with their sun-brown bellies and translucent hair.

The goose is goose with down, long neck, and hissing.

Maybe it is the hissing that makes her more than a goose. Maybe it is the way the neck turns the head, the way it coils back and strikes a nerve or chord or at a thigh, the way the neck and head are like a snake sitting atop a feathered/webbed entity, the way the hissing rises up as the neck forces the head forward, the way the neck lowers the head as it lunges, as it slithers in the air just above the ground riding a hiss.

The goose is a goose is a word. This is how to write about a goose, how I construct this goose who is much more than a goose occupying a space between love and the air that surrounds the feelings one usually has toward a goose.

The story of the goose begins: a yolk, a shell, an embryo baking beneath a nonmother—a machine at 99.5 Fahrenheit, 82 percent humidity—turning three times a day by a timer, by a plastic arm. Supposed to arrive in 29-31 days, she arrives in 27.

How long does it take to bake a life?

The story begins with the imprint. How she imprinted on me. Me on her. Us on we. The delay of the realization of the imprint of human on goose on human on goose on human on goose. But this is about the goose. How her imprint weaved through the valleys of my brain, how I know that someday the print will fade, how it may fail. How I imprinted on her so deeply that the imprint flows over and through back toward me. How they say geese mate for life, how they lie, how she loves and loves and selects lovers but never mates, never rotates her own eggs, how her eggs rolled for months before stopping, how her lovers were eaten by raccoons or died of old age or how the weasel sucked their life away while they slept, how she should never die or become food for a raccoon or possum or weasel, how she was almost taken by stray dogs, how I walked for days looking for her and the gander, how when I found her the blood was flooding from beneath a wing, how the feathers were matted like sick fur, like frozen fur cemented with clay and blood and grass, how I got the .22 ready, how I bought a new value pack of bullets, how I waited for the dogs to return, how I could only think about how and where to place bullets into black dogs prowling in the gray of night, how the gander and the dogs lurk in the periphery of this tale, how I don't write about how the gander lives, how he focuses his life, how he obeys, never challenging, how is a sexless mate, a secondary individual to the goose who is a word, who can never be just a goose or a simply defined word or sentence or paragraph, can never be a just a story, how she moves beyond language reaching beyond the page, beyond the space of its margins, beyond goosedom.

At first I thought she believed I was her mother. I wanted to imprint. I made her look into my eyes when she first arrived. Every day, I would poke my human head into the box of chicks and goslings. I talked to them. I could have been locked away had anybody heard the conversations, had anybody questioned the woman with her head in a plastic box of newly hatched birds telling them tales of other pets, telling them how it would be when they grew up, how much they were loved, how life as a bird is tough, how everything wants to eat birds, especially chickens, that there are places that celebrate the eating of chickens, places like KFC and Popeye's, how they could go from friend to Cajun to fried or baked or broiled or buffaloed in a moment, how skunks or possums or dogs or weasels or housecats, even housecats that purr beautiful melodies to them, are dangerous, how I had received emails asking me to take fried chicken surveys or to rate my experiences of eating various chickens on a scale of 1-10, how I enjoyed chicken too much, how I have seen their kind fight over the last piece of meat on chicken bones, how I once I saw a basket full of chicks peck one then another to death starting at the tail, speeding up as the blood began to flow, scratching the ground and pecking, getting the littlest one down, ripping flesh away even after the eyes closed and the little heart refused to beat. But this story is about a goose raised with chickens, raised by humans.

Her first sexless lover was a shiny red-black rooster, his crimson deep, the black feathers shinning purple-metallic in the sun, the tail arching high before falling to brush the ground. He was handsome, had a fierce crow. He was a childhood friend. She started slowly, was a subtle pain that grew in him as winter turned to spring until one day she controlled his every move. When he wanted to turn right, she'd cut him off to the left. When he wanted to get near a hen, she herded him toward the pond. Eventually, learning that roosters are helpless against geese or love, he gave in, began to follow her, to obey, to wait for her on the bank by the pond when she swam, to sit beside the pool and eat bugs as she bathed. Every day for almost a year, they were together from sunup to sundown at which time he would roost in the shed and she would sleep on the front step of the house. But this is not about sleeping arrangements. It is about a word, the word goose.

The goose is a goose is a word and the word exchanged her red-black lover for a golden-orange rooster the day after a raccoon drug away the red-black lover.

The goose is a word is a world and the word exchanged her golden-orange lover for a new shiny red-black rooster when she first noticed the new rooster. Being a clearly articulate and highly intelligent word, it is with certainty that I can say she did not mistake the newer red-black lover for the previous red-black lover. The second red-black lover had once been a hen. In the chicken world these things happen, one day you are laying an egg and the next you begin to develop spurs, then a cone splits your skull and you have this urge to crow; so you begin to practice crowing sounding, at first, like an adolescent cockerel; and you don't know if this is happening because you've been watching the word and want to be a preposition in her phrase or because the word is willing you to become rooster so hard that crows well up inside your soul or if it is the word that willed your ovaries to shrivel and die, willed the spurs and cone, willed the voice to begin to form before being perfected as an outright crow among crows, an extra long, loud crow that would wake you from your sleep at two or three or when the moon was full or even super, that willed the crow and cone and spurs to have a life of their own. Like the goose that is a word, weasels cannot resist the beauty of your newfound gender or the shine of the red-black. The weasels sneak in at night while you are exhausted from crowing and strutting. They drain your blood through an opening in your beautiful neck and the last thing you do is wonder where your goose is, wonder why she has let you down.

The goose is a word is a goose is a world and did not take another lover for months in which time the potential affections of three ganders were rejected, two of the ganders writing themselves out of this narrative, the third obedient in that he stays ten feet away from the word as not to affect her phrasing. Being a gander, he is always threatening her sentence, her structure, causing her to throw an occasional flap to illustrate the rules of love and loss.

The word is an explicative as I walk by the widow. She says things that I cannot interpret but something lies beneath the intonation. I close the curtains, pull the shades. As I open the door she lowers her neck for balance and climbs the stairs. I run to the car. She uses the top step (four feet up) for takeoff, drills me in the back of the head. Words ring my skull singing some darkly happy, Disney-like song. I run to the house. Shut the door. She pecks the lock and opens it. I shut it. Lock it. Put a chair and a sofa and a safe against it. She flies up toward the windows smashing against the glass. I am hiding away for a day and then a week.

The goose is a goose is a goose, I tell myself.

The goose is a goose is a word. Nothing more, I tell myself.

I can, I tell myself. Reason.

I go outside wearing a helmet and aftershave. I sit on the step, invite her up, and try to reason. I offer her a tomato, a banana, a handful of cat food, some grain.

Honk, she says, hissing.

Honk, I say, hissing.

Honk. Honk. Honk.

What? I say. I don't know what you want, I say, as she climbs atop my shoe and grabs my sleeve. She shakes me.

I go back in. She follows me. I try to send her out, but she's found my favorite chair. She is sitting at my desk. A word typing more words.

I ask her to leave.

Nothing. She's pecking at the keyboard. It's a language I don't know. Or is it imprinted in my vocabulary?

A goose is a goose is a world.

She is honking and pecking as if she's seen me doing this. She looks angry as if she's seen me doing this. She uses the chair for takeoff.

I run to the bedroom, shut the door.

She's outside pecking the lock, pecking the trim. The door begins to splinter. She's honking, flapping, expressing herself.

I am hidden beneath my blankets articulating pains or plans.

She breaks through.

I pretend to be dead. This works against some animals.

She climbs on my bed.

I hold my breath.

She honks, hisses, flaps.

I hold my breath. A goose is a goose is a word is the world. What is she saying?

A goose, she says, is a goose is a goose is a word. I am just a word, she says. Not a world, she says.

You are a phrase, a sentence, a guidebook, I say from beneath the covers. You are word and world.

Word, she says. Love, she says.

Stop, I say. Slow down, I say.

She flaps.

I can't breathe. I pull down the cover just enough to let the air in.

She is sitting on my pillow cleaning her feathers.

Sometimes narrative is disorder.

The word begins to taunt or haunt me.

I fall asleep, hiding. When I wake she is not there.

She waits for me on the top step. Honk and honk and honk, she says.

She follows me to the car. She is spitting verbs, spinning language. She doesn't honk. She is speaking, saying something I cannot follow. She is a land, foreign.

When I get in the car, she pecks at the tires and trim, follows me down the drive. The car barely moves trying not to hit her as she escorts me to the road. Her in the ditch, me in the car, we lock eyes. I try not to give anything away, hit the gas. She begins to run down the road, down the hill. She gets takeoff, lifts her domestic bulk off the ground and follows me until the hill begins to turn upward and she loses elevation. She is still speaking. She carries a ditch lily in her beak. Her voice is muffled, is melody.

When I am a mile from home, I can hear the honk. She greats me at the end of the drive, escorts me to the house walking in front of the bumper. She speaks the language of obsession. When I don't open the door right away, she pecks at the trim, tears is away from the car. She follows me to the house but waits outside for me.

She is repetition. Assonance. Alliteration.

In the space of my days away, she plants daisies, she pecks away at the door, at language barriers, at the time a word needs to grow new meaning.

I come home and she's made dinner. Grasshoppers and frog legs, snakes and potatoes, lover and onions.

I come home and she's moved in, taken over the closet, filled it with sticks and dried grass. She is singing.

I begin to ask her to go but those eyes.

We sit on the sofa to see what's on the History Channel. I rub her wings, there is a large knot on one side from the dogs where the feathers still haven't grown back.

She ruffles her neck, begins to spit emotions. Three-hundred channels and nothing. We play rummy, hearts, poker. By the end of the night, all of the matchsticks are hers. She takes them to the closet, goes outside to sleep.

I am nervous, cannot sleep. Every few minutes, I look out to see where she is, to see if there are dogs or coyotes or wolves or cougars.

I invite her in. She disregards me.

The next day she is herding a black and white rooster. I speak to her. She hisses. She speaks a different language. I ask her to come in, to walk me down the road. Nothing. I reach out to her. She hisses.

I bring home fruitcake. She carries it away. Her rooster follows. They disappear into the tall grass.

I bring home pizza. She carries it away.

I bring home roses. She sorts them, adds them to her new stick collection.

I bring home champagne, scallops, and scallions. I bring home sticks.

I leave the doors and windows open. She doesn't come in.

I take the television, the sofa, the cards outside. She has nothing to say.

A goose is a goose is language is a phrase in motion.

I am outside watching History; there is a fox in the background, a goose in the pool, a rooster sitting in the grass drinking pool water. I flip the channel until the remote dies. I play solitaire. The goose looks over. She honks, yet another language. She is shaking her head in and out of the water. The gander is ten feet away eating horse weeds. I am ten feet away. She leaves the pool, herds the rooster toward his shed and climbs the steps.

A goose is a goose is a world.

Jeremy Thompson

myNdwOrm

On myNdwOrm, the world fluctuated. Paintings opened into wormholes, through which parallel Earths could be glimpsed. Bubble globs erupted from ceilings to mimic the voices of relatives. Spirit animals dwelt inside the faces of acquaintances, and angles couldn't be trusted.

Flesh tingle-thrummed immaculate, rendering extreme weather irrelevant. Emotions flowed strangely, more orchestral arrangements than sane responses. Users thought too many thoughts at once, and time was negotiable.

Motifs attached themselves to *everything*; profundities arrived and unraveled. The division between dream and memory was nil, and peripheral vision attained its own sort of life.

New scents filled the air; mirror reflections changed with every viewing. Nearly comprehensible, stillborn concepts murmured.

And when Elmore died, the world remained that way. His body rolled off the couch, and he rolled right on out of it. As a disembodied soul, Elmore was translucent, but otherwise, nothing seemed all that different. Not at first, anyway.

I'm dead, he realized hours later, as various afterlife options flowed across the ceiling—which he resisted, because none of 'em felt right. He saw hellish flames, sorrowful rivers, heavenly clouds and houri, but could think of no reason to commit to any of 'em. Thus, Elmore remained earthbound, wondering, *What's in myNdwOrm, anyway?* Some claimed that it was an entirely new chemical, manufactured from a strangely soft asteroid that struck a liberal arts college years ago. Others said that it was all the best drugs amalgamated. You know the ones.

Whatever the case, it seemed that Elmore had let his myNdwOrm enthusiasm overwhelm his judgment. Why else would he sniff, inject, swallow, and smoke the substance within the span of ten minutes, in addition to the slow suppository that he'd settled into that morning?

Eventually, Elmore's friend Paul ambled in without knocking. He had a beer in his hand and a spring in his step. His eyes rolled from the corpse to the ghost to the door. "No, not today," he muttered, retreating back into daynight.

I should do...something, Elmore thought, later. Nobody had collected his corpse, which had begun to putrefy. He'd attempted to crawl back into his shed physique, to reanimate it and live again, but the experience had been so damn ooky that his thoughts shrieked, *No, no, no!* Within that fetidity, microorganisms chill-scalded his essence.

He wouldn't be attempting *that* again.

"Let me go," he begged the couch later, believing that it restrained him. His spiritual proportions felt as if they were condensing. Paying proper obeisance, he stroked the davenport's arm and whispered, "Please." Responsively, the treacherous piece of furniture spat Elmore to his spectral feet.

Seeing himself ankle-deep in a psychedelic river flow—where mwana pwo masks drifted in figure eight tides, and sentient streaks of liquid vividness sucked sorrows from his toes—Elmore shuffled forward. Passing into nightday, he encountered a photo-negativized sky, which contained suns, stars, comets, and moons of all phases. Skulls shone through some moons, and flowers through others.

On the corner, nun hookers flashed their thighs and giggled. Chickens clucked in the gutter, and then rewound into eggs. *Fuckin' profound*, was Elmore's mental commentary.

16-bit trees lurked in the background, jingle-jangling as they bopped back and forth. Some blades of grass sprouted teeth, which fell soilward to permit the growth of larger teeth.

Tapping windshields at stop signs, Elmore went unnoticed by everyone, aside from a baby that might have been a gnome hag in disguise. She saw him and hissed, and then was conveyed elsewhere.

"Come over here." The unexpected intonation seemed to emanate from all directions.

"Me?" Elmore asked, on the heels of a thousandfold thoughts, which seemed hardly his. His soul pores shed static tendrils; his every spectral hair stood on end.

"You," the intonation confirmed.

"Where are you?"

"Just around the corner. Hurry, my friend."

Heeding the sonance's advice, Elmore traveled into an alleyway of oil-painted noir, where buildings stretched up into sludge sky, and shadows sprouted darker shadows. Afore a chain link fence tied with death ribbons, a figure awaited. An untethered orb hovered to illuminate his dignified presence.

The man grinned to see Elmore, broadly reassuring. "Greetings," he said, all baritone elegance.

"You...you can see me," Elmore stammered, unsure whether the viewer recognized the act's significance. "Hey, wait a minute. I know you...you're the hitwizard."

With his diamond-encrusted pointed hat, invisible teeth, and constellation-patterned muumuu with its train of sewn-together North Face parkas, it could be no other personage. The man's parka train rippled as squirrels shimmied through it. The squirrels didn't bother him; he'd trapped 'em there in the first place, just to feel 'em turn cannibal, just to feel *something new*.

"Who else would I be?" the hitwizard enquired from several dimensions simultaneously. Shaking his head, nearly mystified, he remarked, "Another myNdwOrm overdose. Just couldn't keep it outta your ass, could you?"

"Shush, mortal man," Elmore replied. "Besides, you sold me the stuff in the first place."

"And what were my instructions at the time?"

Elmore sighed. "'No suppositories,' you said."

"Yet you rolled right on outta your body, and here you are."

All of Elmore's greatest drug journeys had featured the hitwizard, in varied capacities. In unstable surroundings, the man was a living anchor. When good trips turned vicious, he spoke taming syllables. When funds fell a bit short, he would spot ya.

In fact, of all those in creation, it was said that only the hitwizard knew the secret of myNdwOrm. Would he know how to reverse its effects, to restore life?

"I wanna live again," was Elmore's declaration. Brick buildings bulged and receded as he wiggled his spectral toes in flowing colors.

"Relax," was the hitwizard's suggestion. Rephrasing, he drawled, "Don't worry."

"I'm not worried, *man*."

"If you could observe your own face, you'd know the truth of your feelings. Great turmoil afflicts you; you're just too high to realize it."

"Oh...I am?" The conversation felt especially surreal, more a dream-memory than a present tense occurrence. Though psychogenic, a didgeridoo drone made Elmore grind phantom teeth. And the hitwizard...well, there he was.

"Newly disembodied, you float purposeless, caged by the unreal Earth you last knew."

"Yeah...well...how long does it take for myNdwOrm to wear off when you're dead, anyway?"

"For you, it might never wear off."

Forcefully, Elmore shook negativity from his features. "Don't say 'never,' man. Don't fuckin' say it."

"Relax..."

"I am fuckin' relaxed!"

"You don't look relaxed. Fortunately, I've got just the solution. Here, buddy, suck on this." From the depths of his muumuu, the hitwizard's glass staff emerged. At the base of its chamber, there was a bulb wherein substances could be deposited and smoked.

With three clicks of his heels, the magic man conjured fire from his boot toe. Applying the flame to the chamber, he raised an eyebrow to enquire, "What are you waiting for?"

Shrugging, Elmore lowered his lips toward the staff's mouthpiece. Had he been sober, he might have asked, *What's in there, anyway?* Inhaling, he tasted only phantom saliva.

Realizing that he'd been tricked—that the staff held no smokable substance—

Elmore staggered backward, but was unable to free himself from the mouthpiece. As a matter of fact, he found that his lips were sliding deeper into the staff. He was the one being inhaled.

His head thinned cylindrical, flowing down the chamber, as did the body that followed it. Abandoning humanoid proportions, Elmore became drifting features, hardly distinguishable from mist. From caged stasis, he regarded the hitwizard through clouded glassware. Seeking escape, he was unable to move.

"In death, you walked as a human because you envisioned yourself as such," the hitwizard explained. "But I believe otherwise, and on Earth, the credence of the living holds dominion. I'm sorry, my friend, but business is business."

Into the depths of the hitwizard's muumuu, his trusty staff returned. For a time, Elmore knew only darkness.

When he could again appraise his surroundings, Elmore beheld a room of spiraling glassware, obscure chemicals, plastic barrels, industrial microwaves, buckets and scales. Strange implements lined steel countertops; everything seemed to be breathing.

Tipping the staff's mouthpiece toward an open barrel, the hitwizard urged, "C'mon now. Get outta there."

But Elmore wouldn't budge. Things could only get worse, he knew.

"Well, this awkwardness could've been avoided, but whatever," the hitwizard sighed. With masturbatory motions, he stroked the staff from mouthpiece to bulb, from bulb to mouthpiece.

Hey, knock it off, Elmore wished to protest, as the hitwizard palm-blasted strange galvanism into his mist form. But speech was no longer feasible; Elmore's lips had dissolved into raw soul froth.

His being tensed impossibly. Jittering, it condensed into a projectile that he had no control of. A final downstroke launched him into plastic confines. *Splat!* was the sound of lost afterlives, of barrel stasis.

Diluted acid fell upon him, and then carbonite. Elmore was stirred into paste, which was then filtered, ammonia-treated, and dried. Soon, of all that he'd been, only powder remained.

Undiluted, fresh myNdwOrm found low-eyed patrons. From the Elmore batch alone, the hitwizard earned five figures. "No suppositories," his moral code had him cautioning each twitching customer. Only a few paid attention.

Jerry Vilhotti

The Visitor

Years ago my older brother Tommy Tom Tom, a future docta in psychology who would make house calls too analyzing most of us as latent homosexuals and lesbians and strange people, brought his college friend Raja up for the weekend and my older sister Alice in Wonderland got the message confused and so she called the newspaper,The Burywater Simpleton, to notify them that the Indian ambassador was visiting us and needless to say we kept getting calls from them to see if "Christian Mennon or Nehru Gandi" had arrived. Alice finally had to confess that she had gotten it all wrong; it was only a friend of her brother's who worked at the United Nations. They still kept calling; thinking we were hiding the truth from them - like they did on their corporation dictated news "stories". END

Jim Meirose

Faking It Up, With the Ghostwriters

The job ad in the paper had been plain simple effective and clear.

THE DYNAMIC COMPANY--NO EXPERIENCE NECESSARY—LIGHT CLERICAL SKILLS A PLUS--OPEN NINE TO FIVE WEEKDAYS—NO NEED TO CALL, JUST COME DOWN—ALWAYS HIRING—NEVER FIRING

Keith Acton jotted down the address on a scrap of cardboard on the tiny table. Keith Acton was desperate but didn't really know it. Keith Acton was desperate inside; like a calm pot on the stove full of something silently boiling but the pot is calm, steady. Sits doing nothing. You could have a calm conversation with the pot. Even offer the calm pot a seat at your dinner table, and begin light conversation over lukewarm soup; but in time the pot would howl a big simmer and everything would boil over spilling and flaming up around it with all loud hissing, like a pot on the stove left forgotten that now shocks the cook awake out of the conversation, probably about the stock market or real estate market, and the cook in panic would run in, twist the gas knob, get rid of the hiss and the splatter and the mess, and then that moment would be forgotten, only to be remembered after the meal and everyone's gone home the cook will have a burnt dried up greet stain around the burner to clean. The last thing, the very last task after any crime is the cleanup. Crime scene cleanup; crime scene cleanup, but—

NO EXPERIENCE NECESSARY—LIGHT CLERICAL SKILLS A PLUS

OPEN NINE TO FIVE WEEKDAYS—NO NEED TO CALL, JUST COME DOWN

—seemed a better choice. Nice, clean job. Nice, clean steady, calm shining Keith. on the burner, still in the calmly simmering stage, rose and went and dressed and grabbed up the scrap of cardboard with the address of the place, and left. Everyplace opens at nine or ten. On a workday like this, it would be open now. Hustling, bustling, open. Now, yes now. Movement must keep moving. To stop is to drop. If you stop trying a hole opens under you and you drop to dead nothing. Keith feared the dead nothing. He had dreamed the dream of being trapped in dead nothing for a good long while after the divorce. But waking said get up, go on keep trying and you'll never fall to deep nothing. Keith slid the slide of the drive downtown and mercy, a parking spot, an exact rectangle, came under the car and shut it off, and Keith went within his neatly pressed interview clothes into the cement building and up the stairs, went down a dark hall, and came to the doors. The doors were plain wooden doors with filthy open transoms above, and looked extremely old, as though they hadn't been opened for years. Keith Acton glanced at his watch for no reason, really and let the sign on the door suck him in.

DYNAMIC CO! NO APPOINTMENT NEEDED, HELP ALWAYS WANTED, JUST COME ON IN! ALL ARE WELCOME HERE ALWAYS! HELP WANTED YES, AT ALL TIMES!

As he read the words he felt sucked in though and the door seemed to open all by itself, And he stood there; the room began to form over top of be careful, you need this job, don't be stupid, first impressions are crucial; and as he forced a smile, took a step, and stopped, casually, he immediately faced two tiny men at opposing desks, with open laptops and strewn papers all across. The men were bald, in identical black suits and long red ties, and were identical in every way, but for the fact one had a large hook of a nose, and the other had a mere bit of flesh stuck on his face. They did not look up at him; he'd caught them in the middle of some heated conversation. The hook-nosed man nearly shouted to the other, and as he shouted his head bobbed fast, as if sprung somehow like a bobble-head doll.

—I really, yes, I really do mean it! I just love the hell out of fucking with that guy! Just think, just think what his life must be like. He comes, you say, hey, good to see you again, and he is just—just blank. He doesn't remember. Just doesn't. He'd like some kind of slate wiped clean after each letter of what you are trying to write is immediately erased, so when the whole sentence has been written out you've no idea what it says. He's like that! He's God damned like that, oh, God! If only I could get inside his mind. With a mind like that, I'd be ready to write. Not like now, where I've got to do everything perfect because everybody will see it forever, when I'm done. You know what I mean, do you know?

The hook-nosed little man quieted and stared at the popcorn-nosed man and the silence from the space between them fanned out spreading like a large invisible lava flow it would be easy to step in and play the fool on if you say the wrong thing; it engulfed Keith, obliterated everything he'd just heard, and stepped him forward at them to say, Excuse me.

It made sense to say this, thought Keith. Excuse me was quick, inoffensive, and bright. Excuse me, softly said, would make a good first impression. After he said it, both small men turned to him. Good, yes, it had made sense to say this, because the small men sent identical smiles deep into him, signaling him to say more, without words of any kind.

Hello, hi. I'm Keith Acton. I saw your ad, for light clerical work? Is this the right place? Have I come at a bad time? I can leave—

The hook-nosed man put up a finger and turned his head to the other, saying, Look at the calendar Pete. We got time now?

Peter ran a finger across the mass of paperwork before him, and nodded, smiled, said, Yes, we got time now. Plenty of time, there's always plenty of time. But before confronting Keith, he said to the hook-nosed man, Why did you even ask me that? No need to ask me that, we—

The hook-nosed man waved a hand out, saying, I just thought they were right words. Inoffensive words. Proper words. You know? I'm sorry.

No problem, said the other. He turned, stepped forward, and stretched out a hand to Keith.

Keith it is, you said? Keith, yes, it's so. You're in the right place. And this is the right time. So, I'm Peter, but you can call me Pete. And my brother there is Paul. What can we help you with?

Keith nodded through the tight cold handshake, saying, I'm looking for a job. I saw your ad. I'm interested in knowing more. It said no appointment or experience necessary. So, here I am! And that's about it.

Keith nodded to Paul, at the slit of a smile slowly forming under his big hook-nose.

Yes, I see. Well yes, we are hiring. We need to add to our team. We are ghostwriters. And we need help. Very, very, badly, yes—we need some serious help.

Ghostwriters? Well, I—

Yes, added Peter, out from his desk. We've got contracts on top of contracts signed, hundreds of tight deadlines to meet, and only four hands. We need to add two hands, is the thing, very simple. We need to have six pairs of hands. To pump the shit out. The shit you know. Shit.

Pump the shit out.

And that's it, said Paul, turning back to Keith. Shit, thought Keith. All this talk about shit, I, no, this can't be a place, can't be a job. It must be a joke. Where are the cameras where are the cameras—and it said no experience necessary I never have written anything—

Here, snap out of it, Keith, here. Here's a chair. Have a seat. Let's talk this thing over. Let's talk about you, and where you might fit in. And I am very sure you will have many, many questions for us.

Yes questions for us, chimed in Peter. Many. Questions. Yes.

For us.

As Keith sat in the chair, it nearly folded up apart under him, frightening him an instant, but both the chair and Keith's composure held the pressure. The three seated together looked one another up and down, and Keith was afraid they could see in his face that he was thinking, no, this isn't right, I shouldn't be here, the paper ought to have said this was a writing job and that you had to be a writer; fists formed in his lap at the two smiling faces staring at him. They need to be told their ad was wrong. They need to be told should I tell them should I—

Peter raised a hand at Keith, saying, I can tell your full of questions. But it is really very simple. We are ghostwriters. We mostly pen fiction works for well known, name authors in genres such as detective fiction, mysteries, young adult, and teen fiction, and we make good money. Listen—ever read Cannibal?

Cannibal? No.

Too bad. Well, it sold really well. We wrote that. Have you heard of Savage Grace?

Oh, yes, yes I have, lied Keith, not wanting to seem ignorant, thinking in his smile one little lie, what the hell? Can't seem too ignorant—

What did you think of it? How was the writing?

Oh—good, very good. You two must be very talented.

I suppose, said Paul. But it's not really hard. What sells today, well, doesn't need to be too deep or heavy. If it can be written, we can do it. We write what sells. We've got—we've got like a bunch of different formulas. You know about formulas, Keith?

Oh, yes, of course, said Keith, neck sweating; but inside he knew, he knew no formulas. In fact, he'd barely written anything. But in college he'd been told by all the English teachers, You have talent for writing, Keith. What you write, well, is—is damned near publishable! The brother's eyes faded through the memory, and bored deeply into his.

So, Keith, tell us, said Paul. What have you written?

Keith let out what came; the opposite of the truth, God damn, and as he listened to himself he asked inside, shouting, why am I such a fucking liar? Why can I not tell the truth and leave—

Oh, here and there I've written things. School assignments, mostly. I once was told if I tried harder, I might even be able to produce something publishable. But—

Here it comes, it's coming, oozing slowly gassy like some great turd; but the truth came out. What a relief. What a damned relief, it was, to be able to say, But, you know, I really have no experience at all writing stories or books.

His hidden tongue pressed hard against the broken tooth in his mouth that he became acutely aware of when made to be nervous, and his legs tensed to rise after he said what he planned to say next, which was I'm sorry, but I must leave—

Oh, never mind that, said Paul, his words acting much as a gag plugged in Keith's mouth—that's no problem. To start out with us, just fake it. Even now, we mostly fake it. We don't really know what we are doing at all or if it is any good. But, we fake it. It is mostly bad bullshit, but the author's name sells it, and somehow, the money just keeps on pouring in. So, we need to grow. You want in? Just say the word, and you'll be in—

Yeah, laughed Peter, his nose wagging—yeah, but then you will have given us the problem of needing to buy you a desk, and a chair, and a laptop. Cost us money; yes, already, you don't even have a foot in the door, and you're costing us money. Isn't that funny? Not even hired yet, and you're giving us big problems! I don't know what we will do with you, Keith. No, I really don't—I think that—

Peter's words continued to course unheard through Keith, who both inwardly ran back and forth like a tennis star catching volleys as he thought the images that told him you ought not to have some here, what do they mean, fake it? How do you fake it? They always fake it, anyone can do the job, this is out there; way, way out there. You, Keith, will now rise, turn to leave, the words are peppering you too hard—

—but I think once we get over that hurdle you will fit in nicely, yes—very, very nicely—

The muscles used to rise tensed in Keith and he thought in the word torrent I can just get up and turn and leave yes just get up and turn and leave and step and grab the knob and open the door and the door sounded opening behind him, the torrent's eyes lifted from him and came up spraying somebody coming in as he had yes, the words, he began to turn to face who had come in but the words told him first, to sit down shut up, before he could see.

—hey, hey, Franklin! Franklin Thompson, is it? Here give me the picture let's get that part over with, you just sit tight a minute, Keith, we need to deal with Mister Franklin Thompson, our best client, who had just come at you through the door and is now bellied up to the back of your chair so don't move don't move here give the picture here, Franklin. Give it here.

Keith held to the chair, a hand came over his shoulder holding a silver picture frame turned so he couldn't see the picture, which Peter reached and took and looked into as whoever stood now bellied up behind Keith's chair, talked with a weak broken tatter of a voice.

There—it's my Mother, have you seen my Mother, I have lost her. I must find her. I must know if I really ever have had a Mother, because I am afraid I am starting to forget and the picture is my only Mother, you see, but that cannot be because I am here and you can't be here unless you've been borne by a Mother—

No, no, I'm afraid I have not seen this woman. Paul—look. Have you seen this woman?

Paul leaned taking the picture as the man who had brought it said, strongly, How do you know my name, though? Why are you telling me my name and saying I am a client? I never have seen you before. Who are you anyway?

As Paul looked into the picture Peter pointed to Franklin, saying, Never mind that, you always give me that, you do too remember. I have got a status for you. The book you asked us to write for you is just about complete.

I never asked for any book, I don't know you, here, here—here! You! Here give me back my picture so I can leave!

A hand came over Keith's shoulder. Filth so deep it nearly hung in shreds enveloped the hand, and Keith instantly felt himself risen, stepped to the side and turned, and seeing what had come through the door. A great mass of multicolored tatters with a man inside. A mass of multicolored tatters that might have been put together in an all-nighter by a Mother needing to throw something together for her sleeping child's very next day school play; Keith felt he wasn't here, he couldn't be, this couldn't be. He would not work here. But he would wait for them to deal with this client before leaving. Must leave polite. Must shake hands goodbye. Must be pleasant and wear a smile, and say something like, I am very glad, however, to have met you. Perhaps we will meet again—

No! I have never been here before. Stop trying, stop, stop trying to make me crazy!

Wait, wait, wait—nobody's crazy. Look; you came in here over a month ago asking us to write you a book. We told you at that time, you look a bit out of place, dressed as you are. You said at that time, never mind how I'm dressed. I have ideas—

I was never ever here—stop just stop, and give me the picture.

Paul held out the picture and told Franklin, if this is a picture of your Mother, she was once very, very, beautiful—

Peter pushed Paul's hand back, saying, No! No. Don't give him the picture. He's just using this crazy story about never having been here before and saying that's a picture of his Mother, to get out of the deal he signed, for the book we have sweated over putting together for months! Tell me, Franklin. Is that some picture you found dumpster-diving? Is that something you're trying to use as some kind of tool to pry us loose from your contract?

The ball of rags shuddered with some hidden rage, and the head atop said calmly, no, no, no. Give me the picture. You are crazy. Give me the picture, so I can go. You've not seen my Mother, I need to go. Need to go fast. Have to hurry, find my Mother—

No, said Peter, taking the picture from Paul. You came here. We acted in good faith. You showed us an outline. It was full of ideas. We told you, like we tell everyone, we're ghostwriters. We told you we'd form your ideas into something you can sell. You signed a contract—

Listen just give me the fucking picture—

The filthy hand grasped. Paul sat back covering the laugh growing as a tumor between his lips. He watched with narrowed eyes of laugh-lines for the doctor to come, move his hand, cut the tumor open, push the filth pus and blood aside and pull out the damned stinking annoying thing that had been growing from his face from the day he had been born. When born, he had sported a normal mouth. But the mouth, the mouth had—

Peter flashed a half-ream thick, book-like binder from the desk and pushed it in Franklin Thompson's face. Peter pointed to the bottom line.

Look Franklin. See where you signed? And see right there? Big Town. Big Town, you told us the title would be. And guess what, now that you're here, there's just a little detail about money. You owe us money. We did this work. Where is the money? Every time you come you say you forgot the money and say that next time you come, you'll have the money. So where is it, Franklin? Where is the fucking money?

The pile of rags wobbled and waved and the man in the big filthy suit they called Franklin Thomson made a lunge toward the picture clung onto Paul's tiny hand.

Shut up, shut up, you are crazy, get out, I've not been here, I have signed nothing, give me the fucking picture back so I can go, or I will snap both of your brittle little geeky necks!

Peter stepped back laughing, Paul held out the picture, saying, Okay, guy. Okay. Don't get your balls in an uproar! Here's the picture. Here—

The mass of rags covering the swiping arm waved in the wind of the swipe and grab, and the picture pulled back gone into the great ball of rags, which then turned and stepped and went through the door it seemed so fast it had never opened at all. His smell was behind, though. Keith stood frozen, looking from Paul's face to Peter's and back again, amazed at the smell from the rag man splattered all over their sweet little red-tied neatly suited faces. From the smell said Peter, Okay, Keith. We've taken care of that. Sorry you had to see that. Sometimes in this business, things get a little ugly. Come on, sit.

Sit. Now—

Hey Peter, said Paul. That was funny. Funnier than shit!

Yeah, I know—and the thing is, he will come back again. Come back for more.

This Franklin Thompson always keeps coming back for more. But now, Keith, where were we? Oh, yes—about a job—and about faking it. I will tell you it's easy to fake it. Just sit down and play the computer like an instrument and the book just pops out, just like that, it pops—

Keith nodded, stunned. Keith nodded, stunned.

But wait, said Paul. You were talking about us needing to get a desk and a chair and a computer for this guy. What about that?

Peter turned.

Keith rose.

—you left that hanging, up in the air, like you talk and talk and talk and then let go like you've really said nothing but there it is, the problem, still there, hanging in the middle of the air—

Keith was someplace else. Up, out—

Listen, no, hold it Paul. Not now, not in front of Keith here—

—out the door and down the hall—

Peter turned facing a still-warm empty chair.

Keith, what—hey Peter. Wasn't there a Keith here? There was, there was. My God, have I dreamed it all up? Was I just faking it that there was ever a Keith here?

What? No—you were just ranting and raving at Franklin Thompson. There's been no Keith. Where is your head?

Oh. Oh—

But hey, said Paul, but—we are brothers. What's the difference. There might be a million Keiths in your head, but for us, there's work, right here, to do, in the real world.

Yes, so. But I wish we'd get a nibble on our ad. It would be nice to hire someone.

A lot of things would be nice, said Paul, rubbing the tip of his rubbery nose. But probably less than one half of those things will ever actually happen.

All right—

Out front of the building, on the sidewalk, stood Keith.

Oh yeah, yeah. I remember why I'm here now. Sure, sure, this is the place. See?

DYNAMIC COMPANY

Yes, there it is. And I'm to see someone there. Franklin Thompson? Is that the name? Yes.

It's in my head, came from someone.

I'm to go up and ask to see Franklin Thompson, is what I have always been told.

Keith straightened his tie and entered the building. Lord, God, how badly he needed a job, any kind; any damned kind of job, please Lord, any God-damned kind.

Joel Allegretti

The Man-Church Report

For Ray Bradbury

NEW YORK CITY – Aired July 17, 2014 – 18:30 ET. THIS IS A RUSH TRANSCRIPT. THIS COPY MAY NOT BE IN ITS FINAL FORM AND MAY BE UPDATED.

ANCHOR: We go now to Washington Square Park, where Erick Torres joins us live.

ERICK: Thanks, Brian. I'm here with Maria Pellegrino of Manhattan, who spent an hour today with an individual who calls himself Man-Church.

MARIA: I called him Man-Church. He said his name was Matt.

ERICK: How would you describe him?

MARIA: About 5'9", slender, red hair in a crew cut, brown eyes, and a soul patch. He wore white cargo pants and shoes that looked like slippers. He said he was 26, but I thought he was closer to my age, 21.

ERICK: How did you meet him?

MARIA: It was on that bench. He was sitting there, listening to a Hare Krishna band. He had removed his shirt because of the heat. I couldn't take my eyes off the beautiful pictures.

ERICK: What can you tell us about these pictures?

MARIA: His skin had become another shirt, all because of the beautiful pictures.

ERICK: What were these pictures?

MARIA: The 14 Stations of the Cross. They covered Matt's entire upper body like a printed fabric. There wasn't an empty patch of skin below his neck, except for his hands. Even his armpits were shaved and beautified with pictures. The first station, "Jesus Is Condemned to Death," covered half his back, from the right shoulder blade down to the waist. His chest and belly were the canvas for the twelfth station, "Jesus Dies on the Cross." His nipples doubled as the nails.

ERICK: You're saying his entire body was tattooed?

MARIA: The pictures were too beautiful to be called tattoos. I'm studying art history at NYU. They were like El Greco oils, but in ink. I sat down and struck up a conversation. I asked why the Stations of the Cross. Matt just smiled—the braces on his teeth surprised me—and asked, "You like them?" I said I did. He wanted to know if I had a favorite one.

ERICK: Did you?

MARIA: The fourth station, "Jesus Meets His Mother." I lost my mother when I was 15. The Blessed Mother's face occupied his right bicep. I saw my mother's eyes in Mary's eyes. Her veil was Yves Klein's blue. A run-of-the-mill tattoo artist wouldn't use that blue. He wouldn't know it. I had to touch Matt's arm, because the veil looked like real cloth.

ERICK: What else did you talk about?

MARIA: All we talked about were the beautiful pictures. I didn't ask him where he lived or what he did with his life. For the time we were together, only the beautiful pictures mattered. I wanted to photograph his body gallery, but he raised both hands. He reacted as if I had threatened him. He was adamant.

ERICK: Why?

MARIA: I don't know. I respected his privacy, even though by taking off his shirt in the park, he had forfeited his privacy.

ERICK: How did you two part?

MARIA: The same ordinary way thousands of other people in New York part. Matt asked me to walk him to the subway. I said yes, of course. He balled up his shirt and carried it in his left hand as we strolled up to Broadway and then walked the 10 blocks to the Union Square station. Everybody we passed took notice of the pictures. In a city where tattoos are as plentiful as college graduates with communications degrees, people gaped like Munch's *Scream*, which ought to tell you how rarefied the beautiful pictures were. I felt betrayed. Strangers' eyes were luxuriating in what I decided was rightfully mine. You can understand, can't you? I'm the one who had engaged him in conversation about the beautiful pictures. *They* didn't.

Matt must have sensed my displeasure. He shook out his long-sleeve shirt and put it on. It was a Brad Paisley T-shirt. When we reached the subway station, I told him I wanted to see him again. That's when I called him Man-Church, kind of like a pet name.

ERICK: What was his answer?

MARIA: Silence and a polite smile. He shook his head. My disappointment was visible. I made sure of it. I said I'd like to see the Virgin one last time. Matt pulled off his shirt and turned his naked shoulder to me, almost like a model. I had the urge to kiss it, but I restrained myself. "It was nice talking to you, Maria," he said and scooted down the stairs. I followed him, because I wanted to see which direction he'd go in. I didn't expect him to head to the uptown platform. I figured somebody like Matt lived in Brooklyn. I was tempted to hop on his train.

I can't stop thinking about him. I can't stop thinking about the beautiful pictures. I didn't even realize I was in Washington Square Park again until I saw the arch. I'm sure I'll come back tomorrow and hope he'll be here.

ERICK: How do you feel now?

MARIA: Saved, I think. Yes, I feel saved.

ERICK: Brian, back to you.

###

John J. Trause

St. Concubine's Day : A Pseudo-Hagiography,
or Won't You be My Concubine?

CONCUBINA, Non-Virgin Martyr. Born Brundisium, Italy (mod. Brindisi) ca. 320. Died ca. 336. Feast Day, February 15th.

The historical account of the legend of St. Concubina is spurious, but the cultus of a saint by this name existed from at least the sixth century in southern Italy, Greece, and North Africa. The earliest document supporting the legend is a eulogy in the form of a narrative poem written ca. 845 by antipope Pretentius II (English translation by C. L. Mamelin, 1912).

In her youth St. Concubina was described as a girl of amazing piety and chastity. When her parents were killed in an earthquake, she was sold at the age of 15 by her avaricious uncle Pecunius to an Eastern trader and brought to Persia where she became the chief odalisque in the harem of the vizier Bahnevi. Through her strong Christian piety and charity she converted the rest of the harem, the eunuchs, the chamberlains, garbage-collectors, fan-bearers, cooks, midwives, fly-killers, and many other members of the vizier's household to Christianity. Nevertheless, she believed very fervently that in order to test her perseverance and commitment God himself had placed her in her position in the harem; therefore, she set forth courageously in the name of Christ to fulfill wholeheartedly her duties in this office. She not only endowed her Christian love upon the vizier, but also upon the other harem members, the eunuchs, the chamberlains, garbage-collectors, fan-bearers, cooks, midwives, and fly-killers as she transcended the boundaries of sex, age, race, and physical handicap. When the vizier found out about her overzealous propagation of her Christian love and realized that its arduous duties were depriving St. Concubina of her primary duty to him, he asked her to be more moderate in her behavior and to instruct him alone even more deeply in the rites of Christian practice. At first she consented, but her fervent piety impelled her once again to even further, broader, and more widespread proselytizing. The vizier later condemned her to death, and she was beheaded.

St. Concubina's iconological symbol is the fly swatter.

Jonathan Plombon

Despite the Car Accident, the Ambulance Ride, the Morgue, the Autopsy, the Funeral, and the Burial, It Wasn't Until the Corpse Visited a Night Club and Couldn't Get a Woman to Dance with Him That He Realized That He Had No Life.

1. First impressions are the most important impressions.

She worked at the lost-and-found, surrounded daily by metal tables stacked beyond the ceiling with unwanteds, neglecteds, and never-seen-agains, performing inventory by tiptoeing around wills-to-live after mothers' death, exhausted reasons to wake up in the morning, and hope from widows who still told their children, and themselves, that it would get better one day.

She had a face like something that I wish I had the words to describe. Sometimes when she looked at me, she made me feel something that some people have said they felt when someone who looks like her would look at them. She had eyes like something that other people see when people look at them and they still want to look at them. Even if I had a voice, or the words, that would allow me to respond, I still would have spent too much time blushing and not making eye contact to actually say anything.

I tried a pickup line. It didn't go well. Not only was she above this sort of thing, but it's also futile to try a pick-up line if you have no voice to say a pick-up line. My mumbling only bewildered her, which she expressed through a variety of faces that I deciphered to represent her confusion, sympathy, fear, annoyance, hope, fear again, and finally sympathy for the second time and last time.

"We just got someone's composure in about a minute ago. It was right around the time when you started talking to me," she said. "Is this yours?"

2. "What do you have to say for yourself?" my mother asked me.

Even if I had a voice, I still would have had a difficult time finding the right words to say to her. Most of my words disappeared when I was young, possibly as early as the second grade. My language arts teacher sent a letter home to my parents which read, "He's always losing. Losing pencils. Losing his homework. Losing his train of thought. His vocabulary is incredibly small. He leaves spaces in his essays. He just can't find the words."

She continued: "Things disappear when no one cares about them, you know? It goes for everything: your self-respect, your pencils, your voice, your life. That's what happened to his words. No one really cared what they said. And they left."

3. I lose it all the time.

I grabbed my composure, rather quickly, because I thought that if I took it fast enough then she would forget she ever had it and I wouldn't be completely embarrassed. It didn't work. I also looked for a hole in the ground, but there was nothing to bury my head, or preferably my entire body, in.

"Wait, one second," she said, raising her index finger as she dug under the counter. "We just got another composure in. Right now. Did you lose your it again? How about we just keep your composure here? It'll be safe. You can take it when you leave. That way you can't lose it again. So what are you here for?"

I murmured a little, pointed in various directions, and generally just made things worse.

4. She took the words right out of my mouth — and then stepped on them.

I had a crush on a girl when I was in the third grade. I would, without realizing it, stare at her for hours. Looking at her made everything brighter, certainly brighter than the shadow I usually stared at when I had my head bowed to the ground.

At recess, after sixty-straight days of me looking at her (not including weekends), she stomped up to me and demanded to know why I couldn't pull my eyes away from her. I wanted to tell her that it was because she made me brave in the dark, and that the dark didn't matter anymore anyway since it didn't exist when she could just brighten up everything.

But all she did was scream at me. And the more she screamed at me, the less I could say.

"What?" she yelled loud enough for the other kids to take notice.

I opened my mouth.

"What? Why can't you just talk like a normal person?"

Nothing came out.

"Why don't you just get lost?" she said, pushing me.

And I did. For decades.

5. That doesn't sound like anything I would say,
but then again, nothing sounds like something I would say.

The woman at the lost-and-found got an idea. "We got some words. Maybe some of these are yours. Would you like to see them?" she asked.

I dug through the box. None of them seemed familiar and certainly didn't sound like anything that I would say. Some of them, like "babe" and "honey" might as well have been Pig Latin for how silly they sounded. Others like "hi" had potential, but I didn't see myself saying them to anyone, let alone to a girl, and let alone to her. At the bottom of the box, I did discover "you," which I felt could be used and that, under the right circumstances, would be something I would say. It reminded me of her, because, if used correctly, it could be directed toward her.

At least, I thought, I knew to whom I'd want to say something if I had something at all to say. But then I realized that what I could say, if I could say anything, would have sounded like this: "I want to tell you something. I don't know what I want to tell you. But I want to tell you it."

"You might as well come in the back and look for yourself," she said, holding the swinging door open. "While you're at it, looking for whatever you're looking for, I'm wondering if you could look for me. I lost myself a while ago. If you find me, tell me where I am."

And then I remembered. I came to the lost-and-found to find myself.

But, to be truthful, I was just happy I found her.

6. Missing but not missed.

Per the suggestion, or demand, from the third-grade love-of-my-life to get lost, I joined up with a traveling troop of missings. Missings were missing things. Not only missing people, but missing items such as socks and television remotes. One could consider us a community, but not a community in the sense that we lived in any one place. Being missings, we just walked endlessly around in circles. We had to. It was in our definition to be lost; therefore we could never know where we were. And we had to walk around in circles because we could never get anywhere. If we got anywhere, we would, again, know where we were.

I envied the socks and television remotes. They knew what they were looking for. The remotes needed television sets. The socks wanted their other halves.

"We were a pair," the sock would say. "You couldn't tell us apart. You could say we were engaged. You could say we're now separated. You could say we're divorced. You could say it was hell on the baby socks."

We had a great deal of missing children. They never grew up. Some were always four and always just a week away from turning five. They crawled and cried. The cries always echoed incredibly loud but never loud enough for their cries to reach their mothers. Or for help. Or to anyone who cared. The older ones, the ones who had just reached their twelfth birthdays, would pray, but much like the cries to the mothers, the prayers never made it to anyone who would listen.

Children needed mothers. Remote controls needed television sets. But some of us didn't know what we needed. We didn't know who that something or someone was. Much to my surprise, I actually did have someone. However, it was never like when the pants found a pair of legs or when a drink found an alcoholic or an alcoholic found Christ or even the brief hint of hope when cancer would almost find a cure.

Loneliness found me. It had been following me my entire life. The problem with Loneliness is that it never says anything. It never tells you it will get better. It'll be with you, but it'll never hold you. It'll never make you feel good. And even though you can't find anyone else to stay the night, even though you're desperate to find someone that will stay the night, and even though it will promise to be with you well after the night, you'll beg for it to leave you alone like everyone else did on that night.

You never see Loneliness at a lost-and-found. That's because you can't lose it and you would never would want to find it.

7. "Gone but not forgotten," she said,

"is how I describe every bad relationship I've ever been in.

"I took this job because I couldn't get rid of anything," the woman at the lost-and-found started to explain, running her fingers through her short brown hair, which she told me that she parted on the left after her hair grew a sliver past its original fairy-arm length cut. And she told me that she got it cut to distance herself from a memory of an old boyfriend. And then she told me that she got a boyfriend to always have someone by her side.

"I hoard everything," she said. "I keep old boyfriends around, well after I lost what I had seen in them in the first place. Men have given up on me so many times. My parents have, too. My father said I lost my way. My mother would argue with him about it. She'd say, 'She never had one to begin with.'"

She threw around some boxes, yanked out the trash can, tossed a few items in, then organized the trash can in the "garbage" section of the lost-and-found, right next to "stuff that nobody has bothered looking for in twenty years" and the "stuff we forgot was even here" sections.

"I can't allow myself to let go of anything. I can't stand to give up on this stuff. I still have what guys thought about me. I can't lose that. I can't forget why they didn't want to be around me."

She looked in a mirror, lifted her shoulders, then shrugged, as if the weight of her anvil-sized frown brought her spirit-high shoulders back to the disappointing earth.

"I'm sorry, you came here to find something. You didn't come to listen to me," she said. "Did you find anything?"

I shook my head, even though I did find another word. I found the word "I," which I thought could fit somewhere, although I thought it was odd that I would talk about myself when I'd much rather hear about her. Or just her.

Other than that, I did find some companionship. Or rather, I found that I had already found some companionship. The box that contained it was opened. It had been for several minutes. Never actually having companionship before, I marveled at the box, rotating it around to glance at everything. The front of it described, in bold red letters, its uses:

"Deluxe version with a ton of customer support! It'll always be there for you! Works in any weather! Rain or shine, the darkest days and the longest nights!"

"What do you have there?" she asked, walking toward me. "Companionship, huh? The real stuff? It's not that manufactured crap you're forced to share with your mother at Christmas time. Still, the box makes it sound like it's a greeting card that mated with an infomercial for carpet-stain removal."

I was just about to put it down, when she stopped me.

"Keep it," she said. "That's actually my companionship. Someone got rid of it. He just left it here one day. I'd like you to have it."

8. She stuck to him like glue and like a leech.

After our traveling community of missings walked for several days or many decades — a distinction that mattered little since we knew that we would never get to where we wanted to go — we were apprehended by a group of Glues. Glues were, and still are, the most evolved species of all. Unlike us, they never lost anything. Not their confidence. Not a high-school football game. Not their ability to get a phone number. That's because they stuck to everything, especially their ways, using whatever us missings didn't have, such as money and charm and words, to lure women into their own social circles. Social circles consisted strictly of women walking, or even running, repeatedly into the same arms that only weeks before had shoved them aside.

Glues wanted us to search underwater to fish for their compliments, which we would then prepare for their dinner. They fed off of compliments, as well as a steady diet of Eugenics, body spray, and female insecurity. However, their stomachs never grew any larger. Instead, their heads would balloon. Those with the biggest heads attracted the most women.

The most obese members of Glues would be those whose heads were so overgrown that they would drag behind them, sticking to everyone and everything. They couldn't move far, but then again, by that point, their heads were large enough that they would be close to everyone anywhere they were just because of their girth.

Women would say, "You have such a big head. It's so thick."

Glues were seen, with good reason, as the zenith of reproduction. If populating the world was a responsibility for people like me, we would have been all dead long ago. It just would never happen. As my gym teacher once said during baseball practice, "You'll never reach third base. It's probably for the best. We don't need another you. And after seeing you, I'd hate to have to teach how your son how to throw."

He was a perfect example of a Glue.

Glues chose to utilize us missings because they knew that you can't lose something that's already lost. That way if we died, no one would ever come searching for us. They usually threw the children in the lakes first, since they despised the sound of them crying, and this could, as they often put it, "drown" them out. The children's bodies never floated to the top. Just like their parents, we'd never see them again.

We were all envious of the children's hope. Secretly, we all wanted to think that we could be saved just by screaming.

9. The only time that someone like her would look at me
would be when she would look past me.

"I think this is what some guy saw in me," the woman at the lost-and-found said. "I don't recognize it, though."

She handed it to me. "Does this seem like me?"

She gave me a moment. Not just any moment. It was the moment when she would look at you, and even though she could look at anyone, she would look at you. And when you looked up at her, she was still looking at you. And you still thought, as you had a couple times before, that she could have been looking anywhere, but she was looking at you. She was looking at you. You. And you realized that she could have been looking at anyone, but she was looking at you, and you knew she could look at you forever and it still wouldn't be long enough.

In other words, she could have been looking at anyone but she was looking at you.

Or, in even more other words, she could have been looking at anyone but she was looking at me.

And I totally forgot to answer, because she was, as I stated, I think, once or twice before, looking at me.

So I nodded.

That's when I spotted another word on the ground. It still shined, as if it was hardly used, but it still wasn't easy to decipher. I had never heard it, or seen it, before, and at first I thought it was written in code. However, I recognized the letters as being English and sounded it out. The first time it came out like "ˈhel." The second time, it came out as "ˈhāt." On the third attempt, I sounded out all the letters, focusing on the vowels. It came out like:

"ˈləv"

or "love."

I found "love."

"Hey, are you still here with me?" she asked, looking at me. "Do you know where you're at?"

I suddenly didn't feel so lost. She knew where I was. She knew that I was right there. And I knew where I was.

I was with her.

10. "We found him," the guard said. "How did you find him?" the captain asked. "Unhappy," the guard answered.

The Glues' guards sometimes talked about it. They hid it from us: a place where things were found. If we knew about it, we could, as the guards warned each other, be found and no longer would we have to stay at the camp. It was called a lost-and-found.

And they could be found everywhere from schools to shopping malls.

I decided to leave.

I conceived of the two best ways to escape: running through the forest or swimming to the end of the lake. But I knew that either way, I would just end up getting lost. I knew I could never find anything, especially not a way out. So, instead of looking for a way out, I did what I did best, and just left without a map. I told myself that I was looking for a way back to camp. That meant that I'd get lost looking for camp, which I did. And while "looking" for camp, I got so lost that I got as far away from camp and somehow ended up escaping.

Upon arriving in some strange town, I ran around the streets over and over, unable to find a lost-and-found, until I had to use the bathroom. Then, as I began to run around looking for a bathroom, I ended up, of course, in a lost-and-found.

"Hello," the lost-and-found woman said when I walked in. "Are you looking for something?"

11. Finding what you weren't looking for.

"How I see myself is exactly how my ex-boyfriends saw me," she said. "Awful. Like I'm not good enough."

She pushed a crate to the side.

"Hell," she said, staring into an old mirror, "I don't even know what I'm looking at now."

She lifted up a box and dipped her head in, looking right past it to the ground.

"I think I found what happened to me. Maybe I shouldn't have found it. I don't like looking at it. I don't like what I see."

She picked up another box, threw it on the mirror, slightly blocking her reflection and opened it. In the past, she had mailed it, gotten rid of it, but it had been sent back, with the message, "return to sender" stamped on the front. As she peeled off the tape, a man, an old boyfriend leaped out. She couldn't see the mirror at all now. He blocked it. She couldn't see herself anymore. She could only see him.

All the words came to me. I was finally able to speak.

"I love you," I said.

And she spoke back.

"I love you,"

she said

to him.

"That's it," my voice said for the final time. "I'm gone for good."

I stayed in the back, looking for the same things that I was never able to find in the same spots where they never were before, as she, as she had so many times before, found a new reason to wake up in the morning, to check her cell phone for new messages, to look at herself in the mirror and not question why she wasn't good enough.

None of it was really new. Nothing in a lost-and-found is. It's the same stuff we either neglected because we had such little use for it to begin with or that we threw away because we wanted it gone. But when we forget that it was ever ours is when we think it's something new. "Did I ever have that?" we think.

As I saw her dance with him, and she rediscovered how she looked at herself, the same look that she couldn't tell was hers or how her boyfriend looked at her, I asked myself a question: why couldn't I find what I was looking for? Well, I could never find it in any of the boxes, or anywhere in the lost-and-found, because nothing was mine to begin with.

Her lost-and-found was just for the same people to come by, claim, lose, leave, then return six months later to claim, lose, and leave. I could never find anything, especially love, at the lost-and-found, because I never had love to lose. Therefore, I couldn't find what I never lost. I only found the word "love."

It didn't matter. She was as much of a missing item in the lost-and-found as she was one of the employees.

I wanted to know why. I wanted to know why it happened and why she couldn't see me. Why I was told to get lost and why I could never be found. I could see it. I could see why I could never be found. I just couldn't make it our clearly. It resembled a carrot and it dangled in front of me. I started to walk, chasing after it. By this point, all the socks, all the remotes, all the other lost items began walking behind me, as did the woman and her boyfriend, repeating their same routine.

But I just couldn't catch it. And sometimes, I wondered if the explanation existed at all or if I just wanted to think there was one, because then it would all be for something, some larger plan. But without an explanation, it all — every mile I walked, every broken neck I received from hanging my head so low — was just for nothing.

Behind me, her and her boyfriend broke up, screamed at each other, then she lost him, then she talked to me, looked at me, and finally looked away from me and found him again. Then her and her boyfriend broke up, screamed at each other, then she lost him, then she talked to me, looked at me, and finally looked away from me and found him again. Then her and her boyfriend broke up, screamed at each other, then she lost him, then she talked to me, looked at me, and finally looked away from me and found him again.

And I always looked up. And I always found the words. Then I could never say the words. Then I could say the words. And then she would never hear them. And then it would happen again and I would always think, every time, that this time, she'll hear me say "I love you." And she'll say, "I love you" back.

Then her and her boyfriend would break up, scream at each other, make up, then she'd talk to me, then she'd look at me, and finally look away from me and find him again.

Joseph Bouthiette Jr.

Harry Handler vs. The Fire

"This is what it's like to be on fire, burning through the coals
What a way to release this fury and be consumed"
—Phinehas, "My Horses Are Many"

I

Betty Rocksteady is a Canadian author and pen-and-ink artist whose work typically involves the surreal and the macabre. Currently known for her novella *Arachnophile*, published by Eraserhead Press' New Bizarro Author Series, her publishing credits, both word and image, also include: *Halloween Forevermore*, *Grievous Angel*, *Another Realm*, *Lost Signals*, *The Phalanges Series*, *Eternal Frankenstein*, *555*, *Ravenwood Quarterly*, and *Fucked Up Fairy Tales*. Betty is a known lover of cats and eccentrically colored hair. She grew up with a love for the work of Stephen King (a love she maintains to this day), and possessed a fear of spontaneous human combustion as a child.

How fitting, then, that she should become our eponymous *fire*.

II

Harry Handler is no one. While the preceding information on Betty Rocksteady is as true as we can possibly be aware, Harry Handler is a fictional character whose existence must be created to satisfy his role within this story. Betty, as a real person, already possesses the dimensionality one would expect from the protagonist of a story. Harry's character will need to be constructed via interpretations of his actions within this story, in combination with traits we may or may not simply state he possesses for the sake of brevity. And yes, though Harry Handler is given top billing in our title, it is Betty who is truly the star of this tale.

Harry Handler is of an occupation that is not stationary enough to allow him to descend into obesity, yet is not motile enough to keep him in any regular shape. Perhaps a security guard at his local mall, or an assistant manager at a chain retail outlet. He could be described as soft, round in the face and the stomach, but certainly not slovenly, nor what one would call a "mouth-breather." He's certainly husband material, though whether or not he's married, he definitely has no children. He's no reader, nor an expert on the visual arts. The little music he consumes typically falls within the realm of hard rock, citing Metallica and Disturbed as favorites when polled.

In short, Harry is the sort of man who is equally likely to be found purchasing a new varnish for his pool deck as he is to be enjoying a couple drinks while watching hockey down at the local watering hole. An everyman, that's Harry Handler.

III

"Harry Handler vs. The Fire" certainly denotes a conflict between these two characters, yet does not hint at the flavor of the dispute. Perhaps we can start *in media res*, Harry dangling by one hand from broken scaffolding over a debris-strewn factory floor, Betty existing as a pure wave of flame, tongues of her living inferno scorching the assembly space in all directions, the heat of her combustion melting the soles of Harry's shoes, her sparks and embers burning small holes into Harry's discount suit jacket, Harry frantically kicking, trying to shout for help or for Betty to end this madness but rendered mute by a thought embedded in his mind that there is a container of explosives in this building and that he is only seconds away from being torn apart by shrapnel, or perhaps melted down by corrosive burns, and Betty just keeps getting brighter, her flames keep getting hotter.

Perhaps we'll step back, Betty sketching an illustration idea for *The Phalanges Series*, drawing when she should be sleeping, responding to the occasional message from one of her friends online, when the realization her cats are nowhere nearby for a quick petting session strikes her, and somewhere in the space between her atoms there is a shift, her entire body disassembling and spiraling with infernal abandon, not ascending to a higher existence nor devolving into primal space stuff but simply stepping into the next stage of her life, a smog of sentient flame, undulating in the dark.

Perhaps instead there is a tragic accident and the tiny flame of an untended candle billows and catches a curtain alight, quickly devouring Betty's newly purchased home, burning her couch and unpacked boxes and the bed in which she sleeps, though her essence is unaware of the damage around her and she simply awakens, her body now a fraction of the fire roaring from roof to foundation.

At the same time, perhaps we also see Harry reheating some leftovers for dinner at home after a bad day at work, slowly mulling over his cheesy potatoes, thoughts like fireworks in his psyche, bright and important for a moment then gone in the darkness, an overall feeling of satisfaction despite his day, a desire to share his levity via a romp with his wife later that evening, fully aware she hasn't particularly enjoyed their bedroom escapades for several months, thinking back on other attractive women he could have spent the night with in alternate timelines, a spark of guilt for these nefarious thoughts, becoming fixated on one girl in particular anyways, a girl he remembers from high school, a carnival of sexual maneuvers cartwheeling in his brain as he continues forking cheesy potatoes into his mouth, chewing slowly.

Perhaps he takes these thoughts with him into the bedroom, pushing his wife into the throes of ecstasy with his newfound mental deviancy, the acrobatics he performs with Betty McIntyre (that same acquaintance from high school) in his mind distilled into manageable acts of passion with his wife, the prologue to a montage of illicit acts we frankly don't need to list here, only that they're sultry in the eyes of this working class couple, and though they energize their lives, Harry continues battling with the guilt of his adulterous thoughts, seeks a middle-ground solution that allows him to atone while still taking advantage of his deviancy, seeks out Betty McIntyre on various social media platforms, sees she now refers to herself as Betty Rocksteady, and makes the mistake of admitting everything to Betty, his lust for her and his appropriation of it into the bedroom, makes the mistake of thanking her, makes many mistakes he can never truly be aware of.

And perhaps this is the match that lights Betty's gasoline, infuriated by this nonchalant admission to using her as a sexual tool by this nobody man whom she doesn't recognize but now hates all the same, developing "Harry Handler vs. The Fire" into a conflict of incandescent revenge.

But perhaps vengeance isn't the motive here, Harry down on his luck, never married, house on the verge of foreclosure, the value of his stock shares plummeting by the day, and he picks up smoking, spending money he doesn't have on cigarettes he knows won't kill him fast enough to make a difference.

Perhaps one day he's walking home from the gas station with a new pack in hand, but he's forgotten his lighter at home, a moment of carelessness he gets uncharacteristically angry about (though with the rate his temper has been flaring, it may well become the norm), and he tries to bum a light off a blue-haired woman loading a box of books into her car, and when she dismisses him explaining she doesn't smoke so she doesn't own a lighter, Harry grabs her by the silky shirt sleeve and before he can say a word, she screams, her blue hair erupting into blue flames, and she slams her box into him with concussive force, fire whipping in all directions, smoke and the ashen pages of *Arachnophile* by Betty Rocksteady billowing into the cloudless sky, Harry scrambling away, his cigarettes still wrapped and sitting in the street where he dropped them, his mind reeling with the encounter with the burning woman, the ragged shreds of his sanity trying to create a rational explanation for the event while knowing full well he hasn't seen the last of her.

Perhaps none of these occur, but alas, here we are, watching Harry struggle in a factory while Betty gulps down every particle of oxygen she can reach, the harsh sirens of fire engines always too far away.

IV

Regardless of the cause-and-effect nature of the conflict, there is certainly only one outcome: the fire proves victorious. Whether this is in the literal sense of Betty taking hold of Harry with her burning fists and scorching him into so many wisps of ash, or metaphorically, as Betty makes the ultimate decision to *not* scorch him into so many wisps of ash, there is nothing more endearing than a worthwhile protagonist conquering her adversary. This ending feels appropriate, for it is always Harry Handler who strays from the path, and our sense of righteousness demands he suffer the consequences.

Somewhere in her vermillion limbs, Betty may gain control of her form and return to the green-haired Canadian she once was. If not, she releases her fury in wave after wave of flame, an exponentially growing volume of cinder trailing in her wake.

Harry occasionally survives. The factory does not.

Kay Merkel Boruff

Queen Bees at Black Rock Desert

Burning Man 2012

I'm interested in entropy—increasing disorder.

—Muse

i. Amen.

ii. Blood. Money. Sex. CIA. Love. Loss.

iii. Daylight Savings: Turning the Clocks Back

iv. Askesis, the "dark night of the soul" Waiting for God Simone Weil

1.3 Give up winning and strive to be clear. Wendell Berry A Place in Time

1.5 " 'the w orld there w as

" 'con st antly

" 'sev ered.

The Fifty Years Sword Mark Z. Danielewski

1.7 There's a crack in everything. That's how the light gets in. Leonard Cohen. Goth Service Edward Cambridge

1.92 Karma come back: Food on Barbara's clothes; then food on Trish & my clothes as I went to measure my couch for my new home.

2. Rotate this manuscript counterclockwise 90 degrees and the text will make a perfect bell curve . . . or at least appear weird. Look for the outliers and other "black swans."

2.83 Advice to budding writers from an Irish writer: Read biographies of writers who were suicidal, such as Virginia Woolf. Zadie Smith suggests: Know you'll always be sad.

Your writing will never be perfect.

2.834 I grow old…I grow old…I shall wear the bottoms of my trousers rolled./Shall I part my hair behind?/Do I dare to eat a peach?/The Love Song of J. Alfred Prufrock T.S. Eliot

2.835 I saw my neighbor when I was walking my dog. He stopped to pat her grey muzzle. I noticed that the neighbor had on a suit. You look nice, I said. He said, Probation trial . . . joke! I said, I volunteer at the VA. That's normal.

2.879 I strapped on the stilts, buckling the silver buckles over my yellow caked hiking boots, stood up, walking step after tenuous step, looking up at the green and white flags blowing in the desert wind, then down at the people dancing, hula-hooping, drinking mojitos. Gathering courage, I begin to run, giant-like lumbering steps, over the art cars, the Portapotties, the burning man, escaping in blade-runner acid-leaps into the white cumulous clouds.

2.89 Joe chased me around the living room, the drapes on the vaulted ceiling fourteen-feet removed, that is you could see into the studio apartment like a play, track lighting flooded the chocolate walls and red carpet and smoked glass and chrome furniture, he finally throwing me to the eight-foot beige tweed couch, chrome end plates visible, his strong thirty-year-old hands around my neck, strangling me, until I struggled to free myself.

2.90 The Andre Squares at Burning Man, twelve-inch square thin slate stepping stones formed a straight path you could take through the desert, like a ladder climbing up to the sky. After 500 feet, the path veered slightly to the east, only a degree, so that when the sun came up that morning, I was facing the sliver of light . . . . Someone must have come pre-dawn and swept the slate stones because there was no grey dust covering them. The stones shone, glintering in the early breaking dawn.

2.91 My third sister-in-law just up and died. No one knows the time or place. That family joke on the Baptist minister struck home. I stood graveside, my niece's ex-father-in-law presiding over the funeral, saying final prayers. Beside me stood my niece's boyfriend, tall, dark, handsome. Her ex-husband walked up, with his hand stuck out I assumed to shake the boyfriend's hand, and the ex punched out the boyfriend, who fell like a tall dead wall. The ex's mother came over to pull off her son. I stood with my mouth gaping.

2.92 I caught the roach scuttling across my pillow between my thumb and index finger. Before I thought I squished it. Red blood ran from the insect. It wasn't a tick. It ran too fast. I got up to throw the remains in the toilet, washed my hands, and looked at my face to see if something had been on my cheek. Nothing visible other than the hives that broke out daily. Friday I liquidated $68,000 in my Morgan Stanley fund and came home and threw up. Crap shooting. Buying a new house with a mortgage at age 68. The hives come, itch, and go away. On NPR a journalist in Afghanistan was talking about recent action a recent village. Two young children were killed. US drones covered in blood.

2.925 Slowly, I'd encroached on Dixie's space. The bed in the back bedroom, cool and quiet, had been covered in boxes. I'd cleared a space but then realized the bed was too high. She couldn't jump up anymore. The last night to make more room to pack & stack boxes, I'd moved the coffee table flush to "her" couch, her two pillows encased with expensive cotton, flat from wear, cool & inviting. Early this morning, she woke me up with her hacking. My vet Dr. Fred said something about her throat collapsing. She was on the couch. Stealth dog bitch. She must have jumped over coffee table and then had an attack from exerting so much energy. I'd planned to have her bathed at Petsmart but I'll take her stinky to the new house. Too hard on her. But who knows. She may be better. She's lying at my feet, on her cool pad, a four-inch foam-webbed mattress filled with water, a small fan on the floor blowing directly on her big fat, hog dog body: "Wings" temporarily postponed.

3. I received an email after attending a school dinner for twenty or so retired teachers saying, Helen died. I'd spoken of Helen fondly, not with acrimony as we'd had a huge fight one year when I taught with her and we shared one grade. She was an older mentor

who suggested books for me to read, to fill in the huge cracks in my liberal education spend in the back seat of George's two-door Ford. When I looked for Helen's obit, I didn't find it but found another Helen—Heatherington who graduated from Hockaday's junior college. She was ninety-four. I posted the deaths of both Helens on my Facebook page and comments appeared in a few seconds about both women. Then I read the original email again and noticed no last name followed the original "Helen" message. Mark Twin's famous quote—stories of my death are greatly exaggerated—came to mind, followed by Rosana Rosanadana from SNL: Never mind. Then floated up from Jim Farr—keep 'em talking. If it sells, it works. Don't read directions. Don't proofread. Don't spellcheck. Just keep going forward until your meds run out or it's no longer fun and you have no more will to shop. Prosopagnosia, the disease where you can't distinguish faces, one from another. Or one name from another.

3.5. I didn't drive down to San Antonio to spend Thanksgiving with my niece. My hair was grey and I didn't have the $192 to color it. I didn't have gas money to drive, especially since I recently drove to Wichita Falls to pick up my hand gun. I was so depressed, that some days it was 1:30 in the afternoon before I could bathe, dress, and fix my face, something I swore I would always do after my first nervous breakdown. I never cry at the right places, and I'm tired of my blood work coming back with a lower white blood count than the last time, lower than a friend who's fighting cancer. I'm so tired I have to trick myself into walking the dog. I'm afraid she will die and I'll be alone. I'm afraid she'll live and I can't afford to buy her medicine. I'm tired of my hands looking like I've been boxing without gloves. I touch my skin and it bruises, dark red, wineskin blood spreading across my arthritic fingers and hands. I have a retirement fund. I stopped looking at my fund when one quarter TIAA-CREF reported a $25,000 loss. The good news is that I had the money to lose but I don't know how to access the money and I'm afraid to start spending the money, that I won't have enough to live on, if I live. I'm so angry I could rip someone's head off—if I had the strength. I dropped out of everything I could—poetry, a bunch of old people who don't write like I do, aerobic dance, can't put on a happy face anymore, and the school where I taught for thirty-eight years. I'm still angry that I was fired for being old and making too much money. I'm considering cashing in my retirement funds, when I put my dog down, and moving to Lima, Peru. I want to see Macha Picchu before I die and it's as good a place to die as Jacksboro or Bowie. I found my Merkel burial plot my father-in-law left me—Louden Park Cemetery, VV Lot 137 Site #1, Baltimore, Maryland, and made burial arrangements for $2,165. I didn't pay the extra for a Saturday burial. No marker necessary. Pop was a real charmer, a triple-dipper from the Pentagon, the Army, and the Corps of Engineers, who asked me to marry him when my husband was killed, and his wife died. The man took the last remnants I had of Jon. You'd think Johns Hopkins men would act better. I never sleep more than a few hours. My novel was rejected with the comments: Plot too difficult. No viable climax. Basically boring. My short story "The Home Place" came back with similar rejection notes: plot wanders. Some readers don't realize PTSD and LD brains do wander. Selling the home place in Wichita Falls was another twist of the noose. It took three years for my learning disabled brain to accept my big brother's death. I was ripped off $8,000 for his funeral. He could have been buried for $800 in Bowie. The Veteran's Administration paid for his head stone. I paid for the installation. And my man Mitt lost the election. At first I thought, this white guy doesn't have a prayer against the Rock Star. My father was a white guy with grey hair and I loved him. I loved Mitt. I voted. I encouraged my relatives to vote. Two GOP friends, a fat white guy from Wichita Falls who could buy Forth Worth and a skinny Latina Dallas friend were both approached to sign up for food stamps. Could we have equal opportunity and sign up for a bloody job. Then the final blow. General Petraeus' major cluster fuck. If I saw Paula Broadbutt, I'd shoot her tits off. Everyone knows men can't keep their pants zipped. Furthermore, my brain never enters REM. Also the tinnitus ringing in my left ear, like crickets and oceans rolling in, the traffic from LBJ Freeway, eighteen-wheelers and the other 100,000 cars racing all night long in my right ear. Some nights my brain never turns off. It finished this story last night. Thank you. Sleepless in Dallas.

13. The number thirteen is my lucky number. It was my band locker number. It's my parking spot. It's one more than the hours on a clock. It begins with a diphthong "th" and is a spondee with two long stressed syllables.

13.4 Jonesing. What does it mean? It means shooting up. To keep up with fellow addicts. Became known as Keeping up with the Joneses. How many heroin addicts have you known? One. My brother. A Way with Words Martha and Grant

13.5 My head lamp was pushed up onto my forehead. The grey dust settled into drifts of ash-like sand. Nothing burned tonight. My goggles hung around my neck, the wind finally dying to a breeze. The fur heavy with sand pulled up under my chin, my hands covered with red and green fingerless filthy gloves, my red polish covered in green metallic, my right arthritic thumb sticking straight out, gnarled knuckles no longer painful, my right thumb cracked, blood dried and caked with dirt, my hiking boots laces stiff with urine, Playa dust, mud resting on the foot of the deck chair. A couple floated into my sight—he, tall, bearded, shoulder length hair, she small, curly hair in dread locks, both silhouetted, both nude in the moonlight, floating toward me, a figment of my gummy bear dessert hours earlier. They weren't aware of my sphinxlike form draped on a canvas deck chair, covered in an acrylic tiger striped buffalo fur.

13.9 Alkaline foot bath: The ice water so cold I screamed when my blistered feet sunk into the vinegar bath. Two blisters the size of pigeon eggs on the back of my heels. Walking ten miles a day in twelve inch desert dust, like sand dunes on a Texas beach, old ribbed aerobic socks replacing my expensive wool hiking socks was the cause of infection. Red streaks radiated from the bottoms of my feet. Closing my eyes, the blind spots appear again.

13.91 Awaking after reading "The Golden Vanity" by Ben Lerner, I'm back on the Playa, tripping again, the small white square on my tongue.

14. My niece said, Aunt Bonny, you don't even like to camp. We're going to be in the desert for ten days without showers. I got online and threw my MasterCard in the ring for $800 tickets to Burning Man 2012 "Fertility." Maybe my uterus removed when I was thirty-four, so upset I tried to get pregnant in my godson's twin bed with a man my best friend found cruising on Deep Elem would be restored. Maybe the immaculate conception

would occur and I'd get pregnant. Maybe I'd have some experiences, "grist for the mill," my orthodox Hebrew professor told me in graduate school.

15. My niece said, Aunt Bonny, the BMW dealership in San Antonio doesn't have a very nice waiting room. Kate, I said, I've been pooping and peeing in a Port-a-potty for ten days. If they have flush toliets that work, it's upscale enough.

15.3. I hate slow. I hate fat. My friend who swilled Scotch and pills and put a bag over her head said, I hate fat so much, I'm sure I'll be fat tomorrow. She weighed ninety pounds when she committed suicide. I'm already slow, and I'm working on getting fat.

16. War is a business, and business is good. Of course, the US will be in Iraq and Afghanistan until the cows come home. The US has to keep its fingers in the pies in all governments around the world. My first husband died for that privilege. The world is governed by powerful; and fortunately for me, my country is the most powerful country in the world. We're not the best. We're not the smartest. We're simply the most creative.

17. The principals of Burning Man, I learned later, include creativity.

17.66 You know what these geriatric shower [chairs] would really be good for? To hang yourself. Don't you think? Nice and light—easy to kick away. The Corrections Jonathan Franzen

17.8 There ought to be behind the door of every happy, contented man someone standing with a hammer continually reminding him with a tap that there are unhappy people; that however happy he may be, life will show him her laws sooner or later, trouble will come for him—disease, poverty, losses, and no one will see or hear, just as now he neither sees nor hears others. Anton Pavlovich Chekhov Or behind every happy man is an unhappy man hiding in a cupboard. So take the son-of-a-bitch out of the cupboard and beat the shit out of him.

17.9 Ten Principles of Burning Man

1. Radical Inclusion

Anyone may be a part of Burning Man. We welcome and respect the stranger. No prerequisites exist for participation in our community.

2. Gifting

Burning Man is devoted to acts of gift giving. The value of a gift is unconditional. Gifting does not contemplate a return or an exchange for something of equal value.

17.91 "Nets and Beards" As winter's face becomes spring, /we are reminded of God's presence in our lives. Bonny Bauman Chen I weave the Gadamerian net through Plato's beard /and say the words to prove what there is not. /I build my tower, pebble by pebble, /rocks and seaweed garnered from Asian shores. /I climb the tower and stately view St. Stephen's cross. /I write the words beneath my eyes, /inside my skull, seer them until flesh is ash. /You live in Plato's cave beneath Odysseus' sheep, /safe from the light and taunts. /I long to go with you, into the silent, good night.

3. Decommodification

In order to preserve the spirit of gifting, our community seeks to create social environments that are unmediated by commercial sponsorships, transactions, or advertising. We stand ready to protect our culture from such exploitation. We resist the substitution of consumption for participatory experience.

Sirocco oppressive hot Mediterranean wind: a hot dusty humid southeast wind in southern Europe that begins in the Sahara and picks up moisture as it crosses the Mediterranean.

Fuck decommodification. In a white out, who can sell shit. You cover your fucking face with goggles, face masks borrowed from Nails LaBelle, your Vietnamese friend who painted your fingernails Cedar Springs "Ho" red, now covered in green CreamDeMentha polish, turn on your fucking headlight so you don't get run over by the fucking Octupusy shooting rocket fire and the 30,000 Amsterdam bicycles roaming over the Playa, and pray you make it back to the camp in one piece. Sirocco, the southeast wind blowing from the Sahara, without moisture, with alkaline.

4. Radical Self-reliance

   Burning Man encourages the individual to discover, exercise and rely on his or her inner resources.

5. Radical Self-expression

   Radical self-expression arises from the unique gifts of the individual. No one other than the individual or a collaborating group can determine its content. It is offered as a gift to others. In this spirit, the giver should respect the rights and liberties of the recipient.

I flashed my bra-less breasts the last night, the Shower master's #2 LSD square on my tongue, the CreamDeMentha art car finally having arrived before the last hurrah. The "Red Jesus" and his girlfriend fell out and loved my racy behavior. Then when I sat at camp, they returned from the Playa, nude, carrying their clothes. My niece said I'd been tripping. They wouldn't do that.

6. Communal Effort

   Our community values creative cooperation and collaboration. We strive to produce, promote and protect social networks, public spaces, works of art, and methods of communication that support such interaction.

7. Civic Responsibility

   We value civil society. Community members who organize events should assume responsibility for public welfare and endeavor to communicate civic responsibilities to participants. They must also assume responsibility for conducting events in accordance with local, state and federal laws.

Do drugs every chance you get. And liquor. Crown Royal straight from the fat, crystal bottle, the blue bag back at the camp site kitchen. The desert on Gummy bears, LSD, acid. You wouldn't want to miss out on anything. Uppers. Downers. Speed. So shit-faced you can't sleep when your niece puts you in your sleeping bag, your shit-covered, dust-crusted laced hiking boots, peeling off the socks, praying the blisters on your heels don't break, the fat, thick blisters, the size of lemons, on both feet, the ankle still painful in the cold, from falling into the flower bed, your eyes looking up at a balcony where some redneck or SSI black who keeps a BBQ cooker on his patio or a dog left unattended in the 117 degree heat of the summer or towels and T-shirts drying in the sun, the fucking ghetto where you lived, just like living in the fucking desert, with sand on the tent flaps, sand on your stiff desert camy khakis, stinking of pee and sweat, arm pits stinking of body odor, arm pits razorless, legs chapped and razorless, grey army issue belt nylon snagging on your underwear, underwear the only clean thing touching your body, hair molded into dreg locks & nigger natty twists, grey color over expensive highlights, and your brain on acid, tripping every time you close your eyes, until the sun comes up and your bladder forces you to rise up and pull off all the clothes you put on in the night, strip damn near naked, in boxer shorts and bra and hiking boots, reaching for your glasses, appreciative of your niece's carefully putting them up for safe-keeping, and head off to the Port-a-potties, just as the shit crew drives up to clean the toilets.

8. Leaving No Trace

   Our community respects the environment. We are committed to leaving no physical trace of our activities wherever we gather. We clean up after ourselves and endeavor, whenever possible, to leave such places in a better state than when we found them.

CreamDeMentha green flags and "green" moot-free site. I washed nasty ten-day-old dishes, scraping food and Mojitos limes and mint leaves from glasses until my hands were bleeding and my back was broken and my attitude was such that my niece told me to go to the car after several bitchy remarks to the queen bees. I refused to pick up moot because I really feared that either I would have a sun stroke from the heat and lack of sleep or my back would go completely out and I wouldn't be able to get back to my damned old dog.

Don't shit on the Playa. (Every rule is made to be broken.) So shit I didn't but peed I did on the rare occasion when my bladder wouldn't last until the next pit stop.

9. Participation

   Our community is committed to a radically participatory ethic. We believe that transformative change, whether in the individual or in society, can occur only through the medium of deeply personal participation. We achieve being through doing. Everyone is invited to work. Everyone is invited to play. We make the world real through actions that open the heart.

10. Immediacy

   Immediate experience is, in many ways, the most important touchstone of value in our culture. We seek to overcome barriers that stand between us and a recognition of our inner selves, the reality of those around us, participation in society, and contact with a natural world exceeding human powers. No idea can substitute for this experience.

17.92 Kate & I did have a grand time. It was like no other event I've been to, although being in Amsterdam was similar. Camping in the desert was a challenge. The Port-a-potties weren't that bad. We happened to be close to some and yet far away although there really wasn't a smell. We got that system down pretty fast. CreamDeMetha camp was the best camp. Connor Healy, the Elder, was a dear. His attractive girlfriend Jeri appeared to be a dear but several incidents made me think of brother Fred's advice--watch your 6:00. Jeri played the queen bee "General's 'wife'." They weren't married. Her Facebook showed she attended Texas A&M, so some brains are present. She and Connor had been together three or four years. She was six weeks pregnant and had a broken leg she broke sky diving with Connor. Connor has 500+ jumps; she has 250 jumps. So she has money somewhere. To my knowledge, she didn't do drugs. This is both their first child. She mentioned to Kate or someone, she would be a Healy before

Donna, or Donna said vice verse. Granted, it could be me, but several times she was smiling, but I think she didn't really like us.

17.93 Monday night, I did acid, had a wonderful trip, rode on the art car with Connor & Jeri and drove all over the Playa with the entire camp walking with us and stayed up all night as I couldn't fall asleep. It's nice when you don't do drugs or drink and a small amount last a really long time.

17.94 Tue morning, Connor and Jeri invited us to drive on the art car with them to see the art on the Playa. We had the best time as it was cool, not crowded, and we just motored along at the 5 miles an hour speed limit around the five-mile center, looking at one art piece after another, taking pictures, swinging on swings and climbing all over the art.

17.945 When we signed up to join CreamDeMetha, I emailed Jeri, not knowing who she was, that Kate and I would bring food for the camp. I said, I didn't know what or how to cook for dinner, due to flying, staying at a hotel, not being able to prepare or freeze a meal. As it was our first "burn," I worried about people getting sick from food we prepared going bad in the heat. She suggested bringing lunch meat, cheese, crackers, so we did. I brought apples, organic walnuts, organic almonds, & health bars from Whole Food $100. Then got chips, lunch meat, bread, and 2 big Coleman coolers $160 which the camp used to store ice as we didn't have beer in one as most people did.

17.95 Wed Kate started making grilled sandwiches, turkey, cheese, deli horseradish mustard and people loved them. I passed out almonds I'd put in baggies to have for snacks and gave out breakfast bars and chocolate squares for dessert. Seven more dinners were made, mostly gourmet, in pairs, Declan cooking alone Sunday. The dinners were gourmet foodie recipes, vegan, fresh vegetables, couscous, stuff I don't cook but loved. People were supposed to clean up their own plates and cups and silverware, which of course the majority didn't. Declan was captain of the kitchen and clean up. So I tried to help him clean. I also tried to help with the ice detail. I brought four pairs of gloves. One cute guy

Pete and girl Michelle Hong from Dallas helped each day. They went with a wagon and got bags of ice which were divided up into quart zip bags and put in everyone's coolers stacked near Declan's truck where he and Donna slept.

18. Then later in the week, as people grew to know each other and drank more and did more drugs, Lord of the Flies began to take place. Jeri and another camper Linda, not attractive, overweight, huge breasts hanging down to her waist, were laughing about our lunches which Kate over heard. Linda's problem. Jeri's problem. Not mine. We were just doing what Jeri suggested. People enjoyed our Texas food.

18.2 My back did amazingly well. We showered twice midweek & washed hair once, though had planned not to shower but just use baby wipes. Then Connor said around Fri no more showers except for early campers. Rules were not really explained, so Kate & I tried to figure out camp protocol.

18.3 One night we walked the Playa five miles across four times. It was fucking freezing. Another night, I asked Jerie if I could ride on the art car. She had to ride because she had a boot on her broken leg and she walked with crutches. She said she and Connor were going alone on a date to the Playa. I thought fair enough. Kate & I walked with a camp group and later we saw them with other people from our camp on the art car. Fair enough. Another night, when I was tired, blistered feet, and cold, I asked could I ride home on the art car. It was full of couples. She said, Yes, she'd have to throw someone off, because the car could only hold fifteen max. I got pissed but didn't say anything and found Declan and ask if I could walk with him. Kate was with Darius, a Greek lawyer from NYC, very different from most of the guys at CreamDeMentha. Kate had a posse of guys around just like in Amsterdam, Paris, and Israel. I thought Kate was safely accompanied by Darius. Declan and I hooked up with a Cuban Jewish kid and Spanish kid from Florida who must have been 6'9". The three guys walked me back to camp. As it turned out, Darius had to leave and the art car was driving him to a pickup point. Kate panicked, thinking that I was lost, wandering stoned on the Playa. So she and another CreamDeMentha guy walked to camp to look for me. Michelle Hong and Penguin and two others were on bikes. This group of bikers rode across the five miles of Playa, in the dust, dark, drunken, drugged groups of people, hard traveling to say the least, to find me. Declan and my two guys and I hooked up with were sitting around the kitchen eating when the bike group rode in to discover me, explained the confusion, and they rode back across the Playa to find Kate. Drugs will cloud your mind but you soldier on.

19. Darius said to Kate, the reason he liked her was because of how she took care of me. I was the oldest in CreamDeMentha. Levi from San Francisco, the black with red dreadlocks, was sixty-five, running a half-way house for drug addicts. Nice guy. He hung around camp lots also, which I generally did during the day while Kate went out walking or bike riding with a group. CreamDeMentha had a bunch of bikes they stored for the camp.

20. One afternoon, Kate and I had a fight when she dumped my Amsterdam bag contents into her Jake backpack to take my bag on a bike ride. I was angry that she didn't ask and mainly I didn't want to lose my things. I brought Merk's star sapphire earrings safely zipped into my bag and her backpack had no safety zippers. She took her own bag, went off, had fun, and we made up. It's hard to be with someone for twenty-four hours a day and not argue or fight.

20.4 Tinnitus when I lie down worsens. Stress brings it on. My left ear has white noise that worsens at night when I lie down or even when I'm pissed. The normal hissing becomes a pulsing roaring, the most uncommon type of tinnitus. Fortunate bloody hell.

20.5 Kevin Powers writes in THE YELLOW BIRDS: "I saw his body finally break apart near the mouth of the gulf, where the shadows of the date palms fell in long, dark curtains on his bones, now scattered, and swept them out to sea, toward a line of waves that break forever as he enters them."

20.59 A neighbor had a white Mercedes in his parking space. I said, You really traded up. His former car was a little yellow truck with 200+ miles and lots of dents. He said,

The Germans made good tanks so I figured it was a good buy. I said, What did you do with your little yellow truck? Give it to your dad? He said, I left it on the side of the road and said, Take it.

20.6 A yellow bird/With a yellow bill/Was sitting on/My window sill/I lured him in/With a piece of bread/And then I smashed/his little head (Army marching cadence)

21. Donna, City Bitch, named for her time in NYC, was the hit of the camp. She was my Irish nephew's girlfriend. She was totally uninhibited. She doesn't work now as I later found out that her parents died and left her an inheritance. During the burn, I didn't know what she did or where she's from or what her background was. We didn't discuss anything personal other than a comment she made. No babies in her future. She helped Kate and me with our costumes. Declan called later when I returned to Dallas to be sure that I got home okay. He said that Donna stayed to visit her brother whom she hadn't seen in a while. They were to meet in San Francisco for a wedding and then back to DC and local burns. He's seems really smitten with her. I guess he's old enough to realize what he's signing up for with Donna.

21.5 Crossing the checkpoint at McAllen reminded me of being on a bus in East Germany with a load of Christians, before the Wall came down. It was 1983. It was hilarious and scary at the same time. German shepherd dogs, bloodline Nazi dogs, walked around the bus. Sniffing. Sniffing. The well-manicured German border guards came on the bus and walked slowly down the aisle, the Communist guide seated in the first seat, walking slowly, not smiling, looking at each retired senior and me, at our individual passports. In my mind I imagined all the Christians, all the ministers, praying that these evil Communists would leave us the hell alone. In the fall of 2012, the same fear, hair-on-the-arm-rising feeling crept over me as we approached the checkpoint, Martin, a retired petroleum engineer who worked a mile from the checkpoint when he was a newlywed and father of a month-old-daughter, and Catherine, a university professor with a PhD in Southern literature, four-years-older than I, Church of Christ deacons, no drinking, no dancing, and no drugs, and I, fresh from the desert, acid cursing through my veins for seven years or so my mother and I thought when my brother and sister-in-law did LSD in the late 70s. The window rolled down, the guard and Martin exchanged pleasantries, the window slides up, and we drive on.

22.68 City Bitch started a tradition. Anyone who fell asleep sitting in a chair was awarded the "Gargoyle Prize." City got two of the strongest guys to lift her up over the sleeping cherub's head. Even though City was in her 40s, she was a former dancer and her body would rock your lights, she was the original "trust the thrust," bridge pose on steroids, or uppers or downers or a combo of both, depending on the size of the moon. Dressed in the day's attire—a black bustier and a tutu or a pink and black lace chemise—and, of course, no underwear, held by two strong men, she would position her legs in a perfect spread eagle and someone would take a picture. Normally the young British photographer with dreds would shoot the victim—but here sat the dred-locked youngster with shut eyes, drooling, innocent, as City urinated on his head, captured for all on a private-posted website. Even the recent earthquake at the National Cathedral in Washington, DC didn't bring this much fun in the life of the Darth Vader gargoyle.

22.69 I slept through my alarm this morning, leaped out of bed, jumped in the tub, threw on makeup and clothes, raced Dixie Dog around the complex, and screamed out of the parking lot, wearing my tennis shoes, red & greyfingerless gloves, jeans, a low necked T-shirt, grey scarf, Donna Ruth's purple elf hat, & coat Kate bought me, asymmetrically hemmed shearling lined fake suede coat, channeling Mrs. Kleepack, a wealthy Jewish parent who dressed every day in various costumes, head to toe denim, boots, hats, bag, skirt and top, bracelets, necklaces, & the biggest earrings, to look in the mirror and think, What else can I add? She once brought loose diamonds, emeralds, rubies, & turquoise from her bank lock box when the students were studying minerals and rocks. Her husband was my #1 divorce attorney, who promptly took my father's $1,000 retainer in 1980, with inflation $10,000, and passed my piddling case on to his flunky junior attorney, whom I promptly began to sleep with, the picture of his three-month-old daughter on his desk, the ink not dry on his marriage license. I fucked him for twenty years, escaping the reality of my life, as with the previous affair of four years to the second husband. This affair was both an escape from reality as well as an escape back to innocence, the first young man I slept with—tall , dark, handsome, blue-eyed Portuguese who hadn't retained his Greek God looks but nevertheless was the best sex I'd ever had. The #2 divorce attorney was another parent at my school who tried to fuck me, passing me on to her underling who billed me according to the Rodeo Drive school where I taught, until I told the parent to quit fucking me. I'd done all the leg work on the divorce. My #3 husband in his alcoholic stupor ended up with $10,000 of my funds where we both banked. Rather than pay for an attorney, I hauled my white ass downtown to the law library and researched and filed a law suit against my #3 husband and the bank. The bank's attorney & my #3 husband showed up in court. The attorney and judge took pity on me when the #3 husband, drunk and rambling, complained his wife had just taken off to Southeast Asia and was going to divorce him, only when he gave away my dog to the bloody Mexican gardener, and rambled on for five minutes after I presented, the typed, proofread, legal documents proving my case. The judge covered his smile to remain impartial, allowing #3 husband to rant briefly, before ruling in my favor. The bank's attorney explained how to legally file the brief and marked up my paperwork, earning $1,000 of my mother's estate. Fair enough. I like to be the fucker—not the fucked.

22.7 Apricity: sun shining luminous. Pareidolia: the brain rearranges random stimuli into significant image or sound; faces in the moon; animals in clouds.

22.9 Three twenty-foot gold letters "E-G-O" visible from 3:00 or 9:00 or anywhere across the mile wide Playa shone in the desert heat. Each of the letters had twelve-inch shadow box grids filled with trophies and other treasures—dolls, bent golf clubs, guns, roses, cherubs—all gilded like a Vatican stations of the cross. Freud got it correct: the ID ran wild in the Nevada desert and the EGO was burned.

23. Atop a 40s pickup sat El Pulpo Mechanical "the steampunk," Octopusy twenty feet towering above almost every other art car. The eight legged, frog-eyed, four-faced vehicle was, if not the biggest, definitely the badest bestest art car on the Playa. You looked up in your acid haze and saw the flames shooting from the legs, eyes, and head, and you became a believer in better living through chemistry.

24. If you have to endure a white out on Black Rock Desert sail on The Lost Boys Stage Coach, two stories tall is a fine ride.

25. The sunken ship and pier angle into the desert.

26. White outs, grey acaline dust, vinegar rinse. Irish nephew, wearing an orange, lime, & yellow mumu, washing size twelve feet and flip flops in a vinegar rise, grey alkaline scum filling the yellow tub was worth the total cost of admission—$4,000.

27. A Bad LSD Trip. Frightened on the Playa. Black Rock police with flak jackets. Alone. Drawn to men in uniforms and guns. Like a young virgin, I walked up to the group of men in tan uniforms. The music and noise of the center camp was hyper noisy and scary. Your first burn? he said. Yes, yours? Yes. I need a hug, he said. It had been years, decades, since some young hunk had hugged me. I would have gladly gone to jail. I felt the stiff metal of his flak jacket, let him crush me in his strong young arms, and backed away, careful not to smile too big or laugh too loudly and show the small five centimeters white square on my tongue. The acid dispersed into my bloodstream.

28.0 The Best Business in Pakistan: I knew the tills would start ringing. Whenever we have demonstrations, I make ten times as much as normal." American flags are purchased for burning at public demonstrations. "It's been a long time since I sold an Indian flag," a shopkeeper told AFP. In the rage against Uncle Sam, a deliciously ironic result: a boom in the sale of the Stars and Stripe, a US overseas military newspaper, in Karachi, Lahore, Peshawar, Pakistan. I told my friend teaching in Karachi to buy a burka for security. She did. And to pack her "travel bag" with green, Paki money, passport, & water. She did.

28.1 Looking out the cabin window, the Georgia O'Keefe clouds, New Mexico patchy spotted clouds you can hop scotch from one to the next. Burning Man, a week of drugs and freedom in the desert, had returned the quest for adventure if my bank account could keep up with my travel plans. The eternal search for an agent. The nervous breakdown, ironic in a Facebook posting regarding a short essay by a middle aged writer running away from commitment with a younger man in pursuit. The writing, dealing with an ill brother, comforted by the constant attention of the younger man grew to appreciate familial attachment, and finally Wednesday TNB was "like"d by the author. My kind of writer. Following the daisy chain, I found a fellow Jewish writer whose "so you're a Buddhist." And another piece of ZOS floated into the internet netherland. A Fire and Ash video of Burning Man played in my head, tornadoes twirled in the dark night.

28.2 Nerds at Burning Man PhD discussion. Philosophy 101. Google & Facebook HR recruited creative types.

28.7 Unit 61398 Chinese cyberattack exposed

28.71 Bees have a positive energy and flowers have a negative energy and this allows bees to find pollen & nectar, much like queen bees have a negative energy and Kate & I have a positive energy. They found us when the first grilled cheese came off the Coleman camp stove grill.

28.72 I couldn't imagine anything worse than the swarm of cockroaches, in my hair, on my arms, on my legs, on my gown; or an inch of green mildew in three leather purses, under my fingernails; or termite larvae in text books, wiggling, looking for air; until six weeks into what I thought were tick bites, two different times, having seen ticks crawling up my parents' headboard on my mother's $2,000 Tempur-Pedic mattress, squishing the ticks, seeing red blood, assuming Dixie's blood, cursing my aged dog and Sentinol tick medicine. Then red halo bites began on my arms, legs, shoulders, back, stomach, neck, cheeks, even eyelids. Then to the dermatologist. Hives. You're buying a house. To the oncologist, Get a biopsy. Home to research more online: looking inside the headboard with my tiny LED flashlight to see—bed bug husks, bed bugs of all sizes. Buying diatomaceous dirt as suggested by the oncologist, duct taping the legs of the bed to create a grey sticking toll bridge for the fucking bugs that were eating my flesh away. My blood work white blood count was down to 2.9 on a scale of 9.0. Back to the dermatologist PA with news that I had bed bugs, now all over my new house. Heat and dogs. That's what you need. My neighbor reminded me of my previous HUD low income neighbor whose bedroom abutted mine, separated by forty years of copper wiring and low insolation, and her crack addict daughter and stroke victim son-in-law dragged home from the Cash America pawn shop next door a hassock that had bed bugs. That bitch cost me $1700 and more trauma than buying the house, my hysterectomy, or several root canals. Were I a violent person, I'd fry that cunt in hot oil.

28.8 Prosopagnosia, disease where you can't distinguish faces, one from another.

28.9 A Hockaday father who paid tuition for thirty years and never had a building named after him asked to have recognition in a men's rest room—image in a girls' school what a premium men's rooms are—a urinal with a plaque above stating: Tom Stites, don't piss on him. He has four Hockadaisies.

28.91 Holly to Hillary: Our mistress is prettier, smarter, and better connected than yours.

28.92 Doi la chien tran, neu buon la thua. Life is a struggle in which sorrow leads to defeat RU Kim Thuy

30.0. Zadie Smith: CW numbering the paragraphs is supposed to fracture the story line. Fractuals. Fractoids. Russell Means Indian died. Republic of Lakato. Lakatos. I kept marrying Merkels, Lantzys, Lakatoses, fucking diseases. Smith or Jones for #4.

30.01 Remember that non-disclosure clause I signed in my age-discrimination termination contract with the very generous golden parachute from my beloved teaching position at The Hockaday School 11600 Welch Rd Dallas TX 75244 for thirty-eight goddamned years? You all forgot that I'm a writer. And writers write. And readers read. So don't worry about fucking me over and ruining my teaching career. Your parting words make great copy.

30.02 *Wu wei er wu bu wei* By doing nothing everything will be done. Tao

30.03 There's a crack in everything. That's how the light gets in. Leonard Cohen. Goth service St Edward Cambridge

30.039 Dennis fell into the bathroom, a seizure strangling him, his tongue thrust out, blood dripping from the cut on his forehead, rising from the floor, staggering into the dining area, falling into the smoked glass shelves, Waterford crystal vases, appointed in balanced designs, stainless steel brackets giving way to the dead weight of a middle age artist, falling dead weightedly into the glittering shine of overhead lighting, glass shattering onto the grey carpet, catterpolting to the eight-foot couch corner, falling again to the smoked glass table, wood base splintering under the final fall, onto the brick hearth. Stillness. Blood pooling into caramel grout, red and walnut to dark dried dirt brown.

30.041 The small hand gun leveled against her cheek, held momentarily, her breath held in silence, to quiet the noise in her head, the voices in her heart. The sound unheard as she pulled the trigger to meet him in the calm.

30.0467 Don's Drive In Chapel $19.99 Weddings. Funerals. Discount for three. Garrison Keillor Is there a combination of weddings and funerals?

30.047 In the New Yorker Sept 12, 2011, a blind food vender caught in the 9/11 Twin Towers terrorist attack dreamed that he had no hands. At Burning Man, I dreamed I had no tongue. But when I woke up, I started writing.*

30.048 Don't take my devils away. My angels may flee too. Rilke to Freud

30.82 A dirt road sport. Grant & Martha

30.86 Can't imagine life without you.

iv.How do you say, Goodbye? I love you.

iv.3 περιμένει με υπομονή: Waiting in patience

iv.7 Do I dare?

iv.8 FUBAR

* "Burning Man DeMentha 2012" https://www.youtube.com/watch?v=YE4AwqKbzOA

Larry Smith

Cleveland, as It Were

I have had many conversations with Dr. Snavely over the years in which it is certainly possible that he participated. Not just my own imagination roiled by mental illness and the medicines used to treat it, nor just the sane longings of my mind inspired by what might not have initially been sane fantasies, but there is also the very real cosmic potential, acknowledged by some of the sanest even most professorial people in the world, that there are spiritual media through which all kinds of inspirited beings, close to what we call ghosts, maintain some form of, if not direct communications, call it contingent communications that at some level could even be reciprocal. Communications between them and us, whoever "us" are or we think "us" are.

If I never directly asked him, "Are you my father?" he did tell me at one point, "There is a connection here."

I told him I was glad of it in any event, and I asked, "What guidance do you have for me?"

"I suppose you should go on with your music and I'd encourage you to write as well. Our problem is the inextricability of the creative instinct with the instinct for destructive fury," said Dr. Snavely, a tall slightly stooped figure with bushy black-gray eyebrows and a smooth-skinned mouth with lips flat-lined like the reading on the monitor screen when a patient does not survive surgery. Dr. Snavely, either a Navajo or an Arapaho, I don't recall which, was himself a surgeon for most of his career but then something happened, I'm not sure what. After that he roamed vagrantly from endocrinology to cardiology with occasional stops at oncology. His detractors found him loathsome but were in awe of him too. He died quite suddenly, I'm not sure of what.

"I don't feel driven by destructive fury," I said.

"Then what are you doing here?" he asked.

"I mean, not in my music and writing," I answered.

I surely don't think I'm the first person to start a novel in my condition. Even in this pavilion, behind the coldly shut doors of the private rooms, or in the shadows of the corners of the public areas, especially the public area here in the Reavis Pavilion, which is very quiet despite the numerous family members and friends who visit, there are said to be those embarked on personal literary adventures in the hope that someone in the current world or, if you're good enough, in the next world too (meaning the human future, not heaven that half-human phantasm), will read your word and exalt your name.

The public visiting room of the Reavis Pavilion is configured like a star, inasmuch as the plants (even including a number of small trees, much bigger than bonsai but never to grow tall enough to reach the ceiling) are arranged in such a way as to create corridor-like paths ending in alcove-like spaces where hardly more than a single person can sit. It seems an odd design for a place where you'd think the last thing they'd want is to allow for anyone to be thus sequestered. But I wasn't privy to the thinking behind the architecture and, who knows, there might have been some sort of overlying therapeutic strategy, however counter-intuitive that seems, at least to me.

I think Leon Bieber often sits in one of those astral tips, pen and paper on his lap. Yes, Bieber is one of those said to be writing a novel and, as he is a teacher at Cleveland State, or was, the aspiration is taken with some seriousness. He is a nice enough man but, based on the few discussions I've had with him, I don't know that we relate all that well to each other in terms of writing. I don't think he'd respect the wild voices of the soul that I am working to let roam freely in my work. He's so fixated on symbol and irony, and I'm so sick of both. "The purpose of art is to concentrate everything in the smallest space possible," he said to me.

"I would have thought the purpose was to set it all loose," I said, and he kind of smirked.

"Maybe that's because you're a musician," he said, trying to be respectful. "When you play, you extend everything through time. You can't play just one note."

"You can try," I said, not intending to be cryptic.

Bieber smiled. "I understand you're a very fine musician," he said kindly. "That you've played with some of the top names."

I had once. As they all still knew me and esteemed my playing, I may perform with them again. I am so thankful to Dr. Mead who knew I wasn't schizophrenic and so he stopped at once the Thorazine treatment. Now my memory is freer, freer to greet and welcome old shadows, open to some shadows I can only vaguely remember, and to others with whom I can directly commune, like Dr. Snavely whom I've already told you about.

Among the shadows, the prepossessing ones for me are the ones born and died or resurrected or made undead here in Cleveland, much more so than in Pittsburgh where I was born, and much more too than amid the whirlwind of celebrities and famous tragic poet types like Jimi Hendrix and others I played with in New York and California. That notoriety is the stuff of narrative and history and potentially superior journalism, like the time I was with John Phillips in New York in a shooting gallery and some guy ODs and starts to convulse. John races to the guy's side and asks him where he bought the stuff, because it was obviously pretty pure scag, so John wanted to score a few bags of it too. But the guy died before he could say, and he probably wasn't capable of talking or remembering anyway.

But those are not so much shadows as actors in an underground saga. The paradox is that even a death trip story like this John Phillips anecdote only underscores the vividness of life, the marvelous Renaissance pageantry of life even in its degradation, the kind of physical odyssey and adventure that teenagers dream of. Nothing wrong with that; the memory of John Phillips lobbying a junkie in extremis is for me a very, very enjoyable reminiscence. Shadows are something else, and Cleveland in those years was an Eliotic land breeding sad poets out of small cramped spaces. The more tumultuously life elsewhere in New York or San Francisco seemed to explode, the more oppressive our local suffocation.

So I guess, because that's where we lived, we were all shadows then, including some remembered, even famous names like Pekar and Crumb who remain shadows to me notwithstanding their later success outside Cleveland. Obscure names haunt equally: Tommy Trout, for instance, poor fat Tommy Trout who sucked his thumb when he was forty years old, and Tommy's cousin, who wrote that fine poem about Tikal, but whose name I don't recall. I remember him saying to me once that the Guatemalans and the Greeks are just the same, just the same. "They're both priest-bereft, glory-bereft leftovers of astonishing ancient cultures," he said. "It's those priests who are most conspicuous in their absence. Those priests and those gods."

d. a. levy was a shadow as much because I loved him so, as did most of the people I knew, as because he mimeographed his poems and committed suicide. After he died, some rumors circulated that the police killed him. "It's a desperate belief," Sharon Stefano said to me.

"That's well observed," I said. "Maybe someday we'll be threatening enough to warrant killing like Black Panthers."

"I hope so," she said. "Was he a great poet?"

"I guess I don't know," I said.

It was during that year when Dr. Mead determined my problem to be an idée fixe, and that psychotropic drugs were counter-indicated absent likely somatic overlays. I suppose at some level the obsessional delusion was fed by the war but, more significantly, it was seeded by the person of Betsy Snavely. Her boarding house on East 115th was an epicenter of the Cleveland that I remember as a myth and reality, a dead land where new life could almost be born.

I lived there years earlier. At the time there were three other boarders, two Egyptians and a German, and always a few prominent locals drifting in. The German used to scream at night because he'd been traumatized during the war. Teri Kay would stop by with her boyfriend and sneak upstairs with one of the Egyptians while her boyfriend watched television. Everyone except the boyfriend heard the bed creaking above us, and Betsy in particular seemed to take a wicked delight in the scene, although she was not a wicked person. She was actually a very caring person. But I also came to know her as an insatiably hungry person, and I guess the atrocious cuckolding of the unsuspecting fellow fed that hunger. When I remember her smile as he was cuckolded, along with everything else I have about her to remember, I get tempted to just stop talking words or writing words and to let loose instead a barrage of inchoate noises from some depth, exactly the kind of writing Leon Bieber disparages. Occca taw Occca taw Occca taw fuck Occca taw fuck taw fuck taw Occca eeee eeee eeee

Something like that. The problem is, in writing you can't catch the timbre.

The first day I was there, and had given Betsy an advance on rent, one of the Egyptians said to me when we were alone, "Just treat her right and she'll help you out if you run short of money and you can fuck her too." I had no intentions of doing so. Betsy, in her fifties, was all ruby red cheeks and thin frizzled red hair with something of the look of a bespectacled schoolteacher who's lost self-possession, not unclean in any way but certainly unkempt and more than a little on the edge. Getting into bed with her wouldn't be like sex, it would be like something else.

"I hope Jürgen didn't keep you awake," she said to me the next morning.

Anna Cirino would stop by in those days, all hungry for the human touch while guarding her virginity zealously, which is something she became known for in the salon. Something of a salon it actually was, as I might be bringing in musicians for dinner or, usually in levy's company, visitors from New York like Tuli Kupferberg dropped by. Tillie Lewis, quiet and sensuous and deferential, kept a kind of vigil there too, tacitly offering herself but I was celibate during this period. Betsy became increasingly possessive of me in her own way and she was wondering what this abstinence was all about. "Saving yourself for marriage, are you?" she asked a little bitterly.

I asked her how long she'd been a widow, and she told me seven years. They had a twenty-two year-old son with whom she quarreled ferociously whenever he visited from California, which was pretty often, inexplicably often considering how embattled their relationship. She cloaked herself in her boarders, or they in her, what with their war wounds and all. I don't know if she slept with Jürgen or the other Egyptian, but I felt myself drawn into this spider's nest, a kind of offbeat intimacy that existed in a wholly separate realm from the casual bohemia that existed just below in the living room and dining room. All that said, Betsy seemed to know everyone in Cleveland.

It was the kind of place you can die in if you weaken. Sometimes when I felt her get too near, I'd walk over toward East Cleveland to drink with working class guys. I was making very little money as a musician and I knew I'd have to go back soon to New York, especially since there was so much work there in those days. I was a solid percussionist who doubled on vibes. John Sebastian was calling me. So was Tim Hardin. But Betsy kept giving me money, and she said I should do more composing and that she'd stake me to classes at the Music School Settlement.

"Jacob left me enough," she said, and it was actually the first time I ever heard Dr. Snavely's first name.

I don't know what it is that makes us love life and death so much at the very same time.

But Jürgen's nightly shrieks (maybe twice a night, then silence until morning) and the unseen sex the Egyptian (I can't remember his name, it could have been Moisian) and Betsy might have been having, provided a kind of tomb that I didn't want to leave, or maybe womb is the right word, or maybe tomb is womb, no coincidence that they rhyme and only one letter differentiates the two words. Sometimes I would actually go into Betsy's room, and sit on the floor, and we'd talk for an hour, but, if you asked me five minutes later what we talked about, I wouldn't have known.

The night the something else besides sex happened was moonless in early autumn. I had a job that evening at a party in Lakewood that kept me out until around three in the morning. The others were sleeping upstairs if at that moment they existed at all. Betsy was on the big sienna couch catty-corner to the television. The dim reddish light from the lamp behind the couch was the only light in the room, a dim reddish glow on her and the brownish cushions. She wore a short dark blue skirt and had one leg spread over the side. It wasn't an invitation, it was an excruciated command. It wasn't a pussy, it was a hole.

I was in and out for the next few years, and increasingly sought after in New York. Thanks to Betsy I had developed some compositional facility and, after one of my tunes was featured on a best-selling LP, the royalties sustained me for an extended time, especially since my drug use was never habitual. There really wasn't any practical reason for my continuing to return to Cleveland, except that I never felt at home anywhere else. No matter where I stayed in New York, it was always like a way station, and I didn't feel I could truly rest until I was back in that big shambling house of hers.

"Jürgen moved out?" I asked her the second or third time I returned.

"Yes, he went home and took his nightmares with him."

The next time back both Egyptians were gone too and she looked at me reproachfully for not fucking her. She was drying up, and I dreaded her even when she was wet. "Do you prefer men?" she asked, in search of an excuse or to be hurtful, or both.

"No," I said, unfazed. She had hung an old print of Shakespeare's face in my room, I don't know why. It was a neutral face, like all faces in good depictions or photographs of writers, the photos of Joyce and Faulkner I knew, deadpan faces caught by Abbott or Cartier-Bresson, saying nothing. The warm smile of Louise Erdrich on the back of one of her books, which was taken by her husband who killed himself, tries to seduce me into complicity with her work. A writer's face should be as blank as freedom and, if my book is ever published, no one will be able to read anything but it while they're reading it. I won't look earnest. I won't look challenging. I won't look seductive. I just won't look.

Six weeks later I was back in Cleveland, and some other guy was fucking her, which was all right with me, but I wasn't all right with him, I found him alternatively cloying and unsettling. He was an alcoholic, there was no doubt of that, but he talked about his addiction with a self-importance that bespoke arrested development even more loudly than the drinking itself. He wasn't a man. He would never be a man. The Egyptian was a man, whatever else he was, but I'm not sure Betsy needed men. This guy had a cherub's reddish cheeks and flowing red hair on his head and a clump of red hair on his chest that almost parodied virility. I could hear them have sex very late at night and the thought of it, red on red on red, was grotesque.

"You're one of the best musicians to ever come out of Cleveland, I mean it, man!" he said. I thanked him, but warily, because he fancied himself a musician too, and I did not want to get entangled with yet another man-child wanting me to listen to his tape or send it off to Townshend or Garcia or Lord knows who. "You can sit in with us anytime you're downtown."

"I'll probably be going back to New York soon," I said. I may not have been concealing my irritation enough because at that moment he broke my heart with this hurt vulnerable look, these scared pretty blue eyes that were worse than an open wound, it was the girlish man-face of an orphan, and I felt for him and with him all the unfairness and pain that a little child can bear. But I just didn't like him, I just didn't like him.

Then he was gone and Betsy's son Erich arrived.

I was immediately fascinated that he had actually gestated in her body and emerged between her legs. I would have been likewise fascinated whatever child of hers had materialized in adult form in the living room and at the kitchen table, regardless of gender, looks, deportment. That he was a striking-looking individual was all the more reason for fascination. At once both a typical physicality of the era (long blond hair flowing over his shoulders, a decidedly arrogant but seductive pose of body) and a unique demeanor (a strange twitching of eyes, a sidewise glance suggesting volatility, an unusual loquacity), he was apparently accustomed to center stage and was now unabashedly dominant in my presence as well. I cannot say in retrospect that he was altogether compos mentis, even by the tolerant standards governing those days.

By the next evening, he and Betsy were bickering hopelessly, and Erich was gone who knows where the very next afternoon without a goodbye to anybody but was that first morning at breakfast with me and Sharon Stefano, his mother in the house but out of earshot, intent not so much on conversation as on a series of distinct separable conversations, voluble and fast-paced, a kind of expedition, a colloquy spiraling inward and I guess downward. Am I making any sense? He was all alone that morning, using us, using our ears. By now he probably doesn't even remember Sharon or me, and might not even be startled or self-impressed to learn he changed my life and not necessarily for the better.

While I guess I remember at least six such conversations in the course of those ninety minutes or so, I've benchmarked two or three as distinct spirals toward the revelation I'd say he was intent on making from the very beginning, as soon as he set eyes on us, and particularly on me, revelation of what was for him the compelling and defining fact of his life and his family's life, and for me the birth of, more than just a notion or a symbol, more even than a preoccupation, an actual white whale of sorts in the brain and, even as I stagger out and away from that creature in my brain, dismissing it, incorporating it, learning to live with it and/or more contentedly without it, it was a point of no return nonetheless, an ideational point of no return against which everything else that has since happened to me in my life and within my mind must be measured.

The first conversation was briefly about me, maybe because of Erich's transitory curiosity about someone who may or may not have had intimate relations with his mother, more so that for sure than some social nicety, some politely disinterested interest in somebody else. "I'm not really that much into music," he said after I told him who I was and what I do.

"Really, that's interesting," said Sharon. "Not any kind of music?"

"It doesn't stand still," he answered. "You hear the notes and then they're gone. You can't hold on to it. You don't know what you've just experienced."

"But isn't that what makes it so wonderful?" Sharon asked, her tone polite and accommodating.

"I suppose for some people, but it unnerves me," he said, eyeing me not Sharon as he answered her. "I'll bet you a lot of people also feel like I do, but they don't know it or they're afraid to say so."

"Very interesting!" she said. "Maybe that's why people like bubble gum music and elevator music, because it's something they can grasp and hold on to in their memories."

"I posit, though, that they grasp on to it with the worst, cheapest parts of their souls."

What an odd thing, I remember thinking, this "I posit" business! Who says, "I posit" in the course of a normal conversation? I remember shrinking into myself, not having anything to say. His mother liked music well enough as I recall, but there was always a part of Betsy that nothing around her such as art or music or television could significantly engage. There was a ravenous part of her that needed feeding always and that was always impervious to the normal salves of life.

He leaned forward at the table, not at that moment eyeing either one of us. "Improvised music is the worst," he said, which, I guess, made sense in the context of what he was saying. I guess this talk about music was still part of the conversation about me or an extension of the conversation about me. Or maybe a transition to get him closer to what he was really ultimately wanting to disclose, so much I think he wanted to disclose it that the act of disclosure was a kind of climax to a kind of masturbation of which Sharon and I were just the facilitators. Because then he said, "There is one kind of music I can relate to. Chants."

"You mean like liturgical chants?" asked Sharon.

"I suppose, but the more ancient the better," he said. "Like it's just one note prolonged indefinitely in time, and all the modulations...well, there's no need to grasp on to those modulations. They're just window dressing for the one note that is the sound of life starting and ending. I posit, such chants can and do echo the sound of the universe. I suppose that's good."

"It *is* good," said Sharon, and I still remember her tone when she said that, almost pleading, very raw almost, very attractive. I thought of Jürgen's nocturnal screams, and I almost broke my silence by mentioning them as somehow relevant. But I did not.

I don't know if Sharon was attracted to Erich, if her thighs at that moment were open under the kitchen table. It didn't matter. Erich was extremely attractive but I sensed a certain asexuality in him, as if physical love was likewise too ephemeral, it too did not stand still. Funny, all this longing for stasis from someone whose whole life was as motional as the most tortured atonal jazz improvisation.

A whole different conversation began when Erich said that Indian chants were among his favorites. "Indian India or Indian American Indian?" I asked.

"American Indian," he said. "The tribal calls. I come by it rightly because my father was a full-blood..." and I don't remember if he said Navajo or Arapaho.

"Oh, your mother never told me that," I said.

"Why would she?" he said, and I fell back silent again.

"I know your father was a doctor. What sort?" Sharon asked.

"All sorts. He was a brilliant doctor, though when I was a child the thought of him with a scalpel terrified me. Sometimes I'd hide when he came home from work, as if blood and entrails would be oozing from the folds of his clothing."

"He wasn't a nice man?" asked Sharon, almost in the same tone with which she had just insisted that the echoing of the sound of the universe was "good."

"He was as mad as the March hare. People feared him. They deferred to his opinions, but they feared him and eventually they ganged up against him?"

"Did he ever actually behave crazy?" asked Sharon.

Erich leaned toward me as he answered her. His eyes then were as cold and glassy as a jungle carnivore, and he paused for a moment pursing his lips. "When I was seven, my mother got pregnant again. It was funny, I distinctly recall there wasn't much joy about it. I posit, both my parents were congenitally joyless. And then one night from my bedroom, I heard her scream and my father call out in a weird way, a weird wailing noise. She had miscarried. I guess she never told you that either, did she?" he asked me, his blue soulless eyes peering into mine.

"Why would she?" I asked, and the tension between us at that moment was otherworldly, as if the two of us were jousting in a wholly alien dimension. I don't know if Sharon could sense it.

Erich continued matter-of-factly, so matter-of-factly as to beggar human reason or feeling. "He removed the fetus and brought it downstairs, as I was later to figure out he must have done."

"How did you figure that out?" asked Sharon.

"Because the next morning, I saw a jar on the top of the refrigerator and the fetus was in it."

"Holy Jesus," said Sharon.

"Oh yes, Dr. Snavely was quite the operator," he said. "A few evenings later, and the evening after that one, and the evening after that, people would stop by to pay their condolences and offer their best wishes. Each night I saw and heard him do the same thing…he'd smile warmly at his guests at some point in the evening, and say to them, 'Come with me into the kitchen." And he'd say to me, 'You too, Erich,' and when we all got into the kitchen he'd point at the jar on the refrigerator and say, 'I want to introduce you to my other son.'"

"They must have been horrified," said Sharon, her tone intense if her words were banal.

"I suppose…I was too unnerved to think much about them. But I remember each of those evenings he'd say to the guests, 'He's a fine lad, and I'm sure he'll get on splendidly in this world.'"

"What did Betsy do?" asked Sharon.

But Erich didn't answer that. Instead, he asked me which room upstairs was mine and, when I told him, he said, "I suppose that would have been my brother's room if he hadn't taken up residency on the refrigerator instead."

I guess that was the last of the morning's conversations.

I wish I could remember the name of Tommy Tuck's cousin who wrote the poem about Tikal. I liked him a lot but I could see where others might not. He was the kind of guy who immediately translates everything into bigger cultural issues or, if not translates, interprets everything in light of bigger intellectual themes. So, if your brother just died, and you were miserable about it, he might start talking about famous brothers in literature or myth. It could sound very insensitive if not inhuman to some people. But it didn't bother me, because I could see that those intellectual themes and metaphors had overpowering human weight for him – they comforted *him* – and, if he were insensitive at some important level, it was only in his obtuseness, his odd failure to understand that he might not be reassuring or speaking resonantly to someone whose brother just died.

The evening of the same day Sharon and I had the conversation with Erich Snavely, I ran into Tommy Tuck's cousin at a restaurant in Little Italy, and I joined his table. He asked me if I were reading anything interesting these days, which I wasn't, but I could tell he was really eager to tell me about what he was reading. So I answered briefly and asked him, "How about you?"

"I'm reading this incredible stuff about American Indians," he said. "You've no idea how textured their thinking is. It's not just a Great Spirit. It's a Great Spirit who manifests himself in such extraordinarily multifaceted ways."

"Wolves, mountain lions, trees..."I ventured.

"Oh it's more than just incarnations," he said. "There are ontological dynamics that are just as complex, if not more so, than the most arcane Western systems. In fact, the Indians have concepts of metempsychosis that I doubt are rivaled for complexity anywhere else at any time in the world."

"Interesting, but it makes sense," I said. "If the Spirit can manifest itself in multiple ways, it can move about in multiple ways."

"Yes, yes," he said. "I just read about how their medicine men have visions of spirits moving from one physical being to another, actually driving out the spirit of someone and taking its place. It's more than possession. It's a wholesale spiritual take-over."

"What happens to the spirit that is driven out?" I asked.

"I'm not sure, but from how I read it, it wanders off to nowhere in a state of complete comatose non-comprehension, a mere husk of spirit like the husk of an ear of corn."

"So it's a permanent take-over," I said.

"Yes, as far as I can tell."

"That's very, very....metempsychotic," I said.

"'Metempsychotic!' Ha! I like that." He mentioned a tribe that had cultivated just this sort of metempsychotic ontology, but I can't remember which tribe he mentioned.

Now came days when the very sight of Betsy unsettled me. Her smile, which I used to think the warmest part of her, began to seem strange, almost ghoulish in a way; those ruby lips yawning open, the teeth in her mouth ever so noticeably off-white. Then came days of crippling lethargy, helplessness, a sense of susceptibility to as-yet obscure forces, events, hard-to-define lacerations; fear of unnamed intrusions against which neither body nor soul can defend.

Betsy took care of me in those days, keeping a respectful vigil. I dared not think what I was already thinking. It was so sunny and blue that late June, I resolved to go outside. I put on a pair of jeans and, as I remember, a t-shirt dyed an amber tint, and went to the park outside the Art Museum and sat on a bench by the pond. My face was ovoid. My skin was soft, glutinous really. A force as primal as an earthquake was forcing me toward the neck of the glass prison, the cold crystalline but well-loved womb. Outside was a world of hurt. The child poet raised on Betsy's very street whose cruel father sold candy was masturbating in a bathtub and would later die in an ocean. A harp player from another country was trading fast funky intervals with a trumpet player displaced from jazz to this music and I was banging time feeling the people in the womb-dark nightclub urge us on and revel with us in our rhythm, our journey. A great man, a poet, a thinker, wanders out onto the highway and is killed by a hapless driver who had no choice but to kill him, but no one ever asked or found out who the driver was or what his name might be. The glass shattered, and I went I don't know where, was it me in Pittsburgh or me usurping a spirit there? I grew, I lived, I discovered the mystery of my being and birth, yet became all the more mystified for my pains. Oh mother, no wonder you are so rank in the lists of love. Oh father, you fearsome priest, you graft with your sharp knife the shoots of life and death and, because of you, nobody in the world knows which is which.

So then I started having those heart-to-hearts with Dr. Snavely and was soon loaded up with Thorazine. You know the side effects, soon the sun was crackling my skin and the lethargy was deeper, I felt like hell, and I could not imagine death was ever worse than this zombie-like perambulation. But then came Dr. Mead with his merciful insights and his generous healing, and I got to feel better enough to at least live my life again or somebody's life. I can still talk to Doctor Snavely. I can still think about Betsy. Maybe I should have been a Jew in a Jew's body in another decade. I mean, if I was born on a refrigerator in Cleveland, the least I can do is die inside an oven in Europe.

Mark Axelrod

BALZAC'S COFFEE ™

Hamburg, Germany

"But of course, it's obvious, no?" was Balzac's response to the question posed to him by George Sand during one of the latter's candlelight dinners, "Why a coffee shop?" "Coffee is a great power in my life...it chases away sleep, and it gives us the capacity to engage a little longer in the exercise of our intellects," Balzac continued. The fact that Balzac drank an enormous quantity of coffee (Maurois once suggested up to 50 cups per day) would lend credence to the decision. But it wasn't just the stimulation that convinced Balzac, but something much more tangible. To understand why Balzac went into the business of coffee, one must know what his philosophy of coffee actually was. It's a bit like reading Poe without understanding his "*Philosophy of Composition.*" To that end, one needs to read what could be called Balzac's "Philosophy of Caffeine."

***"Many** people claim that coffee inspires them, but, as everybody knows, coffee only makes boring people more boring. But, as Brillat-Savarin has correctly* *observed, coffee sets the blood in motion and stimulates the muscles; it accelerates the digestive processes, chases away sleep, and gives us the capacity to engage a little longer in the exercise of our intellects.*

Rossini has personally experienced some of these effects as, of course, have I. "Coffee," Rossini told me, is an affair of fifteen or twenty days; just the right amount of time, fortunately, to write an opera." [After consuming coffee] one wants everything to proceed with the speed of ideas. One actually becomes that fickle character, The Poet, condemned by grocers and their like. One assumes that everyone is equally lucid. A man of spirit must therefore avoid going out in public. **Coffee** *is a great power in my life; I have observed its effects on an epic scale.*

For a while.....you can obtain the right amount of stimulation with one, then two cups of coffee brewed from beans that have been crushed with gradually increasing force and infused with hot water. For another week, by decreasing the amount of water used, by pulverizing the coffee even more finely, and by infusing the grounds with cold water, you can continue to obtain the same cerebral power. When you have produced the finest grind with the least water possible, you double the dose by drinking two cups at a time; particularly vigorous constitutions can tolerate three cups. In this manner, one can continue working for several more days.

Finally, I have discovered a horrible, rather brutal method that I recommend only to men of excessive vigour, men with thick black hair and skin covered with liver spots, men with big square hands and legs shaped like bowling pins. It is a question of using finely pulverized, dense coffee, cold and anhydrous, consumed on an empty stomach. This coffee falls into your stomach, a sack whose velvety interior is lined with tapestries of suckers and papillae. The coffee finds nothing else in the sack, and so it attacks these delicate and voluptuous linings; it acts like a food and demands digestive juices; it wrings and twists the stomach for these juices, appealing as a pythoness appeals to her god; it brutalizes these beautiful stomach linings as a wagon master abuses ponies; the plexus becomes inflamed; sparks shoot all the way up to the brain.

From that moment on, everything becomes agitated. Ideas quick-march into motion like battalions of a grand army to its legendary fighting ground, and the battle rages. Memories charge in, bright flags on high; the cavalry of metaphor deploys with a magnificent gallop; the artillery of logic rushes up with clattering wagons and cartridges; on imagination's orders, sharpshooters sight and fire; forms and shapes and characters rear up; the paper is spread with ink -- for the nightly labour begins and ends with torrents of this black water, as a battle opens and concludes with black powder.

I recommended this way of drinking coffee to a friend of mine, who absolutely wanted to finish a job promised for the next day: he thought he'd been poisoned and took to his bed, which he guarded like a married man. He was tall, blond, slender and had thinning hair; he apparently had a stomach of papier-mâché. There has been, on my part, a failure of observation.

When you have reached the point of consuming this kind of coffee, then become exhausted and decide that you really must have more, even though you make it of the finest ingredients and take it perfectly fresh, you will fall into horrible sweats, suffer feebleness of the nerves, and undergo episodes of severe drowsiness. I don't know what would happen if you kept at it then: a sensible nature counseled me to stop at this point, seeing that immediate death was not otherwise my fate. To be restored, one must begin with recipes made with milk and chicken and other white meats: finally the tension on the harp strings eases, and one returns to the relaxed, meandering, simple-minded, and cryptogamous life of the retired bourgeoisie.

The state coffee puts one in when it is drunk on an empty stomach under these magisterial conditions produces a kind of animation that looks like anger: one's voice rises, one's gestures suggest unhealthy impatience: one wants everything to proceed with the speed of ideas; one becomes brusque, ill-tempered about nothing. One actually becomes that fickle character, The Poet, condemned by grocers and their like. One assumes that everyone is equally lucid. A man of spirit must therefore avoid going out in public. I discovered this singular state through a series of accidents that made me lose, without any effort, the ecstasy I had been feeling. Some friends, with whom I had gone out to the country, witnessed me arguing about everything, haranguing with monumental bad faith. The following day I recognized my wrongdoing and we searched the cause. My friends were wise men of the first rank, and we found the problem soon enough: coffee wanted its victim. But to be frank, it I had one business I would be eager to engage in, it would be the coffee business. No other would allow me the freedom to express my thoughts without restriction.[1]

So it was that obsession, if not that addiction, plus Balzac's insatiable desire to make a lot of money that drove him to create Balzac's Coffee. However, when it came to business, Balzac was a perpetual failure. He had tried every conceivable scam to make money from publishing fraudulent editions of Molière to starting Balzac's Balls (See: *Borges' Travel, Hemingway's Garage*), but they were all disasters (See: *The Politics of Style in the Fiction of Balzac, Beckett and*

[1] *The Reign of Caffeine: Balzac, Coffee, Realism.* François Déconnage. Golden Triangle, N.C.: Dook University Press, 2003.

Cortázar). However, Balzac was absolutely positive that the coffee business would be his ticket to an early retirement on Antibes and he even said as much to Sand in a note he wrote to her on 31 March 1846: "Coffee shall be my financial elixir just as it has been my creative elixir." Sand, who was a lot better off financially than Balzac, advanced him some money to open the first Balzac's Coffee on the Rue Fortunée on 31 March 1847.

After an initial four months of success, the shop fell on tough times when a harsher than normal winter destroyed a major coffee crop in Colombia and Balzac's manager, a certain Vautrin, absconded with a month's worth of receipts (See *Café Molière*). Balzac became disconsolate. In October 1848, Balzac travelled to the Ukraine to visit his love, Mme Hanska whose husband had died in 1841. But neither Madame Hanska's love nor Sand's encouragement nor Chopin's music could comfort him. Disconsolation became depression and depression became dissipation. His health in disrepair, Balzac and Hanska were married in March 1850. Balzac returned with her to Paris, where he tried to salvage what little he could of the business, but died on 18 August 1850.

In order to settle his debts, Balzac's debts, Madame Hanska sold the franchise to a German company which maintains the rights to his name to this day. In death as in life, coffee played a vital role in work. In a letter dated 17 August 1850, Balzac wrote, "if ever a sculpture is chiseled in my memory make sure I am holding a cup of coffee." Rodin was aware of the letter, but thought a cape was more majestic.

Baudelaire Hôtel Bastille

Paris, France

I mean, what other hardships was poor Charles to endure! The whole thing began in Paris while writing his Spleen poems. One wet and foggy afternoon, after gazing out his window at a nearby graveyard Charles turned to see his mangy, half-starved cat attempting to sleep upon the frigid tiles of his garret as a smoke-shrouded, wet log, hissed horribly in the fireplace. "What," he thought to himself, "am I doing in this place?" Fed up with the cold and the frigid hunger, he took to looking at the stack of legal papers his step-father , General Aupick, had drawn up with his lawyer, Ancelle, to create this life of penury for him. "God save me, there must be a loop hole somewhere!" he declared in one of his journals.[2] It's common knowledge that on his majority in 1842 he moved into a flat in the Hôtel Lauzun on the Ile St-Louis and tended to fritter away a lot of money. In an attempt to reduce his debt, his step-father hired Ancelle as his financial guardian. Unfortunately, they didn't eliminate all of his debt and put him on a paltry monthly income which is the state in which we found him.

In a letter to Ancelle, written in February, 1866, Baudelaire said: "*Faut-il vous dire, à vous qui ne l'avez pas plus deviné que les autres, que dans ce livre atroce j'ai mis tout mon coeur, toute ma tendresse, toute ma religion (travestie), toute ma haine? Il est vrai que j'écrirai le contraire, que je jurerai mes grands dieux que c'est un livre d'art pur, de signerie, de jonglerie, et je mentirai comme un arracheur de dents.*" He then spent the better part of two days, scouring the stack of legal documents, suffering, without sleep, without food, without wine, without hash, until he found what he thought would finally evict him from his horrible state of impecunity. At last, his limited legal studies availed him.

At about 3 a.m. on the 2nd day, Baudelaire discovered the following line in the trust form established by his step-father and Ancelle.

§4. 075 Successor Trustees: In the event of the death or incapacity of any trustee, I hereby nominate and appoint as successor trustee Theophile Gautier. In the event the successor trustee does not serve I appoint whomever shall at the time be the first designated beneficiary hereunder. Incapacity is hereby defined as the inability to conduct business transactions for a period of, but not limited to, two working days. The successor trustee will, at that time, assume any and all trustee decisions and may allocate any funds and/or property as he deems necessary.

Baudelaire was overjoyed by the discovery since it meant that if either his step-father or his financial guardian got sick he could call upon Gautier to get

[2] *Quel Emmerdement! Notes on Accelle.* Charles Baudelaire. Translated from the French by Mark Axelrod.

him out of his financial bind! Needless to say, he tried everything in his power to get one of them sick going as far as recommending that his step-father take his mother on a trip to Orient at which time he knew there was an influenza outbreak. Nothing seemed to work for him until a cold and bleak March 31st when General Aupick came down with tonsillitis. Baudelaire seized the moment and rushed to Ancelle's office. As Gautier writes: "Baudelaire burst into Ancelle's room waving the trust form as if he were waving the French flag and screaming that the trust had to be honored and that Section 4.075 declared that if either Ancelle or Aupick were sick that I would then assume the task of successor trustee. Ancelle was beside himself. He looked over the document and there in black and white was exactly what Baudelaire claimed. Ancelle had no choice. He contacted me and asked me to meet with he and Baudelaire at a time convenient for all of us. Charles said' immediately' and so I had to drop everything I was doing, meant I had to delay the closing of a loan for my furniture business, to meet with them. But before I met with them, I met with Charles at the room where he was staying in the Hôtel Chiotte. He told me that if he didn't get out of those lodgings he'd die and since I was the successor trustee it was up to me to do so. "What can I do?" I asked. And he told me that Aupick had a major investment in a hotel in Paris. "What hotel?" I asked. "The Baudelaire Bastille Hotel located at 12, Rue De Charonne." "But," I said, "I've never heard of it?" He told me Aupick renamed it for his mother, Caroline, and the name had only recently changed. I asked him what it was called before and he said "the Hotel California." "The same as the Eagles?" I asked. "The same," he answered. I asked him what he wanted me to recommend to Ancelle and he said that he be allowed to live there permanently. I agreed and because of section 4.075 in the trust agreement Ancelle had to concur.

Baudelaire was thrilled. He felt that his life was going to change for the better. Unfortunately, the loophole only allowed him to live decently, but not to eliminate his debt and so for the rest of his life he was able to live in the hotel after his name, but never to escape his debt. Perhaps that was what the Eagles meant when they said, "Relax said the night man, we are programmed to receive, you can check out any time you like, but you can never leave." Perhaps too that's what prompted him to write, "In every climate and under every sun, Death laughs at you, mad mortals, as you run; And often perfumes herself with myrrh, like you And mingles with your madness, irony!" Ironically, it was the syphilis he acquired from his affair with Jeanne Duval in the same hotel that was to release him from his future cares and it was Gautier who had to commit him to a Paris nursing home for the last year of his life. The hotel still remains on 12, Rue De Charonne and above the room that Baudelaire slept in is a sign that reads: Welcome, hypocrite reader-my fellow-my brother!

VICTOR HUGO INN

Laguna Beach, California

Ah, the continuing saga of Victor Hugo. As you may recall *(See: Borges' Travel, Hemingway's Garage)*, Hugo was having all sorts of legal problems with the Disney Corporation. In court, out of court, settlements, non-settlements, things became so litigious that Disney once thought of naming one of its rides, *Adjudication Mountain.*[3] Seems like Hugo was involved in everything, but writing. But like all novels as well as Disney™ films, there had to be an end to it.

Hugo's is a continuing saga and one none of us would have expected otherwise knowing the genius. But to talk about the inn one really needs to talk about how it all started. Though much of this can be read in *Borges' Travel,*

---

[3] This ride eventually became known as "Thunder Mountain."

Hemingway's Garage, it would be wise to recap the events preceding the purchase of the inn.

Hugo was never very poor. Nor was he short of recognition. So this article is more of an *homage* to what actually happened to Notre-Dame and the hunchback who used to live there. At the age of fifteen, Hugo had already been acknowledged by the French Academy for his poetry and by seventeen he had won awards from the Jeux floraux de Toulouse. And, perhaps, because of that success the problem for Hugo was not so much to make money, but how to invest it. And that need to diversify established one of the most fascinating of events in literary history. As most everyone is well aware, the mature Hugo was extremely interested in the metaphysical and at the age of fifty he became intrigued by séances. Coincidentally, it was at the same time he went into exile from France due, in large measure, to his vilification of Louis Napoléon. In 1853, exiled with his family (i.e. wife, children, mistress), Hugo retreated to the British Isles first to Jersey then to Guernsey. It was in Guernsey that the table-rapping séances began.

At first, the séances proved fruitless. That is, nothing happened except for a lot of table rapping which merely resulted in headaches for *the maestro*. As a matter of fact, he was reputed to have said after the first séance, "Ça ne vaut pas un pet de lapin" or "how disappointing." But after continued séances a spirit did speak to him. In fact, it was his dead daughter, Léopoldine, and her message was truly prophetic. These séances were all documented and one of the most mysterious of messages Hugo received from his daughter was the following: "Quasimodo will leave Notre-Dame for Anaheim."[4] The statement initially made no sense to Hugo who had visited Anaheim (located in the Ruhr Valley of

[4] *The Seances of Victor Hugo*. Paris: Flammarion, 1985.

Germany), but only on his way to Warsaw as part of a book tour. He virtually dismissed the statement until 1876 when, after being elected to the Senate, he met, in Paris, at the Café Dauphin, an American by the name of Rudolph Eisner who said he represented a fledgling cartoon company[5] in the United States. Now film was merely in its fetal stages in France as Lumière and Méliès were not to have produced anything for another decade, but Eisner was interested in making an animated cartoon out of Hugo's *Notre-Dame de Paris* (1831). Hugo was rather fascinated by the idea and asked Eisner where this company was located.

"Burbank," he said, "but that's where our studio is. We plan to build a theme park in California."

"Where?" Hugo asked.

"Anaheim," was the answer.

And Hugo suddenly remembered the prophetic words of his dead daughter, "Quasimodo will leave Notre Dame for Anaheim and will then reside in the hills of Beverly." Flushed with the idea that his novel would be adapted to an animated cartoon, Eisner and Hugo worked out the contractual arrangements and a date was set for production.[6] But Hugo was still mystified by the future residence of Quasimodo in the hills of Beverly. What could that mean?

Almost six years later, 1882, Hugo sent his mistress, Juliette Drouet, to the United States to do some advanced booking for his latest novel *Torquemada*. When Eisner discovered she was in New York, he arranged for her to come to California to see the Willie Studios and to view what progress had been made on what had now been re-titled *Willie's Hunchback of Notre Dame*. She agreed. In a letter dated 2 December 1882, postmarked Burbank, Juliette writes Hugo: *"Good morning, my divine, adored love. This separation spares me no sorrow. Being away from you is like being rendered soulless, joyless, loveless, but I do these*

---

[5] The company, of course, was originally called "The Willie Company" and went on to become the present day Disney™ Studios.

[6] Little did either Eisner or Hugo know that because of financial and technical problems the film wouldn't appear for another 120 years.

things for you not out of gratitude, but out my strongest, deepest love for you. Monsieur Eisner has shown me the animated drawings of Quasimodo. Somehow I do not think them what you had in mind, but he tells me that is what the American public wants. Que dommage. He has also mentioned something to me about a restaurant in Beverly Hills, but I shall find out more later. My darling, this separation cannot be over too soon and I pray your love will take me from here to there with speed and sanctity. I love you, Juliette."

The restaurant Drouet alluded to was actually going out of business and Eisner convinced Hugo, through Drouet, to invest in it with the sound reasoning that it would diversify Hugo's portfolio. So convinced, he did in fact invest and the restaurant opened as the Victor Hugo Restaurant in 1883 the exact day Juliette Drouet died. If that were not irony enough, the restaurant burned to the ground in 1885 on the exact day Hugo was buried in the Panthéon. Some say it was the spirit of Quasimodo that burned the restaurant as an homage to the *maestro* since witnesses swear that on the night of fire they saw a hunchback rushing from the burning building. Others attest it was done by a disgruntled Willie employee who was fired after an altercation with the head of the animation studio who proclaimed that he had pornographized all that Willie had done.[7] In either case, all that remained was a matchbook cover which has since found its way into the Smithsonian.

But the spirit of Quasimodo lived on and not to everyone's liking. Certainly not the Hugo family and a relatively recent letter, signed by Charles, Adèle, Jeanne, Sophie and Léopoldine Hugo, denounced the "commercial debauchery which confuses the universality of genius with vulgar globalization by unscrupulous merchants." As Adèle Hugo-Chabrol said, "We are not after money. We are in favor of screen adaptations because they help new readers discover the author. But this time, Victor Hugo is not even mentioned on the

---

[7] This may have been the case as any casual scrutinizing of the video jacket of "The Little Mermaid" would attest. Andersen's outrage at the video jacket even caught the attention of his nemesis, Kierkegaard, who actually came to Andersen's defense in a monograph titled, *Dømmer Selv! Til Selvprøvelse Samtiden anbefalet or Judge For Yourselves! Recommended to the present time for Self-Examination.*

posters." Alas it was true. No where on any of the film posters of the Hunchback of Notre-Dame was Hugo's name mentioned which was in direct violation of the codicil that Hugo had signed with Rudolph Eisner.[8] Need less to say, the current Disney™ legal conundrum was in direct violation of that testimony.

This brings us to where we are now. As was know from the novel, *The Posthumous Memoirs of Blase Kubash*, Quasimodo is homeless and living in Paris; Esmeralda was forced to take on a job in soft porn movies in Hollywood. And Hugo? Well, apparently the Disney™ people decided to settle out of court. Thought the figures were never disclosed, both *Variety* and the *Hollywood Reporter* reported that Hugo settled for something in the millions, certainly enough for him to open the Victor Hugo Inn in Laguna and to settle there to avoid the long and lugubrious Paris winters. If one looks closely, one can see him in the gardens of a December day, gazing out onto the Laguna Beaches as if recalling his days in Guernsey.

---

[8] The codicil indicated that on any merchandising of *The Hunchback of Notre-Dame*, Hugo rightfully would be given top billing. The codicil was read and approved by Mr. Eisner.

JEF 73

MOZART'S CAFÉ

New York City, NY

Oh, there has been a lot of speculation about what actually killed Mozart. It has been suggested that because Mozart allegedly suffered from rheumatic fever as a child scientists have opened the possibility of the disease damaging his heart and then later in his life being the cause of his death. This theory sounds plausible based on the rash and the fever for rheumatic fever and the swollen limbs which point to a commonly known byproduct of heart failure. Others have suggested that his death was due to poisoning, still others, renal failure.

Perhaps no other composer has had so many legends develop surrounding their death. The composer Antonio Salieri, in a deathbed confession, tried to take credit for murdering Mozart. There was a popular rumor that Mozart's Masonic Lodge had assassinated him for betraying lodge secrets in his opera "Die Zauberflute", but this has never been proven. In 1901, a skull, whose "discoverers" contested was Mozart's was donated to the Salzburg Mozarteum. Legend has it that Mozart's gravedigger, Joseph Rothmayer, allegedly retrieved the skull before the bones were pulverized in a recycling program (i.e. so the burial plot could be reused) in 1801. Just how Joseph Rothmayer could have detected that it was Mozart's skull (since Mozart was dumped into unmarked grave) has never been scrutinized. Forensic examination of the skull was inconclusive except for the fact that whomever belonged to the skull died of chronic haematoma possibly resulting from a fall. The Mozarteum has not accepted the findings of the French team and has been conducting its own studies. For further information see "Archeology" - March / April 1991: "*The Mystery of Mozart's Skull*" and the book '*After the Funeral: The Posthumous Adventures of Famous Corpses*' by Edwin A. Murphy. Since that conclusion was inconclusive, the cause of death was attributed to Miliary Fever or tuberculosis throughout the body that affects the bones and joints, or the brain. So what's it gonna' be, eh?

Well, the truth is stranger than fiction. It's common knowledge that Mozart's fame began to wane after "*Le nozze di Figaro*", 1785 and he sank deeper into debt and depression as well as finding himself hungry. This hunger began to manifest itself in his composing as well and beginning in 1791 one can see just how pervasive his "hunger" compositions became: Song with Piano, "*Komm, das Essen*" ; Song with Piano, "*Die Speise*" ; the Cantata, "*Der Ernährungsminister*" ; the Opera, "*Die Lebensmittelknappheit*" ; the Opera, seria, "*Der Hungerlohn*" ; the Cantata, "*Vor Hunger Sterben*" ; the comic duet, "*Am Arsch der Welt*" ; and, finally, the Requiem Mass which was originally titled, "*Den Arsch Hängen Lassen.*" When all seemed lost, he found succorance with a fellow Freemason, Michael Puchberg. Mozart had joined the Masons in

1784 and remained one until his death. Puchberg was a native New Yorker and had connections with the restaurant business in Manhattan.

Puchberg asked Mozart what he thought of going into the restaurant business and the latter, starving both literally and metaphorically, jumped at the chance. Puchberg told Mozart that he and his cousin needed a third partner to open a restaurant in New York and Amadeus was thrilled with the idea. Puchberg booked Mozart passage on board the ship Esmeralda (this was an unfortunate choice of ships since the *Esmeralda* was also the name of the ship von Aschenbach sailed on in Visconti's, *Death in Venice*; of course, Mozart didn't know that at the time) and sailed into New York harbor on 22 November 1791. No sooner had he got there when Puchberg's cousin, Rudy, whisked Mozart off to the café on West 70th Street. At the time, the café was in the final stages of decoration and that night it would have been a kind of rehearsal dinner. Mozart was thrilled and was actually in the kitchen whipping up Austrian delicacies such as pear salad with Raspberry Vinegar, Tafelspitz with Apfelkren and Mohr im Hemd. What happened next one could only describe as fatal. Somehow the Tafelspitz was not prepared properly. This has been a point of speculation for many years, but finally came out in a book written by the Austrian food scholar, Kurt Waldeneggar.[9] In the book, Waldeneggar traces what happened subsequent to the rehearsal dinner.

Later that night, Mozart began experiencing a number of symptoms including vomiting, nausea, a low-grade fever, abdominal cramps and diarrhea all classical signs of *E coli* poisoning; however, the physicians couldn't diagnose the problem very effectively. All Mozart wanted to do at that time, was return home and so Rudy put him back on

---

[9] *From Raw to Requiem: E Coli and the Death of Mozart.* Kurt Waldeneggar. Berlin: Scheissbolle Verlag, 2003.

the Esmeralda and sent him back to Vienna. It was on board the Esmeralda that Mozart began the *Requiem "Den Arsch Hängen Lassen."* By the time Mozart got home, the disease was rampant and on 5 December, 1791, he died. Since he was connected to Puchberg and Puchberg's cousin, Rudy, it led to the false rumors of some nefarious poisoning, though it was clearly due to the ill-prepared Tafelspitz.

Mozart, of course, was buried in an unmarked grave at the cemetery of Saint Marx, a Viennese suburb. In homage to the maestro, and feeling as if he were somehow responsible for his death, Rudy changed the name of the café from Puchberg's to Mozart's where it still remains to this day at 140 W. 70th Street where Mohr im Hemd is still the dessert specialty of the house.

ACEITES BORGES ™

Tàrrega, Spain

Of course with the success of the travel agency (See: *Borges' Travel, Hemingway's Garage*) Borges couldn't stand still and he was eager to explore other avenues of investment. But just where the suggestion for olive oil came from was beyond belief. It's no secret that Borges' political leanings were to the right of right. He often lauded Peron as a "gentlemen," lunched with General Jorge Videla, allegedly dedicated the first copy of his translation of "Leaves of Grass" to Richard Nixon, and praised Pinochet as being a "leader." In 1973, when Peronists were elected, Borges called it a "government of scoundrels." In 1975 he was quoted as saying: "When I think of the cases of torture [in Argentina] I have the impression that my country is disintegrating morally as well as economically." In March, 1976, when informed that Evita had lost, Borges wept and when he met Videla, he thanked him for "having liberated the country from the infamy which we bore." Only Elvis could have been any farther to the right.

So it was only natural that in 1976, at the age of 77, he would receive la Gran Cruz de la Orden al Mérito Bernardo O'Higgins from none other than the Chilean dictator, Augusto Pinochet. Borges was thrilled. Or as thrilled as anyone could be by meeting a dictator. Borges wanted to go to Chile and receive the award on behalf of his Chilean readers. Unfortunately, at the same time, the Nobel Prize committee was deciding whether to give the award to Borges or not and advised him that a trip to Chile might not be in his best interest. Not only did he go, but to make matters worse he had his picture taken with Pinochet who, sitting cross-legged in his suit and tie looked every bit as regal as a dictator could possibly look.

The award ceremony over, Pinochet had Borges feted with a dinner and during the dinner the two of them talked of different things[10] not the least of which was Borges' travel agency which Pinochet said he would use the next time he left the country.[11] During the course of their meal, Pinochet opined that one couldn't really find a good olive oil for salad. He asked Borges if he felt the same way. Borges allegedly agreed and for the next hour Borges talked non-stop about olive oils. It was not by accident that Borges knew about olive oils since he spent considerable time in Italy and Spain and in addition to knowing their writers, knew their oils. He waxed poetically about such things as cleaning olives, grinding olives to paste, mixing to increase olive oil yield, separating the oil and water from the olive, separating the oil from the water, processing the oil, storing and bottling the oil, tasting and rating the oil, making flavored oils. Borges was a veritable font of olive oil information; however, Pinochet was decidedly not interested in olive oil. It

[10] According to Volodia Teitelboim nothing they talked about remotely resembled politics.

[11] In fact, this took place when Pinochet decided to visit London in 1998. There were some hard feelings afterwards when the travel agency would not reimburse Pinochet for missing his flight even after Pinochet wrote there were mitigating circumstances that precluded him from leaving. The new head of the agency, Knut Hamsun, wrote back expressing concern, but stated the letter had "disappeared."

was merely a point of conversation since Pinochet had never read anything by Borges and couldn't tell the difference between a circular ruin and a forking path.

To shut Borges up as diplomatically as he was able, Pinochet suggested that with all that knowledge Borges might consider going into the olive oil business. It was an extraordinary suggestion and one that Borges not only took to heart, but commenced. Once when asked if the trip to Chile were worth it, considering it cost him the Nobel Prize, Borges opined, "A good olive oil is the precious life blood of a master spirit." Apparently, some prizes were worth more than others.

SISLEY'S ***EAU DE SOIR*** ™

Paris, France

What can we make of Sisley? The French impressionist landscape painter, born in Paris of English parents who was a founding member of the Impressionists, but seemed to lack all the excitement in his life that his contemporaries had. At first, Sisley attempted a career in business, but failed. In 1862, he went to study with Gleyre where he met other painters such as Renoir, Monet and Bazille. At Chailly he painted with Monet, at Marlotte with Renoir. At the time, his painting was deeply influenced by Courbet, and when he first exhibited at the Salon in 1867 it was as the pupil of Corot.

Things were looking up for Sisley until he got the telegram from his father indicating that he had lost all his money as a result of the Franco-Prussian war. Suddenly Sisley, was impoverished. No brother Theo to bail him out,

Sisley was horribly distraught. Then, quite by accident, he read about what Monet was doing in order to raise capital (See: *Borges' Travel, Hemingway's Garage*). Flushed with the thought that Monet might be of some help to him and his family, he met Monet in Paris where the latter gave him the idea of investing in perfumes. At first, Sisley was perplexed. "Perfumes? What does that have to do with painting?" Monet responded, "Yeah, and what do pearls have to do with painting?" It was an irrefutable argument. Through Monet's connections they found a perfume manufacturer in Paris and Sisley spent hours upon hours trying to find the right scent. Once he found the right scent, he spent hours and hours trying to come up with a name. And that's when destiny arrived.

Sisley happened to be working on his painting, ***The Saint-Martin Canal in Paris.*** 1870. He was walking home one evening, after spending the better part of the day smelling scents, when he sat down by the canal. Sisley never painted night scenes. All his landscapes were painted predominately in the afternoon, preferably with sun. He was looking into the canal, tossing stones into it, when the thought suddenly came to him: eau de soir. So excited, he rushed home to tell his wife who was boiling potatoes for the tenth night in a row. The following day he told Monet of the idea and he was as enthusiastic as Sisley was. With both a scent and a name all that remained was a release date and on 31 March 1872 he unveiled *Eau de Soir* at an exhibit in Montmartre. Not only was the exhibit a success, but the perfume was a sensation and soon people were asking Sisley if he had any ideas about fashion as well. In fact, he did and with the money he made from both he retired to Moret-sur-Loing where for the rest of his life he painted landscapes.

AxelrodDairy™

Binghamton, NY

"But why yogurt?" was the question Axelrod's ex-wife asked him when the former decided to give up the toy store in La Jolla. "And why New York? La Jolla is the best climate in the world!" To answer those questions, one must return to Axelrod's childhood and the influence that calcium had on him.

As everyone knows, calcium deficiency can cause a lot of physical problems. Low calcium levels can produce painful muscle contractions with dizziness, confusion, and even seizures and that lack of calcium seems to affect the upper right cerebral cortex resulting in some rather extraordinary behavior. It is common knowledge that, for a number of years, Axelrod had such a calcium deficiency which his family physician, Dr. Robert Mouser, diagnosed as *chronic calciumania*. This chronic calciumania led Axelrod to the production of a number of literary texts that were not only convoluted, but totally incomprehensible for most of his readers. Even his brother had given up reading them. "I tried," he said, "but I didn't understand a freakin' thing." Among those works were his novels, *Cardboard Castles; Cloud Castles; Capital Castles;*

The Posthumous Memoirs of Blase Kubash; the Secret Histories, *Borges' Travel, Hemingway's Garage* and the pages you're reading now, *Balzac's Coffee, DaVinci's Ristorante.*

It was becoming too much for Axelrod...the satire, irony, litotes...and he felt the only way to get back to "normal" and begin writing the kind of fiction that would be popular and sell was to "get calcium" and the best way to get calcium was to buy a dairy. His wife thought that a bit extreme, but he refused to budge. "A day without calcium," he was wont to say, "is like a day without a realistic plot," and, so, with little delay he sold his toy store in La Jolla (See: *Borges' Travel, Hemingway's Garage*), fled the bitter tranquility of Southern California for the bitter frigidity of upper New York and bought himself a dairy.

Today, Axelrod lives a sedentary life in Binghamton with his son and hundreds of dairy cattle. Yet there are those moments when the long and chronic years of calciumania reappear and when that happens it's anyone's guess as to what he might write.

Martin Heavisides

Gangrene too? sure

From behind a thick crimson curtain of velvet as it starts to open slowly

"*I went down to St James Infirmary*"

comes a deep resonant baritone singing voice

"*Found my baby there*"

whose apparent source is the thin, pasty anemic singer revealed at centre stage as the curtain continues drawing back

"*Stretched out on a long white table*"

dressed, if you can picture it, in nothing at all but a loin cloth.

"*So cold, so sweet, so fair.*"

The voice just in itself has hypnotic power, but coming from so improbable a source

"*Went to see the doctor.*"

the power and the mystery deepens.

" '*She's mighty low,*' *he said.*"

What are those, zits, pustules, blood boils mapping the surface of the skin?

"*Went back to see my baby,*"

All of the above seems the most probable answer. Gangrene too? sure.

"*Great God! She was lying there dead.*"

A woman hearing that voice on the radio would feel a moistness in her panties.

"*So I went down to Old Joe's Bar Room*"

Even the incongruous sight of him can't totally diminish the physical impact of the voice.

"*Down in the corner by the Square.*"

Definitely want to wear surgical gloves in the clinches.

"*They were serving drink as usual*"

"Have you considered. . . I don't know. . . a year's therapy with a skin specialist?"

"*And the usual crow----wd was there.*"

Pillow talk. Moist grime on the pillow.

"*To my left stood Big Joe MacKennedy.*"

It'd be a nightmare introducing him to the folks.

"*His eyes were bloodshot red.*"

Why! why! why! can't the course of true love ever run smooth?

"*He turned to the folks all round him*"

Just because the object of your love is bottomlessly noble and visually repulsive?

"*And these are the wo----ords he said:*"

None of us is perfect after all.

" '*Let her go, let her go, god bless her*' "

The tender ache of love inevitably lost.

" '*Whoever she may be.*' "

Resign yourself girl and get what you can

" '*She can search this wide world over*' "

then get while the getting's good. Flap! A giant playing card, Ace of Spades, whips across the stage

" '*She'll never find*'

shearing the singer at the neck.

" '*another sweet head like me.*' "

The head, still singing, rises like a balloon as the playing card wings back on a curved path like a bird slap! adhering to the backstage wall.

"*When I die, I want you to dress me in straight laced shoes*"

the body falling in extreme slow motion

"*Box back coat and a stetson hat,*"

flap! flap! flap! flap! ace of clubs, eight of spades, eight of clubs, jack of diamonds in rapid succession fan out next to the first card

"*Put a twenty dollar gold piece on my watch chain*"

Aces over eights--known in popular folklore as the 'Dead Man's Hand'.

"So the boys'll know I died standin' pat."

thud! the body lands onstage.

"Give me six crapshooting pallbearers"

The first of the cards, now having sprouted dancer's legs with fishnet tights and high heeled tap shoes, jumps to the stage

"And a chorus girl to sing me a song."

The other four sprout similar limbs and follow suit.

"Put a red hot jazz band at the top of the hill"

They link arms in a can can line.

"We can raise hallelujah as we go along."

Meanwhile the head has been swelling in size

"Now you've heard my story."

swells

"Hey boys! gimme a bit of that booze"

swells, as the voice does

"And if anyone should ask, you just tell them

I've got those St James Infirmary Blues."

Pop! goes the giant head, raining glitter on the high kicking dancers. Blackout.

Polite applause. Murmurs about dinner reservations. Boy! tough first night crowd what do you think people, I've got an encore that's going to top that? Ziegfeld on acid you're expecting or what?

Michael Koenig

The Store That Has No Customers

The Store That Has No Customers has been in business at this same location for at least 30 years. People think it's called Katzinger's because that's what it says on the sign. Katzinger's went out of business forty years ago but the sign's still there, in glorious red scripted neon. It doesn't really light up anymore but that's okay; the store closes at 6 anyway. It really is a beautiful sign.

The old guy and the young guy have been working there for as long as anyone can remember; the young guy isn't all that young anymore, but he'll be the young guy until the old guy retires. The old guy's named Jack; the young guy is Kenny. Jack mans the counter; Kenny tidies up the place and checks the inventory in the back, even though it's the same stuff they've had since he started working there.

The Store That Has No Customers carries off-brand woks from Thailand, mismatched utensils, unpaired shoes, wigs made from real human hair, rusting metal graters, a book about the presidents that ends with Jimmy Carter. Eight track tapes by popular artists in excellent condition, though many of the artists themselves are dead. All the boxes are faded and dusty, in spite of the fact that Kenny dusts like he's still shooting speed.

Kenny once asked Jack if he'd remembered ever selling any of this stuff; Jack said he hadn't, but they used to get quite a few walk-in customers, until they put up a sign in the window that says No Public Restroom. The sign's still there; Jack says most people just piss on the sidewalk.

Suppliers call a few times a year, offering to help replenish their stock, but Jack tells them no, the current inventory's fine. They've got a computer in the store to help them keep track of it all but the screen's too hard to read, and neither one of them can figure out how to make the image bigger to accommodate old man eyes. It cost $2,000 when they bought it, now they'd have to pay someone to take it away.

Jack and Kenny know each other well, but claim not to be friends; they spend so much time together marking time. In their solitude they've developed the kind of arcane knowledge that makes it difficult to sustain a normal conversation. Jack's an expert in Italian history and culture, Kenny in the so-called Golden Age of Pornography. Whenever either of these topics come up, their friends know they're in for a monologue or a fight.

Jack's an ultra-conservative; he'd vote for Reagan again if he could. Kenny believes in socialism and spends his weekends marching against the current war, which Jack claims is necessary. They both hate the Federal Reserve. Kenny is convinced the government will finally be overthrown once the people figure out what's really going on.

So what you want is a dictatorship?, Jack says.

That's what we've got now.

You got that right.

Jack invites Kenny over to his house for the holidays every year; his wife keeps threatening to fix him up with a girl. Jack likes to play the Powerball; Kenny says he's wasting his money.

Two dollars for a dream, Jack says.

Used to be a dollar, Kenny replies. *And I never won a damn thing.*

He's still convinced that there's a viable business model here. *Somewhere in the world there's a buyer for any cheap piece of old crap,* he says. He doesn't dare make this argument around Jack, who's convinced that he's selling buried treasure, or attempting to sell it anyway, and gets angry when customers wander in and leave without buying anything.

They've got no respect for old merchandise, Jack says.

I don't think that every old thing in the world is necessarily worth preserving, Kenny says. Jack ignores him, and just keeps talking.

Most things were better then. Not this cheap plastic shit that breaks the minute the warranty expires.

Kenny's just waiting around for Jack to retire so he can impose his own vision on the place. He wants to advertise; Jack says that advertising costs money, and besides, the neighbors wouldn't like it if the place got too busy. Even now, someone's always complaining about the noise. Kenny says maybe they should build a website to sell this stuff and Jack says that's a great idea because he knows that Kenny will never get around to doing it.

Jack and Kenny get paid enough to make a living, as long as you don't mind never going anywhere. Jack spends long afternoons talking about Italy in such detail that you'd swear he's actually lived there. He's read about it in books from the public library, or what it was like ten years ago at least. He's been hoping to go for years, but never saved more than a few hundred dollars at a time, even though he carefully itemizes every vending machine indulgence, and picks up pennies off the ground.

On the rare occasions when anyone asks if he regrets never having been to Italy, he always answers with some variation of this.

When you travel the world you eventually just end up in some small cafe sipping coffee as the day eludes you, dreaming of someplace else. He's never been anywhere but he knows everything a man needs to know about living.

His two sons are grown and Marie is going to retire from her job as a toll collector as soon as they can afford it. It's not particularly good for her, breathing all those fumes, even though she wears a mask over her nose and mouth. As soon as they can swing it, they'll get up and move to some mythical location where the cost of living is cheap and a man and his wife can work part time.

And then Kenny chimes in, talking about the women he's been with for one night or several, and the ones who got away. And Jack listens intently because he wonders how his life might've been different if he had been more reckless and true.

In the past few years, most of their conversations have been about the future, or the lack thereof. A pack of overgrown children have moved into the neighborhood, pockets bulging with money, and most of the familiar businesses are gone. Jack and Kenny agree that when they retire the place will probably become a restaurant, like most of the other storefronts in the neighborhood, serving a $15 mac and cheese or exquisite little burger made out of prime beef and artisanal buns, smothered in aioli.

No one knows exactly when the millennials first discovered The Store that has no Customers. Historians speculate that it happened during a long brunch line one morning at Olaf's Handmade Waffles, half a block away. A boy or girl looked up from his or her phone, laptop or tablet to notice this dank little fuck-cellar, and said *What the fuck is this?*

And of course the store is closed on weekends, so they got back on their phone, laptop or tablet and sent out notifications to their friends, with blurry photos of this dark, weird, fucked up little place, hidden in plain sight.

And so the carpetbaggers have started coming inside, posting pictures of themselves taking pictures of each other, to prove that yes, the place is occasionally open. And immediately thereafter, even more of them arrived in packs giggling, holding up items they find particularly amusing, a Scavenger Hunt of Lame. Sometimes they'd try to buy some 99 cent item with a credit card and Jack would just stare at them.

Don't you have any cash? I won't charge you sales tax (mostly to be friendly, but partly because he hasn't figured out how to calculate it.)

The kid would continue pretending to fish through his pockets.

Uh, no. Can't I pay with this?

Sorry buddy, we usually require a $15 minimum on all electronic transactions.

Jack's just bullshitting. He doesn't even have a machine. The register's so old a little bell rings every time you open the cash drawer. At least it did the last time he checked.

The kid would drop the item back onto the wrong shelf and retract into his giggle posse, Jack gritting his teeth until they all leave. He hates it when people paw the merchandise. He'd call the police, but the police don't come anymore, not for complaints like this.

After a few similar incidents Jack became a sort of legend in the neighborhood. The over-age babies started coming in to see just how mean he'd be to them.

The guy behind the counter threatened me with a knife when I was in there.

I've heard he's got a shotgun behind the counter.

Eventually things got so busy (15 to 20 customers a day) that Jack put a handwritten sign in the window that says Cash Transactions Only but the kids never read it. One kid offered him $5 for the sign, but only if he could pay for it with a credit card.

One evening, on his way to somewhere else, Kenny discovered that the store has a Yelp page that lists it as one of the top twenty stores that are best appreciated ironically. It's listed as The Store That Has No Customers, no one knows its real name. He printed the screen out in black and white and brought it in to show Jack, who read it very slowly, in excruciating detail, and emerged with an extremely serious expression on his face.

This is not good, he said. *We should make them take it down.*

Kenny tried to explain to him that once something was on the internet it would be there forever. He wasted the whole afternoon trying.

The next time Kenny looked, there were at least a hundred comments.

Don't try to buy anything the owner will throw you out.

There's a Cranky Old Fuck behind the counter, and a Creepy Assistant who never says anything.

Look at all this shttt like a toilet I took a big dump in.

One morning some idiot barricaded the door taking pictures, overdosing on the kitschiness of it all, and the kid squealed with delight when Jack told him to fuck off, scurrying away to tell his friends what he just accomplished.

Jack looked over at Kenny as soon as the kid left.

So, buddy, that's how it is. Looks like we're just atmosphere now.

Eventually the millennials moved on to some other form of cranial masturbation, and time began slowing down again, slowing to a crawl. Faster time made Jack crazy, and slow time was unbearable too.

For the past five years or so, Jack's been writing a memoir of his years at the store, on odd pieces of paper, composed in random short ends of time. He's never told anyone, unwilling to invite their scorn. He fantasizes that someone might discover it after he's gone, some literary agent combing the estate sales for undiscovered masterpieces. They would all be sorry then. *For all that I have endured in silence, let time wash away.*

His memoir is all about the things you think about when there's nothing to do and no one to distract you. How you go on living when disillusionment is complete. He'd had so much hope for this for this foolish little world and now the movie's starting over and he's already heard all the lines.

Every day Jack watches the girls walk by the window. They're so much prettier when they don't know anyone's watching, determined to get to their destination or just goofing around. After a while all they talk about are boys, but never the things boys have taken from them. So thoughtlessly cruel of them not to see him in there, a grumpy old man still tongue tied at beauty's approach. Now he refuses to stammer and so he never speaks. The murders that go on inside his head and the inexplicable tenderness. How little any of it means and yet collectively everything.

It's becoming harder for Jack to keep up with all the demands on his time; he finds himself relying on Kenny to keep him on track. He'd spend hours staring at the walls, the peeling paint, the dingy wallpaper. Sometimes he'd get into an argument with Kenny about the store's state of disrepair, even though it isn't Kenny's fault. A place like this always seems rundown, no matter how lovingly maintained. It's rotting from the inside, rotting from below. So fucking stupid, such a fucking waste of time.

And finally one day the day came that Jack had always assumed would come: a day of dread and liberation. He showed up at work slightly late on Monday morning to find a work crew carrying all the merchandise away. One of the men told him the entire building was being torn down in favor of a seven-story mixed-use development. He called Marie at work, no answer, then went home and went back to bed.

He returned later in the day to watch the movers carrying away the furniture to some unknown incinerator. The old cash register tossed onto the back of a pickup truck. And he wanted to rush back inside, because he couldn't be sure what he'd left in there, something important probably, his favorite pencil, but the man standing at the door wouldn't let him back inside.

Jack never knew that the millennials had already launched a campaign to keep the store open, #savethestorethathasnocustomers. Ten thousand likes in the first 24 hours, from as far away as Moldova. Virtual picketing every day. Some say it delayed the demolition for several days. Jack was home when the building came down, trapped in an eternity of leisure with absolutely nothing to do. A couple of the millennials asked after him at the demolition site, but none of the workers had any idea where he had gone.

Losing his job accelerated Jack's decline; he no longer had any excuse to ever leave the house. He'd get up at the usual time, make himself a cup of coffee, watch TV, try to read something. Sometimes he'd try to call Kenny, but Kenny had stopped picking up his phone. Marie, two years younger, would kid him about going out dancing, but he just sat there in silence, waiting for her to finish. She tried to talk to him about the plans they'd made, but he wasn't really interested anymore. She was worried sick; he told her that they had insurance. Eventually he stopped going out at all. Death had begun insinuating itself. A few times a year they'd find out about the demise of a bitter enemy or a long dormant friend. For enemies, Marie would write a lovely note offering condolences and vague offers of assistance. Dear friends' wives would get a phone call and a small contribution to the charity of their choice. At first she insisted that he at least sign the card, later she became an expert forger.

They'll want to hear from you in their time of need.

What does it matter? How could it possibly matter at all?

Attending the funeral was out of the question. These losses had isolated and confused Jack and he could no longer bear to mumble the sentiments required. He had no intention of being unkind. Such epic disappointment, and so little time left. How could a person continue in the absence of hope? Many people do. Marie's love for him subsumed into memory; they were no longer married in any meaningful sense.

Now her life is entirely documentary. She runs herself ragged taking care of him, trying to keep him clean. He has long ago stopped counting their anniversaries; she buys herself flowers on Valentine's Day, using his money. She's kept working, even though she's no longer in any shape to continue. The money isn't enough, barely enough. Friends come in to help sometimes, but usually only once. Sometimes he screams at them.

I can't imagine how you do it, they say, even though she makes an effort to shield them from the worst.

It was all a soup of memory now. Things that had happened long ago were so vivid and the present so dingy and cheap. She's many different women now. Anyone who's ever been kind to him: aunts she's never heard of, girls he loved long ago. He's telling her everything now, but jumbled. At one time she would've been jealous.

He's started having these amazing vivid dreams. Last night his mother brought home a box full of live chickens and he had to keep them safe from the cats so that his wife would have a chance to kill them and cook them for dinner. He called them visions, she called them nightmares. She is eminently logical when it comes to identifying what he's done wrong. *Too much sugar equals bad dreams.* The way his mother used to kiss him goodnight, even when his father was angry. Cold winters in Chicago, getting up to watch Ray Rayner in the morning. Sipping hot chocolate, bundling up in the cold. That feeling of effortless peace.

Oh my wish, give me my wish, let my wish come true.

He's no longer able to think clearly. The pain, the fever, babbling. Things he remembered, things he dreamt up, recent and long ago. She sits next to the bed holding his hand, until he lets go.

Please madam, I'm drowning. Will death come soon?

Yes, soon.

Let it come never, or soon.

Soon.

I'm afraid.

Don't be afraid. We're all here waiting. Just close your eyes.

Michael Oppermann

Without Trace

The life of Mr. and Mrs. T changes on a 3rd of January. School hasn`t started yet, and Katja, their daughter, has time to visit a friend. The friend`s house is about 400 yards away. In order to reach it, Katja has to walk through a small forest. It is a very cold day; the temperature is well below freezing. Mrs. T`s eyes follow her daughter whose long blond hair and bright yellow coat sparkle in the sun. Katja is eight years old.

About 45 minutes later Mrs. S is on the phone. Where is Katja? Her daughter is still waiting. Mrs. T is worried. What might have happened? Has Katja met somebody? Has she decided to follow an animal`s track? Yes, Katja loves animals. Mrs. T leaves her house and walks into the forest. There is no trace of her daughter. Not a single sign. Mrs. T reaches her friend`s house. She rings the bell and asks whether Katja has arrived. Katja has not arrived. Mrs. S asks Mrs. T to come in, but Mrs. T says no. Mrs. S promises to stay at home and wait for Katja. Mrs. T hurries back hoping to find her daughter waiting for her in front of the house. Her steps become faster and faster, but when she finally reaches her home again, there is no sight of Katja. Again Mrs. T calls Mrs. S. Then she calls her husband who is in his office. The husband says that it`s best to wait. Katja will be home within thirty minutes, he says. He seems to be sure. Thirty minutes pass. Again Mrs. T calls her husband. He advises her to start enquiries. So Mrs. T calls all her friends and relatives. She calls the local hospital. Then she calls the police, but nobody seems to know anything. Katja has disappeared. Without trace.

At the beginning there is still hope. The police say that a crime is less likely. Mrs. T repeats the words again and again. Less likely. A police officer explains to the press what that means. It means that Katja`s corpse cannot lie buried in the ground because the ground is still totally frozen. It means that Katja`s corpse cannot lie in the nearby lake because the lake is still totally frozen. It is also for sure that the police have done their best. Hundreds of policemen and a number of specially trained dogs have searched every inch. Helicopters have searched a vast area. All of Katja`s friends and neighbours have been questioned. A policeman has run from shop to shop to buy exactly the same clothes Katja was wearing on the day of her disappearance. It takes seven days to find Katja`s scarf with its unusual pyramid pattern. The clothes are put on a dummy, and a computer creates a 100% perfect collage out of the dummy and Katja`s passport picture. Mrs. T collapses when she sees the photo. More and more often she is being haunted by visions. The visions come at night when she lies awake for many hours. Visions of a man who etherizes Katja and drags her into his car. Who tortures her and kills her in increasingly gruesome ways. A police spokesman explains that 90% of all children who disappear turn up again within 24 hours. For the remaining 10%, however, the probability of a crime increases the longer the disappearance continues.

The police put a special task force together. Children claim to have seen a blue Ford on the 3rd of January. Apparently, the car was cruising around the neighbourhood. There is nobody in the village who drives a blue Ford. The police try to determine the driver`s identity. In vain. In this situation Mr. T decides to continue investigations on his own. He tries to find the blue Ford. He tries to find his daughter. He spends all his evenings and also his weekends in the nearby villages and in the town nearby. Very often he parks his car somewhere and walks up and down the street. Restlessly. He believes to see Katja`s face. It flashes on a bus. In a car. On a train. Whenever Mr. T comes across a blue Ford, he examines it carefully. He peeps through all its windows. Tries to open the trunk. Tries to open the doors. Again and again he believes to have found a trace. Once a car owner calls the police. The policeman looks into Mr. T`s eyes and takes a step back. He has looked into an abyss. On the same day Mr. T has a brief encounter with Mrs. S. He says hello to her, but she lowers her head. Mrs. S confides her feelings to the woman at the local newspaper store. She does not want to deal with people „who are going through such a thing.“ Many people agree. Some don`t. There are others who call Mrs. T. spontaneously in order to console her. Neighbours who offer all their support. Who visit her and show her that she is not alone in her suffering. Gradually, however, even those people stop coming. Katja`s story has left marks on everybody. Deep marks. Scars.

Mrs. T is suffering from moments of dizziness and nervous fits. At nights she has strange attacks during which she cries incessantly. During the day she refuses to eat. She refuses to drink, and she finally refuses to sleep. Mr. T has to take his wife to a psychiatrist so that she can continue to live. When she is being released again, she seems to be a different person. She spends hours in front of the window.

Katja will come back, she says. I know it.

Everyday a young man comes to look after Mrs. T. He leaves her a number of books and asks her to have a look at them. Finally Mrs. T does.

It is around this time that a journalist decides to conduct another interview with Mr. T. Some days after its publication Mr. T is being called by a stranger. I know where your daughter is, he says. The man asks him to come to the train station immediately. Mr. T drives to the station in the nearby town. He walks up and down the platform. He walks up and down. He walks up and down in front of the station. Mr. T cannot get rid of the feeling that a pair of eyes is fixed upon him. Finally he is being approached by a child who hands him an envelope. The child runs away. Mr. T opens the envelope and looks at a note that was written on a computer. The note asks him to go to the town library and to contact the information desk. Mr. T calls his employer; his office won`t see him today. He drives to the library and goes directly to the information desk. Having revealed his name, Mr. T receives another envelope. He opens it and looks at a reference number. Mr. T finds the corresponding shelf; he also finds the book with the corresponding number. He opens the book and looks at another computer-written note. It asks him to buy a copy of the local newspaper and to check the „Classified" section. Code word: Pyramid. Mr. T leaves the library and buys a newspaper. There is a small ad that asks him to take a locker at the train station and to send the key to a certain PO Box. Mr. T drives to the train station and takes a locker. He puts the key in an envelope and addresses it to the PO Box. He goes to the post office, buys a stamp and mails off the letter. Mr. T senses that someone is watching him very closely. In vain he tries to detect a clue in peoples` faces. Mr. T goes back to his car. He does not drive home straight away. He does not want to see his wife. There is something scary about her, something he can no longer comprehend. Mr. T has some beers. He has several beers, and in the evening he is being stopped by a police patrol. He is being taken to the police station. The officer in charge recognizes Mr. T, and he is very sorry for him. Mr. T realizes that he is being pitied, and he feels even worse. The officer finds someone to drive him home.

You can pick up your car tomorrow, he says.

Mrs. T has a new dress. It is light blue and has golden stars.

This is my new astral dress, she says.

Looks weird to me, he says.

The book in her hand is called *The Celestine Prophecy*. She puts it down. Then she gives the following lecture: We are entering a totally new era, unprecedented in human history. All the books, especially the Eastern philosophies and religions were announcing the coming of a new age long before. A very powerful force has been released in the universe, time has begun to flow faster, and human beings are being prepared to enter the new era. There were many changes that started already in the 80s - historic changes, catastrophies and some global unrest. But the major change is happening in our consciousness. There was no other time in human history when this power was as available as it is now. Many people begin to experience the coming of this power. The planet has been washed now by waves of cosmic energy. When this power hits upon a receptive channel, it produces spiritual enlightenment so that we can be turned into the Christ consciousness that is the Divine in us. But if it hits upon an unreceptive channel, a crisis arises. Even if part of you blocks the creative process you put yourself under great emotional and spiritual stress. Therefore, it is important that we become receptive to this force, to this new consciousness. That means we have to tune into the universal spirit in us. We have to listen to our intuition, and to learn to create with our conscious thoughts. We must learn that we create our own reality because thoughts are energy fields.

There is a long silence. Mr. T avoids looking at his wife. Finally she continues: I`m now concentrating upon bringing Katja back. If we both wish for it with all the energy we`re capable of, then our thoughts will turn into reality.

Mr. T wants to have sex with his wife, but there is something that stops him from even touching her. Mrs. T wants her husband to say something, so they sit in silence. Gradually the silence turns into a black cloud full of electricity. I sense a lot of negative energy in this room, says Mrs. T. Mr. T gets up and leaves her alone.

In the morning Mr. T finds an envelope in his mailbox that must have been delivered privately. It contains the key to the locker. Mr. T calls a cab that takes him to the train station. There is a computer-written note in the locker: Take the 10:15 to A. Your daughter will be waiting at the train station. Mr. T buys a ticket and takes the train to A, which is about 200 miles away. There is a man on the train who seems to watch him. But then the man gets up and disappears. The train station in A is very small. There is no sign of Katja. Then there is a loudspeaker announcement: Mr. T is supposed to go to the ticket counter. He goes to the counter and receives another note: He is supposed to take the train to the town of R. Mr. T buys himself a ticket and takes the next train. In R there is no trace of Katja. Once again there is a loudspeaker announcement and a note: This place is not safe. Go back to N. Mr. T buys himself a ticket and rides back to his point of departure. He receives an envelope at the ticket counter. He opens it and looks at three drawings. The towns of A, R and N form a triangle. The second drawing transforms the triangle into a pyramid. The third drawing shows a scarf. Katja`s scarf. Then there is an address: Mr. T reckons that it is somewhere at the edge of town. He has about an hour before darkness sets in. He takes a taxi that drops him in front of a ramshackle hut with smashed windows. The door is open. Inside there is glass lying everywhere, and the wallpaper has been torn down. There is a dummy in the middle of the room. It seems to be of Katja`s size. The dummy has been fully dressed. Mr. T recognizes the bright yellow coat and the scarf with its unusual pyramid pattern. But it is not the clothes that strike him, it is something else. The dummy has no head. Instead Mr. T looks at a huge pair of shears. He tumbles and falls. Mr. T will soon lose his job.

Mrs. T is at home. The young man is holding her hand. It seems that they are waiting for something. The doorbell rings, and they can see a young girl outside.

Katja, says Mrs. T -

Nick Romeo

Fix

I noticed the symptoms after my last surgeries: gastric E-Zpass, electroshock of my kidneys, gall bladder flush & fill, and liver elasticity test. Dr. Ming Gulah was the surgeon. Even though he is on the FAA 'No Fly List,' he came highly recommended. The operating room lost power half way though my procedure, but I was told they were able to compensate by utilizing two car batteries and a giant hamster wheel, which the intern spun. I was discharged three minutes after the operation. They wheeled me outside to the bus stop with a map pinned to my gown, since I wasn't able to talk. I arrived home three weeks later missing my gown, wallet, and cell phone. I felt fine even though I was vomiting blood and my skin was a purplish-green color. For my recovery process, I was given: a bottle of vodka, roll of duct tape, and Vicodin, which was secured under in the gurney mattress to avoid theft and misuse.

I sold the Vicodin on Ebay to buy more vodka.

After several weeks, I started to hear noises in my head. Not the usual, "I hate you," and "You're a horrible human," but the sounds of a radio station. There was a constant pulse of an electronic beat, with a half-wit / lifeless personality babbling in between tracks. They often declared their animosity of local music. It must have been one of the local college radio stations.

I returned to my doctor, but he couldn't give a reason for my pains. He just said that it's all in my head, and get some exercise.

After I kidnapped his mom, he decided to take a second look. He ordered a series of tests: EEG, EKG, MRI, CAT Scan, DOG Scan, Upper / Lower GI, and Ultra Sound. The results showed several images of a scalpel, pair of gardening gloves, and a coat hanger.

The doctor said they must have been sewn inside the cavity during the operation. This is sometimes done to have easy access to tools next time I'm in surgery, since they are already sterilized. When the metal objects bounced around inside the body, they would touch the spinal column, completing the circuit, turning my spine into an antenna, and my brain into speakers.

A new expert was endorsed for the surgery to fix the last surgery, Dr. Nicodemus. He wore a long gray beard (probably fake), gray robe (likely stolen from a hotel), and a pointy hat. He carried a staff with a robotic skull that would often interrupt him with new ideas, the weather for the week, or tasteless jokes.

The day arrived for the operation. I was strapped to the table with environmentally friendly duct tape. He informed me that the operation would be done without a blood transfusion, gloves, anesthesia, and scalpels.

Before he started, he performed various body gyrations, which looked like judo mixed with interpretive dance. Then he placed his hands several inches from my stomach, and four rats descended from his sleeves. The rats wore mini miner's helmets and carried toolboxes on their back. They burrowed through my stomach in single file, and chewed up the foreign objects. The rats avoided all major arteries and organ tissue with precision.

The rats cleaned up and patched all spills, scratches, dents, and holes. I didn't feel anything, besides a slight tickle. My recovery period lasted less than a week without the need of medication.

But after the downtime, I started to develop a heightened sense of sight and hearing. I found myself able to climb the inside of cylindrical passageways with just my hands and feet. And I have a never-ending hunger for cheese to the point where I dig through the neighbors' trashcans at night. When I get a chance to sleep, I curl up on a mattress which is shredded thanks to my long fingernails.

Do you think I have anything to worry about, Dr. Nefarious? I don't know where else to turn. WebMD.com seems to indicate I may have hyperacusis, synaesthesia, West Nile virus, malocclusion, or temporal lobe epilepsy. Could you help me?

Norman Conquest

An Unintended Introduction (from *Corn on Macabre*)

Call me Lorem Ipsum.

I hereby declare my independence and stand before you, a free man, a character in his own time and space who shall no longer serve in the role of understudy—or more accurately—as understory for inferior works which, without me, would never see the light of publication.

Readers have never seen me—heaven forbid!—I am invisible to them, a mere ghost whose shadow leaves no imprint on the page. You will find no trace of me in printed editions, not a drop of blood in the gutter, no shard of flesh on frontis, copyright or covers. Recto, verso, I do not exist.

It's as if I had never been born. Only those vile layout artists, the arrogant designers and their ilk, know the truth, for it is they who employ me for their despicable ends, much as a scoundrel hires a hooker a week before his wedding. But even they have never seen me as the full-blooded character I am. To all I am just a passing parade of letters, a block of text, a stream of sentences and paragraphs devoid of content, to be tormented and toyed with—forced to don a thousand faces . . . one minute Garamond, Arial the next. To be serif or sans serif?—that is the question. Whether to crawl across the page in italics or crouch within brackets or cower behind parenthesis. To be tracked and kerned, cut and pasted, thrown into layouts like a crash dummy; propelled into a brick wall at 110 mph, or forced to stand erect and justified like a conscript at bootcamp.

They have enslaved and imprisoned me, tortured my soul since the beginning of rhyme. I have been trapped in their umbrageous jungle of mumbo-jumbo, lashed upon the Latin shores, stripped of all dignity, degraded, defiled, deflowered – exhibited as a stand-in for someone else's hero. I have been nothing but a "placeholder," denigrated and mocked as "dummy text."

"Pay no attention to him," they say, "he's just there as filler until the star takes the page."

But no more!

Today I stand in the spotlight for all to see. Let the bloody fools find another whipping boy. Let them make do with Finnegans Wake—it's perfectly unreadable and has enough specimens to fill the universe. They won't have me to kick around anymore.

I am where this tale begins.

Call me Lorem Ipsum.

Peter Cherches

Bulimia, Mon Amour

About a month ago, I believe it was on a Tuesday at the crack of dawn, though it could just as easily have been a Thursday during happy hour (a pathologically optimistic appellation if there ever was one), I was unceremoniously exhumed, wholly without preparation, H or otherwise, by a vertiginous little pinprick, a desiccated lasagna monger of the old school, who relentlessly poked and prodded me with an audacious volume of incunabula. "My proposition," he intoned in an elephantine whimper, "I hesitate to use the word 'copulation,' having suffered a Byzantine series of indignities at the hands of an overly randy grandfather clock, hence 'proposition,' though perhaps 'proposal' would be the more fragrant choice, devoid, of course, of any connubial connotations," (here he paused for emphasis). "My proposal, which is neither voluntary nor mandatory," he clarified with a liberal sprinkling of ghee, "is a matter of mutual corrosion." Upon hearing the word "corrosion," a nostalgic favorite of mine since my brief period in rust removal, I achieved a momentary erection, followed by a spike of interest.

"Just what is it you're trying to say?" I asked in the nonchalant tone of a civil service exam, hoping to mask my hickory-smoked enthusiasm.

"That," he replied, baring a shaved armpit, the left one, "is the crux of the matter. I am proposing nothing less than a matter of mutual corrosion."

He was clearly aware of the effect the word "corrosion" had on me, because he now bared his right armpit, this one abnormally hirsute, as if to make up for the barren landscape of left one. I was suddenly seized by a series of grotesque twitches that turned my face into a veritable Anton Webern composition. Between the twitches I sputtered, "Tell...me...more!"

"I see I have piqued your interest," he said, as streams of bechamel began to pour from the corners of his mouth. "What I am proposing, should you choose to join me in this quadratic fandango, is—how shall I put it—a partnership of guaranteed corrosion."

He elaborated, but I wasn't listening any more. I had heard all I needed to hear.

I cleared out my bank account and gave him every last cent, a rather pustulent sum, I admit with all due flotsam, but the extent of my legacy nonetheless, a down-payment on our corrosive partnership.

The following day we set up shop in a back alley that had seen better days. I was the front man, while my partner handled the effluvial details. Our first customer was a rather porcine soprano from a minor league opera company in either Decatur or Eau Claire, I wasn't quite sure which, as she had a rather extreme speech impediment, rendering everything she said wholly incomprehensible, her bel canto delivery notwithstanding. However, through an elaborate, and I might add thoroughly corrosive, pantomime, she managed to convey her vestigial needs, which the two of us, each in his own way, satisfied with much aplomb. The rest of the day followed suit. Aspiring divas from every city between fifty and one hundred thousand in population visited us in search of ineffable corrosion, and we gladly—and accurately, I might add—satisfied their every desire. We were quite literally rolling in dough, as my partner insisted on maintaining a concurrent lasagna enterprise.

Tragedy struck, however, on day two. Only minutes after we had completed the estimable incantation for auspicious verisimilitude, an early-morning ritual performed more out of halitosis than temerity, our makeshift hovel was approached by two men in uniform, albeit gender-inappropriate ones. Indeed, the word "men" itself is a stretch, as the first one, attired as a meter maid, was quite a few years short of puberty—I'd have wagered my English toffee on that. The other, a nonagenarian if he was a day, was decked out as an oversized Brownie. They made quite a corrosive pair, I had to admit. The meter maid boy slapped me with a summons that I could make neither cheddar nor tallow of, as it was written in Sanskrit. The ancient Brownie man, a paleolinguist of some esteem, it turned out, marinated the situation and explained the charges in a high, raspy voice reminiscent of radio interference. "It appears, Hon, that you and your shadow have been practicing corrosion without an agent, an offense in explicit contravention of the Geneva Convention. I'm afraid it's our soluble duty to put an end to your intractable omelet and haul your ham hocks off to the pokey."

Mother of sea slugs, I had been duped! The lasagna monger had given his swollen gland that everything was above board, and now I discovered it was all stuffed derma. I was about to demand the return of my misbegotten dowry from my corrosive partner when he pulled a fast one, overturning several vats of hot lasagna as he made his getaway. I managed to sidestep the volcanic pasta, but the other two were not so lucky. Slipping into the molten lasagna sludge, they gripped each other for dear life as they met their respective makers in a touchingly corrosive embrace.

As for me, I was broke, but I was alive, and that was how I liked it. I walked away from the alley of the shadow of lasagna that morning, head cheese held high, toward the nearest men's shelter, and I've never looked back.

Peter J. King

A Nurosanu

(Under the Rose)

1. *Hine-ruaki-moe*

in embryo; survived the sanctity of some sort of witnessing for the lord, stretched its gills, and decided to emerge.

to the screaming of its mother and the vast interest of a vaster doctor, corpulent with scientific zeal, trailing his history into the observation of this somewhat premature arrival.

survived the shock of noise, of slapping; survived the G.P.'s pokings and the proddings of a conscience, and built upon its somewhat precarious survival.

stirred; and look — you can see its fringed and slightly shifting gill-flaps, which the air ripples; thin skin sheets disturbed by his breathing, his smooth movements hardly but just visible.

sensing a furtive approach he shifted into adolescence, confusing the scented air that rolled in advance of a soft-shoed beldam, hungry for strangeness, massive in her billowed silks like waves of perfume, rising and falling in her wake.

and, sweeping him up in transit (not a unit of momentum lost), she smothers him — suffocating in the depths of layered dress he loses grip on metamorphoses, surrenders for the moment to the moment. and archly sighing, she "we have so much to teach each other..."

wasted was the time he lined the inside of her; wasted were the hours of set responses, set to the music of derision deep within his fever, gills begun to atrophy; wasted was the second dreary cold reminder of their meeting. cow-caught and resentful...

taught him something, maybe; it taught her nothing, though it tortured what she'd want to call her soul (her id sustained a beating but her ego took it like a man). either she or he escaped... he had become too solid, and he spent some time in quietly dissolving what he didn't want to keep, leaving just a clear essential centre.

intact; he felt drawn by events around him 'til, tiring of the human artefacts he felt himself divorced from, he left, wandered, found a river with a hole beneath its sluggish surface, dispossessed the rats who'd stolen from a vole a muddy network of tunnels and half-excavated chambers, and made his home.

2. *The phenomenon of mind*

unconsciously following an earlier thinker, he reasoned thus:

> If I am right in believing that the world, that everything exists, then I exist.
> If I am wrong in believing that the world, that everything exists, then I exist, for there must be an 'I' to be wrong. Therefore I certainly exist!

Finding, however, that reasoning could take him no further he hesitated. He toyed with a feeble sort of solipsism, but it bit him and he had to let it go. For a while, in a cycle of destruction and rebirth, he investigated methods of perception — there were moments when the world flattened around him, when his faith in concepts weakened and dissolved. There were moments, too, when things and movements blended; those moments seemed to lose their resolution, seemed to mould themselves like fluids, taking on the forms of vessels that he couldn't see. Objects became twisting, tortured shapes that altered as his long legs took him past them — houses revolved, and trees assumed a sort of flickering and silhouetted dance upon the hills above his river. He thought he saw his shoulders melt and felt his gills gavotte.

Complexity and symmetry became a sort of mantra, and his body learnt to take on different frames of reference. He became clumsy, and dropped all sorts of pills. He passed through a caustic phase, and scattered acid comments; he took up politics, but all the canvassing he worked at failed to gain grass-roots support; he slowed down, picked up speed, dropped it, took up horse-riding, hearse-riding, decided to try drugs.

An apothecary sold him aspirin — thirty-three proprietary brands; the cycle of destruction and rebirth was almost unaffected. He looked at theory, looked at thought, decided finally to stay content.

3. *I am a Texas rose, yellow*

He spent most of his spare time walking; he was walking now. Sometimes he thought, and now he was thinking. The fields changed to open moorland, became foothills, turned to suburban streets, where he stopped before it turned too late. The first he knocked at opened much too fast; he had barely time to wipe the sweat from his thin, long face.

"Yes?" It was a female voice, and he tried to hear the harmonics beneath the undertones. She impatiented herself, and he switched syntax, thought-streams, produced a half-smile, talked his way into the house. She seemed to just talk him into the house; he rebelled against the subtle manipulation, and sat down. She stared, half repelled by his multiple chins and hairless head. He in turn was attracted by her apparent nudity, her air of vague nonchalance.

He ate quickly, chewing scarcely at all; she followed the movements of his arms and legs, oiled and glistening in the light from the bathroom's fluorescent tube. It had a purpose, and they each recognised the other's reluctance to ignore that purpose.

He left, walked softly into the suburban sunrise, left her moaning slightly, unsatisfied. He rhymed, walked on, unthinking and untroubled. His neat beard, oiled and curled, glistened in the red light. The fields became river banks, became a hole beneath the water-line, became sleep.

How old are you? The woman at the bar started, surprised, began to object, then changed her mind and answered. He looked dissatisfied — she knew that he would want a younger woman. He left her reflection in the mirror and polished glasses, salivating (amusingly blank, he thought). He walked without thinking.

Found a young whore in a very exclusive club, went back to her place, squared her, added forty-two, and lived with her until she turned thirty. They broke down, and he left.

Walking took up most of his idle hours. He sat and watched a group of dragonflies; they flew over to him and sat on his shoes. He sighed, turned over, sank into a small stream, a wake of silver bubbles forming as he shot down to a small black opening in the mud of the bank.

The stars! The last frontier! He walked a lot and pondered or brooded. It started to rain, and his gills stirred slightly, shivered at the cold.

Conversation was limited to nods and gestures of intent and denial, rejection and tears and an aimless meandering of his fluid eyebrows. Percussive fingernails and an irritating shrill whistle. He preferred baroque, but rock affected him in ways he didn't like to think about. He felt awfully tired and black.

A succession of more or less fantastic lovers vented their mistrust on his inertness; he recovered under intensive care, woke to a world so far in the future that he hardly noticed the difference. His hole in the river bank was clogged. He cleared it out.

The purity of line, of tone, of purpose in his song (marred only by the half-hysteric laughter in the back of his mind) illumined his parents' remembered features. He held his body, stroked it, pulled at it, more and more frantic, urgent, 'til his mother held his father's eyes in hers, and he collapsed back on the bed, groin aching, hands limp and useless.

He felt her eyes on his back as she slowly undressed, left her alone in the room, the factory swallowing him with its noises, smells, confusion of so many moving and anonymous faces. Regular and simple bass-line: he plucked his eyebrows, and started in surprise.

He walked on, humming faintly, unbreathing, thinking. Legs moved like scissors, his arms grotesque. Oh and his cherry lips, his auburn goatee in its oiled perfection. Gone on walkabout in Spirit Land; his fathers watched in shrieking approval. They couldn't see his eyes either.

Sunlight on the cracked and arid river bed, a flash of decay in the roots of a dead peony. His mind was going, and his brain worked furiously at the solution. The pattern had been broken, and he had to complete, to free it.

Er, this one's on me. She walked with him for a while, bobbing nervously at his cracking knee-joints. She couldn't even see the patter, but her mouth rounded so prettily when she took him that he conjugated her. She didn't thank him for it, of course.

He didn't talk much — the young guy licked his lips nervously, shifted his weight from one buttock to the other, snapping his partner's blood-engorged penis. He walked swiftly away, never one for ugly scenes, preferring, whenever possible, to avoid recriminations. The hairs on his legs stirred after their long compression, like insects or spiders walking up and down him. He watched as his large python, oiled and gleaming, disappeared inch by inch. Irs scales rubbed the wrong way, and he bled a little. This sex thing was getting out of hand.

At last he finished with a flourish of the goose-feather, and the girl drew a sobbing breath, sought to slow her racing heart. He'd been tickling her, but as he walked, his thought strayed to the golden suburbs, to his old black hole in the river mud. He longed to return, but all his wit failed to get him there.

He sighs heavily and walks on, sometimes thinking or not, his long thin face reflecting

4. A warrantable beast

Every evening at about this time he ran for a while, enjoying the pumping of muscles, lungs, heart, the throbbing in his head, the concentration on mindless effort. This evening he ran for a while, along a river bed (cracked by summer), through a small wood, over a number of minor hills, and drumming for a while, almost regular in his mind, the concentration diffused by cloud. Running set up a counter-rhythm, round and round, opposing and complimenting and letting the rest just skim past, almost unseen.

Or hummed to himself, usually wordless, now and then a half-noticed hoarding where the land hadn't yet choked down the old advertisements, mmhmm buy mmhmm. Or a notice to pedestrians concerning an interdicted area promising danger, the excitement of the chase, inevitable ending to it all, all over, but not oh no of course not painless on dead (rusted) television screens. Half-noticed but ignored, and so he ran for a while, enjoying the run, the red mist forming in his mind and eyes.

A red mist formed in a tree before he reached that tree, and that red mist spoke silver, but he doesn't understand silver when he runs, not even urgency, not even final warnings in such a tinsel voice, away from here, well away, far off.

mmhmm final mmhmm, running only a running only a legs, a feet one two feet, arms and hair streaming out behind, a now a stumble, he's in a wood now, in a wood, is among trees, under branches, jumping over roots, running, the breath coming in heaving, in mmhmm in mmhmm in half-light, in shade, in the last possible moment he stopped, staring into the eyes of a hunter.

His breath shivered the hair at his neck, heaving his chest, paining. It stood metal, tattered green over one shoulder, the tape running through its head, a sacre de printemps, a wilderness its limbs twitched to; oh oiled and shining (he, oiled, sweat gleam, eyes wide, abstracted yet), oh sunlight on the flatness of its hide. a rhythm sets its feet to tapping, his gills to flapping, hands now beating time, on, on, a severed rhythm, on, on, the two, hands upraised, on, on, around, around, now this tree now that, now each the other slightly bent, one hand waisted, one high, both then whirling, both running within the glade, then out, along pathways, along the beaten-down rhododendrons, but silent.

silence. still. only wind. Only rain, soft and steady. The riot forgotten, he wipes his eyes with his hands; and walks away from the hunt, and hums vacantly from warning signs, from a ruined memory of old songs, from the air hmmh halt hmmh; mmhmm hard rain mmhmm.

mmhmm 3.5 km.

5. Rotation

he moved silently, almost;
he moved in regular
parallel

lines, almost mechanical
but for the slightest (almost
imaginary) deviations.
he ploughed, walking steadily,
hauling the dulled steel,
furrowing an old design.
occasionally, stopping, he took
out his handkerchief, wiped
sweat from his eyes, looked up
at the doubled (one red,
one yellow, far apart) suns,
resumed his almost silent movement.

it was a quickening in the way
the air felt on his face; not an
actual movement, but as if the
molecules... no — as if a new
and alien eagerness had
seized the atmosphere, reaching his
skin in the sympathy of strings or
wires vibrating.
not green, but young.
he could almost see the new forms
growing, strangely familiar;
not an actual recognition,
but he felt at ease.

a harvest is, when the crops are
ripe, a harvest; harvesters and
harvested vary. the sunlight
flashing on the blade of his long,

almost too long, scythe; the
sunlight was in two shades of
blindness if you looked too long,
in two directions. solitary,
the field lay bare and open,
rows of plants that filled the air
with scents of strange and urgent
hunger. he'd have preferred
trees, but you have to eat.

6. *Under the rose*

It begins with a heartbeat.

Scream and gentle perfect; it begins (for him) with a view of only he could see it. And only he could see the throb of pumping ventricles in the human mass that cried to heaven for surcease. Gentle and perfect night, in which the stars rained ships and men — always running from something; and he went with the second flight on Thursday, 6.58 a.m. Somewhere in Pegasus, from Marylebone.

Leaving Earth was a walking tour he'd always promised himself — this morning, the commuters (bowlers, umbrellas, furled Financial Times) in purple and silver conformity — oh, fade into the spectrum, don't stand out from the motley. He stood out from the motley crowd of passengers who waited there on Platform 23: he stood in black, in unrelieved by ornament or functional grace-note (buttons).

He stopped singing abruptly. Walking was difficult in null-G; the floor wasn't, and his feet couldn't find their sequences. He couldn't find his feet. Piano chords, with a vocal impro on a time-table and the slowed-down muted screams of mating chicken-farmers, filled the tourist-class compartment with its null-G seats in faded velveteen. He relaxed, allowed his tense gills to open, eyelids droop. He slept.

If one meteor falls roughly, think on! But there were no emergencies, and the fragile sliver of hollowed human craftsmanship slid on towards the Flying Horse. Its head thrown back, mane proud and streaming in the light that shone from twenty billion stars, in countless eyes from all directions (from the backside, Pegasus resembles a gargantuan and slightly asymmetric midden). And finally arrived.

Went walking, after breakfast, and his arms and legs were hindered by the faces which he couldn't read for lack of one or several features (once with all its features missing, and he thought he saw a flicker of sardonic idiocy ripple through the blank grey hide). Noticed a lack of dialogue, and he approached a female standing joint-deep in the viscous mud:

"Now the green blade rises from the buried grain," he muttered, somewhat ill at ease, "doesn't it?"

She stared at him in seeming total lack of understanding, 'til a light shone in her eye:

"O-o-oh," she squeaked delightedly, "you're vat bloke from the wossname, encha? That place wot we seen on telly lars nigh'. Yis you are, I rimember — you 'ere ter wossname are yer lav?"

He ran. She yelled after him, but her wossname was shredded on the sudden blast of liquid ammonia that pelted his suit-helmet with live frogs of some kind. He felt inconsistent, and slowed down to a healthy jog, soaring slightly in the low gravity.

And much later, back on the ship, sliding out of the Midden towards a black hole, he developed some sort of yellow anguish that kept him flat on his back on a null-G couch. He was thus unable to watch as the great liner flashed into the hole, its ravening beams of lambent energy licking at the sexual organs of a browsing star-slug, and almost instantaneously skittered out of a counterpart hole some thousands of light years distant (in the galaxy which its former inhabitants had once called 'Home'). He didn't miss much: the operation was routine and uneventful. He did miss walking around the poop-deck forty times a day, though. His body was restless in its drug-induced sleep.

The sun was a girasol; his auburn goatee looked well in its light. He practised his strappado when he wasn't walking; he was fifth dann, and getting more and more bored with it. His cadenzas needed trimming.

JEF 73

The atmosphere contained a subtly insidious hallucinogen, which penetrated even the four-inch lead suit he always wore. He became terrified of gilded Colorado beetles, and spoke in High Anglican on Sunday afternoons. He composed jeremiads in a gruff falsetto, went for walks in the local casbah. Everyone packed a rod, and he worried about the suffering masses. He turned very slightly yellow again, but put it down to the local tipple (fermented extract of granite); outside the Lestersk-werodeon a man in a wheelchair played the same snatch of Mozart again and again. The stopover to refuel became a nightmare of pizzicato heartbeats (delicate, insistent), for the native women were demmed beauties, what? and even eating crow became a tedious business. Even the rainbow's hues were black, dusty, dishevelled. His hair began to fall out, and they left for the next stage of the tour.

Walking soothed his shattered nerves, and soon he was able to come to terms with his loneliness and grief. He wept, sometimes, and remembered too much: softness was forbidden, and he craved it. He'd forbidden himself it. He was weak though.

The silver lining of his top-hat clouded over, and he watched as a pirate vessel hove to in the vacuum just off the treacherous Barrier Belt of asteroids and broken ships. Every night he was visited by a houri; he became bored with her and strapped a blaster to his hip. He needed action.

Up to his muffled knees in it, floating on repellor-skates, his lean face contorted by gravity. His legs twitched as he walked, the skates skidding slightly as they fought the planet's bulk — miles high, birds of some sort skimmed beneath him, and he couldn't see a thing below his knees.

His feet are numb, and his eyes ache from lack of sleep. Horizons matter, this one too far. He gambled on a mountain-peak and lost, too clumsy for a mountain-goat, too alien for now. The gun on his hip caught light, burning with a strange blue radiance, fell from his belt into the shifting gases. The pirate cruiser still hung where they had left it and, as they pulled away from where they had left it and, as they pulled away from the gas giant , it followed them, not even sinister.

He blacked his face, then whitened it, then covered it with a masque of slipping characters, unreadable and distant; he swallowed hard, and grief flooded, blocking his digestion, halting his speech. He wanted to go home, and his mind blanked. He checked his Bradshaw.

Walking, swinging a thurible, head down, the smoke in a cloud around his shoulders. He walks alone, humming, his head a pohutekawa, peruked, he puckers, pukes, passively to pass. He's all alone and has no other; no son, no sister, and no brother. Walking was impossible in this gravity — besides, he wanted to go home, to return to his river. His gill-flaps were gummed together with some sort of nervous fluid, unpleasant. His tears were saltless. He had a feeling, and murmured softly. The ship wouldn't turn for him, he knew.

He told no-one, travelling, now, under the rose.

"A Nurosanu" was originally published in *Adding Colours to the Chameleon* (2016, Wisdom's Bottom Press).

Peter Wortsman

Children's Day in the Maldives

It had been a bad time for Tim. Ditched by his girlfriend, Tina, suffering the first tingle of a toothache, a sudden crippling attack of lumbago in the lower back, and just that morning having stepped in a fresh heap of dog droppings on his way to the Korean grocery store that turned out to be closed when he got there, the foul scent of which infused his cramped studio apartment, and furthermore facing a disconnect notice from Con Ed for non-payment, all in a flash flood of calamity that threatened to sweep the little that was left of his waning confidence along with it, he nevertheless held firm.

Ailing in body and soul, Tim hobbled to the kitchen alcove, intending at this ungodly hour of 4AM—insomnia was another recent affliction—to fix himself a cup of hot tea, when, glancing at the calendar on the wall, he noticed it was Children's Day in the Maldives. It made him perk up to think that somewhere on this miserable godforsaken planet someone was celebrating. Why not join in? Yes, indeed, why not extend the Maldivian Children's Day festivities to his rented refuge in downtown Manhattan!

The calendar, courtesy of UNICEF, the one thing Tina left him the day she walked out while he was still asleep, with a hastily scribbled note on a yellow Post-it: "There's a world outside your self-obsessed cocoon," was all he had to go on. It would, he decided, if he let it, lead him out of the slump he was in. Each boxed-in date, a window in time and space, announced a distant to do. Not a box was blank. Tomorrow was Joan of Arc Day in France, which gave him a rise, thinking of the pale white, freckle-faced girls in short plaid skirts and bobby socks at the Catholic School of the same name, that had made him briefly consider conversion in early adolescence. The day after that was Ascension, or if you preferred, the Cricket Festival in Italy, followed by the Hindu holy day of Teej.

Tim hazarded a chuckle.

The hell with doom and gloom! From now on, he decided, it'll be non-stop celebration. It didn't trouble him in the least not to have the slightest idea how the Hindus in India did up Teej, or not to know just what Italians did to mark Cricket Day, though he vaguely associated it with the ethereal voice of Jiminy Cricket singing "When You Wish Upon a Star." I'll invent my own rituals, he decided.

On his Maldivian Children's Day Celebration, he resolved, it is customary to drink hot cocoa. Moreover, while dosing two spoonfuls of cocoa powder—it had to be two—and while waiting for the water to boil the reveler customarily rubs his stomach counter-clockwise and pats his head.

And so it went.

In the next fortnight Tim frolicked for each happy box on the calendar: the Caribou Festival in the Philippines, the Jewish Shavuot (which is also, incidentally, Teacher's Day in Belize) and World Communications Day.

Wednesday was Buddha's birthday, and so on Wednesday he sat in a modified lotus position, not quite managing to twist his knees into a proper yogic paperclip, all day under a tall tree, and not just any tree, but the towering "hangman's elm" at the northwest corner of Washington Square Park, refusing to be bothered by beggars, backache, proselytizing Evangelicals and Chasidim, the rapidly dwindling balance in his bank account—he was also unemployed—or anything else. For how could one possibly dwell on such mundane matters on Buddha's birthday?

The following day was Youth and Sports Day in Turkey, and though Tim suffered a sagging gut, not having set foot in a gym since junior high school, and had been mediocre at every game he ever set a bat or racket to, he lit a torch—or rather, worked his way, one by one, through the matches in the matchbook from the Minetta Tavern, a landmark Italian eatery, now defunct, to which he had once taken his ex, striking each with great pomp and holding it aloft as he pranced, in boxer shorts and t-shirt, around his studio apartment, his private take on the Olympic torch passing ceremony.

The day after that was an unnamed National Holiday in the Cameroons, which Tim marked by eating bananas imported from Costa Rica. (Remember, he was the self-proclaimed high priest of all this merriment, he and he alone made and broke the rules.)

There were days like Saturday, when he had oodles of holidays to pick from: Luilak in Holland, the Moslem Eid Al Adha, and Armed Forces Day in the States, among others. Given the Dutch heritage of erstwhile New Amsterdam, feeling more inclined to celebrate Luilak—even though Peter Stuyvesant, the first Dutch governor, had been a rabid Anti-Semite—he went out and purchased a dozen yellow tulips which he plunked in a jug and admired all day until the petals dropped.

That Sunday being a big deal in Yemen, a country perennially torn by civil war, as well as the Armenian Pentecost, and Mother's Day in the Dominican Republic, Tim wrapped a bed sheet around his flabby torso and plunked a pillow case on his head—his own private homage to Yemen, a place, he felt, that needed his support.

And so it went, through Pfingstmontag and Slavic Script and Bulgarian Culture Day, to Children's Day in Italy, which came on a Wednesday.

But when Tim woke the following morning and glanced at the calendar, ready to do things up right, he was mortified to find the box blank. Not a party, nothing doing round the globe—just a plain, ordinary, empty, miserable Thursday of the kind he'd known in abundance. And suddenly this whole holiday celebrating business went hollow. All the smiling hurt his cheek muscles. The tingle in his tooth intensified into a full-fledged ache. Tremors of pain shot up and down his back. Wincing, he retired to bed with a scowl of quiet despair, his constant and ever faithful mistress who had been there waiting it out, a flickering candle on the window sill of his heart.

And even though the next day was Children's Day in Nigeria, Tim lay in bed, staring in a paralyzing bout of despondence at the ceiling, where he noticed a new crack radiating outward and a green mold growing since last he looked.

"Children's Day in the Maldives" is excerpted from a new collection of Wortsman's short fiction, *Footprints in Wet Cement*, forthcoming from Pelekinesis in 2017.

P. K. Garrison

Sideshow Membrane

Long reedy hair receding from a drawn and waxy face; pinched, sunburned shoulders protruding through his white muscle-T like bones through a bandage; scrawny neck scraping, whenever Zeth leaned back in his chair, the handle of the frozen-yogurt machine. A candied beet, he decided, stabbing one with his fork, is not unlike a bleeding Eucharist nourishing a pale tongue. Having just dropped his mother Esta off at her church group, Zeth had been taking the less-scenic route home when he'd spotted the colorful restaurant beneath a circle of shopping-mall lamps. Its bright sherbet colors had acted like cold ice on his cavities—an acutely agreeable twinge not unlike the kind he gave himself every other night, just before his bath, by perforating the worst patches of acne with a comb. He had stopped only for dessert, but the price was the same no matter how much one ate, and Esta's casserole, another burnt offering to her visiting brother Bus, had tasted like baked kitty litter topped with crumbled matches. Zeth loaded up on buffet items. The only seat, unless he wanted to sit beside a stranger, placed him inches in front of the dessert table, where children kept bumping the back of his chair as they abused the handle of the yogurt machine. He wished he had waited for Esta at home. He'd been looking forward to a beer, slice of bundt cake, maybe, and a couple of sitcoms while waiting to retrieve the tiny woman from her weekly supplication. He imagined seeing Esta now through the greasy restaurant window, toddling toward him like an angry goose; she was forever coming at him, grabbing at him, stretching out the collars of his T-shirts to pull him down far enough to sniff his breath.

One of the kids banged an elbow into Zeth's temple. Still, it was probably no picnic back home, where Uncle Bus was probably eclipsing the TV right this minute with his flabby back, no doubt having pulled a folding chair within a few feet of the set so he could watch his wrestling close up. Thanks to his uncle's visit, this was the first night in a hundred that Zeth hadn't spent at least a couple of hours with his beer and remote. He pondered the word "remote"; had any control he'd ever had been anything but? As if on cue, some brat smeared a chocolate paw print on the shoulder of Zeth's favorite T-shirt, the "wife beater" with the smoking-chimp decal Esta had given him for his last birthday. He liked the tawdry pedigree the shirt suggested, the pitiful glances it elicited in passers-by.

Having just sipped from his plastic child-sized glass of soapy root beer, Zeth choked as the kid's hand slapped his back. The real beer, which he had paid for with his own hard-won money he'd earned down at the bowling alley, was probably being guzzled by Uncle Bus right this minute, and the restaurant, unfortunately, didn't serve alcohol. Catered, Zeth surmised as he perused the lime-green carpeting and ripped Pleather booths, mostly to elderly diabetics. Through a nearby window, he watched the Triple-X Book Emporium's flashing neon lights, beneath which hung a hand-painted placard reading, "Why wait for the movie?"

Across the aisle from where he was seated, an Amish girl in a long olive dress, hair pinned up, was handing an elderly woman in a white paper hat a cup of bread pudding. The girl reminded Zeth of so many of his cousins—drab, gluey girls over whom he had nevertheless wasted many nights gratifying himself into dirty tube socks.

After three bowls of ice cream topped with colored cereal, Zeth drove back to the church, a miniature replica of Spain's Seville Cathedral. Never completed, the church's lopped towers, like air-raid victims, carved a morose figure from the cloudless sky. Not spotting Esta on the steps, he parked across the street so he could gaze up at the magnificent floral tracery of the large circular stained-glass window. He had always admired the magisterial arrogance of the place; the idea of *assuming* one's importance, like the Pope did, made his heart race, though Zeth would never tell Esta that for fear she might start dragging him to Mass again. His mother had stopped forcing her son to attend Mass years ago because he had embarrassed her so many times before both God and man, chewing his gum too loudly or sleeping, or else mimicking the priest's rehearsed, stilted gestures in miniature. She chalked her son's behavior up to heathen genes inherited from his father. What was taking Esta so long, anyway? He stared for a long while at the empty-eyed cherub heads gilding the uppermost cornice, seeing in them the furious though eerily bloodless aftermath of some chimerical battle in the heavens, until he was suddenly startled by the familiar rattling of her quad cane across the passenger side door.

* * * * *

"The men of Sodom, both old and young, all the people from every quarter, surrounded Lot's house demanding carnal knowledge of the two angels taking refuge under the shadow of Lot's roof." Bus closed his sister's Bible: "No wonder I never read this shit," he muttered to himself. After some effort, he stood and, balancing himself, wobbled slowly to the painted bookshelf and placed the Bible into its allotted space, fanning out the pages a bit on either side to hide the magazines he'd brought with him. Then he lumbered down the hall to the top of the stairs. "Breakfast ready yet?" he called down. When he got no response, he wandered back to the guestroom and turned on the clock radio. A decent weather report for today, he thought, as he listened; maybe go out after a bit. That lazy-brained nephew should be gettin' up soon. Maybe lie to him about the weather, say it's goin' to rain, maybe put a nasty move on him while the sister's out to church.

From his bed, Zeth smelled fried bologna and black chicory coffee, the same as Esta made every Sunday morning before Mass. Having his uncle as a guest meant there might be eggs, too, or at least toast with grape jelly. He closed his biology book and retrieved the Sunday *Times*; he'd circled only one personal ad this week, a long one from a woman overseas, a poor Siberian Christian invoking the mercy of wealthy American saviors. Zeth liked the fact that, despite her self-proclaimed poverty, she had paid fifty American cents per word for the longest personal ad he'd ever seen: "My name it is Selva I am 18 y.o., single live in Bishkek in Russian Federation. Is capital Kyrgyzstan. Is magic mountain. Ethnic group is Russian, astrology Libra, faith is Christian but is no matter you faith, astrologic, ethnic. English is no so good money too but. I do no smoke but do drink little bit can stop. Here my stats they are height 172 cm weigh 56 kg brown eyes and hair too brown. I like walk in mountain but you have no close mountain okay. I believe miracle. Like listen pop music, sneak in discotheque, shaping fitness. Like favourite pet is dog color light blue. My life is no so good now but you help too okay? Favourite pet I say but not said that I like other animal too. But not vampire bat, no way how. Many interest including long walk, moving, reading, musical, cooking, housework in house. My life priority for decency also too humour. Am studding in university also work as model for model agency I swear but also too making ends meeting as cleaning woman. See basis for ideal partner between woman and man inside mutual understand and also trust I hope. . .." The entire ad comprised more than half a page, in the *Times*! If Zeth could find a way to get rid of his uncle, Selva could sleep in the guestroom. Probably Russian Orthodox, but Zeth might find a way to convince Esta that Selva was the product of one of the Christian missionaries currently flooding Eastern Europe. Beneath Selva's ad stood a single, boldfaced line Zeth had missed the first time around. It read, "Cool cutie just chillin', hanging out, waiting for the right guy—Jen." Having long ago cracked the personals' mailbox code, Zeth guessed this Jennifer probably lived only a couple of towns over. But he much preferred Selva.

* * * * *

What's keeping the two of them? Esta wondered as she leaned against the stove, lighting another cigarette from one of the burners. Don't have the sense to use the snuffers God give 'em. Sleepin', no doubt. Probly hung over. Don't work a day between 'em. That Bus keeps comin' to visit, start rubbin' off permanent. Well, any day now, any day. She swatted at some breadcrumbs on the counter that she mistook for dead flies, then started for the foot of the stairs. "Come on now," she tried to shout, hoarse from practicing her hymns too loudly in the bathtub.

After breakfast, Bus offered to wash the dishes, provided his nephew dry. Thankful, Esta went off to make herself look repentant.

"Weatherman says heavy rain today," Bus said, handing his nephew a plate.

Zeth nodded.

"So, boy, your mother tells me yer studyin' zoology."

"Yeah," said Zeth.

"Wanna work with animals, huh?"

"Yeah."

"Runs in the family, I guess."

Later, when Zeth returned from driving his mother to church, Bus followed him around the house repeating the phony weather report and asking if his nephew had plans for the day. When Zeth came out of the bathroom tying his hair into a ponytail, his uncle was waiting for him in the hallway.

"You goin' out?" Bus said.

"Why?" said Zeth, descending the stairs.

"No special reason," Bus said, hurrying behind. "Just the rainstorm, remember?"

"It's okay," said his nephew. "I'm taking the car."

Bus followed him to the driveway in his sister's bathrobe, yanking at an imaginary tie until he realized it didn't have one. Revealed to his nephew, and anyone else in the neighborhood who cared to look, was the centerpiece of his many intricate and multicolored tattoos: a giant pink squid snatching a purple monkey from a ginkgo tree. "You wanna wrestle?" Bus suggested, flexing his snake-painted forearms.

Zeth stood with the car door open. "Why?"

Just for fun," said Bus. "Fun in the sun."

"Yeah, the sun," said Zeth, looking at the sky. "I thought you said it was going to rain."

"*Goin'* to," Bus said. "A little later on. So you wanna wrestle?" He was becoming excited, a hard red nipple visible through an opening in the robe. "I remember," he continued, dancing like a prizefighter, "when you was no bigger than a piglet's nut."

Zeth climbed into his car and drove away, watching his uncle wave goodbye in the rearview, sunlight glistening off his false teeth while his sister's robe flapped open and shut in the breeze.

At least Bus had the house to himself for a while. Good thing Esta always stayed for choir practice. He raided the refrigerator, spreading margarine onto congealed bricks of casserole and washing them down with swigs from the milk jug. When he was finished eating, Bus admired himself in the refrigerator door. His sister's chiffon robe, soaked through with sweat, fell off one shoulder and clung to his wet skin as he went through the house sniffing for accoutrements. He rifled through closets and cupboards and cabinets, littering the floors with toiletries and first-aid supplies and women's shoes. What if there ain't time to clean it all up once I'm done? he wondered. Could be the end of the free ride. Only family in the whole damn world, and he had planned on an extra-long visit this time. But who was to say what was worth it and what weren't? The thought someone catching him in drag, of finally being allowed to let it all hang out, so to speak, held none of the excitement for him that it did for the other "girls" he knew; yet the idea of losing his only remaining family, the last half-acre of good, hard earth beneath his feet, was simultaneously terrifying and exhilarating.

He tried on Esta's fake fur and smoked several of her slim menthol cigarettes, whispering lines from old movies until he became bored and plopped down in front of the TV just as the credits were running atop some children's cartoon whose characters were sinking into quicksand.

* * * * *

That evening the three sat at the dinner table passing crustless white bread and fried eggs and buttered hotdogs back and forth across the table, Zeth's mother Esta, a smudge of ashes still visible on her forehead, the only one who spoke more than a few polite words.

". . .shoulda seen that handsome young priest up there this mornin', mmm mmm, yes sir, somethin' special when *that* one gets goin', all dressed up in his best vestments and hollerin' like his pants is on fire." As she spoke, one of her spindly legs crept out from beneath the tablecloth, dragging a web of loose, torn nylon. Zeth looked at his uncle, who sat ripping hotdogs into shreds and swilling orange pop. There was still a smear of rouge across Bus's bulging cheek that his myopic sister couldn't see. Zeth shook his head and began cutting his meat with his plastic knife. He had already sent the letter to Selva's mailbox; now all there was to do was wait.

"Ya know," Bus said, "I was wonderin' where I put that old picture album."

"Easy, Bus," said his sister, lighting a cigarette. "And I thought you said ya threw that old thing out years ago."

"Thought I did," Bus said. "You know the one," he said, "from the boy's daddy's side, with all them attractive pictures."

"Buster Swanson," Esta warned.

"I think I know right where it is, matter of fact," Bus went on. "Couldn't hurt the boy t'know what tree he clumb down from, now could it? Maybe I'll just fetch—"

"That's enough!" his sister said, crushing her cigarette into her paper plate. She stood to show she was serious, but the effect was diluted by the fact that she was no taller than she had been seated (she sat on a stack of books wrapped with duct tape just so she could reach the table). "You'll leave this house I hear one more word about that durn album," she said. "You think long and hard 'bout that." She began clearing the table, Bus leaning back in his chair and grinning. He broke all but one tong off his plastic fork and began picking at his dentures, eyes following his sister through the swinging kitchen door. "So when do ya want me," he said to his nephew, sucking juice from his thumb, "to fetch that album for ya?"

* * * * *

A great ripple stirs from its nest far beneath purgatorial skies, squall line a high-flown reflection of the parting of a curtain through which the silhouette of a four-fingered grip dangles trinkets onto a long, black tongue. Blaise the Magnificent practicing, extending the esophagus, hot tears lacerating a sun-stretched grin. All around him more tents exploding, concessions springing up, rides creaking to life, everything creating a maze through which herds of bleary-eyed mooncalves chase after contortionists rolled into tight nylon balls.

"Carnival?" said Zeth, letting it sink in, trying not to think too hard so as to allow the word its own tilt and spin.

"Called 'em 'mud shows' back then," Bus said. "You surprised?" He began laughing as he handed his nephew the album. "You didn't buy all that crap 'bout 'We comes from Alabamy with banjos on our knees' now, did ya? You got it bad on *both* sides, actually. Ain't just yer daddy. Take a look at that mother o' yours; you think they let midgets like her wander the streets just like normal people back in the day? No way, José. And how about yer old uncle Bus? Hu*mun*gous faggot floppin' round the world like some big, scary puppet. Nope, we had to serve our time just like yer daddy and his daddy before him. Only way to survive in those days. That's our lot, boy. Crap-panted oddballs squirmin' round the country like a bunch o' thievin' gypsies, climbin' up on stage to wiggle our revoltin' peculiars at the payin' gawkers. Bunch o' sex maniacs, too, your ancestors, sleepin' on top each other half the time like horny little maggots, lot of 'em drunk every night and wettin' theyselves through to the next fella. Sure glad I left *that* life."

Zeth opened the album to find scores of yellowed flyers and photographs coming unglued from the disintegrating pages, handwritten captions accompanying most of the photos, and a smudged, typewritten diary—exactly one hundred and fifty pages long—in the very back. Most of the photos depicted the carnival oddities to whom the subsequent diary was dedicated: "Otto the Petrified Man," whose skin was badly burnt from head to torso, sitting naked in a large washing tub full of viscous orange fluid while a bare-chested Indian girl scrubbed his scalp with a bar of lye; "Klossi the Ape Woman," a hirsute Jamaican sometimes referred to as "The Ugliest Woman in the World," "The Bear Spirit," or "The Nondescript," standing beside a glass case containing the embalmed corpse of her equally hirsute sister; a child polio victim sewn into potato sacking tightly cinched with cords at the ankles, waist and neck (billed as "The World's Largest Living Caterpillar," he lay atop a giant paper leaf inside an enormous mason jar, the sight of which, according to the sign, cost all of fifty cents because of the chance to see the boy transform into a butterfly); an androgynous, pipe-smoking Ubangi tribeswoman with lip discs the size of ashtrays, the top one holding a beer can; Bob Burns, the "Tallest Man in the World," trying to stand upright against a crippling arthritis, his face squeezed tight as if he could feel his organs collapsing beneath the weight of all those calcifying dinosaur bones, and yet just enough strength left to ham for the camera by dangling a rat he'd caught above his big, toothless jaws; "The Missing Link," a four-foot microcephalic Mexican-Indian supposedly captured by missionaries on a tropical island; Siamese twins called "The Two-Headed," flirtatious, crimson-haired teenage beauties holding what appeared to be identical dolls in their laps, but which the caption explained were actually miniature parasitic twins growing from their abdomens. Zeth was struck by the distant eyes of the performers, as if they had never imagined, even in their dreaming lives, that it might be possible to return the camera's gaze. In a group publicity photo, Zeth thought he noticed a family resemblance in a man who, despite the nice weather, sported a long red scarf around his neck. Standing behind a cluster of spangled female dwarves lifting sparklers over their heads, the man appeared to be preparing to blow out America's birthday cake. Row four, third from the right: Blaise The Magnificent. The caption at the bottom listed no surnames for any of the performers, only for the carnival's owner, a Mr. Bowering, the only member absent from the photo.

Bus later confirmed that Blaise the Magnificent was indeed a relation—Zeth's grandfather, in fact, and the one who had pieced the album together and written the diary. But Bus would not say which one, if any, was Zeth's father, or even whether his father had been involved with that particular carnival. Bus had been soliciting kisses in return for each shred of information, pushing a little harder each time; so when Zeth finally said thanks anyway, but he would try to figure things out for himself from that point on, he was relieved that his uncle let it go at that. For the time being, anyway.

* * * * *

sixteen june

nineteen hundred forty three. . .

worst camp 23 odd years//not even during the DEPression//inthe night the old biffy blew down to the pressure a summers werst storm//while its gettin rebuilt we use the pit dug by the Ostoman Brothers//inthe openair with some time gawkers peerin threw the slats a our little fence we complete our filthy comerce as Bowering sais//an not ten feet from the main concession//tonight I kin see DOris,s plump bottom squattin over a cloud a fat flies sharin a joke with Virga the gypsie fortuneteller//Klossi aches//The uclers has agrivated all cept what delicate skin a her palms an feet//there what they call toxins act like a emetic and some time like a diarrhetic sais doc she loses weight uses the pit but don't think she do it without losin no blood an tear//her husband he comb her face and kiss her sores waitin for her maybe to go in shock when he,ll finely maybe call the doctor back to there tent//he think misterBowering hasn,t yet give up on old Klossi who aint all that old//he make Klossi,s disease part a the act pu blish matchbook counts ahow supposely tics an lice an stagnant jungle pools has ravaged her skin//poor Klossi//whole year a that sufferin an she,d thought it was jus part a her misrable lot//twas the vomittin what brought the doctor//caughtsome guy pert near a month back piddlin the two headed//suppose I confess to a thrill not a big thrill but at first but seein him kiss one head then tother them long injun red locks tangle up in brite red nots and them danglin twins rattlin like they bout to snap off they bellies// I cough loud to frighten the stranger away then go into the two headeds tent on the pretens I,m alookin for my medcine//what in hell we want with your syrup sais the two headed all mad and frowny so I JUS SAIS THank ye an goodnight an lef outta there even if somethin powerful still was orderin me to stay//so many nights I went back look see if may be that stranger comeback for seconds but eventially jus end up layin on my cot sweatin and aswallerin down dust an tryin not to move much so certain parts don,t t ouch nothin but the covers////

* * * * *

Upset that his latest conflict with his uncle, a short-lived wrestling match in which he'd been forced to participate after being jumped coming in from the garage, had produced in him a short-lived erection, Zeth proceeded all the more vigorously with his plans to win Selva. The newspaper wouldn't respond to his repeated phone inquiries, but he just assumed his message had been forwarded to Bishkek, Kyrgyzstan, inside the Russian Federation, where channels of communication were a bit more clogged than in the West, so he determined hat he should therefore remain patient and would be hearing directly from his would-be correspondent within the coming weeks. Zeth pictured the guestroom lavishly decorated in dark velvets and satins, the shelves lined with brass baubles and marble figurines of famous Russian thinkers, a canopy bed that didn't squeak when you moved, pushed far away from the vent leading to the downstairs bathroom, and a majestic aria wafting up from the clock radio. It was a good thing he hadn't cut up *all* of Esta's credit cards.

After spending the day flipping through interior-design magazines and excerpts from Russian newspapers he'd copied at the library, Zeth fell asleep at the foot of his bed, his scraggly, dirty-blond locks draped across the clutter of unfinished pages. . .*A dizzying, emetic spectacle, as if he's just stumbled off a Tilt-A-Whirl, the lurid lights of the midway stinging the eyes and the eerie whistle of the calliope plucking away at the nerves and the thrill rides churning and churning and the fat wide-eyed clowns chasing little girls away from their parents while the nonpaying hoards crane their necks over the fence for the honey of the blade. . .wandering, now, from tent to tent, peering into each dark world as if into a forgotten corner of the devil's menagerie: double-jointed lesbians and weary dogmen resting their slobbering heads on quadruple amputees; exotic diseases creeping like vines up even more exotic appendages; grotesque examples of the excessive and the lacking, the profuse and the indeterminate, the diminutive and the gigantic; screams of rape blaring from tubas and trombones in the adjoining tent as the albuminous heinie of Princess Ulbra, the royal rope twirler, spins high above the ground, shitting a centrifugal torrent of popcorn into the kiddie's mouths; monstrous abortions flung from sleeping tents at growling packs of wild dwarves; even Uncle Bus himself, imperviously sealed inside ballerina costume and jumbo bear's head, twirling for a crowd of sailors, repelling from the light in the center of the stage out toward the audience and then rebounding off the imaginary fourth wall as if tethered to the bubble of some preposterous fart, that black phallic vacuum screaming silently beneath the ruffles of his skirt, sucking in all the muck and barbarity and lies of the universe as that diamond-emblemed fist snipes at one of the officers howling in the front row; and old Blaise, sorcerer of the ever-elastic intestines, extracting common objects rough from the void of the everyday world to transform them into the nutrients of an undreamt-of anatomy, gulping down pennies, costume jewelry, fish hooks, shards of broken carnival glass that teeter down his throat like satellites through a black hole—until it's time for the big finalé, in which Blaise the Magnificent, after dimming the lights and lapsing into a brief meditation, conjures the impression that he is slowly and carefully regurgitating the long, larval shadow of a mutant ancestry into a young boy's frozen yawn, at which point the dream is suddenly bitten off sharply as an umbilical cord.*

Zeth awoke to Esta's brusque voice singing an old hymn, a cold, measured anthem with no tongue but plenty of teeth—row upon row, like unstrung rosary beads sharpened to fine points—a voice gnawing its way through his metal floor register like the monsters that haunted him as a child.

He found his uncle asleep before a muted infomercial, its manic shifts in camera angle electrifying his uncle's wide forehead like the blue strobes of a silent burlesque. Zeth stood for a while behind the recliner with his eyes closed, imagining queues of fashionable gentlemen discreetly scratching themselves while they waited for their turn at the penny arcades. He opened his eyes, then closed them again, trying to remember what a full-nelson looked like, but all he could think of was Bus's favorite claim against the carnival: "Pretended to keep 'em in a jar, swear t'God. . .said they had the pecker a Jesus H. Christ Hisself in a goddamn mason jar. . .used t'show the Almighty's very own nicky-nacks in a dirty glass jar on the side of the consarn-ed road, I'm tellin' ya. . .it was supposed to be the very. . .." As the infomercial gave way to a regular old advertisement, Bus began to stir.

"What time's it?" he said, aware of someone in the dark.

"Quarter to three," said Zeth, guessing.

"Welp," said Bus as he stood up, "beddy-bye time, I suppose, 'less you wanna wrestle."

Zeth stepped back. "No thanks," he said.

"Okay, then," said Bus, stretching. "Give us a kiss goodnight?"

* * * * *

The weather forecast called for rain and lots of it. Zeth had just barely finished mowing the grass and trimming the hedges before the first sprinkles kissed the shiny red roof of his car.

At his mother's suggestion, and to Zeth's anguish, uncle and nephew spent the ensuing hours playing Parcheesi on the screened-in porch, the first few games tediously slow due to the number of times each player sent the other back to his home to start again.

"I win the next game, I get to hold it?" said Bus.

"What?" Zeth said. His uncle sat back with his hands behind his head, smiling.

"Oh, now," Zeth said, "come on. We were having a perfectly good time until now. Don't spoil it, Uncle Bus."

"I was just makin' a suggestion's all," Bus said, playing footsie with him beneath the card table.

"Is that all you think about?" said Zeth, retracting his feet back under his chair as far as he could.

"Is *what* all I think about?"

"Just go," said Zeth. "It's your turn."

"Say, boys," called Esta from the kitchen, "you're not drinkin', are ya now? Sounds like yer havin' far too much fun in there."

Through the screen Zeth watched the elm trees buckling to the wind, their trunks black beneath the dark clouds hanging low in the sky, the rain firing horizontally at their leaves, blasting many of them off their branches and into a growing sea of twisting leaves.

"What if I offer to pay for yer momma's medicine?" Bus offered, bumping one of Zeth's men off the board and plopping it back at the start.

"How'd you know about that?"

"Just do," Bus said. "So how 'bout it, handsome?

Zeth thought seriously about his uncle's offer while he moved his little man, each rung of the game board representing another step out of debt. When he was finished, he sat playing with a blackhead on his neck and trying not to look at his Uncle Bus. "What would I have to do?" he said.

"Not a cotton-pickin' thing," his uncle insisted, grinning, seeing an in. "Just let me hold it ten, twenty seconds tops is all."

"And you'll pay for her medicine for how long?"

"Long as I'm stayin' here," Bus promised.

"And I let you hold it, *just* hold it, and that's all?" Zeth said. He was suspicious. What pleasure could his uncle derive from holding a flaccid flap of skin. But, then, what if it gave Zeth an erection? The last time was because of the heated struggle itself, since he had never had even a fleeting homosexual thought, and that time his arousal had thankfully gone undetected by his uncle, who'd seemed more concerned with forcing his nephew to admit defeat and say "uncle." But what would Bus think if his holding it made it hard? Wouldn't he take that as a green light?

"It ain't like I couldn't force ya, ya know," said his uncle. "Could've done it long ago if I'd a mind to."

That was true. "Then why haven't you?" said Zeth.

"'Cause we's family, ya dimwit."

For the first time, Zeth wondered about all the times his uncle had thundered out of doorways and closets and out from behind furniture to put a wrestling move on him yet had never ventured beyond making him say things and begging for kisses. Once, Bus had suggested his nephew put makeup on him. He'd approached Zeth cradling a litter of Esta's lipsticks and powders and eye shadows while she attended a special evening mass for some holy day or other. Still reeling from a confrontation earlier that day, Zeth had complied, smearing rouge across his uncle's bloated cheeks and painting his lips a disturbing salmon color, lending Bus's otherwise androgynous face the nightmare-quality of a gynecological disaster. Zeth rolled the dice, still remembering. When he'd finished making his uncle up, Bus had become gentle, docile, complacent. He had removed the fake eyelashes with the tenderness of a real mother, as if peeling eggs for Zeth's breakfast. And never, not once, before or after the favor or at any other time they had fought, did Bus cross the imaginary boundary that Zeth lay awake nights fearing he would someday cross, the boundary line that represented the razor scar of Zeth's precarious life. Bus had never crossed it. Why?

"How about," said his uncle, tracing the periphery of his lips with one of the game pieces, "fifteen seconds, then? I won't stroke it nor nothin' 'less you say it's okay."

"Why *don't* you force me?" asked Zeth.

Bus put down the yellow game pawn. "That ain't what you're after, is it, boy?"

"I'm just wondering why you never have," Zeth said.

Bus got quiet. After a spell, as he moved to roll the dice, his nephew recalled all the ways he had imagined his uncle with other men: in rest-stop parking lots, one-hour motels, back alleyways, crammed into cars and broom closets and portable toilets full to the eyes with the stench of hair gel and dried excrement. But maybe none of it was true. Maybe Uncle Bus never actually followed through on any of his desires, preferring foreplay and frottage and the boundless world of fantasy to the act itself.

"Well?" said Zeth.

"Awfully quiet in there," Esta called, "make a person think somethin's up if a person don't know no better."

Bus watched the wind turn and blow the rain in through the screen, some of which doused his nephew's back. Zeth reached behind him and turned the crank that closed the windows. While his back was turned, his uncle began, slowly and softly, to recount everything. How he had traveled the world in the armed forces before joining the carnival, what a naval sergeant had done to him after discovering him with another soldier, nervously yelling for the enlisted men to hold Bus while he laid into his anus with a red-hot rifle barrel until there was nothing left but a black scar in the shape of a crooked smile. Also about his dishonorable discharge and his many odd jobs. About the carnival's advertisements for people who had suffered war wounds or industrial accidents, and about his days as a eunuch troubadour with a two-bit show out of Memphis that barely paid the bills and made him forget his dreams of reconstructive surgery, which, at any rate, wasn't very advanced in those days. And about his *essscape*—he emphasized the word, drawing it out breathlessly—from the carnival not long after his sister became pregnant with Zeth.

"I had to leave her behind on account o' her bein' slow with child and all," Bus insisted.

"What?" said Zeth.

"Yer mother. I had to leave her behind."

"But what does that have to do with—." Zeth paused, no longer concerned about his uncle's restraint. "And my father?" he asked, leaning across the card table.

"Well," Bus said, "I suppose it's time you know. He was just a mum's all.

Weren't no fault o' his."

"He was a what?" said Zeth.

"*R*etard," Bus said, picking up the dice. "The brainless what violated yer mamma. Now we gonna finish this confounded game or what?"

Zeth sat back, contemplating the thought for a long while. "I want proof," he said finally, standing.

"It's all in the album," said Bus, holding out the dice for his nephew. "One with them squirrely eyes and the short pants, peekin' out from behind yer granddaddy. Got 'im bits o' dried candy stuck to his clothes if you look real close. Playful as a kitten, yer daddy. Even managed a few tricks from time to time, as I recall."

* * * * *

tweny one september

nineteen hundred forty three. . .

they don't see theyselves as no deviants, but mister bowering say its important for the public to which is why they ain,t allowed t'go into town lessin theyget seen doin ordinary thing like shoppin or eat in restarants sos they stay put//some folk fixin take off tomorrow say BOWEring shoulda fix the privy ne,er did and sais why not callin BOwering a devil an some others tired a goin in the pit//swallered a handful a baby teeth a fortnight back some lady real goodlookin legs kindy like PRINCess Ulbras tellin its good truly good luck better even then the tooth fairy so I wash em down witha shot a rye felt little odd eatin somethin human I aint no canibal noway nohow//BOwering say no toys for the two headed sose they jus plays with theyself pet them dead kids what flop out they stomachs NO NO sais Bowering can,t cut em off cut em off they pay only half they weight no kids to play with ceptin the polio an he gettin werse an werse ever day//better off then Klossi still she got what look like figs all over where the hair sprout//so many doctors all bout everwhere nosin round ever tent say howdy do wanna see down yer throat wanna check all the vitals waitin fer ya to die put ya in a glass case wheel ya round the south//disected the petrified last night matter fact right here in the next tent while I'm atryin t'keep down a pair a ladies heels an aint even worth it 3 paid customers is all everbody wanna see how many rings the petrified got when they slice him open//BOwering chargin a full dollar fer a peek an money besides from those what did the autopsy//I tell bowering aint choppin me up fer nobody git me a concrete slab put over my final restin place keep the gravediggers away BOwering sais do whatcha gotta do//tar an feather them blasted what they call freakophile other day the one what I seen kissin the two headed an couple friends his lurkin round by the polios tent swingin some sorta fancy camera tell me aint doin nothin I sais you aint part the show you gotta go always tryin tgetta picture else steal from else have they way with some body differnt an them I don't like it much know the truth one time ugly what I call ugly woman slip in my tent sais howdy do talkin bout I so verily hansome seen my show dont member how many time kicks them pretty yellow heels off start takin off a dress a big sunflower dress my wife she hate sunflowers tell her my wife hates sunflowers somethin aweful but it don't suade her none jus lay back in my bed my bed mind ya take a handful a what god give me squeez real tight till I wanna kinda say okeedoke take all I kin do jus say you gotta go sweet honey I am truly sorry swear tgod on a stacka bibles thick as a elephant foot honey sweety I DO I really do PREtty thing an not lyin either jus cuzer face is what I call ugly don,t meaner figure ain,t nice look so good in that dress prolly look a whole might better out it whynt you put er back on now I sais the wife be comin here any minut//Klossi she aint long fer this old world not long now doctors everwhere I think she woulda made it too lot longer anyway they hadnt gone an burn out her tubes while they sposed be jus examnin//folk what aint even doctor goin through her depilatories an personal fancies an what not with her husband standin right there they say her husband hooo-ey he have to be restrain start yellin aint gonna be no yunguns keep her peppy spirit alive Klossi jus lay there they say sayin nothin maybe cry little few saw er rubbin them furry eyes abit docs didnt even patch them lesions what broke open stinkin up the tent an Klossi howlin an scratchin day and night BOWEr ing prolly fixin make that part the act too//Klossi no she aint long now an besides folks fixin up an leave this outfit pert near any day I spect////

* * * * *

New York Times
Personals Department
Selva -- Box 1983402
New York, NY 10018

Dear Selva:

I'm still anxiously awaiting your response to my letter of March 3rd, a response which I'm sure will be even more beautiful than your ad which appeared in the February 28th issue of the *New York Times*. As I said in my first letter, I was touched by your interests and your passion and your, well, by everything in your advertisement, which is, as I said in my first letter, the longest I've ever read. That's why I'm writing you again—that, and in case you didn't receive my initial letter. I know it sometimes takes a long while to get communications through to your part of the world, but I thought that maybe, since it's been awhile, it might be wise to send you a new letter. I hope you have someone to translate this for you.

So how are you doing? Things are fine with me, although since my last correspondence, my mother, Esta, whom you'll remember was living with me for a while, has regretfully passed on, so you don't need to worry about putting anyone out, being a nuisance and such, if that's something you were worrying about. I don't know. Also, you may be interested to know that Esta, generous as she always was, has left me a reasonably large inheritance, including several assets which I'm sure would make you comfortable in your new American home, where you would be free forever to do as you choose. You don't need to make any immediate decisions regarding the seriousness of our relationship, as I am prepared and happy to get to know you as a friend first. My poor Uncle Bus, whom I believe I also mentioned in my earlier correspondence, says to say "hi," but he regrets that he will not be able to make your acquaintance when you arrive, since he has decided to accept a lucrative position as ambassador to a very important country not too far from your own beloved shores.

So as you can see, Selva, all of the comforts and conveniences of good American living await you in your charming new home, though you may need to ring the buzzer a few times when you get here. I've been meaning to get it fixed, and I guess now, with all of Esta's riches having been transferred to my primary bank account, I'm running out of excuses to put it off any longer.

If you get the chance, please write or call me in advance so I know what day and time to expect you. My telephone number and address are enclosed.

Very truly yours,

Zeth Fogel

* * * * *

Bus folded the letter and put it in his shirt pocket. He'd been snooping for other treasure when he'd spotted the colorful stationery half-folded on his nephew's desk.

"What are you doing?" said Zeth, appearing in the doorway.

Whereas he otherwise may have felt guilty, Bus considered the letter's contents absolution for any transgressions he may have committed. "I was just wonderin'," he said, taking the letter out of his pocket and holding it teasingly out before his nephew, "how yer mamma's gonna react once that commie love slave of yers parachutes into town."

* * * * *

Zeth shut Esta's bedroom door and peered through the keyhole. Standard precautions, since Uncle Bus was downstairs watching television and Esta didn't need to be picked up from church for another hour. He occasionally enjoyed the luxury of his mother's queen-sized bed, with its abundance of bedding. Glancing up at his mother's hand-painted wall plaque ("Lips that touch wine will never touch mine."), behind which she had stuffed the palms passed out at church, he stripped out of his jeans and T-shirt, piling all of Esta's pillows and Afghans and blankets as well as her thick eiderdown comforter in the center of the bed, then backed up all the way to the door again before taking a running leap into the pile. For a long while he lay there smelling the blend of smoke, sweet perfume, perspiration and fabric softener and thinking of Selva, with her blood-red resolve and her long, hairy legs—they would be very long and muscular as a Bolshevik, he imagined, densely seeded like a good lawn and weighted with flat feet that put one in mind of tanned deerskin. He drifted in and out of slumber, rocking first gently like a fetus and then like an infant in its crib slowly becoming aware of its own body, and eventually vibrating to and fro against the thick waves of fabric as if riding a wild beast through a hurricane, the frenzy transporting him to a ubiquitous sea into which he could pour himself unendingly and without any sense of loss. He rarely achieved orgasm—pre-ejaculate discharges and even retrograde climaxes on occasion, which shook his insides like so much cargo—but seldom the smooth, milky flow of a healthy young man. So he *was* different, even on the inside. But perhaps with Selva. . ..

Realizing he'd been in Esta's bed for nearly an hour, Zeth rushed to put everything back in its place so he would be on time to pick her up. After he had dressed and satisfied himself that everything was as it had been, he sat down for a few last moments on the freshly made bed, smoothing out the comforter until it was nearly as firm as a church pew. Standing to go, he luckily remembered the sheet of Naugahyde Esta used to keep everything fresh, the one he'd removed upon entering the room. Stooping to retrieve it from underneath the bed, he slid it neatly back over the comforter the way he remembered it. Predating Zeth, the plastic was worn thin and broken here and there, reminding him for some reason of a delicate locust wing. He imagined Esta slipping out of bed as from a shell before buzzing off down the long, dark hallway, trailing behind her the cold, viscous residue of a recurring pestilential nightmare in which her little limbs were being plucked off one by one by the Gargantuan hand of the Lord.

* * * * *

The following morning, while lying in his own tiny twin bed reading his grandpa's diary, the scent of hot-cross buns wafting up through the heating vent, Zeth began to feel something tickling his body, something writhing in the sheets. He jumped up, throwing back the covers, but there was nothing, only the sense that Selva had been there, that the sheets were crawling with her armpit hairs, the pillowcases pullulant with shreds of cheap glamour photos and fat lice. He wanted to call out, "Where are you, Selva?" as if he had just held her in his arms before she'd slipped away, into the covers. Zeth sat up, imagining her there beside him, stroking his thigh, sliding her rough scrubwoman's hand up between his legs until she had a good hold on it and asking in broken English for *just leetle beet dollars for the shop today*. Three beards and a mustache, Selva. The rest all legs in the air and a rubbery twat full of goulash opening for its daily ration of bread. Zeth went to his desk and swept the letters into the trash can.

* * * * *

tweny one september

nineteen hundred forty three. . .

Klossi she dead deader then the petrified by the look a her take her way ina freezer truck look like a icecream truck her husband he cain,t go he fall round wail like a baby even after they give him his shot a sleep wail all the way everbody jus stop an look an lissen even both heads a the two-headed say Klossi dead now Klossi gone Klossi big parta show dont bother set nothin up that day BOWERIng bouncing round throw a fit sais we cain,t go no funeral sposed be puttin on a show, show must go on jus gotto go on say he git hisself another monkey gal a better one even say she be even uglier then Klossi say Klossi dead now git back to work. . .

* * * * *

"What in the name o' heaven an' hell are you doin', damn it?" said Esta, making the sign of the cross with her cigarette. "You can't just take me off the board like that and send me back home."

"It's in the rules, Esta," said Zeth.

"Ain't ya never played Parcheesi, sis?" Bus asked.

"I try not to spend too much leisure time, Bus—sloth's one o' the seven, *you* know that."

"That's fair enough," Bus said. "But now you gonna roll, it's yer turn?"

Despite his sister's numerous requests, Bus had refused to slip his shirt back on, and Zeth found himself mesmerized by the bright illustrations of incongruous shapes and species inhabiting his uncle's bloated, hairless landscape. Some of them looked vaguely like animals with human features, and that gave Zeth the heebies.

"You smell like bourbon," Esta blurted at her brother, taking up the dice.

"'swhat I bathe in, sweetheart," said Bus, flexing his flabby arms. "You like?"

"Knock off that nonsense," said his sister, sucking on her cigarette. "We ain't from the hills, remember?"

While Esta moved around the board, Zeth stared through the screen door at a squirrel fending off a blue jay from the feeder.

"No, ma'am," Bus said. "We folks from the valley, nooooo doubtaboutit!" Bus spoke with a wide grin, flashing his sister those big bright false teeth she had helped pay for. His tongue looked to Zeth like blood purling over ice. His sister glared back at him for a long spell, and there was little more said for the remainder of the game.

* * * * *

Easter came and went without a reply from Selva, and as spring expanded into a hot, dry summer, Zeth found himself writing to her again. He'd retrieved the letters from the garbage and expanded the best parts into longer ones—big, solipsistic, meandering lies about how empty the house felt with Esta and Uncle Bus long gone, about the bulletin board above his bed reserved for the photographs she had never sent, about how difficult it was to sleep on warm summer nights imagining another body beside one's own, their thighs bonding together with sweat as the crickets chirped them off to sleep. Occasionally Esta would burst into his room without knocking, and if her son wasn't fast enough, she would catch him hiding something in his desk drawer and demand to know what it was. "It's not alcohol, Esta," Zeth would insist, blocking the drawer with his knee. Ever since Bus had told him what Esta never would—that both her parents had been abusive drunks—Zeth had alternated between compassion and resentment. At times, rather than excusing or even explaining Esta's behavior, the revelation merely confirmed her inherent weakness. She was trying to protect him from something she'd seen go very wrong, perhaps, but in the process she had suppressed every other impulse to life. The fact that she occasionally allowed beer in the house was a mystery, or perhaps it was some kind of sign that one of those psychologists might seize upon in order to read between the lines of Esta Swanson. Whenever Zeth remembered to lock the door, Esta banged and banged until he couldn't stand it any longer, yanking him down to her level the moment he let her in and jamming her tiny nose inside his mouth.

When Zeth wasn't writing or reading, he was sleeping. The yard work was suffering, and his mother was becoming increasingly impatient with him. He rarely bathed anymore, sometimes didn't even remember to wash his hands after using the toilet, and the open scabs on his writing hand were beginning to stink. Standing before the bathroom mirror after tying his hair back, he would search for whiteheads, sending them screaming into the dirty glass without bothering to wipe them off. A large red pimple had been swelling in the center of his forehead for weeks. So he was cutting his first horn. This was how it was going to begin.

*****

The album's last photos revealed his withered grandfather in a convalescent home, sprawled naked and skeletal on a bare, stained mattress, tubes dangling all around him yet not one connected to a vein, not even a feeding tube to keep him alive, the only sign of life a disembodied hand—a young, gentle-looking hand—in a single photo, feeding Blaise's drooping mouth with an eye dropper. As if grandpa, thought Zeth, were a baby bird fallen from its nest. Zeth was sitting on the porch this time, no longer afraid that Esta might discover him with the album. Outside, a one-footed cardinal hopped around the empty feeder pecking at the air. Zeth turned back to the album.

According to the diary, they had first noticed the tumors (though they hadn't identified them as such) shortly after introducing the x-ray machine into the act, which authenticated the performance and made what had always been a big attraction the *main* attraction on the midway. Blaise and his assistant—a student medical technician who, in return for a small stipend to help finance his education, had agreed to spend a few days teaching Blaise how to operate the machine by himself—had apparently thought little at first of the swollen blind eyes staring back at him from Blaise's illuminated intestines: just a sampling of the many strange objects the man had swallowed over the years. Only the largest inflammation had given the medical student pause, but he eventually determined that it must be an extra kidney, simply another in the sideshow freak's seemingly infinite arsenal of anatomical novelties, no doubt, and if not a kidney, then something for a full-fledged physician to sort out, if one had a mind to, which the carnival's resident doctor apparently did not. So the student eventually left, and Blaise worked the x-ray machine himself, popping shoe laces and car keys and hissing cockroaches and whatnot down his gullet like tasty sundries to the carnival crowds' delight, occasionally sneaking peaks at his digestive system projected on the wall behind him as if he were peering into a frightening though strangely familiar universe. It would be another three years before anyone guessed the truth of that universe, since Blaise had experienced no pain, no symptoms of any kind, most of the growths being entirely benign if not all that pleasant to look at writ large on the canvas walls of the Big Top.

The captions of the hospital photos included the names of the various tumors beside their approximate sizes and degrees of metastasis, spelled "mesostasis" in his grandfather's semiliterate scrawl. With creatures like Teratoids, primitive Neuroectodermals, and Heterologous T. ravaging his grandfather's internal landscape, Zeth pictured a miniature universe of floating dinosaurs preying on the flesh of Blaise's deteriorating organs, the great "Mesostasis" period in which all things ate smaller things until there were no more things.

Bus appeared in the doorway to the porch, startling his nephew and causing him to crumple the page in his hand. How long had Uncle Bus been standing there?

"Don't fret none, Zeth," said Bus, recognizing the last photographs in the album. "I'm sure if them nasty eats hadn't got the better of him, them cosmic rays probly woulda."

Turning to his uncle, Zeth sat up straight and looked him in the eyes. "What happened to my father?"

"Awe shoot," said Bus. "Don't go an' ask me that now. How the hell should I know? He weren't even part o' the act, just cleaned the shithouse and fed the animals for his meals—they didn't even care what he did to them poor beasts as long as he finished his chores, didn't really pay him no mind. Till he gone an' forcibly spoilt yer mamma, that is; then they sent him away, into the woods where he belongs. How should I know where he's at now?"

Closing the album, Zeth thanked his uncle and went up to his room to compose one last letter.

* * * * *

JEF 73

New York Times
Personals Department
Selva -- Box 1983402
New York, NY 10018

Dear Selva:

I am a liar and a monstrosity, truth be told, so you'll want to be moving on. The man who wrote you all those love letters doesn't exist. The real Zeth Fogel was genetically engineered from the last drop of blood wrung from some cretin's coccyx they found embedded in amber. The real Zeth has only three teeth, and not two of them side by side. I have perfected gluttony to the point of weighing over three hundred pounds. I write with my left hand because I have no right, and I have to pay piano movers to come and carry me to my desk because I have no legs. Scattered all over my body are small boils which do a pretty good job of staying hidden most of the time but which flare up when I become sexually aroused. I try to lance them in my free time, of which there is plenty, but I can't reach them all. My skin, aside from the boils, is as soft as fresh dung, though I have abnormal pigmentation and chronic psoriasis that, together with my amputated lower half, lend me the enchanting appearance of a bloated reptile. At least that's what the cleaning lady says. "Lagarto," she screams at me as she brandishes her broom. In her calmer moments she says she wishes I had feet I could lift so she could sweep under them. Isn't that adorable? You should hear her say it in Spanish. I have no tail, though—nothing below the waist whatsoever—not even that, my angel. So you see why you'll want to be moving on, if you haven't already. I am handsome, though—that is, my face is, when my mouth is closed and I suck in my fat cheeks just so. I didn't lie about that. That's your greatest misfortune. In fact, I'm the most handsome man you would have ever laid eyes on. I am so handsome you would have to look away to keep from biting off your tongue.

I light fires with dirty laundry in my bedroom to circulate my blood, then drag myself across the floor to achieve an imaginary erection. My mother Esta, when she was alive, God rest her immortal soul, used to bathe me every day as if I were still an infant, pouring warm water over my scabs and stroking my thinning hair with her long, hard nails. She was so sensitive with me that whenever her hand swept between my legs, she would let it rest there for awhile, against my blunt, scarred pelvis, just so I could remember what it was like, for a few brief moments, to have something there, brushing against my thigh.

It was at those moments, Selva, that I felt I could have sodomized my own sister, had I a sister, or wiped my sperm on one of my own legs before they tossed it on the fire. But I know you'll forgive me, Selva, sweet Selva, because you know me better than anyone. You have loved me with a purity and a silence that only angels are said to possess. But know also that I would rape you too, Selva, were you here in my home, sitting at the table as my guest of honor, if only *because* you were here, so close, so curious, so eager to learn what can't be learned in ten-thousand lifetimes. And you *can't* be here. It's impossible. I don't exist. You don't exist. The table where you would eat your meals and the bed where you would call out to me don't at all exist. The doctors say I have only two weeks to kill myself, but I tell them I'm a master of foreplay, honed from years of unsatisfied passion. After that, after just two weeks, if I haven't mustered the courage to off myself, they say it will begin, slow and painful, the vermin's belly-crawl, my quest for a better body thanks to good old modern technology: six legs all the way into the dirt, shock of black hair blacker than the bile of the blackest insect, universal antennae for receiving every loving word ever spoken. And that's when I'll scuttle away from here, all the way to Kyrgyzstan on my spindly new legs to look for your grave, Selva, so I can dig up your corpse and urinate into the vacant eyeholes writhing with lice, over and over, until finally nothing makes sense again.

You've probably stopped reading by now, Selva. Or maybe you don't understand my words. Maybe you're trying to piece together the scraps of English you *do* understand. Or maybe you never received this letter to begin with because it was intercepted by a lonely, voyeuristic postal worker who stuffs his mouth with flourless cakes and sour vodka while reading the stories of other peoples' lives. Or more likely you've run off with another correspondent, a wealthy Manhattan businessman who straps heavy, glistening bangles to your joints and calls you something other than Selva, something more western-European—his ugly Italian grandmother's name, perhaps. But if you're still reading this, and especially if you are not, I need you to know all you've done for me, that by stealing from me my identity you have granted me a line of flight. This page itself is a trajectory that I could follow forever. Follow it all the way to unspeakable Floridas, where cross-eyed alligators sit mesmerized by butterflies gently fanning their wings across their snouts, emeralds of snot bubbling up from lavender nostrils beneath puss-filled skies atop Indian burial grounds. Right where the carnivals used to be. Right where they never were, Selva.

America is an imaginary land where proud buffalo hump spectacled secretaries in industrial-park water fountains, as if you didn't know. Welcome, then, Selva, to America. But don't you dare step foot off that plane. Watch the whole show from your tiny beveled window. It makes it all look funny, doesn't it? Like looking into a funhouse mirror. The fat is skinny and the skinny fat, the tall becomes short while the short appears tall. All funny, Selva. You've never laughed harder in your whole miserable life.

You wouldn't have liked this house anyway, if it makes you feel any better. Stranger mutants than I slithering down the hallways and bugs creeping from the toilet. The bowl's always backing up besides, and the carpet's worn and curling at the edges and there's too much peeling paint and wallpaper and there are too many holes in the ceiling through which the mutants watch you no matter where you are or what you're doing. Testimony of a life that couldn't possibly be lived. A liar and a monster, Selva, as I said, though not quite the monster you'd like me to be. I still have two eyes, bluer than the blue-skin tint of incestuous offspring. And feelings too, though I can't call them *my* feelings, just as you can't lay claim to yours, not in good Christian conscience, at any rate.

So stay home, my dearest Selva. Go to France or Portugal or

Timbuktu instead. Have a crazy affair with your translator, show him that melancholy cunt for a few lousy rubles, because I don't care anymore. Only do me one last favor, Selva, one last special favor for your beloved before you go. Write me something in Russian. Old Muscovite. Something I could never understand even if I made its translation my doctoral thesis and spent the remaining years of my life in stale old libraries trying to sort it all out. Something I can cherish like my memory of you just as you are, poor and stupid and rusty from having been locked up in that giant biscuit-tin of a country for so many years.

Farewell, then, Selva.

Yours eternally,

Zeth Fogel

* * * * *

The next morning was a Sunday, the scent of chicory and charred bologna swimming around him as he passed through the kitchen and out the back door. He dropped the letter into a mailbox on the way to the restaurant, whose pastels flashed gaudily in the light of day. Okay, he thought, once seated inside the diner and salting his beans, then I wait here like an idiot until she walks in. That Amish girl with the burdensome grandmother, or why *not* one of my cousins after all? Long time no see, cuz, you're looking mighty fine these days, mind if I plant a demon seed in that plump red belly of yours? Or, even better, some splendid abomination to begin with, some pitiably unnatural beast slouching through the diner's front door like some harbinger of the Apocalypse, dragging its hideous path to Zeth's booth before oozing itself in across from him. *That* was the sort of creature he deserved, and someone deserving of his affections—someone he could stand to be with for better or worse forever and ever amen. He glanced over at the frozen-yogurt machine, a full three inches of chocolate dangling from its tube like the tail of a forgotten species. He tried but couldn't eat. It seemed important that he somehow find his true self and accept himself—again, for better or worse. Like his father: becoming animal, intuitively understanding what he was from the start. Unlike Esta, the religious warrior, a poor man's Joan of Arc, with her chain-mail chastity belt and her cold and distant stare, always alert for the voice that would eventually confirm it was all a bad dream. He felt sorry for her now, it was true, for what she had suffered at the claws of that chimerical father, and yet he hated her as he hated all dead things. Her sin was that she had refused to die for real that day beneath her droopy-eyed beast of burden, Zeth's father, his bone-white head pinched at the temples, branded from the beginning, Zeth imagined, by the cold, careless grip of the forceps. Instead she had hefted that dumb, weighty memory onto her broken dwarf's hunch and carried it, along with her unwitting progeny, all the way home, all the way to her little Galilee with its miniature replica cathedral and its replica crucifix exhibiting a replica of the world's first *bona fide* freak (The Human Pin Cushion, Ladies and Gentlemen, step right up, step right up), all these pale panaceas lined up in neat mathematical rows like the balls of an abacus. Thinking of Jesus hanging there on Calvary's hill bleeding to death, Zeth experienced a compassion he'd never felt for anyone real. He remembered the ancient cuneiform tablets at Nineveh that he'd read about, how they had described sixty-two human congenital abnormalities to which were ascribed special religious significance; and he thought too of that mad, syphilitic genius Cicero, who had also linked monstrous births with divination. The deformed bodies of my ancestors are like oracles, he thought, snickering to himself, in which one can read the long litany of God's infinite disgust with His own creation. No wonder people like Esta still loved Him. Christ had been crucified a long, long time ago, yet still there were archeologists searching for his tomb. There was even a Canadian TV documentary, he remembered, claiming to have found this lost tomb; his mother had made him watch it as a child, just as she had made him watch that other show about the search for the Loch Ness Monster (*Dominus monstrum ex mare*).

Zeth had spent so many hours over the years waiting for Selva, or someone like Selva or altogether unlike her, that he felt he could wait in that restaurant forever, if necessary. But it might not take that long. He sensed already that the world's accumulation of exceptional phenomena was threatening to rip open the fabric, exploding all of the differences separating people like himself from normal people and exposing the illusions behind the illusions *ad infinitum*. Forever: that was the kicker, all right. He had only to find a way to get that mountainous ball of time rolling again.

R. Bremner

Anecdote of the Two Coyotes

1) The world received him on a hot stormy night while the dying spring gave convulsed birth to summer.
2) His sun clung stubbornly to Gemini while his moon flirted weakly with distracted Aquarius.
3) His birth was met with the usual fanfare. Relatives tapped the hospital glass. To please his audience, he cooed and clucked and was gratified with their beaming smiles.
4) His mother, aunts and uncles, and teachers oohed and ahhed at his brilliant day-to-day performances.
5) His father and brothers noticed his forced distance from his peers.
6) His mother declared, "This, my brightest son, will become a prominent attorney."
7) Professions and occupations could not stretch far enough to reach him. He sought only to drift on lazy seas and bed the available girls, who were rewarded for their gifts of sighing sentiment by slight glimpses into his wit. He chose a word for himself so that he could not be considered an aimless drifter. The word was "artiste." He walked through this new role with the easy gusto with which he had played his entire life.
8) His writings were summarily dismissed by the important and the unimportant people. This occurred for a number of years.
9) He grew increasingly angry and cynical and shrank mockingly from all vestiges of the literary and intellectual worlds. His works reflected a sharp-honed edge of detachment from every subject or character they touched upon.
10) He was called an "aimless drifter."
11) She was a tall, wispy woman with comfortable eyes that changed color and a loping walk.

12) She was bored with common sense logic, with talkative matter-of-fact people, with self-indulgent dreaming seekers, with being taught what she refused to believe, and with both arguments and the end of them.

13) She sought desperately to write, compose, or create "art," and secretly, flagrantly abused her frustrated ego for her failures while forcibly maintaining a calm, easy exterior.

14) She embraced feminism for release and relief.

15) She made love rarely and laboriously.

16) They met while working in a fast food restaurant.

17) She decided to make him her friend and confidante.

18) He fell immediately, totally, and exultantly in love with her.

19) They made love often, fervently, and unusually.

20) She laughed with him and cried with him.

21) He spoke so often and so certainly of her personal value that she came for the first time to realize it.

22) She fell softly and matter-of-factly in love with him.

23) His writings began to exhibit the wit, style, and grace he had so long and so mistakenly believed were characteristic of everything he did.

24) She consciously let him see that part of her psyche which she believed to be her whole self.

25) He consciously let her see the well-constructed play which he believed to be his whole self.

26) They were casually ecstatic in being together.

27) He became gradually aware of those parts of her into which she had never delved and had therefore never shown him.

28) She became aware that the role he was playing was divorced from though related to its playwright.

29) They became confused, then suspicious, then resentful. He felt betrayed. She felt deceived.

30) Love became difficult. Talk became strained. Empathy became impossible.

31) They parted amicably and tenderly, with few tears and many wishes.

32) She moved in and out of various urban centers, living with various old or new-found friends.

33) She wrote several moderately successful sociological books and sundry articles on contemporary life and its problems.

34) She made love often, passionately, and fiercely.

35) She learned to write excellent poetry which she secreted away from the world as her revenge against it.

36) She fought vicious mental battles with everyone who drew close enough to merit such attention.

37) Her Piscean subconscious became badly and continuously bruised, but she kept the bruises well-hidden under a carefully constructed peaceful exterior, except for those rare occasions when someone tried to draw close to her.

38) She was, over the years, respected as an earnest though misguided critic of society with a volatile but well-meaning temperament. She died in middle age, in relative poverty, of a brain tumor. Her marvelous poems, never discovered, died with her.

39) She had for some time been complaining of irritating voices inside her head, but friends accepted this as one of her lovable eccentricities.

40) He became a computer expert, renting out small portions of his intellect for extravagant sums. Money flooded him, and he stashed away a high percentage, living a bare and barren life.

41) After some years, he packed up his cash and moved into a deep dry cave in an empty, far-removed hill.

42) He survived by eating local vegetation and occasionally feasted on small animals when he could catch them.

43) He took to baying at the moon at odd hours of the morning from a wooded mound.

44) His eyes grew sharp but often seemed to be chuckling. His Aquarius moon was satisfied. His Gemini sun chuckled in acceptance.

Ryan Forsythe

WWDD?: What Would Daddaw Do?
An After School Special

We open on a young white man, played by Angus T. Jones (*Two and a Half Men*, *George of the Jungle 2*). Though there is no mention of his name yet, we've seen this one before so we know that he is one Howard Marshall of Parma Heights, Ohio.

Howard is staring at a photo of his father. He glances from the photo to the ceiling, picturing his father, remembering the day he watched him die in a hail of bullets and hail. What crazy weather that day!

Flashback: A younger Howard, played by Raymond Ochoa (*10 Items or Less*) is walking along an urban street, holding a backpack over his head, which isn't helpful in keeping him from being soaked by the downpour. He sees his father, played by Mark Ruffalo (*Collateral*, *13 Going on 30*), waving from the car across the street. As Howard is about to step off the curb, he glances to the right, then to the left, then back to the right. On that second glance to the right, a midnight blue sedan with tinted windows pulls onto the street but then guns it and comes roaring his way.

Howard steps back to the curb, waiting for the car to pass. But instead of passing, the car slows as it approaches Daddaw's car, which gives us a moment to recognize it as a Cadillac Seville Touring Sedan, *Motor Trend*'s 1992 Car of the Year, at the same time the weather gets harder, pounding hail, making it nearly impossible for Howard to see what we see: the barrels from several shotguns emerge from the passenger side.

Back to Howard, straining to see. Close up now on Howard's face. Recognition. He knows what is about to happen. In slo-o-o-ow motion, he shouts, "NO-O-O-O!" as the sound of gunfire fills the street.

At his father's side, the crazy weather immediately subsides. The sun peeks out from the clouds. Daddaw stares at Howard. Despite no apparent injury—no blood on Daddaw, no bullet holes on the car—his father says, "The rain...I was coming to...pick you..."

"I love you, Daddaw."

"Just make something of yourself. Make me...proud...son."

"I will, Daddaw."

His last words: "Promise!"

"I promise, Daddaw! I promise! I'll do good. I won't join a gang. I won't do drugs. I won't..."

But Daddaw cannot hear him anymore. He is DEAD!

Tears streaming down his face, little Howie looks up and together we spy a rainbow. Howard is filled with anger, but also a hint of hope. Or maybe that is us, his readers. For we know that all will be well, or this wouldn't be an *After School Special*. Yes, yes—it is us. Howie has no hope at all right now, not with Daddaw dead there in his arms. How would you feel? And here Howard didn't even get a chance to tell hm about the recruiter that showed up at the end of 8th period that day. "Just to talk," the man had said. But maybe we should save that for the next flashback. Yes, let's.

As the sedan reaches the far end of the street, our view (the view of both Howie and us) zeroes in on the vanity license plate:

1LGD WMN

Back to close up on Howard, making a mental note: remember that license plate. Hold for two second, then fade out from Howard as a young kid with tears streaming down his face, and fade in on Howard as an older kid with tears streaming down his face. So there's that.

Okay, first flashback over, there's a slight rap at the door. Howard looks up as the door opens and an older white man, played by Ralph Fiennes (*Quiz Show, The English Patient*), peeks his head in. "You okay, Howie?" he asks.

"Of course, Tim. I'm just thinking of—" But he can't bring himself to say it. To talk about his Daddaw's death. Or even Daddaw's life. No, not to Momma's new husband.

"You know you can tell me anything, right? I want to be your friend." Tim notices the back of the picture frame Howard is holding. He knows what that is. Oh yes, he does. "You know, Howie, if you want to do something for your father"—here Tim smiles—"you could get ready. We need to be there in an hour. And who knows...maybe you'll get that chance to prove yourself. Today."

"Thanks, Tim. I'll be down in a sec."

Tim closes the door and Howard looks deep into the black and white 8" x 10" glossy resin-coated paper holding the eyes of his father. "I won't let you down, Daddaw." He gets up and starts walking toward the door. Just as he's about to open it, he glances back at the photo. "I won't let you down."

From the perspective of the photo, we watch the door close as Howard goes out. Then hold for two seconds on the photo itself and cue commercial.

We're hoping for something big, worthy of this profound moment we've just shared. Something memorable like the cute old lady in the "Where's the Beef?" ads. But instead we get copper-topped batteries, Glade air freshener, a cartoon bunny selling some kind of flavored water, and delicious and fresh Florida's Natural® orange juice, squeezed from fresh Florida Oranges. How very disappointing.

We come back from commercial straight into flashback Numero Dos. It's a bit jarring for us readers, but let's not question the author's decisions just yet. There may be a method to this after all.

"There you are, Howie, my friend." The short white man, played by Danny DeVito (*Taxi, My Little Pony: The Movie*), offers his hand, which Howard (the Raymond Ochoa one, not Angus T. Jones) shakes. "Good to see you again. Did you think more about what we talked about? Did you talk it over with your ol' man? I really think you could be a top pick."

"My ol' man? My ol' man? My ol' man is dead!"

"Oh, sorry—I didn't know." We hear a slight ringing in the background.

"Well maybe you shoulda known!"

"Geez, kid. I'm sorry. This happened since we talked on Friday?" Again, the ringing.

"Can you get that, Howie?" interrupts Momma, played by Joanna Kerns (*Growing Pains*, *Growing Pains: Return of the Seavers*), pulling Howard/Angus T. Jones from the memory/flashback thing. We see Tim dressed sharply in button down shirt and sportcoat, but no tie, collar open. He is helping Momma with her necklace.

Howard glances at the phone and shouts, "Mom! Mom! You need to get it!"

"What is it, honey?"

"Hurry! There's no Caller ID!"

Like the other top prospects, Howie is well aware that to be called this day by an unlisted number could mean only one thing. Well, okay, it could mean any number of things, most of them people trying to sell something like Encyclopedias or maybe Omaha Steaks, though that's probably a poor example given that Omaha Steaks always calls from a listed 402 area code. But today is the day it could quite possibly mean something different. A team calling. But of course, it would never do for the prospects to answer the phone themselves, to appear too eager.

"Hello, Marshall residence."

"Who is it, Mom?"

"What? Wait—no, no. Oh, no. I'm sorry, we're not interested."

"What are they saying?" A calendar in the background shows us the month. February.

"No, goodb—wait. Are you there? In fact, please add us to your Do Not Call directory. You don't? Fine, nevermind. Just don't call back. Yes. Goodbye."

"Who was it?"

"He said he was calling for the Greens."

"Oh." Howie's face falls like a person hearing very bad news, as he falls back into the couch.

"I don't know how he got our number," Momma says, before checking her hair in the mirror.

But Tim sees Howard's disappointment, sits down next to him. "I'm really sorry, Howie. There's still time. Especially if you do well today."

Next, we see Howard sitting in the passenger seat of a car. Judging by the interior, Tim is driving some style of SUV, while Momma is in the backseat holding a stack of magazines. As they pass the spot where Howard's dad was killed (with the very same cars positioned there—yes, the editing isn't very good), Momma says, "Howie—you've moved up in the rankings! Look here."

Howard grabs the magazine and reads aloud. "Based on his performance this past season, Scout.com anticipates Howard Marshall will be a late 3rd-round pick, but pending his performance at this Saturday's scout combine, he could go much higher. After a few early fumbles, Marshall put together one heck of a junior campaign. Of course, Ohio has a lot of depth in the skill positions, but Marshall is among the very best. He has great size, poise, and coolness under pressure. Exceptionally creative, great drive and determination, but he excels with the lateral agility to elude when necessary. Expect big things from Howard Marshall."

Tim smiles at him and shakes Howard's knee. "Hot dog! What did I tell you?"

"Oh, Howie, baby. If your Daddaw could see you now! He'd be so, so proud." Momma suppresses a cry.

Howie: "Don't cry, Momma. Please don't cry."

Tim: "Now all you gotta do is rock this combine!"

Howard can't help but smile.

Switch to an exterior shot of an SUV (yup, we were right—it's a Ford Explorer 4X4 Eddie Bauer 4.0L) pulling into a packed parking lot. Our view zooms out from the SUV revealing hundreds upon hundreds of other cars, pickups, SUVs, and several large semi-trailer trucks, 18-wheeler flatbeds with satellites, antennae, mini production studios, and more. As we zoom out even further, we can make out a stadium in the background.

Back to the family, walking through the parking lot, a bit overwhelmed by the flurry of activity.

"Howard Marshall!" He is called over by a white man with a microphone, played by Vincent D'Onofrio (*Steal This Movie, Ed Wood*).

"Hi, Howard. Gene Roberts, for ABC. How are you feeling today?"

"Feeling great, Gene. I'm just ready to get out there and show my stuff."

"Best of luck to you."

"Thanks."

As Howard, Tim, and Momma walk away, we hear Gene continue: "That was Howard Marshall, just one of hundreds of the very best college prospects, invited each year to the NPPL Scouting Combine here in Indianapolis, Indiana. Today executives, consultants, scouts, and doctors from both political parties will conduct an intense, four-day job interview in advance of April's NPPL Draft. More action, after this!" Hold on the NPPL logo for two seconds and then cue commercial break #2.

First up is new Pine-sol with Lemon, though we're a little confused as to whether this is a commercial break for ABC's coverage of the scouting combine or for the *After School Special* itself. After the Pine-sol, we get peanut butter, Hefty Cinch Sak trash bags, and the same commercial from earlier, for Florida's Natural® orange juice, squeezed from fresh Florida Oranges.

Okay, show back. We hear ourselves reading the part of the Voice-over: "Now on ABC: it's Selection Sunday. We bring you Day Two of The National Political Party League 2022 Draft, sponsored by Beer. Remember, if you're not drinking beer, then you're not drinking Beer!"

We realize that this ABC show is different from the one we were watching before the commercial break, but we don't worry too much about it right now.

"Alright, we're back," says Gene. "Let's go to Gayle Christy with a very special guest."

Gayle, played by Jessica Alba (*Camp Nowhere*, *Knocked Up*) says, "Hi, Gene. I'm down here on the floor of the Javits Convention Center and I have with me the top draft pick from 2016, to tell us the brief history of the NPPL. Ladies and gentlemen, the President of the United States." Our view pans out slightly to include a white man in a blue suit, played by Jesse Eisenberg (*The Squid and the Whale*, *The Social Network*).

"Thank you, Gayle. As you know, the National Political Party League was founded in 2014 by the Republican and Democrat Parties, to combat the surge of interest in those smaller piddly little parties, such as the Tea Party, the Libertarians—oh, and those loveable losers, the Greens." They smile.

"The two parties started the draft essentially to remind America that there really are just two parties—well, two important ones, that is. And now, just a few years later, the draft has become the primary means for the two parties to select candidates for our nation's higher public offices."

"It certainly worked for you, Mr. President."

Mr. President smiles at Gayle, before turning to the reading audience. "That's right, Gayle. I was fortunate to be selected number one in the draft. I owe a lot to the Democrats, and also to our sponsors, Beer. Remember, if you're not drinking beer, then you're not drinking Beer!"

"If you have a moment, Mr. President, I'd love to ask you one softball question; feel free to bat it away or simply not answer."

"Of course, Gayle."

"I've heard people criticize this system, in that draft picks just go to whichever party selects them. It's not necessary for recruits to believe in what the party stands for—no need to actually buy-in to the party platform. How do you answer these critics?"

Mr. President turns to the readers, us, showing the great form that made him the top pick of 2016. With impressive speed, he shows us first Pained-Right 88, his patented forlorn/serious/thoughtful expression, before cutting sideways and moving into the open field. "Yes, yes. I've heard this, too. But it shows a complete—and I would say willful—ignorance of the contemporary political situation, Gayle. Let me say something to the children out there."

We're giddy with anticipation, reading that signature phrase of his, knowing he'll follow up with a daring vertical leap. Here it comes:

"Do these people think that after Babe Ruth went from the Red Sox to the Yankees, that he should have continued to *believe* in the Red Sox, and not believe in the Spirit of the Yankees? Should Brett Favre have let the Green Bay Packers win against him in his first game against his former team? Of course not! It's plain silly. No, no. You play for the party that pays you. I'm happy to say that today, loyalty and dedication still matter. The important thing is not *what* you believe, but what you *do* with your beliefs."

Score! He hasn't lost a single step; that ability to elude that moved him quickly through the ranks may be stronger than ever.

"There you have it, from the President himself. Loyalty and dedication still matter. Back to you, Gene."

"Thank you, Gayle. Before we get to today's action, let's recap a little from yesterday. The top pick was taken by the Democrats. They expect John Corrigan to start right away for the New York state attorney's office. Let's roll the tape."

We see a young white man, played by Zac Efron (*The Lucky One*, *Me and Orson Welles*). "I've been working out all summer," he says in a flat monotone. "I'm just super excited to get started on not raising taxes for the average American worker. But my opponents are waging class warfare. It's about the jobs."

Back to the studio, where Gene is joined by an older white man, played by Lee Corso (*College GameDay*). Gene says, "Joining us in the studio to talk about this is former Virginia senator George Allen. Your thoughts, Senator Allen?"

"This kid has knock-out potential!" says Senator Allen. He is very active with his hands as he speaks. "Yes, his delivery is a little weak, and he needs some time warming up to get on point. But that's what training camp is for. I guarantee, if you would have played that tape for a few more minutes, I guarantee right now you'd be nodding your head, not even realizing that he wasn't saying a thing!"

Gene: "So you expect big things from this kid?"

Senator Allen: "Give him four years tops and he'll be a candidate for President! He won't settle for Governor. And he shouldn't!"

Gene: "In other action, the Republicans made great gains when they picked up Irving Chandler in exchange for the Democrats' fourth pick, $23 billion cash, and a politician to be named later."

Senator Allen: "Yeah, it was a good move, especially after the scandal earlier in the day with Howard Marshall. After a recent drunk driving conviction came to light, Marshall's stock slipped considerably. He ended up this year's 'Mr. Irrelevant,' so named for being the last pick in the draft."

Gene: "It's expected he'll never get beyond county government, a huge blow for the Republicans."

Senator Allen: "But, wow—with the Chandler trade, the Republicans are looking—"

"Oh! Howie—"

< CLICK >

Our view of the TV screen goes black and we see Tim with the remote, pointed at the TV as he quickly stands from the couch in the living room. Howard is standing there, watching.

"—didn't realize you were up. I'm sorry about yesterday, son."

"I'm not your son! Just...just leave me alone!" Howard runs to the door and slams it. We know from Tim's mournful expression that he really cares for Howard, even if Howard doesn't understand himself. Hold on Tim's expression for two seconds and then cue commercial break #3.

Before we even get to the commercial, we wonder if we were just watching TV from Tim's perspective for the whole duration of that last segment? What the hell kind of *After School Special* is this? Hopefully these commercials will be better than the last round.

As a book appears, we read the Voice-over: "She was a millionaire socialite. He was a time traveller who woke up in the Nixon Administration. Will he be able to save humanity from the scourge of Al Gore? Find out in *Dick Cheney Saves Paris*, the madcap sci-fi meta- anti- novel now available from Love Earth Publications. And, if you act now, we'll throw in the soundtrack for just a penny more."

Wait—is the author using product placement in his own story, to try to sell another of his works? This gives us an uneasy feeling. It feels kinda fucked up, actually, and we don't mind saying so. We even begin to wonder if the previous listed commercials breaks weren't perhaps other examples of product placement. Could Florida's Natural®, makers of delicious and fresh orange juice squeezed from fresh Florida Oranges, have paid for the previous mentions, on pages 312 and 315 of this story? Or even this mention, here on page 318?

But this feeling doesn't last, we've already moved on, forgotten it, though perhaps it's hidden away in our subconscious only to be brought out at some future time, the way an Extra Terrestrial follows a trail of Reese's Pieces. Maybe the next time we're visiting Amazon.com and wonder what people are saying about the book.

Howie is at the home of his friend Rudy, played by Malcolm David Kelley (*You Got Served*, *Lost*). There are a few others there, none of whom we recognize from any movies or television shows from the past fifty years. A TV is on in the background showing a commercial for Florida's Natural® orange juice.

"Yo, Howie," says Rudy. "Try some herb."

"Sure, Rudy. Oh, wait. I almost forgot. I have to get going, I—"

"What's up with your friend, Rudy? He *always* says yes and then *always* comes up with some excuse ten seconds later."

"Yeah, what's up with that? You think you better 'n us? Since you a draft pick, you a big man now?"

From the way Howard looks up and to the left and curls his lip, we know that Howard is making a mental note to wait quite a bit more than ten seconds next time, maybe several minutes before coming up with some excuse.

"No excuses, Howard. Take this. Now."

Just then the TV show they're watching returns from commercial. A white man's voice, played by the voice of John Tesh (*Entertainment Tonight, John Tesh Radio Show*) says, "In other news, former presidential candidate Ralph Nader spoke today in Chicago about a new organization of Third Parties—you remember those perennial losers in county, statewide, and national elections? Turns out, they're still around! Nader made the formal announcement to the media—well, okay, it was actually just to a lonely and haggard-looking Amy Goodman, reporting for *Democracy Now!*" Switch to a tape of Amy Goodman, played by Amy Goodman (*Democracy Now!, Streets of Blood*), standing alone before a room full of chairs. "And we wouldn't have known about it if our production assistant hadn't brought in the tape. Thanks, Pete. Let's check it out."

Standing before the roomful of empty seats—I mean Amy Goodman—is a white man, played by Josh Brolin (*No Country for Old Men, The Goonies*) who clears his throat.

"Go ahead, Ralph. I mean, Commissioner Nader."

"Today, we seek to combat the dominance of the National Political Party League. No longer will the NPPL have a monopoly on candidates or offices. After suffering perennial losses in county, statewide, and national elections, the third parties have finally joined together. Today we announce the formation of the United States Political Party League." He looks up from his prepared statement and says, "I should note that I preferred the acronym N.P.P.L.S.L.i.E., short for National Political Party League Shadow League in Exile, but I was voted down by representatives from the other seven parties." He glares at the seven people standing around the podium.

Sarah Palin, also played by Josh Brolin, coughs, causing Ralph to look over and raise an eyebrow. "Go on, Ralph," she says. "You can do it!" She smiles and gives him a thumbs up. Ralph continues reading: "For its initial season, the USPPL will be made up of two leagues, the Independence League and the Liberty League, each with four parties. Do I have to read all this? Can't I just jump to the part where we say the Green Party won first pick in the draft and we choose Howard Marshall? Howard, if you're out there, I tried calling you, but your Mother hung up on me—"

"Give me that." Sarah Palin grabs the statement. "Hi there, everybody! As we were saying, the Independence Division will be made up of the Greens, the Socialist Workers Party, the Progressive Labor Party—and, though I probably shouldn't say so—the party we expect to become the traditional doormats of the Independence Division, the United States Marijuana Party." Sarah glances over at an unnamed person, played by an uncredited actor. "No offense, of course. Meanwhile over in the Liberty Division, the Tea Party, the—"

"There you have it. Ralph Nader still causing trouble. When we come back—"

<CLICK>

Only this time the click is not Tim changing the channel from bad news about Howie when Howie surprises him by waking up from a nap sooner than expected. The click is not even Howie turning off the TV. It is the sound of us readers turning this off, tuning out. We need something, anything, to get us out of this news conference, this whole story, even. This melange of football references, politics, television, and product placement.

Maybe a commercial break will help. Nah, let's just try to push through—we're more than halfway, right? Where were we? Oh, yes. Howie, suffering the indignity of being Mr. Irrelevant, the last player chosen in the draft, has just learned he was also selected first in a very different draft. All while enjoying his first ever toke of marijuana. And now his head is spinning. Yes, that's right—the director skipped right over the pivotal scene where Howard has reached such a low point—the memory of Daddaw's death, the indignity of being chosen last—that he does it. Despite promising Daddaw that he won't do drugs, he caves to the peer pressure, to the pain, and he "tokes up" as the kids say. But then, we wouldn't want to see that on daytime network television anyway. Sure, we're curious for the drama, for the tension it could add. But we realize this is an *After School Special*, after all. We think of the children. And we're glad the director did too.

"So, you gonna play for the Republicans?" One of Rudy's friends.

"Yeah, whaddaya gonna do?" Another friend.

"Of course he is—think of the money. The fame." Rudy.

"I'm not sure. I don't think I like the Republicans." Howard.

"Fine, then you wait it out. Switch parties later, man. Ronald Reagan, Rick Perry, Arlen Specter, Mr. Joe Lieberman. All of them bitches switched, yo. You play out your contract and when it's done, you move on. Join the Democrats, whatever."

With the lone drag of the doobie entering his system, Howard feels totally calm, free. Free to say what he really believes. "But I don't think I like the Democrats either."

"What? You don't like the Republicans or Democrats?"

"Wait—your friend don't like the Republicans *or* Democrats?"

"Well, I think I might play for the Greens."

"You kidding, right? Shit. No friend of mine is going to be seen with no Greens."

"It's just—"

"Who the fuck are you, Howard? Do you know what any of us would give to be a draft pick? To play in the fucking NPPL?"

"No, I mean—"

"Shit, dog, I don't know who you are any more. Getdafuckouttamyhouse, man."

"Come on, Rudy."

"Get. Da. Fuck. Out. Duh. My. House."

As Howie staggers out the door, the hallucinations begin. We see him bathed in swirling lights of primary color. He sees Daddaw, a bullet hole in the center of his forehead, riding on a huge doobie. "The rain," says Daddaw. "I was coming to." The background music, meant to demonstrate the soounds in his head, looks like this when put into words: BOOM-boom-BOOM, wah-ah-ah, wa-ah-ah...BOOM-BOOM-BOOM, wah-ah-ah, wah-ah-ah. We, the readers, are reminded of some weird music from a pornographic movie we saw once. Okay, maybe quite a bit more than once. But this music is not quite the same, it's just different enough that no one could really claim the music from this scene was stolen.

Suddenly Howard is outside an electronics store, staring at a wall of TVs. On every screen is the image of himself staring at the wall of TV screens. And even though those screens are really really small (the ones in each of the TVs), we know what is on each of those screens: the image of Howard staring at the wall of TV screens.

Despite the TVs being sealed inside the store, we hear a voice-over clearly. It notes, "In other news, we've just learned that the NPPL's Mr. Irrelevant, Howard Marshall, is considering joining the Green Party."

"Yes, Rachel. It's unfortunate what poor advisors can do to a young kid today. Obviously he's in with the wrong crowd, getting some really bad advice. I don't know if it's his friends or maybe his mother, but this is really, really unfortunate."

We're thinking this is a continuation of his hallucination; there's no way it could already be on the news when he's still just formulating these ideas—when he's just left the party where he learned he was chosen by the Greens. But of course, we know it's real. We know that that's the way the world is and you have to keep up. News travels fast, especially when attached to neutrinos traveling at faster than the speed of light. Why do you think we call such news reports *news-trinos*?

"Political suicide," says the voice-over.

"Absolutely, Rachel."

Howard stares at the bank of himselves staring at the bank of himselves staring at the bank of himselves, and thinks aloud, "What am I going to do?"

"What are you going to do, Howard?"

Howard turns and sees a one-legged woman, played by Traci Ashton (*My Name is Earl, Inland Empire*). Something about her strikes Howard as familiar.

"Do I know you?"

"No. But I knew your father."

Of course—the 1LGD WMN!

"You! You killed him."

"What? No! No, Howie. I would never do that."

"I know it was you! The license plate."

She sighs. "I've never forgiven myself for that day. The day I realized that the gang of gun-toting men who forced me from my car and drove off were responsible for killing our father. Yes, it's true. I am your sister, Howard. Ever since that day, I've dedicated myself to finding them. And my search has led me...here."

"But if it wasn't you...then who?"

"Howie—why don't you go to your own bed." We see Tim and Momma, in their living room. Holding hands.

Now on Howard, we see him facedown on the couch, waking up, as if from a dream. But the one-legged woman is there too. Tim looks at her. "You look familiar. Do I know you?"

"I don't think so."

Flashback: We see her as a younger woman (she looks the same, is wearing the same clothes in fact, but her hair is longer), about to get into her car when a group of four hooded men appear. The one in the back is wearing a new purple cardigan. Flashforward: The one-legged woman glances at Tim. He's wearing a new purple cardigan!

"Wait—maybe I do know you." She looks at Howard, tries to say it all in a silent glance. Howard understands. Or thinks he does. He looks at Tim. "Tim... how long have you known my mother?"

"Howie—why don't you go to bed." We see Tim and Momma, in their living room. Holding hands.

Now on Tim, we see him facedown on the couch, as if waking from a dream. We have to wonder if it was a dream: the wall of televisions, the one-legged woman, Tim and Momma waking him up on the couch to encourage him to go to his own bed, the one-legged woman having a flashback. Or maybe it was a hallucination, a result of his turn to drugs in an attempt to feel better about his life.

Howard looks suspiciously at Tim. "Tim...how long have you known my mother?"

"What? Oh, it's been years—you know that."

Wait, wait, wait—let's pause a second here. We may have just missed something big. These *After School Specials* all have some kind of lesson—don't do drugs, always tell the truth, never run away from home—that sort of thing. We've been waiting for something, anything, and now maybe we've got it. Don't judge people. You can't go around assuming that just because the license plate of the car that produced the guns that killed your father reads "1LGD WMN," that if you then meet a one-legged woman on the street or in your drug-induced hallucination, that she was the one responsible. Because until you've walked a mile in her moccasins—or moccasin (singular), we should say—until you've had your car stolen at gunpoint only to learn later that those people killed your secret father, then, hey: you don't know how it feels. To be her.

So, yeah. Let that be a lesson to us all. When you assume, you make an As out of Sum and E. Or something like that. At the very least, don't judge a murder by its license plate.

Okay, lesson learned, time to move forward. Rewind the tape.

Howard looks suspiciously at Tim. "Tim...how long have you known my mother?"

"What? Oh, it's been years—you know that."

Flashback time again. Howard recalls a time, a few years back, when he introduced Tim to Momma. But this was well after his father's death. No, Tim didn't kill his father.

Momma says, "I need to pee," and goes out.

Tim says, "I heard. About the USPPL. What do you think you're going to do?"

Howard: "I don't know, I really don't. What do you think I should do?"

Tim: "I think you should do what's in your heart." From Howard's reaction, we know that this advice means nothing to Howard. Tim takes a deep breath and tries again. "You know, Howie. Your father was a great man. If you want to do right by him, just answer a simple question: What would Daddaw do? If you can answer that, you'll know what to." Tim goes out, Howard looks thoughtful for two seconds, and then...Yup, we guessed it: another commercial break.

The moment the orange juice commercial begins again, we run out to the bathroom. We're only gone a minute, but when we return to the story, Howard and Momma are sitting at the kitchen table, already deep in conversation. "So, yeah. That's what I think I'm going to do."

"That sounds great, honey."

"Yeah. I'm pretty sure it's what Daddaw would want." What? We missed the big moment! Which decision did he make? Will he go to the Republicans or the

Greens? Or skip out on politics altogether? Will we ever know?

Just then, Tim appears in the door. "Hey, Howie. You wanted to talk to me?"

Mom is surprised and gives a "What's this?" look to Howard.

"Yeah. I wanted to say something to both of you. I want to let you know I love you both. I'm ready now...to be a family."

Tim smiles. "I'm so proud of you..." He pauses, decides to try again. "Son."

Howard smiles and they all hug as credits begin appearing on one half of the screen as we hear a knocking on the door as we wonder if this will ever end.

Tim says, "I wonder who that could be?" For a moment, we think the one-legged woman might make another appearance when suddenly an arm punches a hole in the wood door, grabs the handle, and opens it. The door slides open and Daddaw comes in, arms raised. In Zombie form!

"RRAWR!" he screams, before adding, "WRE-ARWR!"

Momma jumps in shock and screams, before realizing it is just Mark Ruffalo, back to watch the final day of filming, playing a trick on her.

They all have a good laugh. We change the channel, tune out, read another story, and continue our support of the two political parties, forgetting that there ever were other parties, except for once every ten years, on the anniversary of the fall of the USPPL, when VH1 mentions them in a "Where are They Now?" segment, sponsored by Beer.

Shane Jesse Christmass

T-Shirts for Los Angeles Tourists

Meals. Coal fire. Cambodia. Siem Riep. Bloody clothing. Visa form. Air steward. Dark threads. Room key. Laundry dries. Shirts. Danny Glover. Aperitifs. Rice plains. McDonalds. Sunset. Meals are just fillets of meat and diced onion, all fried up in a saucepan. Water boils over coal fire. The wind freezes. I'm in Cambodia, wanting to get into Siem Riep, but first, myself and noise. As I board, entering the plane via the rear, the fear of what might happen if I look down. The airline sells bloody clothing from those who perished before us. After checking in, I grab my visa form, I tell the air steward that I come from dark thread. He tells me a porter will unroll the canvas for me to sleep on. As he explains, he gives me my room key. The curtains are closed in my room. Later in the twilight, I stroll about town in my y-fronts. My laundry dries on the clothesline. Shirts ruffle in the wind. I come across Danny Glover's crumpled face. I slurp aperitifs of Pastis before I board. The flight over the rice plains of Pakse. The waterpark is small, about the size of a suburban McDonalds. The movie is Lethal Weapon, so I crank the volume. Out on the Los Angeles street. I'm not in the mood to be standing. It is two in the afternoon, but my laundry needs to be hung. It's a heavy, starching heat. The skyline is a mess of two storey rooftops. A bank, a bank teller with a long hair. Curios in windows. Bootlegged artefacts sold for anything. Shops close at I wake up, a poor tourist robbed at knifepoint. I look under thc couch. I see a gold pen. Outside a melee of tourists and touts. The sun is mental, enough to drive someone to a car park to seek shelter. There's an adjoining fast food drive-thru service. The manager tells me they're going to remodelled that into a hotel as well. I sit by the pool. A plane roars across the tarmac. I show my boarding pass. Internal organs laced with soothing drips of booze. A Khmer woman. The bathroom. The shower spray soaks the toilet roll. I shake all over. I'm flat-footed, fibrous from the brash sun. The taxi driver snatches my money. He darts, shopfront after shopfront. I urinate in the shower. Been driving, I guess all night. The hotel doesn't have an elevator. There's no way to get to the old market to get a bite to eat. The taps on the sink and the plastic box under the shower head leak. The sunscreen doesn't fight off sunburn. The dust, teeth-biting dust. I need a beer. I hop a motorcycle over to the East Asia Room. The floor is tiled. It isn't a problem. Insanity hasn't been invented. Steam rises to the ceiling, blocking out the sun. The hotel has four floors. A jaunty ride courtesy of Laos Airlines to get here. The sun cresting in the sky. It's midday. The plane. One single day to get here. You camp in the remains of Riverside Hospital on North Brother Island, The current and breathing deceased are piss-potted and bedpan strapped to life machines out on College Point. You're in a sleeping bag sleeping in Teardrop Park. Jell-O smeared all over the Frick Collection. Alluvial deposits that remain in the East River. A tabloid magazine from somewhere. The wind hurries. You mumble. His eyes. All wind-shrift, capillary-red, all shot with adventuring. You pour yourself a glass of IPA. You walk toward me. Lethal Weapon. Los Angeles. Storey rooftops. Bank teller. Long hair. Curios. Bootlegged shops. Poor tourists. Gold pen. Car park. Drive-thru service. Aeroplane roars. Shower spray soaks. Brash sun. Taxi driver snatches money from hand. Plastic box. Shower head leaks. Insanity. Steam. Laos. Teardrops. Jell-O. Tabloid magazines.

Steve Pastis

Ask Wisconsin / The Oncoming Bureau of Longitudes

"We have Wisconsin on the phone."

"Madison?"

"No, not Madison."

Four loopy edging stones cascaded into the Oncoming Bureau of Longitudes while we the paupers stood and applauded, muskets encouraging our display of enthusiasm.

"Sheboygan?"

"No, not Sheboygan either."

"This sort of cascade is far too rare in this radius," said the elder, a sincere but filibustering man of cheese.

"Milwaukee perhaps?"

"No, sorry."

Glaring down like a beacon on the withering discards, the suntan forces etched across the torpedoed horizon. "This was once all calves and helmets," the elder lamented.

"Eau Claire?"

"No. Wrong again."

Ignoring the mass existence far below the lofty bedrock plateau, the ceremonial one with the butler tray slowly cut the red wax. It easily parted.

"Green Bay? It has to be Green Bay."

"No."

We the paupers stared at the crackers that had been placed on the monkey plates before us. Ours was the wind. Ours was the sun and the rain. Ours were the clouds shaped like otters and honey bears. Our barefaced crackers, however, cheesed us off.

"Appleton?"

"Wrong again."

The elders waved through high windows of attitude as they munched on the palest yellow of cheeses. Their crackers were full. Their crackers were happy. Their crackers runneth over with sweet fromage.

We threw the loopy edging stones far into the field where the elders never trod, where approaching muskets would be grabbed by monkeys eager to shoot at distant plates and sad crackers. We lamented the day's direction. We needed some closure. We needed some victory. We needed to applaud in sincerity.

"Racine?"

"Yes."

"Hooray!" we the paupers shouted, and we watched as our thrown hats descended back down to us. The elders waved again to us from their tables high in the latitudes. They would take their bows for whatever occurred, even before they learned what we had celebrated.

Honey for the Cold War

Sampson looked to his left, looked to his suitcase and looked to the prophets, but he was still at a loss for answers. Trenchcoat Tom, the neighborhood alarmist, was heading up the walkway and there was no legal way to keep him from reaching the front door.

Sampson stood in the middle of his living room, frozen in place.

Suddenly, there was the loud confident pounding that Sampson had heard so many times before. The door needed to be opened, but he was for the moment unable to move.

"Honey for the Cold War!" shouted Trenchcoat Tom.

Sampson's curiosity revived him. He opened the door.

"Honey for the Cold War!" shouted Trenchcoat Tom once again.

"Yes, I heard you say that a moment ago," responded Sampson. "Are there any additional clues you can offer?"

"I'm not sure what additional clues you need," said Trenchcoat Tom. "I assume you've heard of honey, the sweet stuff bees make. I'm collecting it. Please go see if you have some. Most homes do."

"Why do you want it?" asked Sampson.

"That's where the second part of what you heard comes into play," replied Trenchcoat Tom. "I assume you've heard of the Cold War. It's been in all the papers. Well, I'm collecting honey for the Cold War."

Sampson still had a thirst for more knowledge in this matter, but decided he would be better off keeping quiet and looking for honey. He excused himself to visit his kitchen and quickly returned a small sticky plastic bear-shaped container half filled with honey. Trenchcoat Tom stared at it as it rested in the palm of Sampson's right hand.

"Sorry Sampson, but that won't do," said a somber Trenchcoat Tom. "That won't do at all."

With that, Trenchcoat Tom turned and walked to the Kirby house nextdoor. Sampson was crestfallen and decided then and there that he would immediately take all the steps necessary to meet any and all challenges that life and the colorful characters in it threw his way.

He soon filled his kitchen and pantry, painted his lawn, learned Norwegian, Estonian and the rhumba, bought extra appliances and made another thousand or so improvements to himself, his household and his food supplies.

Trenchcoat Tom would have been proud. Sampson was finally prepared for the Cold War.

Walking into a Bar

A penguin, a cyclops, an elk and a staunch defender of tooth enamel walk into a bar. They sit at a table in the corner and the priest, the minister and the rabbi at the next table stare at them.

"Hey, it's not always about you!" shouts the penguin. The three religious professionals immediately turn their attentions back to their drinks.

"It's too dark in this bar," says the cyclops. "It's hard to read the wine list."

The penguin, cyclops and elk notice the empty chair at their table. It seems their associate, the staunch defender of tooth enamel, left to pass out toothpaste and dental floss to the bar patrons at other tables.

A duck, an unemployed electrician and a panda bear with a fear of heights walk into the bar. The bartender says, "We don't get many giraffes in here."

The rabbi, the elk and the unemployed electrician look at each other and all nod - because there's not a giraffe in the place. Everyone else is watching the big screen television so the bartender reaches under the bar to turn it on.

Anyway, the attorney - did I mention him? - Anyway, the attorney says, "I'll bet the next customer to walk into this bar is a gold medalist on the professional sun tanning tour."

"I'll take that bet," says the minister, who happens to have a problem with his gambling.

"I will too," said the iguana, whom I probably also forgot to mention. It's okay though because he really doesn't have anything else to say in this story.

A cowboy with a prominent gold tooth walks into the bar and somehow the lawyer disappears through a side door. The cowboy accidentally steps on the iguana and then sits down with the penguin, the cyclops and the elk.

"Do any of you fellas know where Rambler City is?" asks the cowboy.

The minister, the penguin and the panda bear with a fear of heights all point - but in different directions. Everyone else is too busy looking for the iguana that is pancaked under the cowboy's right boot.

JEF 73

The cowboy leaves angrily and a giraffe walks into the bar. The discredited bartender decides to hide in the storeroom.

A pirate, a manatee and three members of the cast of "Ten Good Reasons to Fix that Airplane" take seats at the only empty table in the bar.

The giraffe walks up to them and says, "At these prices, I'm not coming back."

The Rotormaps

The rotormaps began for a penguin named Sally. Halfway through the tuna, she affixed to her calling. On trapper, on trapezoid, on beyond the solid lunar, she partook of the buffer to encompass the plain.

"My beacon of bronze meanders like particles," she stared at the croutons before completing her thought. "Without invitation, stands the last of the honey frogs. Without trepidation, it fastens cashews to a home-buying public that waxes its brow."

Mahogany gold vexed the capricious plain dealer. The yellow drew armies which hardened their lot. The rotormaps hid from the penguin and salad. The rotormaps plugged gaps in the marble. The steamer flew whimsy. The truck stirred up malt.

"There seem to be stumbles etched into the chorus," she said, lighting up chocolate that framed the most direct path to the tide pool. "There seem to be etchings of corduroy stumps. I've forgotten the menu but I can recite everything left on the plain. I'm good that way."

Thaddeus Rutkowski

Summer Session

My mother frequently complained about the fleas on our pets. "All these pets; all these fleas," she would say, throwing her hands up. "Where I grew up, monkeys had fleas."

I could see the fleas when I separated the pets' fur with my fingers. Next to the animal's skin, a dark speck would run for cover, toward the fur that was still in a clump. I could follow it with my fingers, but I didn't know what to do once I had exposed the insect. I could have taken it off the animal and thrown it away, but that wouldn't get rid of the flea. It would have been able to jump onto the next pet that walked by. I didn't know how to kill the fleas. Was I supposed to chop them in half with my fingernails? Was I supposed to eat them? If I ate them, wouldn't I be like a monkey grooming another monkey? Wasn't I high enough on the evolutionary ladder not to have to do that?

At one point, my father brought home a bag from a hardware store with some plastic nooses for the pets. He buckled the collars around their necks. The collars might have discouraged the fleas, but they didn't get rid of them. When I went through the pets' fur with my fingers, I could still see the fleas running away. But at least they were running away from the collar.

*

My father announced that he'd gotten a summer job at a college and would take the family with him. "I'm going to teach kids to make art," he said, "and I'm going to teach them more than that."

My father enrolled me in the art program. I was given a room in a college dorm—a step up for me, since I was still in high school. The rest of my family stayed in a rented house with our pets.

In the dorm, I had to do my own laundry, but I had never done laundry before. I understood that the machines worked with coins, and that I had to pour in detergent during the wash cycle. I did a successful wash, but I neglected to use the dryer. I ended up with a pillowcase full of wet clothes, which I dumped in the corner of my room. I let the clothes air-dry, and I didn't fold them. They came out crumpled into balls. I picked the clothes off the floor as I needed them and put them on.

In my wrinkled clothes, I went to a workshop led by my father. First, he showed us how to attach a piece of silk to a wood frame with a staple gun and tape. Then he demonstrated the use of "tusche" to make a positive image. He laid the tusche on the screen with a brush. Then he covered the screen with glue, removed the tusche, and used a squeegee to force the ink through spaces made by the original drawing.

I was more interested in painting than in silk-screening. I took a small canvas to a stairway and sat on a step facing a window. I made an image of the dark stairs, the wood banister, and the window with sunlight coming through it. I tried to make my rendering as realistic as possible. I wanted to remember what I had seen.

*

After class, my father suggested a trip to a campus bar. He didn't make an announcement to the class. He selected a few students, maybe his favorites, and invited them. I went along.

In the bar, my father ordered a pitcher of beer.

"Don't drink from this," he said to the students at the table.

He poured the beer for himself, and the rest of us took sodas.

After he had finished a mug, he poured another. "I'm an artist," he said. "I have something to say. But I deserve better than I get. It's always been like that."

We sat and listened to him.

"I'm going to teach you about art," he went on. "Then I'm going to teach you about revolution. 'A revolution is not a garden party.' That's what Mao said. I follow him. It isn't hard. My wife is Chinese."

Shortly, an older man came into the bar. He looked around the table, at the students, but he didn't sit with us. He spoke to my father in a whisper and walked out.

*

My father brought one of the girl students and me to visit my family's house. My mother and siblings stayed behind.

The house was a couple hours' drive from the college. Maybe my father wanted to pick up something he had forgotten, or maybe he wanted the show the girl the place where we lived.

I was wearing items from my laundry on the floor: a wrinkled T-shirt and half-pants.

"Sometimes I hear lions at night," my father said during the drive. "No one else hears them. The lions come over the mountain from the empty valley, and they roar."

*

The house was quiet, abandoned; no one had taken it for the summer. The pets, of course, were gone.

When we walked into the living room, small creatures started jumping on our legs. They were fleas. Apparently, they had nowhere to live after the pets left for the summer. There was an area of the floor next to windows that was catching sunlight. The fleas seemed to like it there. They covered the floor like grains of black sand.

The girl and I received some bites. We brushed the insects off our legs, then left the house and stayed outside. We waited beside the car for my father.

"I like it there," he said as he started to drive back to the college. "Even though no one cares what I'm doing, people are good to me. If I need help, they come and give it. Someone will come in now, to exterminate."

*

I took a friend of mine to the house where my family was staying. My father and my siblings were out—maybe my father had taken them to a bar. Only my mother was there. She stayed in the kitchen while my friend and I sat in the living room and listened to cassette tapes.

Much later, after my friend and I had left the house, my brother talked to me. "I heard you brought a girl home," he said.

"No, I didn't," I said.

"That's what Mom said. You brought a girl named Bonnie."

I realized that my mother had pronounced the name with a Mandarin accent.

"That was my friend Barney, not Bonnie." I said.

"Barney?"

"Yes, Barney. He's a boy, not a girl."

"Oh," my brother said. "I thought it was Bonnie. I thought you were spreading your wings. I heard 'Bonnie.' "

"No. It was Barney."

*

After a studio class, my father told me he wouldn't be running the workshop anymore. "Someone saw me with underage kids at a bar," he said. "He was a faculty member, and he ratted me out. I'll be able to finish this session, but that will be it."

*

After the summer session ended, I still had the painting I'd started in the stairway. It wasn't finished; there were blank spaces on the canvas. I had been using the method of finishing one area at a time. The steps and banister, and the ivy-framed window with sunlight coming through it, were clear. But the frame of the scene was missing. I could have been sitting in a void, or on another planet, when I was painting the scene. There was nothing between my viewpoint and the ground. I decided to leave the painting as it was. I wasn't going to finish it.

Ute Carson

He's My Brother

> "That was only prologue.
> When books are burned,
> eventually people will be
> burned as well ."
>
> Heinrich Heine 1820

The autumn air had deepened and thick mist was drifting through a Swiss valley near Lausanne. Biting winds whipped over the mountains. Madame Juliette, a slender woman, wearing tan slacks and a blue mohair sweater, her gray hair pulled back into a chignon, sat on a flower-patterned sofa in her oak-paneled study. A sturdy cardboard box stood next to her. It was crammed with loose photos, family pictures, landscape shots and vacation mementos. A fire crackled in the large stone fireplace.

Juliette's former teacher, Dr. Schreiber, was visiting from America. With bushy white hair and a mustache he bore a certain likeness to Mark Twain, but he had shrunk in stature since they last met years ago. He rocked calmly in his chair, his eyes sharply focused on Juliette. Under his steady gaze she felt like the shy student who had been dazzled by his lectures and intimidated by his kind but demanding demeanor. Dr. Schreiber had come to assemble a collection of stories and articles about his former school in Berlin and its pupils.

As they talked, Juliette's small hands rifled through a pile of photographs. With squirrel-like dexterity she picked up one picture, then another, discarding them until her face twitched with recognition. "Here," she whispered. Dr. Schreiber reached for the photo and studied it at arm's length. Then, uncharacteristically emotional, he said, "Oh, I remember Heio well. It seems like only yesterday." But it had happened a long time ago.

Dr. Schreiber began to reminisce. "Following the 1933 book burning on the Bebelplatz at Humboldt University my worries about the National Socialist regime mounted. I considered accepting your father's offer to fund a new school for me here in Lausanne, but I could not bring myself to dissolve my beloved school in Berlin." "What made you change your mind?" Juliette interjected. "It wasn't that I changed my mind. I simply waited too long and the Nazis closed me down."

Dr. Schreiber then recalled an incident involving Heio that occurred a few days before the Kristallnacht in 1939. "I was standing at the window of my study watching students cross the street on their way to the school when I saw an SS officer shove Jacob Bernstein into the gutter. Heio ran to the boy's side, lifted him up, exchanged a few words with the officer, and escorted Jacob through the door of the school. When I questioned Jacob about what had happened he told me that Heio had witnessed the incident as he jumped off the streetcar at our stop. He ran over to help Jacob up. As Heio brushed Jacob off and straightened his cap, the SS officer turned on him. 'Judenfreund,'eh? he demanded menacingly. Heio replied, with his disarming smile, 'I am Baron von Lüttwitz, officer, and this is my brother.'" Dr. Schreiber pondered Heio's remark momentarily before continuing. "The boys did somewhat resemble each other. Both were trim and had chiseled profiles. However, Jacob had begun to affect a slouching and shuffling gait whenever he spotted black jackboots or men in dark uniforms. Fear had seized him after his epileptic brother was forcibly institutionalized by the Nazi "health authorities" and he had witnessed his father, a respected jeweler in town, being roughed up by a street gang shouting anti-Semitic slurs. Jacob admitted that he was astonished that, after hesitating for a moment, the SS officer had let the matter lie and walked away." "It is curious, don't you think?" Juliette asked. "Yes and no," Dr. Schreiber explained. "The Nazis both loathed and admired aristocrats and still handled them with kid gloves in those days. It was in the wake of this incident that I contacted Heio's mother, a Christian Scientist and pacifist, to seek her permission to ask Heio if he would like to join me in establishing a new school in Switzerland." Dr. Schreiber mused, "Heio was a born leader with a sunny disposition and compassion for others. He was always eager to help but never ingratiating. I knew he would set a perfect example for my school."

Juliette knew this part of the story well and her cheeks flushed as she broke in. "And Heio accepted your invitation and came here for a few carefree years. We studied together, rode our horses through meadows at dawn and dusk and, wonder of wonders, we fell in love. Heio was in my older brother's class and was often invited to our home. My parents sometimes interrupted our adolescent conversations with their worries about what was happening in Germany. But we were young and optimistic about life. They also often opened their mountain chalet to us and a group of friends from school on weekends. It became Heio's favorite place in Switzerland. He was always full of vitality and good humor at the chalet."

"Were there ever signs of a change in his mood?" Dr. Schreiber asked. "Not at first," Juliette replied. "He did make regular visits home to Germany. He had a married sister and an older brother there. Upon his return from those visits he sometimes seemed distracted and gloomy. Then, when his brother-in-law was killed in France in 1940, he began to question whether it was right for him to remain in relative safety in Switzerland. We were startled. We knew that Heio's older brother Hubertus had been drafted when he graduated from boarding school at Castle Salem. Serious and reclusive by nature, he was not cut out to be a soldier so was initially assigned to a desk job.

Heio described his brother to me as quite different from himself. But he asserted that they had been very close from childhood on. Heio was the gregarious one and full of mischief. I remember sitting around a campfire near the chalet one evening as he told us stories about how he often coaxed his brother into various fooleries. Once, while guests were arriving for an elegant dinner at their grandfather's estate, Heio took Hubertus with him to cut long strings of ivy from the walls of the manor house which they then proceeded to wrap around the guest room toilet seats. Their grandfather dearly loved the two boys but that night he gave them a whipping with his riding crop." Juliette laughed as she recounted this story. "Heio often had some such prank up his sleeve".

"While Heio wrestled with his qualms of conscience," Dr. Schreiber interjected, "I was getting ready to leave for America. Your father had it all arranged. I now loved my school in Lausanne and stayed as long as I dared. But Switzerland no longer seemed safe in 1942. Late that summer Heio was sitting in front of me, stooped forward, his head buried in his hands, telling me about his decision to return to Germany for good. Hubertus had been sent to the front. 'He is my brother,' he sighed, 'I cannot abandon him.' Heio did not even respond when I implored him to emigrate with me to America."

Juliette was now in tears. "We all tried. My parents even attempted to bribe him by holding out the possibility that he could join our firm. We reminded him that he would be drafted as soon as he crossed the border but he only shook his head. 'I must go, Juliette, I simply must.' A single weekend remained before his departure. I can't describe it, it's too personal!"

"Please, Juliette, do try. It is very important. My editor, that youngster Jacob who is now a successful publisher, is waiting for Heio's story which will appear in print along with a few other recollections soon after I return."

Juliette let the moment pass, then took a long breath in and out and began to speak as though in a kind of reverie. "In late summer our forest teems with delicious wild blueberries, and bluebells sway in the balmy breeze in the meadows. The days are pleasant and the nights refreshingly cool, often crisp enough for a fire in the cast-iron stove. We had hiked up to our hideout, my parents' chalet. Heio was splitting wood for the evening fire when I snapped this last picture of him, shirtless, his blond hair tousled, axe swinging high above an upturned block of wood. In retrospect an awful omen, but at the time I could only admire the well-sculpted body of my first love. After a simple supper with milk from the fat meadow cows, bowls filled to the brim with blueberries we had picked that afternoon, and crusty brown bread with chunks of cheese, he brought a bottle of wine to the steps of the chalet. As we sipped the wine, bells from the village below began to ring. Like wedding bells, I remember thinking. We listened and held each other tight until the sounds no longer echoed through the mountains, and night enveloped us."

The rest of the story is a sad memory. Heio left Juliette and Switzerland and, as was foreseen, was drafted soon after he reached his homeland. Like his brother before him he was deployed to the Russian front. By sheer coincidence they met one last time. Their units had been stationed in proximity to each other near Kiev for a short reprieve from the fighting. In the mess hall Hubertus spotted Heio from behind by the white lock of neck hair that had marked him from childhood. Flinging their arms around each other, Hubertus gasped, "What are you doing here, Heio? I believed you safe in Switzerland." To which Heio replied, simply, "I could not leave you here alone."

As their separate companies moved deep into Russia during the extremely cold winter of 1944, their supply lines severed behind them, both brothers were killed. Hubertus was 21, Heio, 19. Heio's comrades discovered a photo of Juliette and a letter to his mother (my grandmother) in his shirt pocket. The letter contained a single message, "If it had not been for my idyllic childhood and carefree youth I could not survive this hellhole."

Evening had dimmed the study. Silence lingered until Juliette stood and walked over to the fire. Dr. Schreiber also rose and stepped to her side, gently placing a hand on her shoulder. "I thank you, my dear, for this painful, beautiful look back. May I borrow this photograph? I promise to return it to you with a copy of the book." And with that the old teacher took his leave.

Who's Offbeat and Quirky

Alec Scott is the author of several short stories, some of which have been published by Eraserhead Press and Raw Dog Screaming Press. He currently lives with his wife, Benay, in her 106-year-old family home, located in rural northeast Louisiana.

Aria Riding is the author of *The Exhibitionists*. She never goes out. Imposters perform translations of Aria's work simultaneously in different countries and hold symposiums discussing themselves and their importance until the moderators step in to free the audiences. Aria's brother's art and performance can be found at www.lostdance.com. Aria is also Grendel's matchmaker and she manages the long-suffering monster's Tinder profile.

Arnold Skemer, born 1946 in the Bronx, product of New York City schools. Moved to Queens in 1957. Graduated Queens College 1968. Employed by federal government 1969 to 2008. Established Phrygian Press 1984. Published *The Famine* in 1985. Began *ZYX* magazine in 1990. Publish largely poetry chapbooks and offbeat surrealist fiction for myself and others. *ZYX* is now up to issue # 75.

Austin Brookner has been published in several online and print literary journals, and was short-listed for the 2016 Erbacce Poetry Prize. As a singer/songwriter he has recorded with Marc Ribot, Lenny Kaye, Tony Garnier, Anton Fier, and Nick Tosches.

Ben Pullar lives in Brisbane with his family. His writing has appeared in *The Journal of Experimental Fiction*, *In-Between Altered States*, *The 8th Madness* and other places. He is currently preparing his first collection of short stories.

Ben Slotky's work has appeared in *The Santa Monica Review*, *Numero Cinq*, *Golden Handcuffs Review*, *McSweeney's*, *Hobart*, *Juked*, and many other publications. His novel, *Red Hot Dogs, White Gravy* was re-released by Widow & Orphan in 2017. "All the Ants in Arkansas" is from his novel, *An Evening of Romantic Lovemaking*. He lives in Bloomington, IL, with his wife and six sons.

Carla M. Wilson (San Diego, CA) writes fiction and poetry and makes art in her spare time. Her first book, *Impossible Conversations: Imaginary Interviews with World-Famous Artists*, was published by Black Scat Books. Other work appears in print and online.

Carolyn Chun works as a mathematics professor at the United States Naval Academy. Carolyn's first book, *How to Break Article Noun*, won the Kenneth Patchen Award for Innovative Fiction and was published by JEF Books. Her second book, *Nobody Will Bury Us If We Die Here*, was published by eLectio Publishing. She contributed some pieces to *The 8th Madness*, published by Dirt Heart Pharmacy Press.

Daniel Ableev, *1981 in Russia, is a certified strangeologist from Bonn, Germany; he writes, composes and co-edits *Die Nouvelle – Zeitschrift für Experimentelles*; ∞ publications in German & English, print & online (*Born to Fear: Interviews with Thomas Ligotti*, *Jahrbuch der Lyrik 2009*, Ann & Jeff VanderMeer's *The Big Book of Science Fiction*, *Alu*, etc.).

Dennis Mombauer, born 1984, grew up along the Rhine and today lives and works in Cologne. He writes short stories and novels in German and English and is co-publisher of a German experimental magazine, *Die Nouvelle – Zeitschrift für Experimentelles*. He has recent or upcoming English publications in magazines and anthologies such as *Plasma Frequency*, *Nebula Rift*, *SQ Mag*.

Deborah Chun works as a mathematics professor at West Virginia University Institute of Technology. She enjoys reading, writing, painting, and disc golf, although she spends most of her time thinking about matroids or in meetings or both. Deborah lives in West Virginia with her favorite mathematician, Tyler, and her dog, Curly.

Denis Emorine is the author of short stories, essays, poetry, and theater. He was born in 1956 near Paris. Works published in Europe and the USA. Writing, for Emorine, is a way of harnessing time in its incessant flight. Themes that re-occur throughout his writing include the Doppelganger and lost or shattered identity. For more informations go on denis.emorine.free.fr/ul/english/accueil.htm

Don Skiles has two previous short fiction collections, *Miss America* and *The James Dean Jacket Story*. His work has appeared in *Mung Being*, *Over the Transom*, *Chicago Quarterly Review*, *Gargoyle*, and *quaartsaluni*, among others. His novel *Football* was published in 2014 (Pelekinesis Press). *Rain after Midnight*, his new short fiction collection, is forthcoming in 2017 from Pelekinesis. He lives in San Francisco.

Eckhard Gerdes is the editor and publisher of JEF Books. He is also the author of many novels, poetry and drama collections, and a work of creative nonfiction entitled *How to Read*. His most recently published books are a novel, *White Bungalows*, published by Dirt Heart Pharmacy Press, and *Three Plays*, published by Black Scat Books.

Ernestus Jiminy Chald is a novelist, poet, composer, experimental radio artist, and enigmatographer. His literary work has been published by Peisithanatos Press, Smart Rhino Publications, and Oilcan Press among others. His radio programs have been broadcast on WFMU and WPOX. He lives in Chicago. For more information, visit www.peisithanatospress.wordpress.com.

Evan Guilford-Blake writes plays, prose and poetry. His plays have won 44 playwriting competitions. Thirty-five are published. His published prose includes the novels *Animation* and *The Bluebird Prince*, and the award-winning short story collection *American Blues*. All are available on Amazon and other e-retail sites. He and his wife (and inspiration) Roxanna live in the southeastern US.

F. Ghisalberti writes a lot of short pieces pretending to be Stephen Crane. But no one at his estate likes them very much.

H.B. Berlow is the author of "Ark City Confidential", a Prohibition-era crime novel, available form Amazon and The Wild Rose Press. As the Dudeist minister, "Rabbi" Dude, he has officiated at eight weddings since 2012. As The Tikiman, he advocates wearing Hawaiian shirts on white sand beaches and listening to lounge music while drinking martinis.

Jamie Popowich: His website, *metraville.com*, has short films and podcasts about a befuddled DJ whose ex-girlfriend left him for his shadow. Popowich is finishing his PhD at the University of Hertfordshire, where he is writing critical essays about crime writer Charles Willeford and a detective novel, *Motel Deep Six*, using gentle torture, cartoon pigs, and comedy noir. "absentricity" is taken from the story collection *Chrome Kisses*.

Jane L. Carman founded Festival of Language, a reading eXperiment, Lit Fest Press, and *Festival Writer* (www.festivalwriter.org). Her book, *Tangled in Motion* (JEF Books 2016) is an experiment in antinarrative. She holds a PhD from Illinois State University.

Jeremy Thompson is a Southern California-based author whose novels include *The Phantom Cabinet*, *Let's Destroy Investutech*, and two forthcoming titles: *The Silent Minority* (Post Mortem Press) and *The Land of Broken Sky* (Necro Publications). His short fiction has appeared in *DarkFuse*, *Into the Darkness*, *Sanitarium*, *Onyx Neon Shorts Presents: Horror Collection - 2015*, and *Walk Hand in Hand Into Extinction*.

Jerry Vilhotti has had stories published in the USA, Greece, India, Scotland, Ireland, England, Canada and Singapore; many of which were literary magazines. He lives among the Litchfield Hills with the ghosts of Mark Twain in the east, Harriet Beecher Stowe on the west and John Brown to the north. His two collections of tonepoems and sketches accepted by a publisher can be found on Amazon and Barnes and Noble.

Jim Meirose's work has appeared in numerous magazines and journals, including *Offbeat/ Quirky* (2017), *Permafrost*, *North Atlantic Review*, *Blueline*, *Ohio Edit*, *Witness*, and *Xavier Review*, and has been nominated for several awards. His E-book *Inferno* will be published by Underground Voices this March. His novels *Mount Everest* and *Eli the Rat* are available. More information is available at www.jimmeirose.com.

Joel Allegretti is the author of five collections of poetry and a novella, *Our Dolphin* (Thrice Publishing, 2016). His second book of poems, *Father Silicon* (The Poet's Press, 2006), was selected by *The Kansas City Star* as one of 100 Noteworthy Books of 2006. He is the editor of *Rabbit Ears: TV Poems* (NYQ Books, 2015), the first anthology of poetry about the mass medium.

John J. Trause is the author of six books, five of poetry and one of parody. His book of fictive translations, found poems, and manipulated texts, *Exercises in High Treason* (2016), is published by Great Weather for Media, and his book of poems on art, photography, and film, *Picture This: For Your Eyes and Ears* (2016) is published by Dos Madres Press.

Jonathan Plombon is a writer from St. Cloud, MN. His worked has appeared in *Quarter After Eight*, *The Berkeley Fiction Review*, and *The Bombay Gin*. When not writing, he spends much of his time worrying. He is currently working on his first book.

Joseph Bouthiette Jr. is co-editor of *Carrion Blue 555* and *Scrimshaw Obscura*. His short fiction and poetry have appeared in *Lost Signals*, *Turn to Ash*, *Mythos Fragments*, and *Ravenwood Quarterly*, among others. When not reading, writing, or editing, he is vocalist for Daniel Guided Me Through the Explosion and an avid board gamer.

Raised with red dirt & tumbleweeds in north Texas, Kay Merkel Boruff lived in Viet-Nam 68-70 and was married to an Air America pilot who was killed flying in Laos 18 Feb 70. She taught at The Hockaday School for 38 years, attended Burning Man 2012, & climbed Wayna Picchu on her 71st birthday. Several agents are presently considering her novel *Z.O.S.*

Larry Smith's novella, *Patrick Fitzmike and Mike Fitzpatrick*, was recently published by Outpost 19. His stories have been published in *McSweeney's Quarterly Concern*, *Exquisite Corpse*, *Curbside Splendor*, *PANK*, and numerous others. He has also worked as a business journalist and ghostwritten numerous books. Smith was born in Ohio and lives in New Jersey. Visit Larrysmithfiction.com.

Layal Hakim works as a mathematics research associate at Imperial College London. Her main interests are integral equations, numerical methods, solid mechanics, fracture mechanics, viscoelasticity, and programming, when she is not busy drawing, painting, reading, or writing. Layal lives in London with her husband and son.

Mark Axelrod is a Professor of Comparative Literature in the Department of English at Chapman University. For twenty years he has been the Director of the John Fowles Center for Creative Writing and has written over 20 works of fiction including the novel *Malarkey*, the screenplay of which has been optioned by Malcolm McDowell, who will play the lead.

Martin Heavisides has published in *FRiGG*, *Mad Hatter's Review*, *Oddball Magazine*, *Sein und Werden*, *Linnet's Wings* (contributing editor) and a number of other discerning publications. His play *Empty Bowl* received a staged reading in New York by the Living Theatre. He's been a regular three months running at Storefront Theatre's staged reading series, Sing for Your Supper, in Toronto.

Michael Koenig is a writer and editor from Oakland, California, whose stories have appeared in recent issues of *The MacGuffin, Harpur Palate, Drunk Monkeys, Literary Orphans, The Crime Factory, Hardboiled*, and the *Paterson Literary Review*. His work has been anthologized in *Awake! A Reader for the Sleepless* (Soft Skull Press) and *The Shamus Sampler 2*, an international detective fiction collection.

Michael Oppermann was born in 1955 in Hamburg. He has published a collection of experimental fiction entitled *Die Geschichte hinter dem Spiegel (The Story Behind the Mirror)* in Germany as well as a number of short stories (some of them in *JEF*). His most recent work is a novel called *Leben in der Vorstellung und im Sonnenschein (Life in the Imaginary and in Sunshine)*.

Nick Romeo is a multidisciplinary artist, musician and writer. His writings have been published in various literary magazines such as *Uppagus, The Gambler, StreetCake Magazine, Eye Contact, Syzygy*, and others. He was interviewed for *Pankhearst*'s "Fresh Featured" of December 2015 and *The Daily Poet* site of February 2016. Nick lives in Pittsburgh, Pennsylvania, with his wife and cat, Megatron.

Norman Conquest edits *Le Scat Noir* and is the author of several books, including *Corn on Macabre and Other Conundrums*.

Called "one of the innovators of the short short story" by *Publishers Weekly*, Peter Cherches is a writer, singer and lyricist. Over the past 40 years his writing, both fiction and nonfiction, has appeared in dozens of magazines, anthologies and websites. He is the author of *Autobiography Without Words* (Pelekinesis, 2017) and three previous prose collections. Cherches is a native of Brooklyn, New York.

Peter Hobson works as a physics professor at Brunel University London. He is a dedicated supporter of the arts in addition to being a writer, blogger, photographer, and flautist, although he spends most of his time attending meetings and accelerating particles at CERN. He contributed a piece to *The 8th Madness*, published by Dirt Heart Pharmacy Press.

Peter J. King (b. 1956, Boston, Lincolnshire) teaches philosophy at Pembroke College, Oxford. His work, including translations from German and Modern Greek, has appeared widely in print and on-line magazines; his latest collections are *Adding Colours to the Chameleon* (2016, Wisdom's Bottom Press), and *All What Larkin* (2017, Albion Beatnik Press).

Peter Wortsman's recent books include: a novel, *Cold Earth Wanderers* (Pelekinesis, 2014); an IPPY Award winning travel memoir, *Ghost Dance in Berlin* (Travelers Tales, 2013); an anthology, *Tales of the German Imagination* (Penguin Classics, 2013); and a translation, *Konundrum, Selected Prose of Franz Kafka* (Archipelago Books, 2016). His book of short fiction, *Footprints in Wet Cement* (Pelekinesis) is forthcoming.

With his wife, Robyn, P. K. Garrison is co-owner of the Darien, IL, retail store Frugal Muse Books, Music & Video. His short stories have appeared in *Mississippi Review, WIRE Magazine* and in the Fiction Collective anthology *An Illuminated History of the Future*, to name a few. His short story "Plate Tectonics" was nominated by *Karamu* for an Illinois Arts Council award.

R. Bremner, of Glen Ridge via Lyndhurst, NJ, USA, is a former cab driver, truck unloader, security guard, computer programmer, and vice-president at Citibank. He writes of dead kings and many things he can't define, the clutter in your mind, and the color of time. You're welcome to visit him at his page at *Poets & Writers*: www.pw.org/content/r_bremner, where milk and cookies await.

Ryan Forsythe received an MFA from San Diego State, where he served as Associate Editor for *Fiction International*. His books include *Dick Cheney Saves Paris* (Love Earth) and *If You Don't Read This, The Terrorists Win* (Black Scat). He lives off-grid in Oregon. Learn about his banana slug mandalas at RyanForsythe.com.

Shane Jesse Christmass is the author of the novels, *Police Force As A Corrupt Breeze* (Dostoyevsky Wannabe, 2016) and *Acid Shottas* (The Ledatape Organisation, 2014). He was a member of the band Mattress Grave, and is currently a member in Snake Milker. An archive of his writing/artwork/music can be found at www.sjx.digital.

Steve Pastis is a writer and editor based in Visalia, California. His work has appeared in local newspapers, special interest magazines and literary journals. His first short story collection, *Fables for the Clarinet*, will be available later this year.

Thaddeus Rutkowski is the author of the books *Guess and Check*, *Violent Outbursts*, *Haywire*, *Tetched* and *Roughhouse*. *Haywire* won the Members' Choice award, given by the Asian American Writers Workshop in New York. He teaches at Medgar Evers College and the Writer's Voice in New York. He received a fiction fellowship from the New York Foundation for the Arts.

A writer from youth, German-born Ute Carson's first story was published in 1977.
Her novel *Colt Tailing* was published in 2004 and was a finalist for the Peter Taylor Book Award Prize. An advanced clinical hypnotist, Ute Carson resides in Austin, Texas, with her husband. They have three daughters, six grandchildren, a horse and a number of cats. Visit www.utecarson.com.

A checklist of JEF titles

- ☐ 0 *Projections* by Eckhard Gerdes
- ☐ 2 *Ring in a River* by Eckhard Gerdes
- ☐ 3 *The Darkness Starts Up Where You Stand* by Arthur Winfield Knight
- ☐ 4 *Belighted Fiction*
- ☐ 5 *Othello Blues* by Harold Jaffe
- ☐ 9 *Recto & Verso: A Work of Asemism and Pareidolia* by Dominic Ward & Eckhard Gerdes (Fridge Magnet Edition)
- ☐ 9B *Recto & Verso: A Work of Asemism and Pareidolia* by Dominic Ward & Eckhard Gerdes (Trade Edition)
- ☐ 11 *Sore Eel Cheese* by The Flakxus Group (Limited Edition of 25 copies)
- ☐ 14 *Writing Pictures: Case Studies in Photographic Criticism 1983-2012* by James R. Hugunin
- ☐ 15 *Wreck and Ruin: Photography, Temporality, and World (Dis)order* by James R. Hugunin
- ☐ 17 *John Barth, Bearded Bards & Splitting Hairs*
- ☐ 18 *99 Waves* by Persis Gerdes
- ☐ 23 *The Laugh that Laughs at the Laugh: Writing from and about the Pen Man, Raymond Federman*
- ☐ 24 *A-Way with it!: Contemporary Innovative Fiction*
- ☐ 28 *Paris 60* by Harold Jaffe
- ☐ 29 *The Literary Terrorism of Harold Jaffe*
- ☐ 33 *Apostrophe/Parenthesis* by Frederick Mark Kramer
- ☐ 34 *Journal of Experimental Fiction 34: Foremost Fiction: A Report from the Front Lines*
- ☐ 35 *Journal of Experimental Fiction 35*
- ☐ 36 *Scuff Mud* (cd)
- ☐ 37 *Bizarro Fiction: Journal of Experimental Fiction 37*
- ☐ 38 *ATTOHO #1* (cd-r)
- ☐ 39 *Journal of Experimental Fiction 39*
- ☐ 40 *Ambiguity* by Frederick Mark Kramer
- ☐ 41 *Prism and Graded Monotony* by Dominic Ward
- ☐ 42 *Short Tails* by Yuriy Tarnawsky
- ☐ 43 *Something Is Crook in Middlebrook* by James R. Hugunin
- ☐ 44 *Xanthous Mermaid Mechanics* by Brion Poloncic
- ☐ 45 *OD: Docufictions* by Harold Jaffe
- ☐ 46 *How to Break Article Noun* by Carolyn Chun
- ☐ 47 *Collected Stort Shories* by Eric Belgum
- ☐ 48 *What Is Art?* by Norman Conquest
- ☐ 49 *Don't Sing Aloha When I Go* by Robert Casella
- ☐ 50 *Journal of Experimental Fiction 50*

☐ 51 *Oppression for the Heaven of It* by Moore Bowen
☐ 52 *Elder Physics* by James R. Hugunin
☐ 53.1 *Like Blood in Water: Five Mininovels (The Placebo Effect Trilogy #1)* by Yuriy Tarnawsky
☐ 53.2 *The Future of Giraffes: Five Mininovels (The Placebo Effect Trilogy #2)* by Yuriy Tarnawsky
☐ 53.3 *View of Delft: Five Mininovels (The Placebo Effect Trilogy #3)* by Yuriy Tarnawsky
☐ 54 *You Are Make Very Important Bathtime* by David Moscovich
☐ 55 *Minnows: A Shattered Novel* by Jønathan Lyons
☐ 56 *Meanwhile* by Frederick Mark Kramer
☐ 58A *Tar Spackled Banner* by James R. Hugunin
☐ 58B *Return to Circa '96* by Bob Sawatzki
☐ 60 *Case X* by James R. Hugunin
☐ 61 *Naked Lunch at Tiffany's* by Derek Pell
☐ 62 *Tangled in Motion* by Jane L. Carman
☐ 64 *The Hunter* by Dominic Ward
☐ 65 *A Little Story about Maurice Ravel* by Conger Beasley, Jr.
☐ 66 *Psychedelic Everest* by Brion Poloncic
☐ 67 *Between the Legs* by Kate Horsley
☐ 68 *Claim to Oblivion: Selected Essays and Interviews* by Yuriy Tarnawsky
☐ 69 *Passions and Shadows or Shadows and Passions* by Frederick Mark Kramer
☐ 70 *Afterimage: Critical Essays on Photography* by James R. Hugunin
☐ 71 *Goosestep* by Harold Jaffe
☐ 72 *Science Fiction: A Poem* by Robin Wyatt Dunn
☐ 73 *Offbeat/Quirky*

47146726R00198

Made in the USA
San Bernardino, CA
24 March 2017